About the author

My ultimate dream has always been to become a writer and I have dabbled for years, making up stories and writing down my ideas. During a convalescence period in 2015 following a surgical operation, I really got to grips in starting *The Copycat Killer*. With having to work full time and taking care of my family, it hasn't always been easy to find the time to write, but I persevered with what has become a labour of love over time. I hope you enjoy reading it as much as I enjoyed writing it.

THE COPYCAT KILLER

Sarah Shelly

THE COPYCAT KILLER

Vanguard Press

VANGUARD PAPERBACK

© Copyright 2020
Sarah Shelly

The right of Sarah Shelly to be identified as author of
this work has been asserted by her in accordance with the
Copyright, Designs and Patents Act 1988.

A CIP catalogue record for this title is
available from the British Library.

ISBN 9781784656 98-0

Vanguard Press is an imprint of
Pegasus Elliot MacKenzie Publishers Ltd.
www.pegasuspublishers.com

First Published in 2020

Vanguard Press
Sheraton House Castle Park
Cambridge England

Printed & Bound in Great Britain

Dedication

For my mum, who has always been my biggest fan, best critic and relentless supporter. I love you.

PROLOGUE

THEN: BEFORE THE BEGINNING

He watched fascinated as the cat swung gently from its position of being strung up by the back legs. He had sliced open the belly and watched as the internal organs fell forward and were now precariously balanced half in and half out, threatening to spill entirely from the cat's body. At first the blood had gushed red and fragrant onto the wooden table in front of him, spilling on to the tiled floor, but it had now slowed to a solid, persistent drip. The soft ginger fur of the cat appeared wet and black in places and the blood had already begun to dry.

The cat had died almost instantly, which was disappointing, its now glassy green eyes staring sightlessly into the ether, its mouth slightly open, showing its small, white teeth as if it had died with a grimace on its face. Its claws had ejected immediately, a natural defence mechanism he presumed, but had since retracted as the cat had expired. It fascinated him to think that this small animal was a miniature replica of a much larger cat, able to rip apart a bird or mouse with its teeth and claws. He would like to kill a larger cat, a lion for instance or just something larger in general. He craved to feel that power evaporate during the kill, to be able to absorb it into himself. To kill made him feel powerful. He knew his power was being mastered every day.

At first, he had killed violently and indiscriminately: only birds, mice and rabbits. He had set traps and watched as the terrified creatures cowered in fear. He enjoyed their fear; it fuelled his passion for ripping their tiny bodies apart, breaking their necks and slicing them up. With each kill he felt their small power wash over his body as they died and knew he was honing a craft that was destined for bigger and better things. He had wondered how it would feel to kill something as large as a dog. Dogs, although stupid, were harder to trap. They seemed to sense his power and ran away before he could entice them to him. Cats were more curious and easier to catch. 'Curiosity killed the cat'. That saying came from somewhere, and now he knew why.

But now the powerful feeling was becoming less and less. The thrill of the catch and kill did not achieve the same sense of power he had felt in the beginning. At first it had been exhilarating and the adrenalin would be pumping. Now it was brief. A flash of excitement and nothing more.

Sighing, he picked up his scalpel and cleaned it on the towel he found in the shower room. His only regret at this stage was missing the aftermath of his work. He wouldn't be able to see their reaction and that was disappointing. He sighed again and stood from his crouched position by the table. The drip, drip, drip was slowing significantly, the blood beginning to congeal already. Soon rigor mortis would be setting in, in fact may have already started. The corpse would rot. It was all over.

There was no adrenalin left; he felt empty. The current anti-climax following each kill was proving difficult for him. He wanted the rush to last, the thrill of the kill to be maintained at least until the next one.

He knew the problem.

Killing small insignificant animals presented no challenge any more and the euphoric feeling of the kill faded more and more quickly each time. He needed a bigger challenge. He needed to feel that rush of adrenalin and excitement he had got the first time he had started to kill animals.

He had killed something bigger... once. It had not taken much in the planning and certainly not much in the execution. In fact, although the act at the time was deeply satisfying, that feeling had disappeared.

It wasn't practical to romance over killing. Everything to this point had been for practice and now he needed to kill for real. He needed to focus on something more, to fulfil his purpose and destiny.

The answer was clear and he had known it was inevitable, like spring follows winter. He just hadn't realised - unconsciously knowing what needed to be done, but not doing it. His heart flipped a beat; he began to salivate from the anticipation of what he was contemplating. He knew what he needed to do and it would take considerable planning, but it was not beyond his means or capabilities. He was ready and he knew just who the victim would be. He could hardly wait and turned to exit the scene of the murdered cat before him. That chapter was already over and forgotten as his head filled with plans of what he intended to do and to whom.

School the following day was abuzz with the gossip that a murdered cat had been found in the girls' changing room by Miss Martin, the PE teacher. She was currently in the staff room, hysterical by all accounts, being commiserated with by the rest of the PE faculty. The caretaker had been given the gruesome job of removing the cat's remains and the police had been called. It was all laughable really. All this fuss for a cat!

He stood outside Mr Roy's classroom with the rest of the class, the statutory requirement of that particular teacher being that all pupils had to line up outside his classroom to await *his* arrival before being allowed into the sanctuary of learning. He stood at the back of the line as always, slightly away from his peers, his dark eyes hooded and watching. He did not engage with anyone and they seemed to sense his silent malevolence and equally kept their distance.

He heard her voice before he saw her. He closed his eyes for a moment, savouring the anticipation before he opened them and stared in her direction. She was flanked by her two cronies, lower standard, copycat versions of their adored leader. She wore the statutory tight t-shirt displaying her tanned midriff and a mini skirt so short, it left practically nothing to the imagination. Her shapely legs were bare and looked incredible, disappearing into the black calf-length boots she wore. Her long blonde hair was curled and hung loose down her back, a bright red head scarf tied atop her head to keep the hair from her face. She wore brightly coloured bangles and far too much make-up than was required. She epitomised everything that screamed slut at him, yet he was completely transfixed on her fluid form, as was every other boy in the class line.

Of course, she didn't glance in his direction as she passed, *he* was beneath her notice. In contrast, his intense stare was trained on her every movement, her every breath. This attracted the glance of her friend nearest him, on her left – an insignificant wannabe copycat in similar clothing, but shorter in stature and lacking in looks, trying way too hard to be like her friend. The girl looked to the left, catching his eyes as he glimpsed her for the briefest of seconds. She turned to the front again in a quick fluid moment, but the word 'freak' she muttered was not lost on him. He ignored it, was used to it. Everybody called him 'the freak' and he could not have cared less. It meant that everyone held their distance and that, as far as he was concerned, was the only thing that made entering this place of education on a daily basis worthwhile.

The quietening down at the front of the line suggested that Mr Roy had arrived. She had made her way to the front with her friends and was now standing next to Andy Mitchell, perhaps the most popular boy in the school. She preened before her conquest as he did before her, two peacocks trying to best each other in the 'I'm the most awesome ever' contest. He sneered in distaste. It was all so superficial and pointless. They both deserved to die – him quickly, her more slowly. She would one day, but her time was not yet. Andy Mitchell on the other hand might be a different story. He grinned to himself at thought.

Mr Roy ushered them into the classroom, his flinty glare at each and every face ensuring that they were silent as they took their seats.

"I need to collect the books from next door, I am sure I don't need to remind you to remain in absolute silence in my absence." His tone broke no opposition as the class sat in silence.

However once he was out of the room…. "Oh my God, did you hear about Miss Martin?" *She* was asking anyone in her general vicinity. Usually, he could not bear to listen to their inane chatter full of pop music, who watched what and details of the current flavour of the month and tuned out, but today he felt himself tense in anticipation. She didn't wait for anyone to answer but proceeded to inform the class about the gruesome discovery in the girls' changing room that morning by Miss Martin.

"Apparently the cat had been chopped up into little pieces and everything, Miss Martin has had to go home she was so upset." She had regaled the group with her tale, adding just the right amount of exaggeration to ensure the most impact. One of her friends became quite upset, her eyes filling with tears. He almost laughed out loud, wishing he had indeed chopped the cat into little pieces. In his mind's eye he could almost see small ginger pieces of red meat flung around the changing room and the caretaker, Mr Hobbs trying to decipher what it was he was actually picking up. It might prove to be an amusing diversion at some point when he had nothing better to do. However, for the sheer entertainment value right now, he was glad he had come to class today after all.

"What are you smiling at?" Her shrill voice exclaiming in horror brought him from his reverie to the attention of the entire class. Thirty pairs of eyes turned in his direction; the sudden silence was deafening. He hadn't even realised he was smiling; he was so wrapped in his thoughts of ripping the cat apart even further that he had lost himself for a moment. He removed the smile from his face and glared at the faces around him, wishing in that moment that he had a Kalashnikov rifle and could cut them all down in a furious hail of bullets and blood. He could kick himself for his sloppiness and allowing himself to be caught out like that. The saving grace was that many of his fellow students failed to meet his eyes and turned away when he looked in their direction.

His glare fell on her and her companion, Andy Mitchell, who was shaking his head and grinning. "What a freak," he muttered and turned to the front of the class, as Mr Roy entered the room with a stack of collected text books. This entrance ensured he was no longer the focus of the class, as they turned almost in unison to face the front. He really needed to be more careful in future. It wouldn't do to arouse suspicion so early on. He had so much more work to do and many things to accomplish. He was only at the beginning of his journey and couldn't afford to throw a spanner in the works now. He would need to work on schooling his emotions much more rigidly in the future.

He could feel his anger building inside, threatening to explode but inwardly directed to himself. Usually his anger was his friend; it allowed him to complete his tasks. Now he wanted to punch something and could feel his fist pulling into a tight knot, his fingernails digging in to the palm of his hand – a comforting exercise within itself which stemmed some of the anger. His fingernails dug in so hard they drew blood. He opened his palm and stared at the half mood shaped crescents of red. He wanted to lick his hand, to taste his blood, but unfortunately there were too many witnesses and he was still incurring surreptitious, suspicious glances from the other students. It never ceased to amaze him, the influence one or two people could have over those around them. There was nothing particularly special about *her* or Andy Mitchell or any of the others for that matter and yet their popularity stretched across the whole year group and to those below.

His stare fixed on the back of her head, following the flow of the blonde hair that fell gracefully over her shoulders. He could imagine how soft her hair would feel to his touch; how her unblemished skin could be marred by his blade as he drew it across her slender throat. There would be other places to use his blade; he could imagine cutting into her belly like he did the cat. He imagined stepping up to her, thrusting his knife into her soft tanned stomach to the hilt, ensuring that she was so close their bodies would be touching and he could look into her eyes as her life was extinguished.

Immediately he felt warm, his pulse had quickened and he found that he had to reign in that soulless part of him that felt the urge to kill. This was why he was tempted so often by those around him – why he was tested so strenuously on a daily basis. He was destined for great things. He had always known it to be so, but he also knew he needed to work on his skills, become the master of his craft and he knew he was far from that at the moment.

His eyes strayed involuntarily to the back of her head once again, the pictures reforming in his mind's eye. As if she sensed him looking, she turned suddenly, glancing at him over her shoulder, her green eyes meeting his dark ones for the briefest of seconds. He saw her unease in that one glance and almost smiled once again. As much as he wanted her now, her time was yet to come. Their time together would be beautiful but it would take considerable time and planning. It would be the most wonderful tribute, a homage to the start of his career, but alas there was much to do before her turn would come.

He needed to concentrate now. A plan was forming in his mind, the necessary work that was required to become the ultimate killer. He would make a name for himself, would go down in the history books. Would his persona be a mystery? That would remain to be seen.

He reached home eager to start making his plans. He raced past the kitchen where his mother sat preparing the dinner and ran upstairs to his bedroom.

His sister sat cross-legged on his bedroom floor, one of his books in her hands, while she flicked through the pictures. She couldn't read properly yet, only able to pick out the odd word. She grinned up at him, unrepentant at being found in his bedroom going through his things.

"Hello, Randall," She crooned in her baby voice. He smiled at her. It was the only genuine smile he ever gave, since she was the only person he had ever cared about. His five-year-old baby sister came over to him immediately and threw her little arms around his legs. He scooped her up and allowed his senses to take in her sweet scent as they hugged each other. Never had he expected to feel how he did. He had thought he hated her until the day she was born, when her tiny form had succeeded in reaching the part of him that no other living being had ever done. He would do anything for that child, for he loved her unconditionally.

CHAPTER ONE

NOW: MARY NICHOLLS 31st AUGUST

MARY

It had been one of those days yet again. Nothing was going to plan and everything seemed like harder work than usual. She had been feeling like this for a few days now – like a black cloud was hanging over her, threatening rain – rain that would undoubtedly splash all over her parade, and then some.

Mary was a pessimist – always had been. Some people might say a realist – having a glass half empty was a pretty good way of avoiding life's disappointments, and let's face it, Mary had had her fair share of those. It was a flaw in her personality, a fault she put down to inheriting from her mother, except in her mother's case everything that went wrong in her life was down to the fact that she lived her life out of a bottle of drink.

Mary sighed, holding her silver pen in her hand, flipping the top with a soft click, click, click as she brooded over her past.

Her private life was a mess! Marcus, her husband of fifteen years was loved up with his new secretary. Nothing new on that front. It had sadly become a regular occurrence for Marcus to play away from home and she had long since come to terms with the fact that nothing she said or did would change the way he behaved. At first, he had been full of apologies and promises never to do it again, but something had died in her for him after that first time she caught him out. Finding out her partner was so full of deceit and so clandestine at sneaking around had knocked her off her feet. She had threatened the end of their marriage, threatened divorce, threatened to take him to the cleaners, everything she supposed a scorned woman threw at her duplicitous husband. In the end however, she had had to admit that she couldn't do it alone, didn't want to give up her lifestyle and certainly not her house. It was easier to turn a blind eye and admit defeat than leave it all behind. She knew it was a superficial existence. She lived for the materialistic world she had created, oh… and her cat.

When his affairs were over, he returned home, the handsome playboy who would never grow old, who could still make her heart beat a little bit faster and talk her into bed and for a while, things would once again become some semblance of how it used to be when they were first married. Her very own Hugh Hefner fighting his own demons of growing older by surrounding himself with *the younger model*.

When ultimately being confronted with the truth that she was just not enough for Marcus, what was left of their marriage had been killed off, yet the sham remained. The fake marriage it had become was the face that was shown to their friends and family. There was no barrage of questions or recriminations from anybody that she was a career-driven childless spinster in the making, while her husband remained dotingly at her side, while he in secret lived the proverbial life of Riley. Deep down their families must have at least suspected something was off, if not actually knowing the truth.

In some respects, it was *her* fault. She had always been a driven, career-orientated woman who was determined to be nothing like the alcoholic mess of a mother who had spawned her. She had carved out a successful career and had money, a house and cars. She had security. The only thing that had eluded her perfect existence was the ability to have a child. She suspected that if that piece of information had presented itself prior to their marriage, Marcus would not even have deigned to walk her down the aisle.

Whether it was her age, or her hormones, she was finally missing what she had never had. She might have all the materialistic baggage, but really there was no-one to share it with. Marcus did his thing and she did hers; they were like ships passing in the night with separate bedrooms. She had wanted to be loved, to know what it felt like to be loved. To understand that feeling that there was only her and no-one else in another's person's life. A sad smile touched her mouth briefly. Did anybody really have that kind of security? When all was said and done, wasn't she just looking for a fairy tale that didn't exist?

A small huff escaped her as she answered her own questions. In the end, greed and deceit were the only things that endured. There was love, but it came at a price.

Mary, despite knowing how it felt to be a wronged wife, was no better than the women who knowingly bedded her husband, being fully aware of her existence, the dutiful wife at home scenario. But Mary could claim no special prize for that, when in fact she was doing the self-same thing. She was having an illicit affair with somebody else's husband.

Franklin Hart, Managing Director of Hart, Smith & Dawson had been her immediate boss for seven years. It had been a platonic, serious working relationship until seven months ago, when after a particularly big deal had gone through, followed by several bottles of expensive champagne later, they had ended up in bed together. It was an affair that had continued despite them both admitting they had made a terrible mistake initially, vowing to put it behind them and forget it ever happened.

Franklin was of course married and also happened to be the father of four beautiful children. Mrs Roselynn Hart was an exceptional hostess, wife and mother. Mary had always felt inadequate around her. She didn't work per se, but she ran their house, a palatial eight-bedroomed country-style manor, with of course the help of her staff, cook, nanny, groundskeepers and cleaners. It was the reason Roselynn looked so immaculate, not a hair or fingernail out of place. Mary couldn't even dislike the woman; she was hardly an empty-headed Barbie doll who looked good on Franklin's arm, rather to the contrary. She was a savvy, smart, genuinely nice person which made the affair all the more guilt-ridden in its illicitness.

Deep down, Mary knew she was burning a candle at both ends and sooner rather than later there would be no wick left to burn and the affair would be over. In truth, Mary dreaded that day. There was a semblance of safety in her clandestine affair in that it would never go any further than what it was. Mary felt that both her and Franklin felt secure in that knowledge, that neither one expected anything more than the other was able to give. They had not declared their love for each other; they were not planning to separate from their respective spouses or give up their lives. Still, there was a side to the story yet to be told but for now it would remain her own secret as she was unsure which weapons she would later need at her disposal.

She was digressing. She was doing that a lot lately, staring off into space, ruminating about the past and imagining her future.

She glanced at her computer screen. The screensaver had kicked in, the company name bouncing around the screen from side to side in a hypnotic sort of way. Mary reached out and flicked her mouse, her computer zinging back to life instantaneously.

Her report and Powerpoint presentation were finally ready. There was nothing more she could add that could improve it further. This was her final presentation for new business to be presented to Franklin and his directors tomorrow morning. She was sufficiently satisfied that they would be impressed. They ought to be too since she had worked to a very strict deadline and knew she was up against stiff competition, her main rival being David Crisp, the current man about town and rising star of the company who was clearly making a beeline for her job.

She was safe at the moment. She was in Franklin's bed. She winced at that thought. Was she really going to play *that* card and discount her own professional accomplishments up until now, basing career and future success on whether she slept with the boss or not? That was *so* not her. Although it did provide food for thought. Mary immediately pushed that thought from her mind. She would bring it out and dissect it later when she had time to procrastinate over what would happen when the affair was over. She really needed to accept their affair as being what it was, two people happy with their casual arrangement with no claims or demands being made on either side. It had worked thus far.

Despite that thought, Mary sighed. The thought of breaking up with Franklin filled her with dread when she actually considered it. When had things actually changed for her? She couldn't pin down a definite date. The affair had become quite intense suddenly, perhaps for the last two months. They were seeing a lot of each other, and whether it was a honeymoon period, or whether it something more lasting, Mary didn't know. She had a sudden realisation that she had developed feelings for Franklin. When had that sneaked up on her? She was sure it had all been so casual, but now she was thinking about the affair ending and she couldn't bear it. Her mouth felt dry and she suddenly felt close to tears. This was not her at all. She could feel all the fear and anxiety she had mastered hiding so well, fighting with her psyche to raise its ugly head. She put her head in her hands and ran her fingers through her hair, loosening the chignon she had so carefully put in place that morning. She removed her hair clips and shook her hair free, rubbing the back of her neck in a soothing gesture. She was tired. That's all this was. She needed to go home, have a hot bath and a camomile tea.

Mary glanced at her watch. Already nine forty-five p.m. The cleaners were at the far end of the office, the hum of their cleaning equipment a muffled sound in the otherwise deserted place. They were probably cursing her, wanting to get on with their own jobs and go home. No doubt they had cleaned all the other offices in the building and were awaiting her exit.

She reached over to her computer and saved the documents before shutting down. She jotted a few notes on a post-it note for her secretary who would no doubt be in before her in the morning.

She stood and stretched her arms behind her back, turning her head this way and that to remove the kinks in her neck before pulling on her jacket hanging on the back of her chair. Taking her post-it note and her bag, she left her office, closing the door behind her. She placed the post-it note on her secretary's desk which resided outside her own office, before making her way towards the lifts. She waved to the cleaners as she left and received a single salute in return. 'Yes, definitely not happy to be kept waiting', she thought as she made her way to the lifts and pressed the down button. She took a moment to rummage in her bag for her keys. The carpark would be dark and deserted by now, and although she could ask the night-time security guard to walk her to her car, the man gave her the creeps. Despite a remaining childhood, irrational fear of the dark, she would rather that than have Brad's company to her car.

The soft ping of the lift's arrival attracted her attention, the doors opened and she stepped in, hitting 'G' on the board.

Brad was an aging forty-something who clearly still thought he was a hit with the ladies, despite the fact that his stomach overhung the top of his trousers and his chest, visible through the slightly too-tight shirt, gapped unattractively, rendering the unlucky onlooker a glimpse of the sparse grey hair on his chest. He reeked of cigarettes most of the time and usually had a serious case of body odour which got worse in the summer, accompanied by sweat patches in his arm pits and down his back. He had a leer that made a woman feel as if he was mentally undressing them, or as if he had actually seen them naked. Either way, he made most women feel uncomfortable and it was the reason he was now on the night shift. Fortunately for Brad, he had not overstepped the boundary of complete decorum, keeping his actions limited to the pastime of perversely leering at women and therefore they were unable to get rid of him entirely.

As the lift doors opened and Mary stepped out, she was startled to discover him standing right in front of her. He grinned broadly as she almost careened directly into him and his hand touched her arm briefly to steady her. She stepped back, not wishing to be touched by him.

"Just about to do my rounds, Ms Nicholls, thought everyone had gone home already." His voice did not match his looks. If you closed your eyes, his voice would be a soft, soothing sound on the radio, perhaps a voice to read you a story to lull you into a relaxed state. However, the reality check meant that unfortunately you saw the person before you heard the voice and, in that case, all bets were off.

"Just heading off now," Mary said quickly, creating a distance between their bodies immediately by side-stepping away from him. If he had any idea that he made her feel uncomfortable, it did not show on his face. No flicker of emotion touched his eyes, which Mary noted always seemed flat and lifeless. His smile however remained and Mary suddenly felt a chill echo down her spine. "Well, I'm off," she said with false cheeriness, turning towards the exit.

"Would you like me to walk you to your car?"

Mary was already at the exit door, and still her heart did a little skip of trepidation. She pushed the main door. "No thanks, I'll be fine. Have a good evening." She was through the door and going down the steps, the chill of the night air giving her goosebumps. The soft huff of the door closing behind her broke off any response from Brad. She didn't care what he said, as long as she was away from him. There was something about Brad that just didn't sit right with her. Call it women's intuition, but there was something definitely off about him.

Mary kept walking, refusing to even glance behind her, having the feeling that he was watching her, still standing in front of the lifts. Whether he considered in his mind that it was part and parcel of his job to ensure that she got to her car safely or not, it was a great deterrent in making her forget about how worried she was being in the dark carpark alone.

Mary climbed into her car and took a surreptitious glance back the building. Sure enough, there he was. Well, he was actually locking the main doors, but still, she knew he had been watching her walk to her car.

As she started her car and pulled out of her parking space, her headlights lit up the dimness of the glass reception area. Brad was now no longer in sight, probably having gone up in the lift to commence his check of the building. She felt relieved that he was no longer there and her mood lightened slightly. She switched on the radio, which was playing a favourite song of hers and merrily started to sing along as she drove home.

The house was in darkness as she pulled up. Damn, she had forgotten to set the timer again. She hated entering a dark house. Her childhood fear of the dark reared its ugly head once again.

Marcus of course, was on one of his *business* trips. The term business was used loosely, although Mary did have to admit that he was a successful structural engineer which did take up a lot of his time. He was currently somewhere in Dubai overseeing a new build and would likely be home next week if all went to plan. However, in true Marcus style, the chances were that he would then fly to Japan or the South of France with his secretary in tow of course, for a little down time.

However little Marcus thought of their relationship, or in truth the fact that she was no better, didn't diminish the fact that she missed his presence around the house. She hated coming home to an empty house.

Mary knew she lived in a good area. She and Marcus had picked it especially because of that fact. They had neighbours of course, but the houses were nicely spaced apart with large grounds to each plot, giving the homes a sense of solitary privacy. Many of them had gated fronts and it had been a discussion between her and Marcus for some time to have something similar installed, just for an added sense of security. Crime, as far as she knew was down to a minimum in her area and probably in part due to the fact that most of the houses had security systems; hers was no exception on that front. And there was neighbourhood watch of course. No stickers were visible in this street though... too tacky.

Despite all that, she couldn't help but feel vulnerable and alone when it was just her, and wished they had already had gates installed so that she could feel more secure.

Mary let herself into the house, locking the deadbolt behind her, feeling an immediate sense of relief. She went into the house, first switching off the alarm system on the panel near the front door. Kicking off her shoes she went through the rest of the ground floor, systematically flipping on the lights as she made her way through the hall, into the living room and finally back out into the hall and into the kitchen.

Marmalade, Mary's ginger cat sat on the kitchen table and greeted her with a small mew as he jumped down and began twisting himself in and out of her legs. She reached down and picked him up, stroking his soft fur and feeling his immediate vibrating purr as he enjoyed the attention.

"Yes, I missed you too," Mary whispered against his head as she rubbed her face on his fur. She placed him back on the floor and moved to the back door, unlocking it and opening it just enough to let the cat out. This being their night-time routine, Marmalade went out through the door without so much as a backward glance and disappeared into the darkness of the garden. Fickle, Mary thought, smiling to herself before closing the back door. She turned and switched on the kettle.

Making her way back through the hallway, she collected her shoes and went up the stairs. In all honesty, this was her favourite time of the day, when she could come home, put her pyjamas on and slob out in front of the TV for a while. It was her slovenly indulgence.

Again, she flipped on every light, banishing the dark corners, even in her bedroom. The other rooms in the house, that weren't being used, had their doors closed so that she didn't have to look at the black maws of darkness like astonished open mouths. All evidence of the dark was eradicated from her sight.

She unzipped her skirt and removed her tights, letting them fall to the floor, before removing her blouse followed by her bra, also dropping this to the pile of clothes at her feet. She felt the freedom of liberty as she removed her knickers and stood naked for a moment, the act of having no clothes on giving her a childish sense of autonomy, goosebumps spreading over her skin as a sudden chill enveloped her body. Still she avoided viewing herself in the mirror however. There were just some things she didn't need to see.

Taking fresh pyjamas from the drawer, she put them on the end of the bed before entering the en suite. Walking over to the claw-footed ornate bathtub, she put in the plug and turned on the mixer tap, adjusting the temperature until she was sufficiently satisfied. She chose a bubble bath and applied a liberal helping to the water, where immediately bubbles began forming. Turning, she grabbed her make-up wipes from the counter and began carefully removing all traces of her make-up, before washing her face. Glancing at herself in the mirror, she huffed out a breath as she inspected the lines around her eyes. She was going to have to get Botox if the lines kept increasing at this rate.

Grabbing her brush, she pulled it through her dark brown, shoulder length hair, removing all the tangles. She kept it tied up for work, but now it shone to her shoulders, only the tiniest slivers of grey visible under the harshness of the unforgiving bathroom light.

She pulled her hair into a bun and secured it with a scrunchy. She turned back to the bath, which was now full, and switched off the taps. Gingerly she tested the water with her toes and then climbed into the steaming bubbles, easing herself into the water and lying back with a satisfied sigh.

The frantic day began to disappear from her mind, as did thoughts of the stress she would also endure tomorrow. This was her time. She closed her eyes and enjoyed the warmth of the water enveloping her entire body, the scent of the lavender bath bubbles filling her senses with its calming aroma.

Mary had dozed off. She woke with a little start and sat up in the water, slightly disorientated for a moment. The water was still warm so she hadn't been out long, but her sense of self-preservation was telling her it was stupid thing to do. She stood up, allowing the water to run in little rivulets down her body, before leaning forward to release the plug. She pulled a large fluffy towel from the rail beside the tub and wrapped it around herself, stepping out of the bath onto the mat. She padded into her bedroom. Her pyjamas were neatly laid out on the bed. She couldn't remember laying them out like that, but she must have done. She must be extremely tired. She glanced at the clock and realised that it wasn't so very late, only quarter to eleven. If she went to bed now, she would be awake at four a.m. She would just have to make herself last a little bit longer.

Returning to the bathroom, she rinsed the bath out, dismissing all the bubbles, and towel-dried her crevices before pulling the scrunchy from her hair.

Switching off the bathroom light, she moved to the bed and pulled on her pyjamas before wandering back downstairs to the pristine white kitchen to make herself a camomile tea. She was pleased to note how clean the house looked. Pepe, her Spanish cleaner always did such an excellent job. The house was spotless and Mary didn't have to worry about coming home to the morning's washing up or a dirty house, not that it was ever really dirty with only her and Marcus living there.

Mary stood by the kitchen counter and dipped her teabag in the cup absently. She yawned and noted that it was now eleven fifteen p.m. It suddenly occurred to her that she had left the back door unlocked when she let the cat out. Opening the door, she peered into the blackness of the back garden.

"Marmalade," she called softly. Only the gentle rustle of the leaves in the trees answered her as they were buffeted by a gentle wind. He was no doubt off doing his night-time cat activities, she assumed, and reclosed the door, this time locking it firmly. She realised it was testament to the fact that she was perhaps getting used to being on her own and feeling much safer than she thought that she had forgotten to lock the back door, and this was not the first time recently.

Picking up her mug of camomile tea, she walked barefoot into the living room. Aside from her own bedroom and the décor it displayed, this was her favourite room in the house. A haven of calm tranquillity. Almost everything was white, something that could not be had with small children running around. The floor was a light parquet wood with white walls, white sofa and white rug. A Louis XIV fireplace framed a real fireplace which had long ago been blocked up and replaced with a modern fake fire, giving all the reality of a real log fire, but none of the dirt and soot. White bookshelves covered the walls on either side of the fireplace, filled with a collection of interesting books, photographs in frames and other knick-knacks collected over the time of her and Marcus's marriage together. Nothing tacky – everything screamed sophistication and taste, at least in Mary's eyes.

The starkness of the white was broken up with light wooden furniture, end tables that housed lamps and ashtrays that would never be used (not in this room at least) and pictures on the walls. Many of the pictures were black and white, tasteful photographs where there was an implication of nakedness, but nothing revealed with strategically placed hands or angles. They were among some of her most favourite possessions.

Mary sat down and relaxed into the white billowy softness of the sofa. She sipped her tea, now feeling totally relaxed. The muffled sound of her mobile phone alerting her that she had received a text came from her handbag in the hall. She would read it soon, but at the moment was enjoying the blissfulness of a quiet house. She would look at it later, or in the morning, or never. She smiled at the thought of her rebelliousness against the technology.

Another ping of a text interrupted the silence almost immediately, wiping the smile from her face. "No rest for the wicked," she announced to herself and padded into the hall to grab her mobile phone from her bag.

She had actually received four texts and three calls, all from her mother, and all the in space of time since she had arrived home. The relentlessness of the texts led Mary to know that her mother was in financial difficulties once again. It was the only time she ever heard from her these days and it only took opening and reading the first text to confirm her assumption. Mary sighed and sat back down on the sofa, flipping through the other texts, each one becoming more insistent than the last, before listening to the one voicemail that had been left in three calls. Her mother's shrill voice insisted that her daughter call her back immediately, irrespective of the time. Yes, her mother wanted money, yes, her latest boyfriend had left her, and yes, she was probably drunk to the point that she could barely see, judging by the amount of spelling mistakes in the texts. Any moment now, her mother would probably pass out in a stupor. There would be no point in Mary ringing her now as it would only end in a barrage of insults and a heated argument. It was a scenario that had played itself out multiple times in the past. Nothing would ever change and quite frankly it was not something that Mary needed right now. It never ceased to surprise Mary that her mother had lived this long and that her liver still managed to function.

Mary knew that every family had skeletons in their cupboard, that behind every closed door was a story to be told. Marcus was the only person who knew Mary's full story. She had never even divulged it to Franklin. Mary described her mother as no longer being alive when she met people. It was easier than fumbling through the reality of truth or finding a way to lie and in turn, remember that lie.

Mary was an only child, a product of a one-night stand on any one of a numerous amount of drunken evenings. Her mother had no recollection of exactly how many men she had slept with, much less which one could have possibly been Mary's father.

Some years ago, when Vera was going through a detox programme, Mary had attempted to question her during that brief moment of lucidity as to whether she had any recollection of who she had slept with that evening, at least giving Mary a focal point to start with. Mary was not surprised to learn that her mother's recollection of events was sketchy to say the least, and she knew very few of her *gentleman callers'* names then, or indeed since. There had been no love in any of the relationships she had had and no particular evening had been outstanding enough to provide a clue as to the paternity of her father. The only saving grace at the time had been that at least Vera finally looked remorseful as she admitted the facts to her daughter. There had been some evidence of guilt for the cruel life she had led her daughter to live, although in truth it gave Mary very little comfort.

Mary's had been a difficult childhood with no good memories. She was a walking cliché, having suffered every humiliation and degradation in the book. She had been forced to grow up quickly. She was a constant reminder to her mother that she had 'lost money' in those weeks post birth, and as she put it, being forced into a bringing up a child she didn't want. That mantra had preceded Mary's life from day one. Her mother had saved her love for the men she entertained on a regular basis, if one could describe *that* as love. There had been no cuddles, no kind words, no encouragement and definitely no love for Mary.

Mary's first memory had been of the dark smelly cupboard space under the staircase, just off the kitchen where a filthy mattress had been thrown. It had once been used as a cellar, now Vera used it to store her daughter.

She could have been no more than three when she was first placed in there, her tearstained dirty face looking forlornly up her mother who just told her to keep her *'trap shut and not make a sound or it will be the slipper'*. Mary knew her mother was as good as her word as far as the slipper was concerned. It had been used often, and sometimes with little provocation.

There were no good memories from that time on. Birthdays and Christmases were almost non-existent unless her mother had a generous man who provided extra money for extra favours. Otherwise the money was spent on what little food she could get away with; the rest went on her booze, cigarettes and appearance – and in that order. Sometimes the men stayed around for days, with one or two staying around for a few months. However, each relationship ended the same way, sooner or later; they became bored and moved on or her shrew of a mother nagged the men into going away. It continued that way for Mary until just after her tenth birthday.

Suddenly things changed as Vera finally met a man who seemed different from all the others. He was pleasant, softly spoken and for the first time in her life, Mary found she didn't have to be shut in the cupboard as he didn't seem to mind her being around. He was an angel from heaven as far as Mary was concerned. He was nice to her, spoke to her and didn't make her feel like a stranger in her own home. Sometimes he brought her sweets or little gifts of comics and even on the odd occasion would give her a couple of quid, asking her not to mention it to her mother. As if Mary would have done. Vera would have taken the money and it would have gone on what she wanted for herself.

The man unfortunately had been interested in obtaining payment for the gifts he brought Mary, something she was completely unaware of at the time. He kept asking Mary to come and sit on his lap and sometimes she obliging did, ever grateful for a kind word or a treat. One day he whispered seductively in her ear, "When Mummy goes down the offy, I've got a special treat for you today." Mary was so excited she could hardly wait for her mother to make her daily trip to the off licence to buy her booze, wondering what her treat was going to be.

It was also a sad fact that all too often, when any of Vera's boyfriends showed any interest in Mary, her mother would become insanely jealous, no matter how platonic things appeared to be. On this occasion, Vera must have had some kind of mother's intuition attack on her conscience. She was back from the off licence in double quick time and as she walked through the door, she found her latest man sitting in an armchair with his erect penis released from his trousers. Mary had been just about to touch it like he asked. Clearly embarrassed at being caught, he stood up and put his now flaccid penis back in the confines of his trousers. Vera was livid, her face resembling the colour of purple in such a frightening way that Mary considered she might have a heart attack.

Needless to say, Vera blamed Mary for the events. She beat her with her slipper that night so much that Mary had trouble sitting down. While she beat her daughter, she had screamed at her that she was never to touch the *one-eyed python* again. Did Mary understand? Mary didn't but when she gasped that she did through her sobs, Vera stopped the relentless beating. In her own way Vera may have been protecting her daughter, but she never called the police. Thankfully the man never came round again.

Henceforth, Mary was ushered immediately out of sight when Vera's gentleman callers came round, usually to the cupboard under the stairs. The cupboard was dark, damp and full of who knew what creepy crawlies. It was a place that Mary loathed and felt so afraid every time she was put in there. It was pitch black apart from the line of light from the hallway at the bottom of the cupboard door, and all she had was a filthy mattress to sit on. It was cramped and, on some occasions, Mary had not only felt the brush of a spider or two running over her body, she had also felt mice scurrying around her. She had urinated in fear on more than one occasion and when she did, her mother would beat her with an old slipper for doing so as punishment.

Mary would watch as Vera would wash and clean herself up, plastering her face in make-up and donning her most revealing clothing. She would barely speak to her only daughter and when she did so, it was usually with a contemptuous, spiteful remark. She would be drinking from early in the day so by the time she was getting ready, her viciousness would take on a whole new turn. Sometimes Vera would catch a glimpse of Mary watching. "You won't ever look like this," she would spit while she applied her make-up, expertly despite the amount of alcohol she had already consumed at that point. "You're a fucking dog-ugly piece of shit, just like your father. Now fuck off, you give me the creeps staring at me like that." If Mary didn't immediately move, her mother would pick up an old slipper which always seemed to be to hand wherever she was, and wave it threateningly. "You want a beating? Now fuck off like I told you," she would scream and, in that instant, Mary would make her move. She was adept at staying out of her mother's way, particularly when she had consumed more alcohol than usual. On some nights Vera would allow Mary to just go to bed. She would seem mellow and quite pleasant, but those times were few and far between. Once Vera was ready to go out, she would instruct her daughter to climb into the cupboard under the stairs. She had tried crying and begging her mother, promising to remain quiet in her room rather than be put in the dark, but when she did so, Vera seemed to get an almost gleeful, spiteful look on her face which seemed to persuade her to fiercely grab her only daughter by the arm, drag her and almost throw her into the cupboard, locking her in. There were also occasions when her mother became so drunk and absorbed in entertaining the man she was with, she forgot about Mary altogether or Vera would just fall into a drunken sleep. When she could hear her mother up the following morning or sometimes even the afternoon, she would tap on the cupboard door, desperate to use the bathroom or grab something to eat. More often than not, her mother would fling open the door, slipper in hand and swipe at Mary as she ran past. It would be all that Mary could do after that to disappear from her mother's presence or receive another beating, only to be flung back into the filthy cupboard. It was a daily routine that played itself out every day of Mary's existence.

When Mary was ten, Social Services stepped in. The school, having become increasingly concerned about the absences and malnourished, dirty look of the child that attended their school each day, had reported the situation to Social Services who immediately on discovering the situation had removed Mary from Vera. Mary remembered her mother standing, wearing what looked like a silk kimono and not much else, with one hand on her hip and the other holding a cigarette. She had watched dispassionately as her daughter was taken from her. "If I had known you'd come and take her away, I would've called you meself," was Vera's parting shot. She was still drunk, weaving from side to side, her eyes bloodshot, her make-up smeared and she absolutely reeked of stale alcohol.

Mary was then in and out of foster homes and placements as well as being returned to her mother intermittently. Nothing was strikingly memorable about anywhere she went; she was there and then she wasn't anymore. It wasn't until she was thirteen that she was placed with an older couple who had no children of their own. Mary called them the bookends although their real names were Martin and Judy. They used to sit in their own armchairs, one either side of the fireplace. Mr Bookend would read his paper and smoke a pipe and Mrs Bookend would do her knitting. The house smelt of baking and had a homely feel to it. They even allowed Mary to have a night light on so that she could comfortably rest without fear of the night terrors that seemed to pursue her once she was left alone in the dark. They were kind and encouraging. They didn't own a TV but had a large gramophone player on which they would play 1930s and 1940s records, or they would listen to the radio. The Archers was a regular feature in their living room. They would read extensively and had a large collection of books and in a very short amount of time, Mary found solace in some of those books herself. It was a world away from everything she had ever known and for a year of her life, Mary was the happiest she had ever been. She attended school regularly and started to enjoy it, she made some friends and found that academically she could excel and with the Bookends' encouragement she seemed to go from strength to strength. She never wanted to leave and felt like this was the family she was supposed to have. The Bookends couldn't have any children of their own, and they seemed to feel the same way.

Disaster came, as it always seems to do when you least expect it and when you're entirely happy. Mr Bookend suffered a massive stroke. He passed away that night in the hospital, never regaining consciousness, with Mrs Bookend by his bedside and Mary waiting in the hospital corridor. She had never felt so bereft in her life. She hoped that she and Mrs Bookend could get through it together. That, however was not the case. Mrs Bookend said she could no longer look after Mary. She told Mary that their last year together, despite being one of her happiest, was something she felt that she could no longer give justice to without her husband by her side and that Mary deserved something better. She said that something inside her had died along with her husband. Mrs Bookend committed suicide the evening Mary was returned to her mother. She left a note behind that explained she could not live without her husband.

Mary was devastated. Not only had she lost the two most important people in her life, she was returned to a woman who did not now, and had never cared for her. She was also not surprised to note that nothing much had changed as far as her mother was concerned. She was still a drunk and was still bringing men home. The only difference now was that Mary had grown – as tall as her mother but considerably weightier, having been well fed and well looked after. Vera had tried to bully Mary, but had come up against a formidable adversary to which Vera's response was "You stay out of my way, and I'll stay out of yours." It was the only time Mary had agreed wholeheartedly with her mother on anything.

Mary had been determined to never end up like Vera. She continued with school, attempting to live some semblance of her life around her mother's lifestyle. She got a job, waitressing in a local restaurant in the evenings which kept her from the house and allowed her to earn her own money, which she squirreled away in a post office savings account. One day she vowed that she would leave Vera and live like the Bookends.

That of course was something that had never happened. Mary often ruminated on the relationship the Bookends had and their love for each other. She had never really found that love herself although when she had first met Marcus, they had been besotted with each other. Even now, with all the materialistic baggage her life carried, she was still lacking a certain something.

Mary sighed and checked through her phone for any message from Marcus. He had agreed to ring her at seven p.m. each night and with the time difference it would then be ten p.m. in Dubai. However, when he had called that evening, earlier than scheduled, she had still been at work and their conversation had been cut short. Still, there had been little to say to each other. These days they seemed to have virtually nothing in common. The how are you, how's work requisite questions were over and done with within a few seconds and then nothing, just an awkward silence and eagerness to get off the phone. His job did not particularly interest her and her job had never interested him. In fact, she would be surprised if Marcus even knew what she did for a living.

Sometimes Mary wondered why they stayed together. It was merely a marriage of convenience now. They cared for each other, at least Mary knew that she still cared for Marcus deep down, however the heat and passion of being in love had long since passed, and Mary could not help but wonder if not being able to have children together had played a tremendous part in that. When they were together at home, although they were good companions, they rarely saw much of each other. They certainly didn't sleep together any longer; Marcus had moved to another bedroom after she had complained about his resonant snoring. And since then making love had even become a virtual thing of the past. Marcus took mistresses, usually his secretaries, but then who was she to complain about that! What's good for the goose and all that.

Mary put her mobile on the side table by the sofa. She'd hardly touched her tea, having spent so long ruminating over the past. She drained the entire cup and placed it on the side table alongside her phone. She switched on the TV, tuning in to some late-night chat show. She was starting to feel a bit strange, kind of wobbly like being drunk, but at the same time very sleepy. Before she knew it, Mary was lying back on the sofa in drug-induced state. The comforting mumble from the TV became a monotonous drone in the background and she had heard nothing that was said.

HIM

The house was quiet now; only the soft low sound of the TV drifted up from the living room below. He quietly opened the door to the bedroom he had been hiding in and stepped into the hallway. As he had done many times previously, he walked quietly down the carpeted staircase and to the entrance of the living room. He stood there for a moment watching her sleep, her face in repose and unlined, giving her a look of being much younger. His mouth curled up slightly on the corner in a half smile. He was going to enjoy this and look… she was happy to see him.

He had watched and waited as he had done for many weeks. He knew her movements, knew when she came home, knew when the housekeeper was there. He knew everything about her.

He had watched intently from the moment she had arrived home. She was later than usual tonight but he had known she would come eventually. He knew her routine inside out, knew she was creature of habit and while the lights lit up the inside of the house like a Christmas tree, he waited.

When the lights flickered on upstairs, he moved from the shadows. His place across the street, away from the brightness of the street lights had afforded him a good place to hide – a quiet road where none other than the odd dog walker could be seen, however not at this time of night. The suburban jungle played its part to a tee. No-one ventured from their house after ten thirty p.m. meaning that he could wait and observe in relative solitude and had done so on many occasions previously.

He had practised and honed his craft in preparation for this moment. A life's pursuit coming to fruition and he could barely contain his excitement. But he must! There was no room for error.

He moved silently onto her property, dressed in black from head to toe, a black balaclava covering his face and head. It was too hot for such attire, but completely necessary.

Making his way to the side of the house, he vaulted himself over the fence and into the back garden. There was a side gate, but it was locked with a padlock. He had no need of a key for that. He did however, have keys to the rest of the house. Those had been obtained surreptitiously on one of his many reconnaissance missions in the past few weeks. The stupid Spanish housekeeper, despite having a very good command of the English language, had been easily duped into allowing him access to the house while masquerading as a man from the gas company. She had dutifully shown him to the boiler and given him free access to the house, while she went about her duties. It had been too easy to find the spare house keys, hanging in a box beside the front door. He had of course returned them to their rightful spot a couple of days later, once he had had duplicate keys cut and gained access to the house while no-one was at home. The simpletons had even written down the code to their alarm on a post-it note and left it on a glass bowl on a hall table. These were all mistakes people tended to make because they thought they were safe in their homes, that nothing bad could ever happen to them.

He moved in the shadows around to the back of the house and came to the kitchen door, where he carefully backed against the wall and looked in through the glass. The kitchen was deserted, as he assumed it would be. Moving to the back door, he turned the handle and was gratified to find the door unlocked. He opened it freely and stepped into the kitchen. Sometimes he had found the door locked and sometimes not. He had observed her letting the cat out on several occasions from the darkness of the back garden and for the most part she dutifully locked the door behind her. This presented no challenge on entering the house later that evening as he now just used his keys.

However, this evening, she had left the door unlocked as if she expected him somehow. He liked to think that she did and that at this very moment, she was waiting upstairs for him, ready for him to take her, her legs spread wide, while he fucked her senseless and then slit her throat. He could feel himself growing hard at that thought. His cock felt uncomfortable against his trousers, straining for release. He rubbed his hand against himself in an attempt to relieve the pressure slightly before moving across the kitchen. He was pleased to note that she had got a cup down from the mug tree and placed a tea bag in the cup ready. This was going to be so easy.

Taking a small phial out of his pocket, unscrewing the top, he poured the contents of the Rohypnol he carried into it. The liquid was colourless and tasteless and would easily be disguised in the tea when she made it. He replaced his phial back in his pocket.

On silent feet he moved from the kitchen and into the hallway. He heard the faint sounds of a tap running upstairs and knew she was preparing her bath. That was good, that was *very* good. He wanted her to be clean and ready for him. It was important.

He started up the stairs, keeping watch on her bedroom door, should she suddenly come out of the bedroom and throw the plan into chaos. As he reached the top of the stairs he turned left and headed towards her bedroom door. A small groan of satisfaction came from the en suite he knew adjoined her bedroom, alerting him that she had gotten into the bath. Knowing that he shouldn't deviate from his meticulous planning, he stepped into her bedroom, feeling that he needed to see her. His heart was pounding with excitement and he was struck suddenly, knowing now what people meant when they hoped others couldn't hear it. Would she hear the pounding of *his* heart?

He stepped close to the bathroom door and looked through the tiny gap between the door and the door jamb. He wanted so much to go in, he could almost taste it. She was lying almost motionless, her head against the back of the bath, her throat exposed invitingly. Involuntarily he took a step into the bathroom. He found himself gazing upon her still form, steam permeating the air around him, the scent of her bubble bath assaulting his nostrils. He could so easily take her life now. He could take his knife and slice it across the milkiness of her soft throat. He swallowed the saliva that had formed in his mouth, the anticipation of having such power in hands, overwhelming him for a moment. Then something inside him stilled. As easy as it would be to take her life and absorb that force into his being right now, he knew it could not happen like that. His mission was too important to fail so early. The tasks he had been set had been carefully laid out and meticulously planned in order to avoid detection and capture. He had to become, and in order to become, each and every detail had to be followed exactly. There could be no other way.

Regretfully, he turned back into the bedroom. Seeing her pyjamas folded neatly on the bed, he carefully opened them out and laid them separately and ready for her. With one last look towards the bathroom he left the bedroom and moved to the bedroom next door – her husband's room.

Silently he opened and closed the door behind him, knowing she did not venture here. This was her husband's room and in contrast to the white, pastel tones of her bedroom, this was clearly a masculine retreat of dark wood and dark red walls. He had been in this room many times, rummaging through the wardrobes and the drawers, each new piece of the puzzle he found describing a part of Marcus Nicholls' life and an adventure of discovery.

Marcus Nicholls was a sadist. He enjoyed the rougher side of sex and loved to be dominated as well as be the dominator. He kept his dirty little secrets in a compartment at the back of his wardrobe, which no doubt had remained undiscovered by his wife or his housekeeper. It had been easy for *him* to discover because *he* was the master of all to be purveyed. There had been items of sexual debauchery such as a fake penis of extraordinary size, leather attire and equipment like whips and chains, handcuffs and a ball gag as well as two photo albums full of photos. Self-proclaimed images of his depravity. *He* had enjoyed several hours poring over some of those photos and imagining himself in similar scenarios, except that his idea of ending the fun would have been to cut the women up, slivering pieces off them while they were still alive, tied up and unable to do anything about it. That thought had brought shivers of excitement down his back.

He wondered if Mary knew of her husband's double life. He doubted it. She most certainly knew about his affairs. There were times when she had seemed so melancholy and wistful. He had wanted her to see him then. Had wanted her to see that he was her saviour. She had been chosen, and he had picked her. That made her special.

He had enjoyed watching her in the beginning. She was a temptation and he had almost succumbed to his lustful urges on many occasions, wanting to know what she felt like when he killed her. There was something special about your first love, and he felt like he did love her, although really, she wasn't his first.

He had been through all the aspects of her life, been through her personal things. He knew the intimacies and secrets she held and at times he had found her intriguing.

Very soon however, she had disappointed him. This was, he acknowledged, an expected discovery. Throughout his life he had encountered not one woman who could claim anything other than being a whore. Even his own mother had not escaped that prestigious title. The discovery of that strengthened his resolve, made him believe that what he was doing was righteous and true.

It had happened by accident really. He had been watching her for a couple of weeks and at first thought she was not the woman he was searching for. She worked and came home, worked and came home. There seemed to be nothing more in her life except her job and when her husband was home, Marcus. He couldn't understand how he had found her and began to wonder if he had in fact found a woman who could be worthy of his forgiveness. He had vowed if this was so, he would leave her alone. The irony was that she was just better at protecting what she really was and he was duped into believing it. That had made him so livid with anger, he could barely see anything but a red mist.

The day she had betrayed him, she had in fact had sex with her boss, and it wasn't even a magical moment they could be proud of. It was a quick fuck in carpark!

He had watched Mary and her boss Franklin Hart go for a meal together. There was drinking; a considerable amount of wine and champagne was consumed. The sex had taken place in a carpark at the back of the restaurant. She had removed her underwear and he had taken her against the wall. *He*, having followed them to the restaurant, watched from his vantage point behind a bush at the back of the carpark. She was giggling and couldn't stand straight. Franklin had better control and was maybe was not so drunk. He was clearly planning to drive them both home. As they reached his car, he suddenly reached out and pulled her to him, and they were suddenly kissing each other. He had not expected this and suddenly his entire being stilled as he watched the scenario before him unfold.

Franklin was pushing her to the back of the restaurant, away from the carpark lighting and into the shadows. Their kissing continued, hands exploring each other.

He could see perfectly clearly, his eyes having adjusted themselves to the darkness. He watched as Franklin pulled her blouse from skirt, his hand disappearing underneath the fabric where he grabbed her breast. She groaned suggestively. He pulled her skirt up slightly and she bent to remove her tights and knickers.

Everything that was sacred was almost on display to the whole word. While she removed her underwear, Franklin unzipped his trousers. He entered her while she stood against the wall. Her bare leg was wrapped around his leg as he fucked her. The wet smacking sounds were clearly evident across the carpark.

He was shocked and devastated. He expected her to be a slut and a whore, but never had he conceived in the past few months that she was entirely promiscuous, having no respect for herself to give her body to a man in the street. Everything changed for him then. He knew that he had found her. The first of many. Had anyone been watching his face at that time, they would have observed the steely consternation in his face. The eyes that displayed no emotion, but glittered darkly in the night, a fearful hatred on his face that should have made Franklin and Mary fear for their lives.

He watched until it was over. He watched as Franklin zipped up his trousers and bent to pick up Mary's handbag where she had dropped it on the floor. He watched Mary as she readjusted her skirt and tucked her blouse back in. She accepted her handbag from Franklin and put her retrieved tights and knickers into her handbag, before bending to pick up her shoes. He watched as they joked that two buttons had broken off her blouse and he watched as they both got into Franklin's car.

His scathing appraisal of them both burned in his mind for a long time after they had left the restaurant.

Their affair had continued since. He had observed many rendezvous since that first night, although none quite so tawdry as the quick fuck against the wall of a restaurant.

He had been in the house many times while Franklin and Mary had sex, when her own husband Marcus was away. They met often for their solicitous self-gratification before Franklin Hart would scuttle off, back to his own wife and family. Oh yes, he had been there as well and observed that particular set up. The whole thing sickened him. No-one could be trusted. He was the righteous one, he was a messiah and he would have no hesitation in wreaking the vengeance that he needed to.

He had made his way downstairs silently from the bedroom. He stood at the entrance to the living room and observed Mary where she lay on the sofa. The Rohypnol had done its job and she snored softly, unaware of anything in her surroundings. He was ready. It was time.

His stare was intense and dark, his almost black eyes fixed and unblinking just like a snake, on the sleeping woman before him. The smile on his lips displayed no sense of happiness or pleasure, but was a mask of pure evil, a predator with its prey in its sight. It would have been disconcerting for any ordinary person to see at that moment, but of course there was nobody to see it, of that he was assured.

His gaze flickered over Mary, observing her breasts and the rise of fall of the pyjama top that encased them. Her breathing was deep and even. She was in a half-sitting, half lying position, her body slightly slumped to one side, her head at a peculiar angle. It was quite overwhelming for him in that moment, being so close to Mary. His Mary. She was his now. She belonged to him. He had been so close to her many times, he had touched her when she slept, ran his fingers across her cheek or her breast, touched her hair and allowed his lips to touch hers, but never without inhibition or danger. He wanted to touch her now, feel his skin against hers. He could do so, he had hours of pleasure ahead of him.

He stood back and removed his balaclava, carefully putting it the right way around and laying it on the arm of the sofa. He had been wearing surgical gloves since he entered the house, and kept these on as he removed all his clothing except for his socks. He stood naked before her sleeping form, his cock standing ready to attention. He was going to enjoy this so much.

He moved towards Mary and pulled her by the thighs so that her legs were mostly off the sofa, her feet on the floor, although not flatly. The fluidity of her body meant that her legs and feet flopped down in her relaxed state, leaving the rest of her upper body at a peculiar angle. The movement made her eyes open and she stared at him for a moment before giggling. He smiled at her. She knew who he was of course.

He pulled at the waistband of her pyjama bottoms and shimmied them over her hips and down her legs, lifting her legs and removing them one by one. He flung these across the room which got another chuckle from Mary. She was clearly enjoying herself, and he was sure it couldn't all be drug induced. Carefully, he pulled her forward again and half lifted her to a sitting position with her back leaning against the sofa. Her legs seemed to flop out before her and she reminded him of an oversized rag doll. Her head flopped onto his shoulder for a moment and she sniggered. "I wanna get naked," she slurred almost incoherently.

"Of course you do and I am going to help you," he told her gently, allowing her head to flop back onto the sofa cushion. She murmured something else incoherently and her eyelids fluttered. He paused for a brief second to see what would happen, but her head just lolled from side to side in a drunken floppy sort of way. She did not seem at all perturbed that he was undressing her. It was essentially like undressing a child. She was a lot heavier than he had anticipated, her body almost a dead weight in her induced state. He pulled her arms out of her pyjama top one at a time and eventually pulled it off over her head. Again, he threw this across the room where he had earlier thrown the bottoms. He stood above her, gazing down at her now naked form. She was positioned in such an awkward way as to appear unnatural but he didn't seem to notice or care as his eyes devoured every inch of her body. He had viewed her in this state many times of course. Her naked form was no stranger to him, the soft curves of her stomach, hips and breasts tempting him provocatively on many occasions. Now however, he got to touch and feel at his own leisure to relish her body as he had wanted to do for so long. She shifted in her sleep then, her legs flopping open slightly to allow him to view her most inner secrets.

He could feel his mouth salivating in anticipation as he gazed at the juncture between her legs, the soft curls that shone in the glow of the lamp light of the living room as though she were appearing to offer herself up to him. She was of course. His head tilted slightly to one side as he regarded her. If only Mary could have known how he felt about her in that moment, what a privilege it was for her to be the first in his becoming. He sighed theatrically and collected himself.

He glanced down at the white rug in front of the sofa and decided it would provide an adequate bed. He leant forward and began the job of manoeuvring her body into a lying down position. It was hard for their bodies not to come into contact with each. He was sweating, not only with anticipation, but also with the exertion of moving her body. Her sleeping form was heavier than he might have considered and he was not entirely gentle as he hoisted her body to the floor. When he was satisfied with her position, he turned back to his own clothing and removed a condom from his pocket. His mouth was dry with anticipation. For so long he had coveted this moment, he hoped it was all he expected it to be.

Placing the condom over his engorged penis he bent down and pulled Mary's thigh's apart. He almost ejaculated as his penis touched the entrance to her vagina, but steeled himself against doing so. He needed to savour this for as long as possible.

Again, once he had commanded himself to remain controlled, he pushed his penis into her pliant body. It was like coming home. At once his body came alive, the nerve endings all over him seeming to carry an electrical pulse as he began to move in a slow, steady rhythm. She made a soft mewling sound, her movements suggesting that she was enjoying herself as her arms found their way around his neck and her legs around the back of his thighs. He stilled for a moment again. Her head was thrown back, her eyes closed. Her tongue darted out and licked her lips, moistening them. He began to move again, this time faster. She moved with him, her pants and groans mounting as she neared her own orgasm. His balls were making a satisfactory slapping sound against her body as he pounded into her. His whole body was covered in a thin film of sweat. He had never felt so alive. All of the times when he had been alone, servicing himself by his own administrations, had not felt like this.

At the moment of ejaculation, he knew he loved this woman in that moment with his entire being. His one regret was that she would never know of his love, nor of the part she would play in the evolving of his being.

He collapsed on top of her for a moment to catch his breath, before moving to a more comfortable position beside her. His face was turned towards her.

She turned her head towards him. "Thank you." She murmured and closed her eyes. Determined to savour every second of their conjoining, his fingers, still encased in the surgical gloves, moved along her body, tracing the line of her stomach to her breasts where took his time to cup and tweak her nipples. He wanted to suck them, but couldn't afford to leave any DNA from his saliva. When the time came for him to dispose of a body in water, he could afford to taste and discover those other delights, which had so far eluded him.

He was becoming excited again. He removed the soiled condom from his cock and tied the end, encapsulating the semen that resided there. He took a second condom from one of his pockets and removed the packaging, placing it over his penis. He was almost ready to have sex with her again. He grinned down at her. She had a small satisfied smiled playing around her lips.

"I'm going to take you once more, Mary, then I'm going to cut your throat," he told her honestly. She seemed to smile in agreement. He was pleased, but then after all she nothing but a dirty little slut. Still, he could not refuse such an invitation?

He took her again, this time with more ferocity, slapping her hard around the face as he ejaculated. She squealed in pain, but he was still inside her and had her body pinned to the floor. Still she had nothing to fight him with. He couldn't help but feel disappointment and resentment consume him as he watched her lie there. She had just pretended to enjoy it. Isn't that what whores did? Lie back and pretend it was the best sex they had ever had, but thanks and leave the money by the bed as you leave?

Instantly he felt angry. He wanted to kick her hard between her legs or take his knife and stab her impetuously over and over again.

He took a deep breath. It wouldn't do to rush this. He had a schedule and it had to be stuck to. There was no telling how long the Rohypnol would keep affecting her. Everything he had read suggested that different people reacted differently. It could take as little as two hours before she began reviving, or as long as twelve hours. Whatever happened, it wouldn't do for the Rohypnol to wear off and her to be fully revived before he was finished.

Standing up, he removed the second condom, again tying the end with a knot. He would dispose of those later along with his clothes. Turning, he walked silently back into the kitchen and chose the largest kitchen knife he could find. It was a large carving knife and would do excellently. During his previous reconnaissance in the house, in the early days of his planning, he had thought to bring his own equipment for the work he had to do. A scalpel was small and could be easily hidden, but a large knife was another matter entirely. He needed a large knife for the bulk of his work. It was then that he had thought of using what was at his disposal within Mary's home. Mary seemed to have the best of everything. What she thought screamed taste just because it was expensive was a misinterpretation that many people had, but in the case of her kitchen implements, she had in fact purchased some of the most superior steel money had to offer and hence the large knife sitting in the block on the kitchen worktop, although never having been used for the purpose it was intended, was now a perfect weapon at his disposal.

Now that he had had his fun, it was time for his real work to start. This had to be carried out meticulously.

He stood above her once more before kneeling down on one knee, straddling her body. Gently he placed the knife down on the floor.

She lay looking up at him so innocently that he could almost believe that she was innocent of any crime, but he knew like he was looking into the deepest recesses of her soul. She was far from innocent. To see the things he had seen could broker no argument from that quarter.

Kneeling now on both knees, still straddling her body, he leant forward and ran a gloved hand across her face and smoothed her hair back from her forehead and cheeks where it had fallen naturally. He placed his hands gently around her neck.

He had never strangled anybody before and had no concept of the effort it would take.

Despite her drug-induced state, some awareness or survival instinct must have kicked in immediately. Her eyes popped wide and fixed on her attacker. He wondered what was going through her mind, whether she was trying to place where she knew him from. Did she recognise him for sure? He was fascinated as her mouth moved silently like a fish out of water, gasping for air. Her body was semi-slack but her arms were flailing, although not really doing anything helpful. In a matter of seconds her face showed confusion, then horror as she realised the seriousness of her predicament.

She blinked up at him, her blue eyes fixed on his face as if memorising what she saw. He watched the emotions play over her face for a moment. It had only been a matter of moments since he had put his hands around her neck, but already she seemed to coming around a lot quicker than he would have anticipated; already his arms were starting to burn a little. It took immense pressure to strangle somebody.

MARY

Mary saw black dots in front of her eyes. Somehow, she knew she was going to lose consciousness. Her brain at first had been very sluggish. She felt like she was in a dense fog but it wasn't all around her, it was inside her head and body. She felt like she couldn't move properly, like every move she made took an immense amount of effort. Was she drunk? She tried fruitlessly to remember her evening. What had happened? Had she been out? Where was Franklin? Where was Marcus? Who was this man? She knew this man. The realisation dawned on her. She knew his face. She had seen him before, she was sure of it, but it was just too difficult to remember where. Her thoughts flew by in a matter of seconds, each moment bringing her closer to unconsciousness or death as the man continued to strangle her. Too late perhaps, the dawning realisation that she was not fighting for her life, despite a dwindling lack of oxygen, broke through her consciousness. Mary's brain seemed to jump start into working in double quick time. At that first moment when she had realised she knew her attacker, she had also understood with a sense of dread that the feeling that she was being watched and followed had not been a figment of her imagination at all but very likely her intuition or sixth sense which had kicked in with uncanny accuracy. She felt the fruitlessness of her situation however, as she realised her early warning system had in fact failed to actually prevent this moment from happening.

Realising too, that her worst fears were coming true, that everything she had been so afraid of, the shadows and the dark seemed to spark a sudden awareness in Mary's being. Was he planning to rape her, murder her, both or simply strangle her to death? As the black spots began to fill her vision, Mary's one last coherent thought was that the police always checked fingernails for the attacker's skin. Her arms reached up towards his face which had seemed so near at first, but now it was like he was disappearing down a long tunnel. She couldn't seem to reach him; her arms flailed as if there were no true destination in mind at all. Had she been more awake or alert, she might have thought to try to buck and kick in order to try and dislodge her attacker, but as Mary Nicholls descended into a black unconsciousness, only one final thought filled her brain… "Why me?"

HIM

He knew the moment she lost consciousness. His arms were screaming under the pressure of strangling her; it had taken much more out of him than he had realised it would, and that was with very little fight coming from Mary. He reduced his hold on her throat, waiting in case she had somehow tricked him. There was a fine line between unconsciousness and death. In truth he had not been concerned if she did die; she was going to anyway, but as the realisation dawned on him about what he had actually accomplished, he felt like shouting from the rooftops.

He watched Mary's breathing, the gentle rise and fall of bosom. Dark pink bruises were already forming on her throat and he cocked his head to one side as he regarded his handiwork. This was just perfect.

Satisfied that the first part of his work had been completed, he took a step back. The muscles in his arms and neck were screaming from their exertions. Had she been fighting back, it might have taken considerably more effort on his part; he might not even have been able to successfully strangle her. He was glad he took the time to keep himself in shape. He felt sweaty and slightly breathless, although he was unsure whether that was because of his administrations or whether he was feeling slightly excited. His heart rate had increased.

He stood up and rolled his shoulders in an effort to loosen the tightness. He had no benchmark to compare for how long she would be out, so he needed to work quickly now.

Kneeling down beside her, he smoothed her hair away from her face. Seeing her face was imperative.

He rearranged her arms so that they were by her side. He stood and looked down at her, satisfied at last. Yes, she was finally ready.

Turning, he picked up the knife he had taken from the kitchen from the floor where he had left it. He was startled by Mary's sudden whimper. He couldn't very well have her waking up and screaming, drawing unwanted attention to him, spoiling his plans and ruining his evening. The anger roiled through him, coursing through his body like a red-hot poker. A mist seemed to manifest itself and cloud him mentally and before his mind could produce a coherent thought, his foot had connected with her head, kicking her so hard to the side of her head that her whole body jerked to the right side. She whimpered again, attempting to bring her hands up to defend herself. This was not going according to his plans. She was supposed to have stayed unconscious for longer but already she was waking up. The kick to her head should have put her out again, but it had not and now he was perturbed. Despite his attention to every detail, he had not formulated a back-up plan and for the briefest of seconds he had no idea what he was going to do.

His gaze fell on Mary's naked form. Her head was flopping from side to side slowly and she seemed sluggish. Her hair had fallen across her face once more, but she made no move to push it back. One more swift kick would likely put her out, but on the other hand he might actually kill her and that would spoil his plans completely.

He realised he was holding his knife. He felt a prickle of disappointment as he had wanted to do other things to her before she woke up, but this perhaps might be even better. Kneeling quickly over Mary's body he placed one knee either side of her chest. He positioned his knife. He looked down at her, a mixture of pleasure, distaste and finally ecstasy crossing his face. She was becoming more alert at a pace quicker than he would have liked;

she was trying to move her hands and arms, her head rolling from side to side as if she was trying to bring herself around.

MARY

Mary Nicholls opened her eyes and stared up at the naked man above her. The realisation dawned on her in those final moments of her life, what had happened to her. She knew this man, of that she was certain. She couldn't remember his name, but his face was undoubtedly familiar to her. Other things became apparent to her. Her neck and throat hurt immensely. She knew he had tried to strangle her, perhaps even to kill her. She also knew he had had sex with her. Not only was the fact that he was naked an indication of this, but she could feel an uncomfortable wetness between her legs suggesting that she had been excited enough to orgasm. He had raped her and the only way she could think of him being able to do that without her knowledge was that he had used that date rape drug. The name of it escaped her right now, but she had heard of the symptoms. The question that burned in her brain now however, was how he had got into her house – had she let him in and if so, how had he managed to drug her?

It was a strange jumble of thoughts that assaulted her mind as she slowly regained consciousness. Her body still felt sluggish as if she was weighed down and she knew instinctively that that was another side effect of whatever he had given her.

Too late, she started to wonder what she was going to do about all this, when out of the corner of her eye something bright and shiny caught her attention.

She realised a millisecond too late what her would-be attacker's intention was towards her. She opened her mouth to scream, but he moved with lightning fast ferocity. With a practised hand using the knife, he sliced open her throat.

HIM

It felt like a hot knife going through butter, and as he cut, he knew that it was deep enough to have cut through major tendons. Her artery having been hit caused her blood to spurt out in an arc, cascading across the room and landing on her table, lamp, photographs and wall. Her life's blood was already pumping onto the white rug, spilling onto the wooden floor, flexively keeping pace with her heartbeat as it pumped out of her body. He watched in fascination as her hands moved to her throat, a reflex action. She was going to die and she knew it. Gargling noises came up through her throat as she tried to speak and then blood bubbled up through her throat and fell from the corners of her mouth. He had severed her wind pipe and he smiled as she began to choke on her own blood. It wasn't a pretty death by any means, but he found it absolutely fascinating to watch. He was hunkered down by her feet, the knife loosely in his left hand, the point disappearing into the white carpet as he twizzled it back and forth gently watching Mary's demise.

Her hands remained against her neck for what little help they were. Blood oozed through her fingers and ran in little rivers down her hands and arms, joining the ever-increasing pool already forming under her head and shoulders. His heart was racing with excitement. The evening was back on track.

Mary's life extinguished before his eyes, her futile last struggles for breath no more than wet gurgling sounds. It was mesmerising to watch and he could not have removed his eyes from her face in that moment.

At last the final semblance of Mary Nicholls' life ebbed from her body, her body growing still in death, her eyes staring sightlessly into space, resembling pieces of glass on a waxwork model. Her life's blood, as he had hoped it would, ran out in a large puddle, ruining her white room, forever staining the white rug. He had moved away from her, but sat close enough that he could still see every minute detail as it played out before him. The seconds passed, becoming minutes and yet he still sat silently watching his prey. He had felt the frantic rise and fall of her chest as she struggled to gather a breath, the butterfly wings of her fluttering hands as she tried to reach out and grab him. Each moment of her death replayed itself in front of his eyes like a DVD playing over and over again. He recalled how each struggling inhale seemed to suck down the blood and she choked.

It all stopped like a switch had been thrown into the off position. She no longer moved. There was no rise and fall of her chest, her eyes stared sightlessly. She had known she was dying and had tried to speak to him in those final seconds. He wondered what she had been trying to say.

Now he would need to set the scene before rigor mortis took hold of the body. He moved towards her carefully. He didn't really want to disturb the pool of blood. Bringing himself into a standing position, he turned once again to his clothes carefully placed on the end of the sofa away from the carnage and blood. From inside his pocket he pulled out a small pair of booties for his feet and sat on the edge of the sofa while he placed them over his socks. It wouldn't do get his socks soaked with her blood and leave tell tale footprints throughout the house. The police, while he knew were inept at best, it wouldn't do to give them any additional clues.

With the booties in place, he stood once again and reached forward toward Mary's body. He pulled her hands carefully away from the gaping hole in her throat. Blood continued to trickle from the wound in her neck, but with no heart pumping to continue the flow, it was little more than an ooze. He placed her arms, one either side of her body.

Now he was ready to begin phase two.

Standing up, he paused for a moment to contemplate the thing that was once Mary. He had loved her as he had loved others. She was not his first by any means, but was perhaps one of the most important to him. She had certainly become so over the months he had watched her. How he had enjoyed the watching, the chase, the meticulous planning that made him feel so powerful and superior.

Mary had no knowledge of the part she was about to play, none of them did and he wished suddenly with a moment of wistful nostalgia that he could have shared that with her so that she would understand the purpose of her death. The fact that she was a whore was immaterial really, all women were whores in varying degrees, but there were those who were meant for a higher purpose despite their indiscretions and how they lived their lives.

He was thankful to Mary and in that moment felt an intense sense of gratitude towards her. In an involuntary movement, he suddenly reached down and stroked his fingers across her cheek, almost an adoring tender expression of reverence that in any other circumstance might have been interpreted as an act of a lover.

"You are more special than you know," he whispered softly, finally rising to his feet. A natural calm instilled his body. Was this how a surgeon felt when they worked on a body? He thought so. He took a deep breath. With the preliminary phase over, he was ready. With a determined look of concentration on his face, he bent once more to Mary's body.

CHAPTER TWO

Phoebe Dalton sat at her workstation. She had worked at Hart, Smith & Dawson for almost three years and for the most part enjoyed her job. Mary was outstanding to work for. There were not many employers who gave a single mum a second look, but she was grateful to Mary for giving her that chance and whenever she could, she repaid Mary for the times she had allowed her to leave because her child was sick or she had to leave early due to parent's evening or a school play. Mary had never treated Phoebe as a lesser mortal for being a mum, although the same couldn't be said for some of her colleagues at work.

Phoebe had a theory that perhaps Mary really wanted children. At thirty-nine her biological clock must be ticking, and she had a successful career, a husband and was settled, but Phoebe's theory extended to the fact that she thought that Mary or her husband couldn't have them. It was never a consideration in Phoebe's mind that perhaps neither of them wanted children.

Mary had been considerate enough to buy her son, James, a Christmas present, and she even remembered his birthday and brought him gifts then too.

Because Mary was so thoughtful, Phoebe was happy to reciprocate whenever she could, hence finding herself in the office today at eight a.m. instead of the usual nine a.m. Thank God for her mum, that she could take James to school on the odd occasion it was required.

It was a big day today. Mary had been working on a proposal that could push the company into the twenty-second century. There was a massive presentation to the managing director Franklin Hart and his two partners, as well as the other directors in the company.

When she arrived this morning, Phoebe had found a post-it note on her desk, giving the save location of the Powerpoint presentation Mary had been working on. It had been an ongoing task for weeks, but Phoebe knew what a control freak and perfectionist Mary was and knew it would be just about perfect. Phoebe found the location in their shared drive and pulled up the presentation, setting about printing out the handouts for the attendees of the meeting.

She had just finished typing up the agenda and realised that it was close to 8.35 a.m. and Mary hadn't arrived at the office yet. This was unusual for Mary, who was not only a perfectionist and workaholic but had never been late for anything in the whole three years that Phoebe had worked for her.

At 8.40 a.m. Phoebe was starting to fret, having glanced at her watch for the umpteenth time only to find that the second hand didn't appear to be moving. She wondered if Mary had broken down in her car, or maybe had had an accident. It was a brief assumption. She was sure if that had happened, Mary would have called. She would never be late for something so important and she did, after all, have a mobile phone.

She dialled Mary's home number and listened to the persistent ring at the other end before it kicked into the answerphone message.

"Hi, you have reached the home of Marcus and Mary Nicholls... ", yada, yada, yada. Phoebe listened through the message and then left one of her own, asking Mary to call her as soon as possible. Then she tried ringing Mary's mobile number. Again, she listened to Mary's voicemail message before leaving her own.

Having tried the home phone and her mobile at alternating intervals, at nine thirty a.m. Phoebe was seriously worried. It was so uncharacteristic of Mary to be late and not let anyone know about it and as far as she was aware no calls had been received at all.

Not knowing what else to do at that precise moment, she left her desk and made her way to Franklin Hart's office.

Selina Jackson, Franklin Hart's PA sat at her desk outside his office, typing so hard on her keyboard, Phoebe was sure she would break it. Phoebe stood before Selina's desk, waiting. It must have taken a whole minute before Selina finally stopped typing and looked up. She peered at Phoebe over the top of her glasses. "Yes?" she snapped.

"Is Mr Hart in his office? I need to speak to him about Ms Nicholls."

Selina's lips pursed in a disapproving way and she sighed heavily. Phoebe inwardly raged. Just who did this woman think she was? God she was like the gestapo, with her I'm going to look down my nose at you attitude. Selina Jackson pressed the intercom button. "Mr Hart, sorry to trouble you, I have Ms Dalton, Ms Nicholls' secretary here to see you." Her voice dripped with disdain as she spoke both Mary's name and hers. Phoebe stood and glared at her.

"Send her in," came back the curt reply down the intercom.

"You may go in," Selina sniped regally, although there was no need as Phoebe had heard Franklin Hart speak.

"My ears work just fine thanks." Phoebe couldn't help herself and marched haughtily passed Selina's desk, tapping on Franklin Hart's office door.

"Come." She pushed open the door and stepped into the sumptuous sanctuary which was Franklin's Hart's office.

Opulent became a whole new phrase when you walked into Franklin Hart's cream carpeted office. Phoebe had heard tell that Franklin's wife, who had a flair for interior design, had decorated his office. It smacked of taste and look expensive.

Franklin Hart sat behind his dark mahogany wooden desk, his body encased in a black leather office chair. On one end stood his laptop, beside which was his diary, opened to a specific page, his telephone and intercom. A piece of art which Phoebe could only describe as a small statue of a well-endowed woman held up a globe made of metal wire. A large gold desk lamp stood at the other end of his desk, framed with a large teal coloured shade. Two Queen

Anne designed chairs sat in front of his desk, a bold red, green and brown pattern adorning them. To the right of the room in the corner was what could easily be described as a dining room table. Made of the same mahogany wood as his desk, this housed six red leather sturdy chairs around it. A large display of orange and yellow flowers adorned the centre of the table. To the right of this below a large picture window sat a red leather Chesterfield sofa, flanked by two comfy armchairs in a cream and red stripe. The sofa was adorned by cushions and a large oriental rug stood beneath that and the chairs. A large clock decorated one wall, the pendulum swinging, the ticking heard in the otherwise silent room. Pieces of expensive looking art brought the other walls to life. It was a functional as well as comfortable space. It was also bigger, Phoebe noted, probably than her entire apartment.

She found Franklin Hart to be imposing and was instantly nervous around him, her hands wringing in front of her. Phoebe spoke quickly, wanting to relieve the burden of her worries about Mary not attending for work. Phoebe explained that she had tried countless times to get her on her house phone or mobile. She finished her summation stating that she believed something must have happened to Mary; could she have slipped in the shower perhaps?

Franklin Hart listened to the young woman's explanation apparently appearing dispassionate, but quite frankly he was alarmed. Mary Nicholls, in the ten years he had known her, had never had a day off sick. She rarely took holiday and was as much a workaholic as him.

Franklin stared at the woman before him for a moment. She was pretty in a girl-next-door sort of way, but didn't really do anything for him. Too timid for one thing. He liked women with a bit of clout, a bit of a sting in the tail and a definite ability to stand up to him. This little mouse was neither of those things and actually, far too young. He drew the line somewhere.

Franklin had always considered himself quite a traditionalist with an old-fashioned set of values that he adhered to whenever *he* deemed it appropriate. He was set in his ways and was wary of women in the workplace. However, in Mary's case he had been proved happily wrong. If there were any woman who he deemed could fill his shoes, it was definitely his Mary. '*His Mary*'. Well, a faux pas perhaps, she was hardly *his* really.

He had high hopes for Mary; he considered that she had the business head of a man, despite her womanly exterior. She had impressed him several times, earning her an unlikely position in his company.   He had wondered whether she would up and have children at some point, but she had not seemed at all interested and so he had given her more and more responsibility. He had a serious 'jones' where Mary Nicholls was concerned. She had put him firmly in his place on several occasions. He respected her, which few women, other than his own mother and his wife Roselynn, had earned in his opinion. He also got one hell of hard-on when she was around and acting out, playing the big 'I am boss'.

In Franklin's mind they had danced around each other for years, neither one acknowledging that theirs was more than just a working relationship, however, nothing had come of that until one night about six or seven months ago. After obtaining a very lucrative deal, they had gone out to celebrate. The evening had gone off with a bang in more ways than one and Franklin had in fact had sex in the restaurant carpark with Mary. It had been quick, hot and heavy, but deeply satisfying and exciting and Franklin for one, could hardly wait for a repeat performance. At first Mary had held him firmly at arm's length, but it hadn't taken long before they were pawing at each other again, and now they were both embroiled in an affair as well as a working relationship. So far, it was fun. Franklin knew he may well rue the day when it was all over, but Roselynn had forgiven him before; she would do so again. He would perhaps secure Mary a good position with one of his colleagues if it came to that, and they could all move on.

Today was one of the most important days in the company's history. Each of the high rollers in the company had been putting together the deal of a lifetime, which would undoubtedly set him among the most serious players, earning him a six-figure salary and a huge amount in the bank to boot. He would be minted. Of all the pieces of the puzzle, Mary had been working on the ultimate part, and now she was missing in action. She knew only too well what this deal meant or what it could mean for both him and the company. It crossed his mind briefly that perhaps she had gone to one of his competitors. Maybe that's why she wasn't here this morning. He pushed the thought from his mind immediately, refusing to give it any substance.

Franklin steepled his fingers on his chin as he regarded the worried-looking young woman in front of him. Had something happened to Mary? Was she now lying in her shower, as this woman surmised, having slipped and banged her head? It was certainly not like Mary to be late, be a no-show or not even ring. "Take a drive out to her house if you don't mind, er, er… "

"Phoebe," she finished for him, recognising that he didn't know her name.

"Er, yes, Phoebe. You do drive I take it?" When she nodded, he continued, "Give me a call when you know more. Hopefully it's just a simple mistake. I will postpone the meeting until eleven a.m., that should give you ample time."

Phoebe nodded again and turned to leave the room.

David Crisp was perched on the edge of Selina's desk when she came out. There was something so smarmy about him that he physically made her skin crawl. He grinned salaciously at her as she stepped out of Franklin's office, closing the door behind her. He was a typical male that thought himself God's gift to women. He always wore light grey suits and waistcoats with brown brogue shoes and brightly coloured ties. His black hair was cut in a short back and sides style with the top being gelled within an inch of his life. He had clearly had his teeth whitened and used a sunbed regularly. Phoebe suspected that he even went so far as having his nails manicured as they were perfectly round and looked shiny. The thought of him evening putting a hand on her had her wanting to run for the bathroom to be sick.

"Sucking off the boss man?" he drawled. Selina giggled behind her hand. "Oops, I mean sucking up? Or did I have it right the first time?" He smiled with what he must have supposed was a winning smile. Phoebe glared at both him and Selina and walked on by to her own desk.

"Stuck up tart." She heard David stage-whisper to Selina, who again giggled.

"Fuckwit," Phoebe murmured under her breath, grabbing her bag and her coat and making her way to the lifts.

Phoebe knew the reason for his disdain and it came down to the fact that he had tried it on at the office Christmas party and failed several times. Although she had heard that he had tried it on with several other of the junior secretaries and by all accounts had managed to snag one. That particular woman had left shortly after Christmas. There were rumours that David had had sex with the young woman although she claimed without her consent. Fortunately for David Crisp it had never come to more than a rumour, but Phoebe had a feeling there was no smoke without fire.

Phoebe took the lift downstairs, checking her mobile as she went. Not a call or text from Mary at all. Phoebe could feel nervous knots crawling all over the inside of her stomach. She had a terrible feeling that something was very, very wrong. This was not like Mary at all. She placed a further call to her home number and mobile obtaining the same response as previously.

Phoebe parked her car next to Mary's on the drive. The house was quiet, as was the street as she got out of her car. Nothing seemed out of the ordinary. She walked up and knocked on the front door, but received no response. She bent down and looked through the letterbox, but everything looked as it should be. She called through the letterbox. Again nothing.

Phoebe walked to the side of the house and tried the gate to the back garden, but it was firmly padlocked. She wondered if she should call the police. But they would break down the door and then maybe there was a simple explanation and Mary would be furious and possibly sack Phoebe for doing it. She pulled her mobile phone from her handbag, and stood staring at it. She just didn't know what to do. A small red car suddenly pulled in to the drive behind her.

The engine cut off and a tiny Hispanic-looking lady climbed from the driver's side, giving Phoebe a quizzical look. That's got to be Pepe, thought Phoebe and began walking towards the lady. Mary had raved about her amazing housekeeper. "Hello," Phoebe called, giving a little wave. Pepe smiled politely with a 'can I help you' look on her face, but moved to the back of her car anyway. She opened the rear door of the car and removed some dry cleaning before moving to the boot of her car and taking out a couple of supermarket shopping bags.

"My name's Phoebe Dalton, I'm Mary's secretary," she explained quickly. The small woman looked up at her and for a second Phoebe wondered if the woman could speak any English. "Mary didn't come into work this morning and we had a very important meeting. I came to see if she was okay as I can't seem to get her on the phone." She continued anyway, her words coming out in a rush.

"Okay," Pepe replied, shrugging, and moved towards the front door, keys at the ready.

Phoebe watched as the tiny woman juggled what she was carrying in order to release the keys and unlocked the house. "Oh goodness, let me help you, I'm sorry I wasn't thinking." She moved toward Pepe, hands outstretched.

"It's okay, I can manage, I'm used to it." Although Pepe was heavily accented, she clearly understood and spoke English perfectly.

Phoebe followed Pepe through the front door and into the hallway.

"The alarm's not set." Pepe gestured towards the small box on the wall with her head. Phoebe glanced at it and then turned to look around the house. There was a faint odour in the air. She wrinkled her nose, unable to place it immediately, but there was also something more. The house was deathly quiet.

"Mary... " Phoebe called into the silence. She had been to Mary's house before as a guest and did not feel comfortable entering further without permission.

Pepe, of course, had no such misgivings. She strolled through the hallway towards the kitchen. Phoebe followed, not knowing what else to do.

The kitchen was immaculate and spotlessly clean and like everything else in Mary's life, perfect. The white, modern kitchen cabinets gleamed in the late morning sunshine and Phoebe stood and watched for a moment as Pepe placed her shopping bags on the kitchen table and went to hang the dry cleaning up in the utility room. She returned to the kitchen, starting to unpack her shopping bags.

Phoebe shrugged, turning to walk back to the hallway. "Mary... ?" she called again, louder this time. Again, the deathly silence of an empty house greeted her back.

All the doors to the hallway were closed but Phoebe could still detect that peculiar smell. She sniffed the air for a moment, wondering what it was.

There were two doors to her right and one to her left. She opened the first on the right and was confronted with a pristine dining room, a cream-coloured room, where the only splashes of colour were the furniture and a feature wall, painted a dark burgundy red. A shining mahogany dining room table, surrounded by eight matching chairs, sat perfectly central to the room with a beautiful display of flowers upon it, the smell emanating from them denoting that they were real. Phoebe knew that such a large flower display would cost a fortune. A real bar sat in one corner of the room, while an old-fashioned jukebox adorned another corner.

Other pieces of expensive looking furniture were around the room, while large French windows cloaked with striped burgundy and cream coloured curtains gave a view of the garden, but no Mary.

Pepe appeared at the entrance to the room as Phoebe turned to leave, closing the door behind her.

The next door to the right was also shut. Phoebe pushed opened the door to what was the living room and froze as the scene before her unfolded itself like a grisly nightmare. Before she had a chance to react, Pepe began screaming hysterically. She backed away from the room, making the sign of the cross and spouting a torrent of Spanish that was being said so fast, Phoebe had no chance to get what she was saying. She stood on the threshold of the living room, in complete shock, her mind not fully comprehending the scene before her which was like something out of a horror movie.

Mary Nicholls lay on her back, her eyes starring sightlessly into nothing. Her dark brown hair was fanned out around her head as though carefully arranged.

Mary's mouth gaped open slightly; blood had trickled out of her mouth on both sides. Her neck was made up of two open garish wounds that looked as though they had been sliced open and then scooped out like a melon with a spoon. The wound had bled profusely, creating a now dark red stain like a halo around her head, neck and shoulders. Most of it had seeped into the once white carpet and some had spread even further to the oak flooring.

She was completely naked. Her legs had been pushed open and her arms lay by her sides. There were stab wounds all over her body, and an especially large cut on her stomach. It looked as though someone had slashed at her in a frenzy. The entire scene was macabre and abhorrent.

Pepe was gone. She was not screaming any longer, but mumbling in another part of the house.

Phoebe had no idea how long she had stood there, but a rational part of her knew it was mere seconds. The scene before her would be carried in her mind's eye for the rest of her life. Realising that her handbag still resided on her shoulder, she reached inside and pulled out her mobile phone. Her hands were shaking almost uncontrollably as she failed two attempts to enter her pin to unlock her phone. She also couldn't seem to take her eyes away from the scene before her, like she thought it might be a hallucination. Unable to make her feet move in any direction, she finally looked away from the grisly scene before her and down at her mobile phone. It took all her concentration to dial the numbers – 9-9-9. "Nine nine nine, which service do you require?" came the disembodied voice down the phone.

"Police," Phoebe said, her voice giving rise to a calmness she did not feel.

CHAPTER THREE

1st SEPTEMBER

Detective Chief Inspector Virginia Percy stood looking at the body of Mary Nicholls with consternation. Scene of Crime officers and forensics were all over scene, photographing everything. The house was a melee of sound and action.

So far there was nothing to alert the police to who had conducted such a crime.

Ginny checked her notes. The alarm had been raised by Mary Nicholls' secretary, Phoebe Dalton, who was currently at the Main Road station being interviewed. Mary's cleaner, Pepe Vasquez, who was so traumatised she could only speak in Spanish, mumbling the same thing over and over again, was currently on her way to the local hospital. One of the uniformed officers fortunately remembered his schoolboy Spanish and had loosely translated that she had been muttering, "the work of the devil" – however as far as being a plausible witness at this stage, she was far from it. Phoebe Dalton looked to be the best bet at the moment.

Forensics were currently combing the scene, and the body was just about to be moved to the morgue. Everything was being photographed. Ginny knew she would have her work cut out. She had only been in the job of DCI for just over three months and this was her first full blown murder case.

She turned away from the crime scene and wandered through to the kitchen, her paper booties making a soft swishing noise as she walked. Detective Sergeant Patrick Paterson, her colleague and best friend since they were children, watched her approach.

"Ma'am." He acknowledged her formally with a nod as she stepped into the kitchen. Their relationship, always had been purely platonic, more like that of a brother and sister. They had gone to the same school, lived on the same council estate and had eventually entered the force at the same time. They had similarly followed working in the same places. Ginny liked to rib Pat about being a higher-ranking officer, but only when they were off duty.

"Any tea going?" she asked hopefully. Pat picked up a cup and passed it to her.

"I had a feeling you might be looking for one." He grinned ruefully. She gratefully accepted the warmth the tea had to offer,, lacing her fingers around the cup, and sipped her tea. Her hands were freezing despite the weather being extremely warm for the time of year. She looked around the kitchen, appraising the beauty of it, nothing out of place, empty surfaces and only what was needed on display. It was a far cry from her own kitchen at home which usually ended up being a dumping ground. Ginny glanced around, acknowledging it was just her and Pat, that there was no-one else around.

"I just don't know if I'm ready for this, Pat," she admitted in a hushed voice. She never would have said such a thing in front of any of the other officers.

"If you weren't, you wouldn't have got the job in the first place. You're gonna be fine, Gin." Pat tried to placate her, but he could tell she was seriously shitting a brick. Murders happened all the time, but not on their patch, and certainly not to a new DCI in the job just three months. He could imagine how Ginny felt, knew how he would feel himself if he was in the same boat. Still, he had faith in her. She was the best copper he had ever met and he didn't just think it because they had been best friends for three quarters of their lives.

"Has an initial house-to-house been done?" she asked hopefully, taking a seat at the kitchen table.

"Nothing to report, nobody heard anything at all. Woman next door said she is a very light sleeper and hears every little noise in the street, but claims not to have heard anything last night. Same story at the other houses nearby."

"Well extend the questions, see if anyone remembers anyone lurking around, maybe there was unusual activity at the house. What appears normal might actually be a clue for us. Find out about the comings and goings. Neighbours tend to notice things without realising that they've noticed things. Does she have parcel deliveries, that sort of thing."

Pat nodded. "I'll get the uniforms on it straight away. What about the husband? Do you think he could have done it?" he asked hopefully.

"According to Phoebe Dalton, he's in Dubai but we have the name of the company he works for and I've got Mark on it, checking it out. Once we find out where he is, we'll get a uniform for that neck of the woods to go and tell him, assuming he's not hiding out around here somewhere covered in blood." She grinned at the flippant comment.

"We checked the shed... " Pat offered helpfully, grinning back. It was good that she still had a sense of humour. He had the feeling she was going to need to need it before they caught the perp for this.

"What about a murder weapon?"

"Looks like it was one of her own knives from the kitchen. Perp left it by the body, bold as brass."

"Fingerprints?"

"Let's hope."

Ginny looked about the kitchen. It was a lovely space, just right for someone who loved to cook. However, from what she'd heard about Mary Nicholls so far, she was a straight up career woman and not into the domestic scene.

Ginny placed her empty cup on the kitchen table and stood up. She wanted to view the rest of the house. She needed to build a picture of the woman that lived there. So far everybody, as far as she was concerned, was a potential suspect, from the housekeeper to the husband.

Mary Nicholls was being carefully lifted and placed in a body bag as she went back past the living room. The forensic team would be there well into the next day, recording and gathering all the evidence they could. With any luck, there would be a skip full of DNA hanging about and they could catch whoever did this as soon as possible.

Ginny noted the colour scheme of the house presented itself throughout the whole place. Everything was either cream or white with a splash of colour here and there. It was not a house that exuded the presence of children or one that children ever came to visit.

Ginny entered the bedroom of Mary Nicholls. The bed was immaculately made and had clearly not been slept in. Up here too, the forensic team were going through everything with a fine-toothed comb. She tracked their movements for a moment, acknowledging their recognitions of her presence with nods and smiles.

She moved towards the en suite bathroom and glanced around. Nothing was out of place. A couple of make-up wipes in the bin, a hairbrush on the counter top but nothing else. Mary Nicholls' clothing had been found in a heap on the bedroom floor and removed for forensic testing, as had her pyjamas from the living room, where they had been found strewn across the room. Ginny preyed that some clue could be found on the body, such as DNA under the fingernails or semen in the vagina. Anything that would give them a lead at this point would be fantastic. Ginny had the feeling that otherwise, this case could cause a lot of sleepless nights and a good many more man hours searching for their perp.

Back at the station, the incident room was in full motion of noise and bustle. An official-looking picture of Mary Nicholls had been put up on the white boards, her name scrawled by the side, but very little else at this point. Despite the team being made of seasoned officers, this was far beyond anything they had encountered before. Every patch had its fair share of stabbings and the odd unexplained death, but this was huge and Ginny was in the front firing line. She felt like the novice she was, but wasn't about to let it show.

Steve King was perched on the edge of one of the desks, his large frame threatening to obscure everything else in sight. Steve was not a small man in any shape or form. At least six feet, five inches, he must have weighed anything between twenty and thirty stone and could easily have made it as a pro-wrestler at some point. Although large, he didn't appear flabby, his heaviness pointing to bulk rather than fat. If you punched him with anything other than a sledge hammer, he would probably swat you like fly. He was perched on the edge of a desk, the phone receiver almost disappearing in the paw of his large hand. His shirt was half tucked in, half out and his tie was skewed somewhere about the side of his neck from constant pulling to relieve the pressure of the knot which was clearly strangling his huge neck. He had a large jowly face with grey hair that had been buzz cut into a least a number two. It hid his bald patches well. He had sharp eyes and watched everything carefully; rarely did anything get past him.

Mark Roberts in contrast was his complete opposite. At around five feet, six inches, he was stick thin despite the fact that all he ever seemed to eat was take-aways and rubbish. He had wiry, curly, ginger hair which seemed to fight any attempt to do anything with it other than form an auburnhalo around his head. He had a friendly face and bright blue eyes. He epitomised the phrase 'happy-go-lucky'. In the three months he had worked with Ginny, she had yet to see him with a frown on his face or a miserable disposition. He was also quite the joker and tried to cheer anyone up when they were feeling depressed or down in the dumps.

Gerry Dines was perhaps the granddad of the group, being the eldest by about twenty years. He had a mop of white hair which was wild and untamed and on occasion looked like somebody had stuck a load of cotton wool on top of his head. He was a little too portly these days to be considered fit, but was so close to retirement that nobody seemed to mind.

Finley O'Malley had jet black hair and bright blue eyes. He stood around five feet eight inches and fell somewhere in the middle of Steve King and Mark Roberts in both age and stature.

Francine Blackman was Detective Constable on the squad, having joined the team one month after Ginny. It was also noted that she looked peculiarly just like her boss. Both women were around five feet, three inches with the same slight build and similarly coloured blonde hair. The only difference was their facial features and eye colour. Where Ginny had a small nose, blue eyes and a rosebud mouth, Francine had brown eyes, a slightly larger nose and wider, fuller lips. Francine also like to wear an incredible amount of make-up.

The only other member of the team at this point was Charlene, their uniform and Ginny's go-to admin. She was so called because her mum had been a huge Neighbours fan back in the day. Charlene's brother was ironically called Scott. Charlene however, looked nothing like Kylie Minogue. She had brown hair and brown eyes always covered with her glasses. The only make-up she ever wore was mascara. She was tiny at around five feet tall and almost appeared child-like in stature. Ginny felt like a giant standing next to her. Ginny had noticed Charlene giving surreptitious looks in Mark's direction many a time, but so far he had failed to notice, or had noticed, but she just wasn't his type.

Pat strolled in behind Ginny and now her team was complete. She was going to have to request more officers unless they were lucky enough to find an immediate lead, or get something from the forensics that pointed them in the right direction straight away.

Ginny walked over the white board and turned to face her team who were now quiet, expectantly looking at her.

"Okay." Her voice came out so quiet. She could kick herself. She glanced over a Pat for a split second, who nodded in her direction, a sign of encouragement.

"Okay." She said again louder this time. "What do we have so far?" She glanced around her team expectantly.

"Nothing from the house to house at all," Mark offered helpfully, grabbing his notebook. "A Mrs Sayers who lives three houses down, recalled that she thought she saw a man lurking outside Mary Nicholls' house about three weeks ago. Total dead end, couldn't remember what he looked like, what he was wearing, nothing."

Ginny lit up. "Sounds like she could have seen something though. Go back to her, take a picture of the husband, see if you can get her to recall some more details, what time of day etcetera, you know the sort of thing, Mark." He nodded, making notes.

"What about the husband?" Ginny requested.

This from Steve King. "Just got off the phone with his company, Ma'am." Ginny winced openly. She hated the official titles, particularly Ma'am. "Apparently, he was supposed to be in Dubai, but they haven't heard from him since last Friday. They're not sure if he's still out there, somewhere else, or simply back home."

Ginny looked thoughtful for a moment. "So, he could potentially be our killer. We need to do background checks on Marcus Nicholls, and of course Mary. We need to find out every detail about this woman's life, who she knew, where she went. Check with the airlines, see if you can track down Marcus Nicholls leaving Dubai and whether he's back in the UK."

"We spoke to Phoebe Dalton, her secretary." This from Francine. "Got a statement."

"Anything useful?"

"Not a lot. Seems Phoebe only knew her boss at work, not socially. Mary brought her son Christmas and birthday presents, but as far as Phoebe knew, Mary was pretty much a workaholic. Came in early, went home late, that sort of thing. She seemed to think Mary's husband was currently in Dubai, he's an engineer. Phoebe reckons reading between the lines, their relationship didn't sound too good. They rarely saw each other, and for all intents and purposes, lived separate lives." Charlene concluded.

"This is sounding more like the husband all the time. We need to find out if there was any insurance on Mary Nicholls' death. Maybe her husband is a bit of a playboy or a gambler and has run out of money or something. That's going to be our line of enquiry in the first instance, locate the husband. Pat and I will head over to where Mary worked, see if we can unearth a few skeletons over there."

The office of Hart, Smith & Dawson sat in a prestigious part of town. The offices were a five-storey purpose-built building, the exterior resembling a hotel instead of offices. From the carpark, three steps led the way to the large glass fronted reception area. It was decked out in marble floors and marble walls, with a bank of elevators to the right. Large plants were dotted around the area with white leather sofas for guests. A TV played adverts, advertisements of the company's achievements. A receptionist sat behind a glass table, her blonde hair perfectly twisted into a chignon, her make-up expertly applied. She smiled politely as Ginny and Pat approached the desk. "May I help you?" She sounded like a telephonist of the 1950s, all clipped tones and exact pronunciation.

"We would like to speak to Franklin Hart if possible." Ginny and Pat produced their police badges almost simultaneously. The receptionist seemed to pale behind her make-up, but she already had a phone in her hand and was punching numbers. Ginny noted the long red fingernails and wondered how the woman coped with such long nails and dressing, doing up the buttons on her blouse for instance. It was an enigma to Ginny.

"Franklin Hart's PA will be down to collect you in just a moment, if I could get you to sign in." She pushed a visitor's book towards them with her red talons. Pat took the offered pen and started to fill in the details.

"Perhaps you would like to take a seat?" Looking in Ginny's direction, she gestured towards the pristine white leather sofas with her red manicured talons. Ginny shrugged and moved to the sofas. She spotted a water machine and helped herself to a tiny cup before sitting down. Pat strolled over, offering her a visitor's badge to attach to her jacket. Ginny noted the receptionist kept looking at Pat under her eye lashes.

"Somebody's got their eye on you," Ginny whispered, hardly moving her mouth. Pat always attracted female attention everywhere they went. He was a handsome man, Ginny couldn't deny it, but they had never had that kind of relationship. Not to say it hadn't crossed either of their minds, but after one quick drunken fumble when they were about fourteen, they had never 'gone there' again. Ginny had told Pat kissing him was like kissing her her brother, it had felt wrong and he had readily agreed.

Pat joined Ginny sitting on the sofa. He looked around the sumptuous reception area. "Quite a bit of money in this place I reckon," he murmured softly to Ginny, studiously ignoring the glances from the receptionist.

"How long do you think Hart will keep us waiting?" Ginny took out her phone and flicked through her messages, then checked her watch.

The arrival of the lift was announced by a soft ping and out stepped a mid-twenties woman (as far as Ginny could guess), who was immaculate from head to toe. Her blonde hair was tied back in a perfectly, not a hair out of place chignon. Her make-up looked expertly applied. She wore a simple white fitted shirt and a dark grey skirt to her knee. She wore black stilettos. She was slim and statuesque and Ginny in her plain navy trousers and blue jumper felt considerably under-dressed and inadequate.

"Wow, this place certainly does pick their staff according to looks," Ginny whispered to Pat, standing up. He nodded in agreement.

Blondie strode purposefully towards Ginny and Pat with the tip-tap of her heels on the marble flooring.

"Detectives?" Selina Jackson enquired politely as she reached them.

Pat and Ginny offered their badges as identification. Selina took her time to look at each badge individually, before again meeting Pat and Ginny's eyes. "I'm Mr Hart's PA, Selina Jackson. If you would like to accompany me to the elevator, Mr Hart will see you now." The coldness in her demeanour could not be ignored as pivoted and began tip-tapping back towards the lift. Ginny and Pat dutifully followed. "You could freeze ice on her backside," Ginny mumbled and Pat almost burst out laughing.

"Do you think we've entered the realm of the Stepford secretaries?" he whispered back.

The mirrored interior of the lift allowed Ginny to check out Selina Jackson while Selina Jackson checked out Pat. Ginny couldn't help but wonder if Hart, Smith & Dawson picked their female staff based on their looks. So far Mary Nicholls, Phoebe Dalton, the receptionist and Selina Jackson were all extremely attractive women, with slim figures, long legs, perfect hair and perfect nails. Pat was right, it was like being in a Stepford scenario.

They alighted the lift on the fifth floor. Here they stepped out into a large open plan office which housed several desks, each separated by a partition. A large skylight in the ceiling provided lots of natural daylight. To the left, a large glass fronted board room allowed extra light to come through, having a bank of windows. The vertical blinds here were pushed back. It was easy to view the large table central to the room, complete with smart white board at one end and several comfortable black leather chairs. Several other glass offices flanked the sides of the large open plan area, however many of these had their vertical blinds closed, allowing the occupants some privacy.

Selina Jackson turned right on exiting the lift and walked down the carpeted office. Here there were no glass offices, but dark wooden doors, some open, some closed, allowing Pat and Ginny to glance into various offices as they passed. Outside some of the offices were other desks presumably placed to house the secretaries who worked for those particular executives. At the end of the office Selina stopped by a desk and moved around until she was situated behind it. She leant forward and pressed an intercom button on her desk.

"Yes." A clipped response came back almost immediately.

"The detectives are here, Mr Hart." Selina replied. The way she said the word 'detectives' made Ginny feel like she was saying a dirty word.

"Send them on through." Another curt reply. Selina moved back around her desk and opened the large teak coloured panelled door. She stood back and allowed Ginny and Pat to enter.

"May I get you anything, tea, coffee, water?" She enquired politely as they passed her.

"No thanks." Ginny replied straight away, noticing how nice Selina smelt. Was there nothing imperfect about this woman at all?

"I'm good thanks." Pat responded and received Selina's first smile in his direction since they had arrived. She stepped out of the room and closed the door behind her.

Ginny and Pat were greeted by the sumptuous surroundings which were Franklin Hart's office. He sat behind a large mahogany desk on a large black leather chair. He regarded his visitors warily.

"I'm DCI Percy, this is DS Paterson," Ginny began, her identification at the ready. Franklin Hart stood up and waved the ID away. "No need for that. I'm Franklin Hart." He offered his hand which Ginny and Pat both took in turn to shake.

"Have a seat." Franklin gestured towards two armchairs before his desk. Ginny and Pat dutifully took their seats.

Franklin Hart, like the rest of his staff, was immaculate. Ginny's best guess was to place him around mid to late forties. His hair was black, broken up only by greying temples. His hair seemed to be styled without a strand out of place. He had dark eyes that almost appeared black, framed with long black lashes. Crow's feet at the corners of his eyes suggested that he laughed a lot or squinted often. He was sporting a rather nice tan and was clean shaven. His clothing, although Ginny couldn't predict for certain, looked as though he might have been wearing a designer suit. The dark grey jacket hung on the back of his chair, but otherwise he wore matching dark grey trousers, a crisp white shirt and lilac coloured tie. He looked very much the part of the wealthy executive business owner.

"Do you know why we're here?" Ginny began softly. Franklin Hart looked from Ginny to Pat expectantly for a moment and then it was almost as if he crumpled before them. Suddenly the confidence he had been sporting a few seconds ago was gone and in its place was a broken, tortured soul.

"I'm so sorry." He grabbed a handkerchief out of his trouser pocket and dabbed at his eyes before blowing his nose. "It's all come as such a terrible shock."

Ginny had to admit she hadn't been expecting that. Pat looked over at her and she could sense his uncomfortable unease. There was always something disconcerting about seeing a man in tears, especially one so suave and sophisticated looking as Franklin Hart.

"Take your time." Ginny spoke again. "Shall I get you a glass of water or something?"

He shook his head, clearly trying to collect himself. After one last dab at his eyes he coughed and sat back in his chair. He swung to the right slightly and looked out of the window. "I'm terribly sorry." He repeated, still looking out of the window as though embarrassed and not wanting to make eye contact.

"Look, I hate to come here at this time, but I'm sure you can understand, we need to know who might have done this terrible thing to Mary Nicholls. We are going to need access to her office and her computer including her files. We also need to know about your staff, every single person who works here who might have known Mary. Is there anything you can tell us?"

"Everybody liked Mary as far as I'm aware. She certainly didn't have any enemies that I knew about." Finally, Franklin Hart seemed to have collected himself together enough to face the officers before him once again

"Were there any staff, perhaps in the past, who she fell out with, may have had to sack for any reason, anybody past or present you could think of who might have held a grudge?"

Franklin considered this for a moment. "I honestly can't think of anybody. She was one of the most conscientious workers I have ever known in my life and she always gave one hundred and ten percent. Her secretary may know if she had fallen out with anyone recently, I'm certainly not aware of anyone myself, but I'm sure if anything serious had happened, it would have been brought to my attention. What about her husband?"

"We're attempting to locate Mr Nicholls' whereabouts at the moment. Did you know him?" Pat asked.

Franklin shrugged. "Somewhat, but not very well I'm afraid. He accompanied Mary to a couple of events we had, but for the most part he works away."

"Sounds like you didn't have much time for him?" Pat surmised, judging by Franklin's body language and clear disdain.

Again, Franklin shrugged, but didn't make eye contact. He seemed to be picking at an invisible piece of lint on his shirt sleeve. "Like I say, I didn't really know him that well, only bits and pieces from Mary. I knew she wasn't happily married."

"Did she tell you that?" this from Ginny. Franklin's eye contact was brief and Ginny detected the slightest blush coloured his cheeks. Ginny pursued her line of questioning without giving him a chance to answer. "Were you and Mary Nicholls having an affair?" Ginny was nothing if not direct with her questions. Sometimes the filter between her brain and her mouth failed to recognise each other, and out it popped the moment it was in her head.

Franklin Hart stuttered and blustered for a moment as if looking for a reason to deny it. "We were," he eventually admitted, "but nobody knew about it, it was just a little affair." He shrugged helplessly. "Nobody needs to know this information, right?" he asked hopefully as an afterthought.

"I'm afraid we can't guarantee that it will remain a secret, Mr Hart. How long had the affair been going on?"

Franklin paused as though thinking for a moment. "I suppose it must have been around seven months altogether."

"Do you think Mr Nicholls could have known about the affair, somehow found out?"

"I expect he could have done. Mary had put up with Marcus's affairs for many years. For all intents and purposes their marriage was over. She might have enjoyed some revenge by admitting to him that she too was having an affair."

"Was she the kind of woman who might want to take revenge on her husband like that?"

"I would have to say no, but it might have come out in the heat of an argument I suppose."

"Did Mary say she argued with Marcus recently?"

"She mentioned that she argued with him all the time. I think virtually every time he came home from a business trip in fact. Invariably, he extended his business trips, he has a holiday home in the South of France and I think an apartment in Japan. He has a passion for his secretaries and very often takes them away with him. He tends to hole himself up in one of his retreats until he has had his fling, then he comes home."

"And would you say that after all that he would expect to come home and find Mary waiting at home like the dutiful wife?"

"I suppose their marriage might have been like that in the beginning. I know that Mary put up with a hell of a lot. I believe his affairs started around three or four years into their marriage, around the time her career started to take off."

"Could he have resented that?"

Again, Franklin shrugged. "I really couldn't say, I didn't know him well enough and Mary never mentioned that."

"But she mentioned that her and Marcus argued a lot?" Franklin nodded in confirmation.

"If you think of anything else, Mr Hart, perhaps you could call us." Ginny retrieved a card from her pocket and put it on his immaculately polished desk.

"One last thing Mr Hart." Ginny lent on the edge of his desk. "Where were you last night?" Franklin Hart looked stupefied by the question for a moment. "I was at home with my wife." He responded simply. Ginny had no doubt he was telling the truth, something about his demeanour suggested that he was being entirely honest, however she also knew how good an actor a person could be. Until his alibi was properly checked he would also fall into the category of suspect, although to Ginny at that moment, Marcus Nicholls was looking like the favourable candidate.

"It's going to be so strange around here without her you know." Franklin spoke softly and Ginny was unsure whether he was speaking aloud to himself or to them. "I hope you catch the bastard that did this." This was spoken louder and with considerably more venom.

"We definitely will, Mr Hart. Thank you for your time today." Ginny and Pat got up to leave.

"I'll ask my secretary to provide the list of the people who work here to take away with you. Please feel free to question whoever you need to."

"Thank you, Mr Hart, we'll be in touch." Ginny opened the door and stepped back into the open plan office. Selina Jackson turned her perfect head towards them as they left the office. After a quick dismissive glance in their direction she turned back to her computer. The intercom buzzed on her desk.

"Yes, Mr Hart." Her focus was on her boss's needs.

"Please provide the police officers with a list of everyone who works here and their contact details and then come into the office for dictation, I need to send an email round."

"Yes, Mr Hart." She responded in a clipped professional manner. She stood up, gathering her notebook and pencil. "Perhaps you could leave me your contact details, Detective, and I'll send you the information." For some reason, Ginny did not like this woman. It wasn't the fact that she was taller, prettier, more perfect or better dressed; there was just something about her demeanour that stuck in Ginny's craw. If she wasn't in the middle of massive murder investigation, she might just have hauled the woman down the station.

"I'd prefer to take it away with us if we could. I'm sure you understand the seriousness of this situation." Ginny kept her voice pleasant and even, but the scathing look she received from Selina Jackson suggested that no, she was not happy to provide *that* information now. Sighing heavily, Selina put her notebook and pencil back on her desk with a little too much force. Oh yeah, definitely not happy, oh look she has her best resting bitch face on already, Ginny thought to herself as Selina sat down at her computer, looking over the top to give Ginny yet another contemptuous glance.

"It will take a little time to gather it all together and print it out."

"We can wait." Pat spoke, sensing the animosity growing between the two women straight away, drawing Selina's attention to him. She gave him a weak smile and started tapping on her computer. "Did you know Mary Nicholls well?" he asked.

"I knew Mary Nicholls as well as any of the executives here, Detective," Selina responded, not taking her eyes off the computer screen. She said 'detective' again like it was a dirty word that was distasteful to her.

"Was she well liked?" Ginny piped up.

Selina shrugged. "She was a nice lady, I suppose people liked her." No emotion, just her tone dripping with disdain.

"Did she have any enemies, any arguments that you're aware of?" This from Pat again. He could sense trouble brewing a mile off and always knew when Ginny was getting pissed off.

"I wouldn't know that information I'm afraid." The clipped, bored sounding tone of Selina Jackson's voice was really grating on Ginny's nerves. Somewhere, somehow this lady had had dealings with the police or someone in her family had. She clearly didn't like the police and certainly didn't want to answer any questions. She appeared slightly on edge in their presence and Ginny wondered if Selina Jackson actually had something to hide.

"Look Miss Jackson... "

"Ms." Selina snapped rudely.

Ginny glanced at Pat, who raised his eyebrows in response. That did it. "Okay then, Ms Jackson." Ginny deliberately emphasised the *Ms* sarcastically and stepped right up to the edge of Selina's desk. This time because the woman was sitting down, Ginny loomed over her. It was intended to intimidate. "One of your work colleagues has been brutally murdered. I don't know what your problem is with the police and quite frankly I don't care, but what I do want to do is find out who killed Mary Nicholls. Now if my asking any questions offends you for some reason, I really don't give a shit. So perhaps you can try to be a bit more helpful with your responses or perhaps you would prefer to do this down at the station?" It was an idle threat. They had no reason whatsoever for taking Selina Jackson to the station, but an idle threat usually worked a treat with those in an uncooperative frame of mind.

Selina Jackson's fingers stilled above her keyboard and she turned to stare at Ginny. Ginny had encountered mouthy little shits who thought they could be Charlie big potatoes with the police, she had encountered football hooligans and she had encountered some of the nastiest trash to walk the planet, but Ginny could never remember seeing anyone look at her with such vile hatred as Selina did in that moment. She didn't flinch and she didn't seem bothered by Ginny's threat.

"I have done nothing wrong, Detective, and *I am* trying to be helpful. I did not know Mary Nicholls particularly well as I said, especially not well enough to know if she had any enemies. What I do know is that she got on well with her secretary Phoebe Dalton, so perhaps you should direct your questions to her. Now if you will excuse me, I have work to be getting on with." She deliberately turned her head back to her computer. A few seconds later, her printer started to whir and several sheets of paper came out. She pulled them off and handed them to Pat who, in those few seconds, had moved over to Ginny and was standing next to her. He could almost feel the anger coming of Ginny in waves and was glad that Selina Jackson kept her mouth closed thereafter. He had the feeling that Ginny was about to explode like the proverbial volcano, which could end with Ginny hauling Selina's arse down to the station.

Pat took the offered sheets of paper from Selina. "Thank you, Ms Jackson." He spoke politely, grabbing Ginny's upper arm in a firm gesture. She knew that touch from Pat. He was the calm one, she was the one with the quick temper and fast reactions. When he grabbed her arm like that, she knew she was on the verge of going too far. Much as it pained her not to rile Selina Jackson some more, she had to admit defeat on this one. If Pat said it was enough, she knew it was enough.

"Let's go." She said simply and turned, without another word in Selina Jackson's direction and made her way to the lifts with Pat following in tow. Another word wasn't spoken between them until they reached their car.

"That woman proper wound you up, didn't she?" he asked, getting into the driver's side and putting the key in the ignition.

"That obvious was it?" Ginny laughed. "Honest to God, Pat, I don't know what came over me in there, but I wanted to slap her so hard."

"Police brutality," Pat joked.

"Big time. Stuck up cow." At least they could both laugh about it now.

"Where to next?"

"Let's go and get the lowdown from our favourite forensic pathologist."

CHAPTER FOUR

Pat drove Ginny the five miles to the coroner's office where Melanie Watson worked. She had been a crime pathologist for six years and was a well-seasoned expert in her field. Not much got past her.

They both got out of the car and Pat immediately lit up a cigarette. The smell wafted over Ginny and her craving level shot up immediately. She had only given up smoking three weeks ago and it had been hell on earth since. With the stress of this new case, she was craving cigarettes more and more. In such close proximity, she could have cheerfully strangled Pat and stolen every last one of them from him. Fuck it! "Light me one of those."

Pat's eyebrows rose until they almost met his hairline. "You sure Gin? I mean you said if you asked… remind you about giving up, wouldn't want you to blame me later."

"Give me a fucking cigarette, or do I have to order you as your superior officer?" Ginny growled. Pat knew a poor reformed smoker when he saw one, he had been there, done that himself on several occasions. In fact, being a reformed smoker was the reason (at least one of the reasons) he was divorced now. He took a cigarette from the packet, lit it from his own and passed it to Ginny.

She dragged on the offending little stick of nicotine like there was no tomorrow, but at least she felt suddenly calmer and more in control. "Sorry about that." She apologised with a rueful grin.

"No harm, no foul. Just don't blame me when you're feeling guilty later." His voice was quiet but firm.

"I won't." Ginny's voice was also quiet now, her mind reverting back to the case. At the moment there were no leads, no suspects. Forensics had not turned up anything helpful as yet. There were fibres but nothing specific, but they were still working on it.

Ginny hoped that the pathologist would have more helpful information. When they left the station this morning, the press already had wind of the story and were clamouring for details. Ginny had grimaced at the thought. On occasion the press could be helpful, but mostly they were just a hindrance to the enquiries.

Pat glanced over at his boss, looking at her profile. Ginny was a good-looking woman, no doubt about that. He knew she had had a tough time getting to where she was because of her looks, having to work twice as hard as any man to prove she had brains.

Her father had been fairly high up in the Met, but somehow that had never cut Virginia Percy any slack. In fact, it was the opposite. She had had to work harder than any man or woman he had met so far on the force to get where she was. It had taken a severe amount of grit and determination to suffer the humiliation of not being born a boy, yet trying to follow in her father's footsteps and make him proud. Pat respected her and loved her, albeit like a sister, but above all he knew she was one of the police officers who had the most integrity and sincerity. She was in a job that was not only her chosen profession, but a calling.

Ginny had blonde hair scraped up into a neat pony tail, not styled in any particular way. She had worn it that way more or less since he met her. She had startling blue eyes that looked almost silver on occasion in the right light. She wore no make-up except for a touch of mascara that enhanced her eyelashes. Her skin was pale with a smattering of freckles across her nose, almost faded now that she was getting older. Her nose was small as were her ears which were adorned with plain silver stud earrings. Her body was curvy but she favoured baggier clothes hiding a figure that was trim but womanly. She preferred to wear trousers or jeans with trainers and oversized tops. The only time she wore a suit was on formal occasions, such as meeting with her superiors However, she was essentially a tomboy and although not particularly tall for a woman, had always been of the opinion that whatever a man could do, she could do better and she had set out to prove just that.

She had been the only woman in their team until recently and she had received a definite amount of ribbing and requisite tormenting, which to be fair, she had taken in her stride, even joined in on occasion. She had proved she could give as good as she got. But she had worked hard on each case they'd had so far. She was earning some respect from the other men, but it was a far cry from being taken seriously. There were some who presumed incorrectly that she was where she was today because of daddy. And then there were those who thought she had slept her way to the top. The force was nobody's fool at the end of the day, but there was a lot of conjecture and rumour and despite what the top brass dished out, a certain amount of prejudice.

Ginny walked beside Pat. He was tall and fairly muscular – muscular because of the rugby he had played in his younger days. He still liked to work out and therefore had lost none of his tone. His once black hair was slightly receding and he had a smattering of grey working its way in from the sides of head at the ears. He needed a shave, but then Ginny didn't think she had ever seen him when he didn't; he appeared to have permanent stubble around his chin and face. His nose had been broken a few times from his rugby and had set slightly crooked, but this gave his face an intriguing quality. It did not diminish his looks. He had grey eyes, framed with thick black lashes that would have been the envy of any woman and his lips were full and sensuous. He looked nothing like a policeman, and given different attire may have passed for a bouncer in a club, but he was definitely not GQ magazine material. She couldn't see him in a sharp suit. He still sported the semi-student look of jeans, checked shirts over t-shirts and his staple footwear of Converse. He never wore a tie and usually looked like he had grabbed whatever was hanging around either in the wardrobe or in the washing basket and thrown it on.

When Pat was aged nineteen, he got his then girlfriend pregnant. Pat had not long joined the force and really wanted to make something of his career. Michaela Stratton was a dizzy little redhead who as it turned out had a very calculating mind indeed. She had set her sights on marrying Patrick Paterson and that's exactly what she intended to do. The only problem was, Pat didn't feel the same way.

Many times, Pat had tried to break it off with Michaela but she was having none of it. She threatened time and time again to kill herself if he tried to leave her. Pat felt trapped and could see no light at the end of the tunnel. Ginny encouraged him to leave Michaela anyway, wanted him to call her bluff. Equally, Michaela wanted Pat to have nothing to do with Ginny. She was jealous of their relationship even though it had a proven plutonic track record. Michaela wanted Pat to herself and saw Ginny as a rival nevertheless.

When Pat tried again to break off their relationship, Michaela broke the news that was pregnant. Pat was devastated. He didn't feel ready to be a father and certainly had no money to do so. At the time he still lived with his parents, as did Michaela with hers.

Unfortunately, Pat came from a Catholic family who would accept no other outcome to the situation than for Pat to marry Michaela. It wasn't until two months into their marriage that Pat finally asked his wife why she wasn't showing yet. It was four months into the pregnancy, yet Michaela had no visible symptoms that Pat could identify, although he was no expert. Michaela had broken down almost immediately and explained that it had been a false alarm, that she had got her period just before the wedding. Michaela said that she hadn't wanted to let everyone down at the time, so she kept it to herself., except she had told her mum. Pat was beyond furious. He knew somehow that there had never been a baby all along and that Michaela had trapped him into a loveless marriage. Pat started staying out to all hours. Sometimes he wouldn't come home at all, camping out at Ginny's place.

Michaela tried to hang on to their marriage, he gave her that. She was determined to see it work even though he was damn sure he didn't love her, never had and had told her that multiple times.

They carried on like that for two years until they were like virtual strangers passing in the night. Eventually, it was Michaela herself who called time, realising that to remain in the marriage was a futile exercise. They had gone through their divorce, Pat allowing Michaela to keep what remained of their short time together, him preferring to blot it from his memory like a bad dream. He had since vowed never to marry again and had so far kept that promise. Michaela he knew had moved on, married again and had a couple of children now. That information had come from Pat's mother as if she expected a reaction of sorrow at missing out. Pat was only sorry that he had allowed the sham to go on as long as it did.

Melanie Watson sat behind a desk with stacks of files on one side and a computer on the other. Apart from a pot that held a few pens, that was the entire contents of her desk. The entire office was supremely neat; even the stacks of files were precisely lined up. There was nothing out of place, but then looking at Ms Watson (as she had introduced herself), the neatness was a theme that continued personally.

Her hair was red. Not bottle red, but natural red. It was a startling colour against the pale translucency that was her skin. Unfortunately, she had scraped it all into a severe looking bun at the nape of her neck, giving her an austere quality, but a couple of wiry tendrils had managed to escape, framing her face and softening the seriousness of her look. She had freckles, but they seemed to appear below the skin rather than decorating it. Her eyes were a startling green, perhaps enhanced by the redness of her hair but the wire rimmed glasses that they were hidden behind did nothing but detract from the beauty that she could have been. Her nose was perhaps a little too large for her face and distorted her image slightly so that you could never say she was truly attractive. It made her lips appear too thin by contrast. She had the sort of face you could stare at for hours finding the imperfections and perfections before you could decide whether she was truly beautiful or merely attractive, but unfortunately neither Pat nor Ginny had that kind of time.

Melanie stood up to shake hands with both Ginny and Pat. She was tall for a woman, at least five nine, and extremely thin. Her shoulders seemed to carry a slight stoop of one who had attempted at some point to make themselves appear shorter. It was difficult to guess her age accurately, but Ginny placed her somewhere between thirty and forty-five even though her face was relatively unlined, and she may infact have been younger

"Have a seat." Melanie Watson gestured towards the two other chairs in the room with a slim white hand before re-taking her own chair behind the desk. Ginny noticed that she smoothed her skirt behind her before she sat and once seated her posture was excellent. Clearly only standing gave her a complex.

Ginny and Pat sat in their respective chairs.

"What can you tell us about the victim?" Ginny was straight in with her line of questioning, never one to beat around the bush.

Melanie Watson's thinly plucked eyebrows that perfectly matched the colour of her hair, rose just above the line of her glasses for a moment as if she was shocked that their conversation would have no preliminaries, but she said nothing so it was difficult to tell.

"Well, the victim, as you know was a thirty-nine-year-old female." She glanced at her notes in front of her on the desk, pausing before continuing, although Ginny had the feeling that she knew exactly what her report said, verbatim. "She had been strangled prior to death; the bruising to her neck matched that of fingers placed thus around the neck." Melanie gestured with her hands as if she was holding somebody's neck in her hands. "There was substantial bruising to the throat, suggesting that she may have taken some time to become unconscious and for him or her to be using substantial force. There was a large bruise to the left side of her head, possibly a kick or some heavy instrument was used. Five teeth had been removed post death and there was a slight laceration to the tongue. She had a bruise along the lower part of the jaw on the right side of her face, again a punch or possibly pressure from a thumb perhaps if he held her face while he removed her teeth."

"Why would he remove her teeth?" Ginny interrupted.

Melanie shrugged. "Could be some kind of trophy; I believe they were not found at the scene of the murder?" She had made it sound like a question.

"No, no teeth were found." Melanie nodded with a smug look on her face, like Ginny's admission had confirmed her suspicions.

"On the left side of the neck about one inch below the jaw, there was an incision about four inches in length, running immediately below the left ear; the incision was made by a strong blade. On the same side about an inch below that, and commencing approximately once inch from the ear she had a further incision which stopped approximately three inches below the right jaw. That particular incision had severed all the tissues down the vertebrae and was probably the cause of death. The carotid vessels on both sides had been severed. That incision was about eight inches in length. The knife found at the murder scene was undoubtedly the blade used to kill her. He used excessive force and violence in the execution. There were other cuts to her lower abdomen, a three-inch wound from the left side. The cut was jagged and deep enough to severe tissues. Several incisions were made on the abdomen itself, running downwards on the right side as if the knife had been used in a repeated stabbing motion downwards." Melanie gestured again for the police officers sitting before her, acting out a stabbing motion as if she was holding a knife. "The bruising to her neck was substantial. Clear marks where the fingers had pressed could be seen to the left and right of her throat. As I suggested he used both hands to strangle her, and it wouldn't have caused her to die, most likely would have rendered her unconscious. Judging by the amount of blood from the severed neck wound, I would suggest that this was the primary cause of death, the rest of her injuries would have occurred post-mortem. The assailant had large hands, I would suggest too big for a woman but obviously this cannot be ruled out entirely, however the amount of force used in order to strangle her... That would have taken some doing, particularly as she try to put up some semblance of a fight."

Ginny paused in her note taking and looked up at Melanie, who nodded. "She had small bruises on each of her hands," Melanie gestured to the bottom of her palm and wrist. "The bruises were not consistent with any kind of bondage. There was also a large bruise on the left side of her head down to her temple a good five inches in length; that blow had caused a skull fracture and may have been carried out by some kind of implement, but I would rather think he kicked her and with sufficient force too."

Ginny looked up at Melanie. "And you say the same implement had been used for all the injuries?"

"Without a doubt." Melanie confirmed. "Each of the knife wounds had the same characteristics and was undoubtedly the work of the knife found at the scene. For the removal of the teeth which thankfully was carried out after death, he most likely used pliers unless he had access to some kind of dentist's equipment."

"Isn't strangulation usually considered a crime of passion?" Pat queried. Melanie's sharp green eyes transferred themselves to him and immediately he felt like a bug under a microscope, but she smiled and nodded enthusiastically. The smile interrupted the severity of her features and made her suddenly appear less austere.

"It is usually considered something a lover may do, yes, but in this case, I believe he used it as a means to an end." She referred to her report once more. "There is definite sign of penetration in the vagina, but no evidence of semen, which would suggest he was wearing a condom. There were no fingerprints, indicating that he was wearing gloves, probably some kind of surgical plastic, however there were some black fibres found on the rug. . We are running these through the lab and should have some idea what they belong to later today. It also seems that although he may have stepped into the blood, no evidence of footprints per se could be found which would indicate that he was perhaps wearing some kind of bootie to cover his feet, however the size once again would indicate a male foot, a size 10 or 11 shoe perhaps. I would say that the person you are looking for came fully prepared to carry out his attack. It was premeditated and staged, I would also add, and carefully thought through. He knew he would have time to complete his tasks, maybe knowing her movements beforehand, knowing her husband would not be coming home. It might suggest he knew her. Finally, something that the victim may or may not have been aware of was that she was pregnant."

"Pregnant?" Ginny repeated and Melanie nodded gravely.

"I would say very early on, barely showing, possibly about ten weeks. She may well have been unaware herself. That's about it for my report."

Ginny turned back to Melanie; all three stood at the same time and shook hands. "Thank you, Melanie, we'll be in touch if we need anything else."

"Of course, Detective, I will ensure a copy of my report is sent to you as soon as it's typed up. Oh, one last thing … "

Ginny, who had already turned towards the door, stopped and turned back, waiting.

"I should have mentioned it earlier, I apologise. The assailant who carried out this attack was left-handed."

Ginny and Pat sat in the car outside the coroner's office, each smoking a cigarette. "We've got our work cut out with this one, Boss." Pat broke the silence first.

"No prizes for stating the obvious," Ginny responded quickly, but smiled over at him. He grinned back, meeting her eyes.

"Why would he take the teeth?" He was speaking more to himself. Ginny glanced over at him but he was staring through the windscreen out at nothing.

"A trophy, as Melanie suggested?"

"Could be, but why the teeth, do you think there's a significance?" He turned to her and silence descended in the close confines of the car for a moment while they both regarded each other.

"Maybe he was removing the teeth so the body couldn't be identified." Pat finally surmised, "But maybe it was a bit like hard work and he gave up."

Ginny frowned. "I don't know. I'm sure there's a significance in it, but I really don't know yet. I doubt its got anything to do with identifying the body, she was in her own home and we know what she looks like." She finished her cigarette and flicked the butt out of the window. "Do you think Franklin Hart was the father of the baby?" Pat shrugged in response.

"Do you think he knew?" he asked.

"No. He would have mentioned it today. I think Mary had only just found out herself, probably coming to terms with it. However, if the husband found out or she told him ...." Ginny left the sentence hanging in the air, both herself and Pat thinking the most obvious at that moment.

Back at the station the team were assembled, ready and waiting, thanks to a quick call from Pat as they travelled on their way back. Ginny marched into the room in full DCI mode, her pony tail swinging from side to side.

"What letter are we up to in the alphabet, Mark?" was the first question directed at Mark Roberts, sitting with his feet up on the desk, reading the newspaper – well, reading was a loose term since he was clearly leering over page three. He jumped like a kid caught with his hand in the cookie jar, newspaper on the floor, feet down from the desk.

"Erm, is it C, ma'am?" He sat to attention like a puppy waiting for a treat.

"You asking or telling?" Ginny continued, striding to the front of the room and flinging her handbag on one of the desks.

"It's C." Mark confirmed.

"C – okay, let's go with operation Christine for this one, guys." She said loudly in the now quiet room. "And don't call me ma'am." She turned back to Mark Roberts, who nodded emphatically.

At the front of the room, three large white boards adorned the wall side by side. The PR brochure picture of Mary Nicholls stared back prettily from the board. The picture was very staid and staged – Mary, with her hair perfectly styled framing her face, her blue eyes twinkling and an enigmatic smile. She was wearing a pale grey suit jacket and white blouse. She looked exactly how you would imagine a successful female executive to look; could have been considered a poster girl for them. Ginny was struck once more how the women who worked at Franklin Hart's company were quite distinct in one way or another. None she had seen today and including Mary herself could be considered ugly. Pat had hit the nail on the head mentioning Stepford and Ginny found herself considering for the first time that day whether Franklin Hart could indeed be considered one of their suspects.

"Okay, listen up." Ginny called loudly. The hub of low voices in the room quietened like magic into silence. Ginny grabbed a whiteboard pen.

She turned to the men and two women in the incident room. "Okay, before I come on to what we have so far, I'm going to assign the tasks for this particular investigation. Pat, deputy SIO with me." Pat nodded, knowing that as the next superior officer of the group, he would be the deputy senior investigating officer.

"Steve, you've earned your stripes recently, office manager." Steve King nodded. "Fin, you've worked with Pat before, outside enquiries, Gerry… you're on crime scenes and Mark house to house. Francine, I need you for media and as for the rest, we'll just divvy it up between us." There were murmurs around the incident room, some happy, some disappointed. Ginny had long known that you couldn't please everybody and she didn't even try. They would soon adopt their roles as assigned and she was sure rise to each of their challenges.

"Okay guys, this is what we have so far... " Ginny turned to the whiteboard and started to write bullet points while speaking fluently to her team, explaining the deductions of the coroner. She turned from the whiteboard.

"We are looking for a left-handed assailant, probably male due to the amount of force used in the attack, particularly the strangulation."

"Do we have anything on the husband Marcus Nicholls?"

"He should be arriving back at Gatwick nineteen hundred hours, Boss, we've got two uniforms picking him up." This from Gerry Dines. Ginny nodded at him.

"Anything further from the door to door?"

"Nothing new ma'am... er, Guv." this from Steve King. "Nobody heard anything or saw anything, complete dead end."

"Well, I want them back out there asking about visitors to the Nicholls home. Did they notice a man around, not just on the night of the murder, but any other time? Did they see any comings and goings from the property during the day? What about when the husband was home? I am sure in that middle-class street, there are more clues than they think. If everyone focuses on the one night in question, we're not going to get very far." Murmurs of approval ran through the room. Ginny wondered if she was the only person thinking here. After all these were seasoned police officers. "I want CCTV checked for the night of the murder. I want people coming into the street and leaving, what cars were used and where did they go. Roberts, you go with O'Malley and speak to Pepe Vasquez; she and Phoebe Dalton are our key witnesses at the moment. The housekeeper may know something significant." Mark Roberts and Fin O'Malley rose from their seats, grabbing their jackets in unison.

"The rest of you can check the internet and find out everything you can on Mary Nicholls, where she associated, who her friends were, how many times a day she took a piss. Alright?" Several nods from the men in the room came with murmurs of approval. "I want any line of enquiry exhausted. As you know Marcus Nicholls must be our prime suspect at the moment, but I want checks carried out on Franklin Hart. He might not have had much of a motive, but I'm not going to discount him at this stage. Ginny picked up her bag. "I don't need to tell you we need a result on this. We're a brand-new team operating together and we are going to be watched to see how we handle this and how quickly we turn a result. I want everyone working their arses off." She put her bag her over shoulder walked into her office, closing the door. She leant against it for a few seconds, catching her breath.

Sitting down at her desk, she looked through the list of names provided by Selina Jackson. Nothing jumped out as significant, just a list of names, addresses, contact numbers and what they did at the company. Suddenly, down near the bottom of the list, was a name she recognised. Richard Ladden.

Richard Ladden, if it was the same person, had once been a uniform in the force. Ginny hadn't had much dealings with him, but she recognised the name. If she remembered correctly, he had been on the take, accepting money for bribes. The Police Complaints Commission had been heavily involved and he had eventually been removed from the force.

She had no idea whether he had been arrested at the time, but now it seemed as though he was working at Hart, Smith & Dawson. That was an interesting fact.

There was an address on the list Selina had provided. Hopefully it was still current.

The address was located on a local council estate, which turned out to be maisonettes rather than flats. Pat pulled the car into one of the allotted carparking spaces that displayed the same corresponding number as the maisonette they were visiting.

It was a fairly quiet time of day, with very few people about. A young woman pushing a buggy strolled past them, eyeing up Ginny and Pat suspiciously as she passed, clearly knowing they were police. It would no doubt be around the estate by teatime that somebody had had a visit from the 'filth'.

The maisonette they wanted was situated in a block of four, two upstairs, two down. They needed the maisonette ground floor right. There was a main door allowing visitors into an entryway. Each maisonette had its own front door. Richard Ladden's was painted council green.

Ginny rang the doorbell. They could hear the dingdong resonating inside the flat, but there was no response. Next Pat banged on the door with his fist. "Alright, alright for fuck's sake," came a disembodied voice from inside the premises.

The door opened a crack, still with the chain on and a bleary-eyed unshaven face peered out. "Fuck me," was the response as the door closed and the chain was rattled. Richard Ladden, dressed in nothing but a pair of boxer shorts and a seen-better-days dressing gown that gapped giving them a generous view of his flacid white stomach and skinny pale legs, stood back against the wall, opening the door wide enough to allow them entry.

Ginny went first, with Pat behind her. "Second door on the left," Richard instructed, closing the door behind them and grabbing a packet of cigarettes from his dressing gown pocket. He paused to light his cigarette then followed them into the living room, coughing harshly

The curtains were still closed in the dingy space. Two old sofas provided the seating in the room, which was bare of carpet on an old tiled floor. A scratched coffee table sat between the two sofas, covered in old newspapers, post and an overflowing ashtray. An old model TV sat in the corner on a stand, a newer looking digital box beneath it. There were no photos, nothing of sentimentality. Ginny perched herself on the edge of one sofa nearest the door. Pat took up residence beside her.

Richard stood hovering in the doorway, taking a drag on his cigarette. He sniffed loudly, which was followed by him using his hand to wipe at his nose. "You want a cuppa or something?" he offered.

"No thanks." Ginny declined; she had an inkling of what his kitchen might look like judging by what she had seen so far, and she had no intention of catching a dose of botulism. Pat also shook his head. Richard shrugged and moved to sit on the sofa adjacent to where they were.

"What do you want then?" No preliminaries, Richard was straight down to it.

"We've come to ask you a few questions, Richard. We understand you work at Hart, Smith & Dawson." Realisation dawned on Richard's face.

"Ah, the Mary Nicholls murder," he stated and nodded his head as if he should have known from the moment the police walked into his flat. "Well it wasn't me." He opened his arms wide, displaying the sight of an emaciated chest and a gap in his boxer shorts that revealed a lot more. Ginny averted her eyes quickly.

"We'd just like to ask you a few questions, Richard, that's all. We will be speaking to everyone who works at the company," Ginny confirmed, keeping her eyes averted to the mess on the coffee table. "Would you like to put some clothes on?" she added.

"Why, I'm going back to bed when you've gone."

"Maybe just cover up then, mate." Pat added, pointedly looking at Richard's crotch.

"Oh." He pulled his dressing gown around himself but showed no embarrassment, made no apology.

"Did you know Mary Nicholls?" Ginny began her questions.

"Not really," came the sullen response.

"When you say, not really?"

"Only in passing, weren't like we was BFFs or nothing."

"Are you the only security guard?"

"No there's two others." Richard pulled his cigarettes from his pocket and lit a further one from the butt he was now holding.

"What are their names?"

"Brad Parker and Patrick Founder."

"Who was on shift the night Mary Nicholls was killed?"

"That was Brad."

"So, where were you?"

"The pub, then home."

"Anyone to corroborate that for you?" Richard shrugged. "What time did you leave the pub?" Ginny continued.

Richard shrugged again. "When it closed I s'pose, it's usually 'bout that time."

"What shift do you do?"

"We usually have a split, I do two till ten, Brad usually does the night – ten till six and then Patrick does the morning six till two."

"I don't recall seeing a security guard when we visited the company."

Ginny looked at Pat to verify her query. He shook his head. "Just a female receptionist," he confirmed.

"Oh yeah, that's Jess, top bird she is." Richard nodded again. "Patrick's off sick at the moment, got a bad back or something. They haven't replaced him."

"How long has Patrick been off sick?" Ginny asked.

"About two months now. I reckon he might get the sack if he doesn't come back soon."

"Did you ever see anyone visit Mary Nicholls at her place of work that she might have been worried about? Was she being bothered at all?"

"Not that I ever saw." Richard confirmed.

"Have you seen anybody lurking around the company at all? You must have to do rounds? Has Brad ever mentioned anything?"

Richard paused as though thinking for a moment. "Well, now you come to mention it." Ginny eagerly leaned forward, hoping that some useful information would be forthcoming.

"There is this little black cat, that keeps coming around in the morning. I just thought he was a stray." He chuckled at his own mirth.

"Do you realise how serious this is?" Ginny sprung to her feet.

"Yes, I fucking do and I also know that the only reason you came around here first was because you still consider me a bent copper. Well I might have been once, but that don't make me a murderer, so don't think you can fit me up." Any perceived friendliness was gone.

"I'm not accusing you of being a murderer, Richard, I just thought you might be willing to help because you were a copper, and a good one at that from what I heard. I actually thought it might have been possible you noticed something that nobody else would've necessarily seen, but I can see I've wasted your time, and ours." She turned to go; Pat rose from the sofa.

"Look, I'm sorry alright. I didn't mean to be flippant, but you are the first colleagues I've seen in a very long time. Nobody bothers with me anymore. I used to have a lot of friends in the force, but now they ignore me like I'm scum."

Ginny looked back at Richard. She felt sorry for him really, but he had done the crime, now he had to do the time. "Look, if you think of anything, give me a call." Richard nodded again. He allowed them to let themselves out of his home.

CHAPTER FIVE

Ginny sat before the Detective Chief Superintendent's desk, a bundle of nerves. He, on the other hand, was sitting back in his chair, seemingly totally at ease with life.

"What's the update, Percy?" The deep, baritone voice of DCS Sparkes filled the moderately sized office in which they sat.

Ginny viewed him with the same respect that she showed her father. He too was a DCS, but with another force far away and definitely left some big shoes to fill. DCS Sparkes was slightly younger than her father, but nonetheless intimidating. A tall man without an ounce of fat all over his body, he even made the force uniform look good. However, that was all Ginny could say in his favour. His face was small and beaky with sunken eyes that were so small they almost disappeared into his head. He had a hooked nose but a wide mouth, thick lips and a pointy chin. His hair was completely grey and white. His complexion reminded Ginny of a farmer – slightly red as if he had been outside for a long time, although clearly more to do with the amount of alcohol he consumed on a daily basis rather than being outside.

He had no time for women on the force, and made it clear without actually saying so out loud. It was nothing that Ginny hadn't encountered before. The force was made up of discriminatory bigots despite the ever-present media hype to the contrary. However, that was an 'all boys network' commonplace mentality, despite the precedents that had been set in place against sexual discrimination. The police force was one of the worst places where it was rife, with the best cover ups that it ever happened. Only those women who set their caps at going far within the force were the ones who felt the full brunt of the discrimination. There were of course the odd exceptions, but for the most part, it was still very much a man's world.

DCS Sparkes knew that Ginny's father was at the same rank as himself. He was of the opinion that Ginny had only got as far in the force as she had because of her father. It was an opinion that had been shared by many. He was firmly of the opinion that strings had been pulled

He had read her file of course, knew of her accomplishments and some were impressive – a fact he couldn't deny. Had she been a man, he would no doubt have supported her one hundred percent in her pursuit to be promoted through the ranks. As it was, he fully expected her to either fail miserably and return from whence she came, or go off and have babies. In his experiences, there was no in-between.

Now a manhunt was on the cards. A brutal murder had occurred on their patch and it fell to DCI Percy to investigate and bring the perpetrator to justice. He hoped she was up for the challenge, but he had a feeling that it was only a matter of time before he was looking for a replacement to head up the motley crew she called her team. In fact, he already had somebody in mind, but time would win out in his favour, of that he was absolutely sure.

Ginny sucked in her breath and began answering him regarding the update.

"There are a few leads, sir. The husband at the moment seems to be the prime suspect. He was reported to be in Dubai, but following our investigation leads, it seems he left there three days prior to Mary Nicholls' murder. Through the flight records, we have been able to ascertain that he got on a plane in Dubai headed to the South of France, but so far, no further leads. He could be using a fake ID, have made his way to the UK and committed the murder. It's a long shot, but not wholly unlikely. Other than that, we are continuing to follow up on other lines of enquiry. However, it seems that Mary Nicholls' life didn't stretch much beyond work and home.

We're going through her computer files both at home and work, but so far it's turned up nothing."

"The boss, this er… " DCS Sparkes looked down at his own notes.

"Franklin Hart, sir." Ginny finished helpfully.

"Yes, him. Any leads there? Could he be one of our suspects?"

"He has a cast iron alibi provided by his wife, but that doesn't make him totally innocent in my book. Mary Nicholls was pregnant and if she had told Franklin and he was somehow upset about the connotations of that, it might put him in the frame. ."

DCS Sparkes nodded and leaned his elbows on the desk. He looked Ginny directly in the eye. "I don't need to tell you, Percy, that we need to get a quick result on this one. I'm getting it in the neck from above already. We can't have a brutal attacker running around on our patch. Find the husband, bring him in. Hopefully, it is him and we'll have this done and dusted."

"Yes, sir. The team and myself are working especially hard."

"Good to hear." He didn't sound that sincere in Ginny's opinion. She knew what his thoughts were and that he had little faith in women on the force. She was just going to have to prove him wrong on that front. The eye contact was broken, and she was clearly dismissed. Ginny stood up and left his office. She had had her fair share of discrimination since she joined up and had probably encountered every kind of bigoted male and no doubt DCS Sparkes would continue to be part of a long line of the same until she retired.

Ginny walked down the two flights of stairs which led to her incident room and office. It was late in the day and only Pat remained. He greeted her with a salute. "Wanna grab a beer?" he offered.

"You must've read my mind." She sounded weary and slightly beaten, "It's been a hell of a day so far."

"Don't let the bigwigs pull you down, Gin, it's only been a week so far. These things can take a while and even if we had

Marcus Nicholls in custody, we would still need to find out how and why. It's not a quick process."

"You always know how to make me feel better, Pat." Ginny smiled ruefully. "Come on, it's your round."

CHAPTER SIX

He sat at his computer watching the screen as face upon face scrolled past. Sluts, all of them. Parading themselves like items for sale where anyone, anywhere could view them. It was disgusting and shameful. They should all be ashamed. *He* could make them all ashamed!

At last his finger hovered over the mouse. At last he had found her. She was perfect. Just what he was looking for. The next link in the chain. He chuckled gleefully to himself as he clicked onto the picture in front of him. More information uploaded itself in an instant. Whoever had invented this website was pure genius. In days of old, it would never have been this easy to find out this kind of information without weeks of study and watching. Now on a plate he had everything he needed handed directly to him. All he had to do was read – everything he needed was there, down to where to find her at that precise moment. It was like they wanted to be caught, wanted him to find them. All he had to do was go to her. All he had to do was watch and wait for that golden opportunity. The opportunity to meet his prize. He was so excited, he could hardly wait. She *would* be surprised…

NOW: ANNA CHAPMAN 8TH SEPTEMBER

ANNA

Anna Chapman was late for work again and her boss was going to kill her, well slight exaggeration, but she was probably going to be sacked at the very least.

She needed this job even though it was thankless and shitty, with shit wages and shit customers. Really, she needed to stop saying shit, it was becoming a mantra. Anyway, she hated her job, well that wasn't quite true, she didn't hate it all the time, just most of the time! She checked her watch for the umpteenth time although she knew that the hands still read the same time. It was eight forty-five a.m. She had to be at work in exactly fifteen minutes and the bus wasn't even on its way yet. The bus ride took twenty minutes. She was sooo going to be late… again!

Anna had only lived in the area about eighteen months. She had moved to attend the university to study a degree so she could go on to be a teacher, but had suddenly discovered, somewhere into her second year, that she didn't actually want to be a teacher and had dropped out. She had stayed in the area however, as she had made some good friends and her rent was cheap. It was better than living at home with her mother, since neither of them had seen eye to eye about a single thing since Anna was about seven years old.

Anna was small and petite at exactly five feet, two inches tall. She had been described as pretty on many occasions (in a pixie sort of way) and had never failed to have her fair share of male attention, although most of the men who were interested in her were quickly discovered to be arseholes and never failed to disappoint. She always moved on to the next with a fresh, open mind, only be disappointed in a matter of weeks.

Anna had naturally dark blonde hair with brown and red undertones so when it caught the light it could appear different shades. She kept it boyishly short. She had thought about dyeing it several times but just couldn't pluck up the courage. Her friend Kelly currently had bright pink hair and Anna envied her braveness, wishing she had the same adventurous spirit.

Her eyes were brown and her features were small, with a small slightly upturned nose and a rosebud mouth. She liked to wear a lot of black eye make-up, which made her eyes appear huge and dark. She also preferred to wear mostly dark colours or black. That was one good reason at least why her job suited her so well; her uniform was black.

Today she wore black skinny jeans, a black tight-fitting t-shirt tucked into her jeans and black trainers. She wore an oversized denim jacket to complete her outfit because it was chilly, the weather dipping in temperature as they moved into September. No predicted Indian summer yet again.

Anna fiddled with her hair, fingering her fringe. She could feel the gel she had put in it earlier and knew she had applied too much in her rush to get ready; it felt brittle and stiff. She touched her ears briefly and could feel the large silver hoops she had put on this morning. They matched the silver and fake crystal studs she wore in the many piercings she had in every available space up the length of each ear.

Anna peered down the road. Still no sign of the bus. Collecting her phone from her pocket, she checked her messages once again. She had posted a status about being late and already several of her friends had commented. She grinned, feeling better already as she saw the comment Greg had added about joining him in bed instead

Finally, trundling around the corner at what must have been two miles an hour, came the bus. Anna puffed out a breath in relief, clouding the chilly air in front of her. She hopped from foot to foot trying to mentally will the bus to go faster. After what seemed like an eternal amount of time, it at last stopped before her at the bus stop and the doors swooshed open. She climbed aboard in the warmth and flashed her bus pass. The driver nodded unimpressed as the doors swooshed closed again behind her. There was nowhere to sit on the crowded bus so she stood and held the bar wishing that the driver would break the speed limit driving into town. There was no way on hell's earth she was going to be at work by nine.

At 9.09 exactly, the bus pulled up at the bus stop in the high street. Anna flung herself through the doors, thinking look out little old ladies, here I come. There were already several people at the bus stop and she barged her way through, no sorry or excuse me, in response to the murmured tuts. Finally, she was free and immediately fell into a jog, running towards the restaurant. Usually she would have sauntered to work despite being late, but as Mr Castellani had in fact spoken to her the day before about the error of her ways and that always being late was unacceptable, she thought she had better hustle.

She ran around the back of the restaurant and entered through the staff entrance, which was really the kitchen but Mr Castellani did not like staff coming through the main body of the restaurant, even before it opened, which was stupid in Anna's opinion; the customers were going to see her anyway. Hanging up her bag and coat, she put her phone in the back pocket of her jeans and grabbed her white apron before casually strolling through to the restaurant.

Nico Castellani was behind the bar stacking bottles. He stopped mid-motion and gave her a fatherly look of disappointment. "You are late again Anna." The obvious statement made her grin unrepentantly at him, hoping to win him over. It didn't seem to be working as he scowled on response. When she had first started working there, she had found his accent quite sexy. She liked the Italian lilt, and the way he pronounced her name. Now she was used to it, it could be quite irritating and she was sure he put it on all the more for the customers.

"Sorry Nic, the bus was late." Anna shrugged in what she thought was an apologetic way and began tying her apron behind her back

"Did we not have a conversation yesterday about being late?" She could see that he was very pissed off at her. She put a contrite look on her face.

"I am really sorry Nic. I'm gonna try harder, I promise."

"Not good enough… you late tomorrow… you fired." Oh yeah, he was definitely pissed off, the accent was out in full force. He turned his back on her, continuing to stack his bottles.

Anna breathed a sigh of relief; at least she wasn't fired today. She really was going to have to make a concerted effort tomorrow though. She had the feeling that Nic had been pushed to his limit. She had been quite accomplished with her little girl lost routine for a few months now, and had managed to sway him in to forgiving her each time she was late or had done something wrong. Clearly, that particular honeymoon period was over.

"Get on and set the tables." Nic snapped when Anna hadn't moved immediately, lost in her reverie for a moment. There was no doubt he was definitely not a happy man today. She had better watch her step.

Nico could be pretty scary in his own way. He had been born in a tiny village, somewhere in Italy that Anna had never heard of, and his family had emigrated to Britain when he was two years old. His father had started the business that Nico now ran. It was a semi-traditional Italian restaurant and it was popular in the town with its corner booths, red and white chequered table cloths and dozens of pictures and photographs decorating the restaurant, including many containing famous faces of yester-year. A couple of them were signed and Anna had often wondered if they were real signatures. The photos looked real anyway. The other pictures were picturesque views of places in Italy. Anna had stared at them on countless occasions, wistfully imagining herself there some day. She had never been further south than Kent.

Nico had employed an Italian chef who spoke perfect English, but swore all the time in Italian, which was highly amusing and had in fact proved to be quite educational. The air and feel of the place was kind of clichéd; you almost expected to find Marlon Brando sitting in a corner booth ordering spaghetti.

Nico himself was tall, dark and had probably had been very handsome when he was younger. Now he was an aging middle-aged man, a little squidgy around the edges, but not bad on the whole for an older man. Anna wondered now and then if he had 'mob' connections. Sometimes men in suits would come to the restaurant and Nico would sit with them in the furthest corner booth, talking in hushed tones. Those men never seemed to pay for their meals, nor any of the drinks or anything else for that matter. That in itself grated on Anna's nerves because she knew that no tips would be forthcoming from those particular tables.

She had originally had an instant crush on Nic when she had first started work eighteen months ago in his restaurant, as all the waitresses invariably did. Nico flirted with them all shamelessly but never took it any further than that. As time wore on, she had got to know Nico better. He was married, happily it would seem, but he had no children. His life was the restaurant where he seemed to spend every waking moment. Anna had never known him to miss a day of work, not be there when she arrived in the morning and was still there when she left, late at night. She had met Mrs Castellani on occasion and her first impression had been 'what does Nico see in her'. She was a plain Jane, which obviously hadn't changed much as she grew older. Still, as Anna got to know her better, she found out she was one of the kindest people she had ever met. She knew that it was probably Mrs Castellani's influence that kept her in the job. Mrs Castellani tended to mother everybody and Anna was no exception.

Most of the waiters or waitresses worked at the restaurant for a short time before they moved on. Anna had worked for Nico for eighteen months since she had first moved to the area and was currently one of the longest reigning members of staff. It was probably the only reason she scored points with Nic and managed to keep her job. Anna was well aware of the fact that he could sack her for being late all the time, which she seemed to be doing lately on a regular basis. Anna also knew that she would only be able to push Nico so far before he snapped. She couldn't afford to lose this job, that would mean returning to her mother and there was no way on earth she ever wanted to go back there again.

Anna's relationship with her mother had always been a difficult one. Her mother, Phillipa Snelgrove was stuck up and middle-class. She had married Anna's father on discovering she was in fact pregnant with his child. Obviously, it would have been too much for Phillipa to bear to bring up a child on her own, and with parental pressure and persuasion, Jacob Chapman had been made to marry her.

As Anna knew only too well, people who didn't love each other should never get married. Jacob Chapman had not been in love with Phillipa any more than she was with him and subsequently, the divorce that had been impending since day one of their marriage, happened. Anna was too young to remember any of it; she was only eighteen months old when her parents parted, but Phillipa had never tired of informing her daughter about the disappointment that was her father, not to mention the fait accompli of having a child out of wedlock.

Jacob Chapman had been like a ghost in her life. He had visited her on some occasions in her early years, but she hadn't now seen him she was six years old and his face was nothing more than a nondescript blur. Phillipa had finally fallen in love, and married the very safe and dependable, not to mention comfortably off, Richard Snelgrove. He was a mousy little 'yes' man as far as Anna was concerned. Of course, he clearly adored Phillipa, yet he never seemed to stand up for himself. Phillipa ruled his life as much as her daughters with an iron like vice. He never argued with his wife and although he was never anything but kind to Anna and tried to treat her like his own daughter, she found him to be an insipid, spineless shadow of a man. Anna was convinced her mother only married him because he was pliable, easily bullied and had a fair few quid in the bank that allowed Phillipa to live the life she had always craved

When Anna was old enough to start making her own decisions, her mother quashed any thoughts that did not match her own expectations for her daughter. Phillipa had spoken to Anna about the 'birds and the bees' and was very adamant that her daughter would not have sex before marriage. "Any union may result in offspring. Offspring outside of wedlock is not acceptable, Anna."

It was a mantra that had played and replayed itself. Anna felt confined and restricted by her life. She stopped bringing friends home because when they left, invariably her mother would give a disappointed little quirk of her eyebrow and Anna would know immediately that she disapproved. Anna was pushed towards children of other families who Phillipa regarded as 'worthy' of her daughter's friendship, yet somehow those friendships never seemed to pan out.

Phillipa expected Anna to really make something of her life, to become a doctor or a lawyer, or if that failed to marry a doctor or a lawyer. Unfortunately, Anna was not an exceptional student and would never academically achieve the heights her mother wanted her to. Phillipa's answer to this was to arrange a private tutor for her daughter in a supreme effort to push her up the educational ladder. Unfortunately, it had quickly become apparent that Anna did not have anything more than an average educational ability and even Phillipa had been forced to give up the dream of having a doctor or lawyer in the family, although many times she accused her daughter of not trying hard enough.

There might in fact have been some truth to that. Anna didn't want to be a doctor or a lawyer. She didn't want to be anything anyone told her to be. She wanted to be herself.

Despite her mother, Anna had somehow made it through school and had come away with good enough grades to take 'A' levels. She had then announced to her mother that she wanted to go away to university to train to become a teacher.

In Phillipa's mind, this was the next best thing. She agreed to allow her daughter to attend a university of her choosing and even financially supported the move.

It was a dream come true for Anna. She had finally managed to escape her mother, with her mother's own blessing. Phillipa, of course had overseen everything that needed to be done, including arranging accommodation for her. Anna was happy to go with the flow since she knew ultimately that she was getting away from the claustrophobic lifestyle her mother wanted to wrap her in, to finally live her own life the way *she* wanted to do it.

During her first year of university, Anna had gone through several emotions. At first it had been exciting and a challenge. She loved the social side of university and quickly made many friends. However, the academic side of things failed to achieve a winning goal. She found her classes boring and knew that even if she qualified, she had no intention of looking after other people's snotty-nosed kids. Life was seriously too short.

Without informing her mother, she moved out of her halls of residence and found herself a little flat just outside town. In some respects, it was like residing in God's waiting room, due to the number of elderly and retired people around her, but it was cheap and it was her own place and she loved it. Her mother continued to believe that Anna was studying hard and continued to pay a sum of money into Anna's bank account each month. Because this wasn't quite enough to live the life she wanted to, Anna was forced to find a job and had subsequently started working at Castellani's.

Phillipa continued to be proud of the daughter she could finally gloat about to her friends; a teaching profession afforded her the sort of credibility she desired.

Anna hated to think what her mum would make of the fact that she had dropped out of university; she would probably make her come home straight away. Her life would go from zoom to doom in one fell swoop. Not that her life was zooming anywhere exactly, but at least she wouldn't be forced to live in the confines of her mother's ideals. Which in truth, she never had anyway. Anna always had the sense that she was never quite good enough for her mother, that she was expected to be something more, but she just couldn't live up to that, and in any case, didn't want to.

Anna had discovered a new-found sense of freedom and she had no intention of going back. Her life might not be the most exciting, but she was enjoying herself for the most part. It was certainly better than going home with her tail firmly between her legs.

Anna now tolerated her mother in small doses; she dutifully sent her texts and called to update her about the fake side of her life, the part she knew her mother wanted to hear. If her mother ever found out it was all lies, it would be a disaster of cataclysmic proportions.

Anna set to work setting the tables with the red and white checked table cloths, cutlery, glasses and napkins – the paper kind of course. The restaurant opened at eleven thirty a.m. in time for the pre-lunchtime crowd.

The rest of the day flew by in a blur for Anna. She worked her tables with smiles and pleasantries. Sometimes she really enjoyed the social aspect of her job. It gave her the opportunity to meet lots of different people and for the most part they were happy and polite.

On her break, she checked her phone for updates, posting a new status on her social media page before texting a couple of her friends regarding the upcoming evening before eating her lunch. That was a definite perk working at the restaurant. She got free food.

The end of her shift came at six o'clock. Grabbing her jacket, bag and tips, she left the restaurant and made her way to the bus stop.

With her attention firmly settled on her phone, Anna never noticed the man watching her. But then she hadn't noticed him on the occasions when he had sat in her restaurant, she hadn't seen him the countless times he had followed her home or to her respective boyfriends and she certainly hadn't seen him when he had sat invisibly outside her flat. He had been free to watch her like the invisible man.

He watched her from his position across the road now. He had no need to rush, he knew where she was going, knew where she lived. He knew her movements better than anybody. He knew *her* now. And like a snake watching its prey, he would know exactly the right moment to strike. It was inevitable, like the sun setting in the west.

Anna sat in Greg's flat on the worn sofa, taking a drag of the cannabis-filled rollie offered to her by Tanya.

Anna, Tanya, Greg and Tom had been sitting in Greg's flat since about seven o'clock that night. Anna had come straight from work to find Tanya and Tom already there. In fact, to Anna's annoyance they had been there since three o'clock that afternoon, smoking and drinking. They were mellow and very drunk when Anna arrived, which pissed her off straight away. Despite already smoking a couple of rollies of cannabis with a good few slugs of vodka, she was still not feeling it.

Greg was being an idiot as well and really getting on her nerves. She had been looking forward to this evening all day, and now she felt like it was a huge anti-climax.

Greg lived in a squat. It had boarded up windows and some rooms smelt of urine. Thankfully, they were the parts nobody used.

Somehow, Greg and Tom had managed to get the gas and electric put on; apparently it had something to do with tapping into a neighbour's supply. They had water too. All mod cons in a flea-infested rat hole. Greg and Tom used to also share the squat with another man called Toby, but Toby had mysteriously disappeared about a month ago and hadn't been heard from since.

Anna had been seeing Greg for about two months now. They had met one evening when Anna had been out with her friend Lisa. While in the pub, Lisa had seen her friend Tanya who was with Tom and Greg and the rest, as they say, was history.

Anna liked to think of herself as a bit of a party girl. She was never short of male attention and had had several different boyfriends since moving from home. She was hoping to find the one, someone who would treat her really nicely, whom she could settle down with. So far all she had met was losers. Somehow, at first she had felt Greg was different.

Greg strolled into the room, with a cigarette dangling precariously from the side of his mouth, his eyes screwed up from the smoke. He was carrying a half-empty bottle of Jack Daniels. He was bare-footed, and wearing jeans slung low on his hips and a dirty looking t-shirt promoting some long-forgotten band from the '80s. The t-shirt had seen better days and needed a good wash. It made Anna feel a bit squirmy to look at him walking around barefoot on the filthy floor.

The squat was dirty, no… it was beyond dirty, it was so disgusting that it actually made Anna feel sick. There were food containers everywhere, and overflowing ashtrays or receptacles that had been used as ashtrays. The smell of cannabis permeated the air. They never cleaned and a thick film of dirt coated every surface that did not have something residing on it.

She didn't come to Greg's too often because the squat was so disgusting, but usually after a few drinks she forgot all about it. Tonight however, she just couldn't fail to notice the grime and dirt all around her and all she really wanted to do right now was leave.

"Alright, babe." Greg's voice was gravelly from too many cigarettes and weed as he flopped down next to her on the sofa and flung an arm over her shoulders. She hated to be called babe and she wondered if he did it because he actually forgot her name. Hadn't she read somewhere once that if your man called you babe, it was because he couldn't remember your name, or he had more than one woman on the go at once and didn't want to mix your names up?

Anna got a waft of his body odour combined with an underlying unpleasant smell that suggested he hadn't washed any part of his body for some time as he attempted to snuggle up to her on the sofa. Ash from his cigarette dropped onto the leg of his jeans and he swiped at it, smearing a blackened stain across his leg. Anna grimaced as she watched his hand. She hadn't realised before just how dirty Greg's fingernails were. He propped one leg on the other, his right ankle balancing on his left knee and she was treated to a glimpse of his feet, which were in fact so dirty they appeared black. Anna swallowed hard, trying not to let her dismay and disgust show on her face. How could she not have noticed these things before?

"Is the water working?" she asked simply. He chuckled and took a drag of his cannabis cigarette before passing it to her. She shook her head, declining.

"Water's working fine, babe, why?" She knew she didn't have to answer. His response was automatic, she doubted if he even heard what she said.

In truth, she had only been dating Greg a matter of weeks. Anna had been quite attracted to him because, truthfully, he was everything her mother would abhor, and that was always the name of the game Even if her mother never knew about Anna's *real* life, the fact that Anna knew her mother would hate it was enough. An act of unknown rebellion.

Greg had seemed really good looking to her once, with his dirty blonde hair that flopped in no particular direction, probably because it was so long, the beard he sported and his smiling blue eyes. He was of slim build and quite tall. The fact that he lived in a squat had not really bothered her before. It was a means to an end. He had trained to be a computer programmer, but had never actually got a job doing just that. In fact, he had never worked a day in his life. He claimed benefits and thought himself clever for doing so. He promised Anna that one day he would make a lot of money and move into his own place. It was a rehearsed mantra that she was sure he was so used to spouting that it was as normal as getting up in the morning.

She knew that Greg also sold drugs on the side. On the nights they went out, he would spend a lot of time disappearing into bathrooms, or there would be surreptitious handshakes where goods were exchanged for money. Anna had ignored it all, thinking it was nothing to do with her. Had she been off her face or drunk every time they met? There were certainly nights she had no recollection of at all. Greg could have sold her for sex and she wouldn't have known a thing. Why was it just now that she could see it all with perfect clarity?

Tanya and Tom were getting a bit hot and heavy at the other end of the sofa. Tom's hand was under Tanya's t-shirt, and she clearly wasn't wearing a bra. As Anna watched in disgust, he pulled up her t-shirt and took her nipple into his mouth. Her head was thrown back in ecstasy and she groaned loudly.

"Get a room, you two," Greg said, laughing, "Then me an' Anna can have the sofa." Tom looked up from sucking Tanya's left tit. "We could always make it a foursome." He leered in Anna's direction and winked.

"Don't stop," Tanya whined, completely out of it.

"Yeah, maybe later," Greg responded to his friend, grinning luridly. Anna was appalled. That was so not happening.

Tom got to his feet, pulling Tanya with him and dragged her towards the squat's only decent bedroom. There was no door and everything could be heard as clear as day. They were not quiet.

As soon as they had left the room, Greg turned to Anna, and began nibbling his way along her neck. Usually she would be very up for anything Greg wanted to do but tonight she just wasn't turned on, and certainly wasn't in the mood to do anything with the other people in the next room. She felt uncomfortable and just wanted to leave.

"What's up, babe?" Greg questioned, sensing Anna's reluctance.

"I'm just not up for this at the moment." She tried to explain as the sounds of the couple in the bedroom having sex drifted in.

"Yeah." Greg crooned, one hand rubbing his crotch suggestively. "You wanna see what I got for you, babe, you wanna feel how hot for you I am?" He was trying to be seductive, his voice low, but to Anna at that moment he just sounded like a dirty old man. He made a grab for her t-shirt, trying to untuck it from her jeans. Immediately her hands went to his, trying to still them. The thought of his dirty fingernailed hands touching her clean skin made her feel sick.

Undeterred by her hands on his, he continued to try and untuck her t-shirt.

"Stop," Anna told him firmly. His mouth that had been nibbling away at her neck, working its way to her ear lobe, stopped and his head came up to look at her face.

"What's the matter with you?" Greg asked harshly, all semblance of his passion disappearing in an instant.

"I told you, I'm not up for this." She repeated. "Not here, not tonight," she said firmly, her eyes flicking towards the doorway that led to the bedroom where the sounds of the couple having sex was reaching some kind of heavy breathing, moaning crescendo. Anna felt her cheeks colour.

"You weren't bovvered the other day," Greg whined.

"I was drunk the other day," Anna reminded him. God, she must have been drunk if she had failed to notice on countless occasions what a shithole Greg lived in. In fact, she must have been drunk *every* time she came here because she couldn't for the life of her remember it ever looking this bad. Still, he did come to her flat more often.

Anna stood up and tucked her t-shirt back into her jeans.

"Where you going?" Greg looked up at her, confusion filling his face.

"I'm going home, Greg, I'm not in the mood for this, I don't know why, but I'm not, I'd really rather just go home." She was trying to explain, albeit not very well, and not really sure if she was making sense to him at all through the fug of the drugs and alcohol he had consumed. Greg stood up unsteadily and made a grab for Anna, catching her wrist in his hand.

"Come on, babe." His tone was wheedling which infuriated Anna even more.

"No, Greg, I really would rather go home." She grabbed her denim jacket off the arm of the sofa.

"Well fuck off then, fucking cock teaser," he retorted venomously. He released her wrist instantly and turned to grab his bottle of Jack Daniels off the floor. He stood a slug and flung himself back on the sofa.

"There's no need to be so nasty." Anna cried indignantly, "I'll call you tomorrow."

"You don't wanna fuck, then fuck off," Greg repeated nastily. "Fucking prick teaser, that's all you are, you snotty, stuck up bitch." He added, giving her the finger as he threw the Jack Daniels bottle back and took a further slug. She knew it was the drugs and alcohol talking, but it didn't hurt any less. She picked up her bag and pulled on her jacket.

"I'll speak to you later." She said, quietly turning for the door. She looked back at him quickly before she stepped through, hoping that he would come after her. He was on his feet alright, but he wasn't looking at her. In fact, Anna was sure he didn't even see her as he shambled his way to the bedroom. She stood transfixed in the doorway as he walked through to the bedroom, oblivious to her presence.

"Got room for another one?" she heard him say before the sound of female and male laughter drifted through. Anna felt tears well up in her eyes as she turned and headed through the door. How could she have been so stupid? How many times had this happened? Anna felt like the biggest fool.

It was only nine o'clock, but it was dark; ominous clouds were creeping in and threatening an impending rain storm. Anna walked alone to the bus stop, wiping at the tears that ran down her cheeks. She was annoyed with herself for crying. How many times had he had sex with anyone who would agree to it when she wasn't around? She thought that they had something sort of special together. She thought that he maybe he loved her, there were times when he had murmured those words and the romantic part of her assumed that they may have had a future together. Clearly, he didn't feel the same.

She waited at the bus stop, pulling her mobile phone from her pocket. She stared blankly, willing a text message or a call from Greg. She didn't want to speak to him, just wanted the satisfaction of being able to ignore him, but for once her phone was silent. And no wonder, since he was probably fucking Tanya's brains out at that precise moment. She felt sick.

She peered down the road into the gloom, wishing the bus would come along. She was sick of waiting for buses today. All she wanted to do was go home and remove the dirtiness that was Greg's squat off her body with a hot shower and climb into bed.

The bus wasn't coming and her mind was in overdrive. She couldn't get the imagined pictures of Greg and Tanya out of her head. The more she thought about it, the more she thought about scenarios that had happened between Greg and Tanya, little touches here and there, like when he used to grab her bum or make a lurid comment. It was making her angry. He had clearly been having sex with Tanya for a long time. It had been going on right under her nose the whole time and she had no clue. It was obvious now. He called her babe, hardly ever Anna. He called Tanya babe too, she had heard him. He spent most of his time off his face on drugs or drink. He didn't work, claimed benefits and he lived in that filthy squat. What had she seen in him? She was in two minds whether to go back and have a go at him right now, to walk in and pretend she was just returning and catch them all in bed together. No, she didn't need to see that. The images in her head were projecting a vivid enough scenario as it was without seeing the real deal. She closed her eyes and leaned her head against the back of the bus stop shelter.

"Are you okay?" The soft voice took her by surprise and made her jump. She opened her eyes and looked at the man before her. "I thought you might be unwell." He looked apologetic for bothering her.

"No, no I'm fine really, just had a really tough day," Anna replied, standing up straight and collecting herself, "You just startled me."

"I'm sorry." He went to move away, looking at the bus timetable.

"It's okay, honestly." She liked the look of him, liked his voice. He looked familiar to her although she couldn't place him. Perhaps he had attended the university. He looked sort of sad.

"Are *you* okay?" she asked. For some reason she wanted to keep talking to him.

"No actually, I just caught my girlfriend with another man," he admitted ruefully, putting his hands in his pockets and shrugging his shoulders at the same time. He was clearly very upset about it and Anna felt like she'd found a kindred spirit. She felt like she wanted to comfort him, he looked so forlorn.

"Do you know what? The same thing just happened to me... I mean I just caught my boyfriend with another girl," Anna explained quickly.

"It's shit, isn't it?"

"Totes." They fell into silence, neither one seeming to know what to say to the other.

"Do you wanna grab a drink or something? Looks like the bus isn't coming and to be honest, I could do with cheering up." There was a vulnerable hope in his face that touched Anna's heart strings. She felt sure she knew who he was and that they had met before. She wouldn't usually agree to go for a drink with a complete stranger, but then if she knew him... he wasn't a *complete* stranger. There was something sort of charming about this man with his good looks and soft-spoken voice. All of a sudden Anna found herself thinking that this would be kind the of man her mum would be happy for her to take home and she found herself agreeing.

"Sure, I'd love to get a drink." She found herself smiling up as his face lit up in a smile.

They turned from the bus stop, walking back the way Anna had come. There was a small pub a few yards from the bus stop. "What's your name?" Anna asked as they were about to step over the threshold.

"My name's Roger," he informed her.

"Well Roger, I'm Anna, it's nice to meet you."

They approached the bar together and Roger drew a twenty pound note out of his pocket. "What would you like?" he asked. She really liked his voice. Perhaps it was the after effects of the cannabis or the vodka she had consumed in Greg's flat earlier, but Anna felt sufficiently mellow now. Thoughts of Greg, his dirty flat and his indiscretions were being pushed further from her mind in Roger's company.

"Could I have a vodka and lemonade please?" Roger nodded and turned to the barman for their order. "Just popping to the little girls' room," she stated and heard him ordering her a double vodka as she moved away. She smiled to herself as she went into the girls' bathroom. A few moments ago, her world was in turmoil; now she was feeling like she had done a complete three-sixty. Roger seemed charming, generous and very nice. She went over to the bathroom mirror to check herself out; since she had been crying, she thought her make-up might look a complete mess, but thankfully it was okay. She turned her head from side to side, looking and trying to look at herself from every angle. She didn't think she actually looked too bad considering she had been at work all day. Her make-up could do with a touch up, but it would have to do since she didn't have her make-up bag with her.

Roger seemed really nice and she was sure she had met him before. At least he looked clean and she was sure he didn't live in a squat. Well, at leastshe hoped not.

It was early days, but she was hoping that Roger would want to see her again after tonight and on a proper date, she could blow his socks off. She giggled at that thought to herself. She locked herself in the toilet cubicle and used the toilet. She wondered whether she should freshen up down below. No. Roger seemed like a decent sort of man, he wouldn't want to have sex with her tonight, and besides he had just caught his girlfriend with another man. Probably not feeling too sexy right now. She bit her lip as she considered that final thought. What if he just wanted a drink and some company? What if he didn't want to see her again? She couldn't think about that now. She could at least get his number. Who knew what might happen? They were both on the rebound.

She washed her hands and fiddled slightly with her hair, trying to give it a little bit more bounce. She checked herself out in the mirror once more before returning to the bar.

She found that Roger had grabbed them a small table by themselves, not that the bar was very busy and crowded tonight, although there were several people milling around. She smiled at him as she sat down opposite and he smiled back. "Thanks for the drink." She lifted her glass and took a sip. The vodka was strong. It warmed her throat. Roger lifted his glass of coke to his lips; his eyes met hers over the top of the glass. "Aren't you drinking?"

"I don't drink," he replied in that soft way he had of speaking. She could listen to his voice for hours, just close her eyes and drift off to sleep listening to it. Another good reason to take him home to mum, she thought, especially being teetotal. Now all she had to do was find out what he did for a living.

"How long were you dating your girlfriend?" she asked, trying to appear supportive, although in all honesty she didn't give a shit, that bitch was history.

"Not very long, she was a slut."

Anna burst out laughing. Him saying slut sounded terribly funny coming from such a nice voice. "Clearly." She agreed.

"What about your boyfriend?" he asked, smoothly moving the subject on to her.

"Girl meets boy, boy is so wrong for her, but would annoy her mother, but boy is a waste of space." Anna said cheerfully; the vodka was starting to do its job. "You on the other hand... " Anna pointed in his direction and giggled playfully. She was already getting drunk. She had only taken a few sips, but she thought maybe with what she had consumed at Greg's her tolerance level was down low.

"Me?" Roger replied smiling.

"You would be perfect to take home to my mum." Oops, there it was, out there in the open – she had said it. Anna would have winced had she been a bit soberer.

"Well drink up, my darling, we'll have a good night." Anna smiled at him once more as she lifted her glass. He had just called her *darling*. She was in flirt heaven right now. Maybe she should have freshened up after all; she had the feeling she was going to enjoy herself tonight.

She never knew what hit her, never saw it coming. The punch to the left side of her face was as sudden as it was intense, sending her spinning around so fast she lost her balance and went down to her knees. Her face felt like it was exploding except she couldn't help but find it funny. She started to giggle hysterically as flashes of light danced all around her; she felt disorientated. She tried to stand but was immediately pushed to the ground by a sharp blow to the front of her head this time. She lay sprawled on the floor, on her back as a dark shape appeared above her. Her brain could not comprehend what she was seeing at first. It was a man, it was *the* man, the man from the bar. She liked him a lot. Her mum would like him too. She couldn't remember his name though. He was smiling down at her. This is it, she thought. Her last coherent thought was that she should have freshened up down below.

HIM

He could only triumph in his own success. How easy it had been. He had expected more of a challenge, had expected to work harder than he had, but in the end, Anna Chapman proved herself to be what he expected, *a dirty little slut*.

It had all worked out so much easier than he had anticipated. He had thought that he would need to ply her with several drinks before she needed the bathroom, but in fact she had made that move straight away. He had ordered her a double, intending to get her pretty drunk anyway and while she was gone, he had emptied the phial of Rohypnol into her glass. It had all been so simple and straightforward. She was falling down drunk when they left the bar, and it had only cost him one drink. She was leaning into him heavily, telling him that she loved him, loved his voice as he half carried, half dragged her from the bar. The barman had given him a commiserating look as he led her to the door, clearly thinking that she was a lightweight. He had bundled her into his car easily enough, it was a stolen model of course, a beat-up Volkswagen Beetle, which could not be traced back to him. Then he had driven her back to her flat. It had been easy to fish her keys from her bag and he had carried her into the apartment, unseen by anyone in the vicinity.

He dropped her semi-conscious body unceremoniously on to the floor in the small hallway while he took the opportunity to scout around. It was a sparse, but clean little place. He had not had the opportunity to get in previously, too dangerous, too many people. The people living in this particular part of town tended to be more elderly or retired. They were therefore at home during the day and suspicious. It wouldn't do to attract any unwanted attention. He wandered into the small living room that also had a cooking space and was intended to be a dining room too, he assumed. There was a sink area and one cupboard, all rather worn, but kept clean, he was surprised to see. One sofa, probably well-worn since it was covered with two large throws, stood under the large sash window. There was a small coffee table, a standard lamp and TV. The floor was uncarpeted but had been swept and was kept clean, with a pretty rug in the middle of the room.

The rest of the flat consisted of a minute bathroom with a shower, small sink and toilet. In the bedroom was a rail which housed a few clothes, mainly dark coloured, and Anna's bed – the largest and undoubtedly the most expensive item in the flat.

Having viewed what he needed, he was sufficiently satisfied that his work could begin.

He had punched Anna in the head twice and she was suitably semi-conscious, along with the effects of the alcohol and Rohypnol in her system. He dragged Anna into the living room, since there was more room here. He had already put on his surgical gloves. She was wearing a dark-coloured top and black jeans. These presented much more of a problem to remove than Mary's pyjamas since they were so tight. Anna smiled at him with an unfocused expression and giggled intermittently as he wrestled with her body to remove her clothing. It might be smarter in future to carry a pair of scissors and cut things off. He would have used the knife but there was a risk he might have caught her skin. The point was to be precise. Everything had to be perfect, he could afford no mistakes.

He was sweating profusely by the time he had her stripped down to her underwear. Thankfully, these items presented less of a challenge in their removal than her clothing.

Finally, she was naked. He looked down at her semi-conscious form. She was tiny. Her breasts were small, tapering into a slim waist, barely flaring out to her hips. She had shaved completely, her pussy bare. He knelt down and pulled open her thighs, unable to stop himself from looking. She glistened invitingly at him and instantly he felt himself growing hard.

Going into Anna's bedroom, he removed his clothing and laid it on her bed. Taking his condom from his pocket, he rolled it over his engorged penis. Oh yes, he was going to enjoy himself even more with this one, more than he did with Mary. He could hardly wait; his mouth was watering in anticipation.

He sauntered back into the living room. Anna had remained exactly as he had left her a few moments before. He loomed over her small frame.

"Anna, my darling," he crooned softly. She turned to him smiling and licked her lips. An invitation if ever there was one.

"I'm going to fuck your brains out now and then I'm going to slice up your cunt and eat it for breakfast." She giggled, none of what he said really registering in her drug-induced befuddlement.

He entered her with such force that she yelped in pain, but he had no qualms about any discomfort he might have caused. This time he was frantic in his rhythm, he pounded into her with such a ferocity and hatred as he raped her. Beads of sweat covered his entire body and yet he continued to roughly pile-drive his body into hers until he came. He felt physically drained, was panting as he climaxed, but rolled away from her and onto the floor. Wouldn't do to leave any DNA. He was always one step ahead.

He didn't want to fuck her again. She was not like Mary; Anna was a filthy little slut who would have slept with anybody who showed an iota of interest in her. He just had to know what she felt like, just once and now that was over, he was satiated. He had also used a lot of energy this time and he felt the need to sleep. That, however was not an option; he had work to do.

Reluctantly he raised himself from the floor and looked down at Anna. She looked like she was sleeping peacefully. Dark bruises had already formed on her face where he had punched her and he giggled.

Standing up, he removed the soiled condom from his cock and tied a knot in the end, taking it through to the bedroom to leave it with his things. It wouldn't do to forget it later. While he was there, he took his scalpel from his jacket and wandered back into the living room completely naked, wearing nothing but his forensic booties, a fresh condom and a pair of surgical gloves. He rummaged through her cutlery drawer. He was gratified to find a large knife, big enough for the job in hand. He just hoped it was sharp enough. Still, he had the scalpel and a couple of other implements at his disposal. They were purposefully brought for the job in hand and small enough to be hidden in the lining of his coat. He placed his items ceremoniously onto the small coffee table.

The cut was not deep enough. He watched as the blood seeped from the cut. The gentle rise and fall of Anna's chest suggested that she was not yet dead. He knelt beside her and lifted her head up by her hair. He had rummaged through Anna's things and found a scarf which he found perfect for the job. He now placed that under her head. Then he released her head allowing it hit the floor with a loud thump. She barely made a sound. Gathering the two ends of the scarf together he ensured that it was tight enough, then fastened a knot so that the scarf formed a gag through her mouth. There was no real need to gag her; her drug-induced state would ensure that, except in order to 'become', but there were certain things that had to be done to set the scene. Even if, by some miracle she were to wake up now, she would probably choke on her own tongue. He smiled down at her. She was being a very good girl indeed.

Picking up the knife once more he held her chin with his left hand while he used the knife to make a deeper cut in her neck. Blood splashed up as he hit the carotid artery but at last, he was satisfied that the cut was deep enough. Preciseness was very important to him.

Now that he was satisfied that she would shortly cease to breathe, the young nubile body tempted him once more, her small breasts greeting him with their perkiness. He could feel himself growing hard again; the tightness of his cock felt uncomfortable, begging for release. Bending down, he ran a gloved hand almost lovingly across her breasts before moving down to lower regions. It was a moment before he realised what he was doing. He snatched his hand back like her skin had burned him.

"You dirty, filthy slut, look what you made me do," he hissed, a look of pure disgust on his face. He stood up abruptly and delivered a sharp, swift kick to her chest. An audible snap sounded as his foot connected with one of her ribs, breaking it on impact. That assured him some sense of wellbeing immediately. It had hurt his foot and he was angry, wanting to kick her again. How dare she try to tempt him again, she was evil, pure evil. How dare she think she could command him with her disgusting whore's body? *He* was the master, *he* was the taker. He kicked her again for good measure. He was breathing hard, a mixture of excitement for himself and disgust directed at her. His erection was straining, begging to given the chance to take her once more. He pondered this thought for a moment. It was what she wanted. She was trying to tempt him with her whore's wiles.

"It's meeeeeeee," he shouted at her, thumping himself in the chest. "I'm the one," he shouted again. She didn't move, she didn't respond. Her life was slowly ebbing away, her life's blood forming a pool around her head like a scarlet halo. He was happy to accept this as her assent and agreement.

Turning to leave the room, he entered the tiny bathroom and turned on the taps at the sink. He splashed cold water on his face. He needed to regroup. Anna was doing things to him he didn't expect. She was using her womanly wiles on him, her whore's tricks. He needed a shower. He needed to refresh himself. He looked towards the small cubicle with a covetous expression. He certainly had the time to spare; nobody would be coming to see Anna Chapman tonight, not even her vagrant, layabout, good for nothing, boyfriend.

The shower was tempting, but he could not afford to leave any trace of himself. He went to great lengths to ensure that his identity remained a secret. It had to be the case or he would never be able to carry out his work. He glanced at his own face in the mirror, willing himself to mentally calm down. Reaching the coldest, dead spot inside himself, he closed his eyes. His breathing became rhythmically slow and any erotic thoughts he was having disappeared. His erection too with those thoughts disappeared and ten minutes later, he was feeling like himself again. She was clever, but not clever enough. He turned and left the bathroom. He had a job to complete.

Now when he looked at Anna, she was nothing and she meant nothing to him. He was not moved by her appearance or her nakedness. There was only the job in hand.

He moved her legs, pulling them up so that he feet were flat on the floor and her knees pointed towards the ceiling, then he allowed her legs to flop open left and right. From his position at her feet, he could clearly see everything. She was trying to tempt him again, but he remained strong and he was proud of himself for that.

Turning the knife, it glinted in the light, he was smiling as he knelt down and plunged it deep into her abdomen, tearing across so that her intestines were clearly visible. Using both hands, he pulled them from her stomach and draped them carefully by her hips. Cutting precisely, he severed their mesenteric attachments, picked up the intestines and stretched them out, arranging them carefully by her shoulder. They had been heavier than he thought they would be and the smell was beyond disgusting. Still, an artist must do what he must, for work.

Returning to the abdomen area, he carefully pulled the stomach open so that the glistening remains could clearly be seen. This time he used his scalpel that he had retrieved from his coat earlier. Then he set to work.

He was sweating by the time he had finished but he stood back to admire his handiwork. He had removed the upper portion of her vagina and two parts of the bladder. These were nestled in sandwich bags that he had brought with him and now resided in his coat pockets along with his scalpel and his used condom. He would dispose of them later.

He leant forward and loosened the gag from around her mouth, pulling it so hung around her neck; authenticity was important to him. Anna's mouth remained open. The gag sat loosely around her neck just above where he had cut it. He had done an excellent job, it was far better than the last one and although the sweat made him feel uncomfortable, he was proud of his night's work.

He stepped over the body of Anna Chapman. The blood was everywhere. Thank god for his booties but they were saturated now Returning to Anna's bedroom, he sat on the bed and carefully peeled of the blood soaked booties, folding them so that the bloody part was inside. He added them to a sandwich bag. He then pulled on his clothes, first his jeans. Now fully dressed, he pulled on his coat. The pockets were bulging with his goodies. Stepping to the threshold of the living room, he took one last look at his handiwork. Pleased with himself, he turned and left, moving to the front door of the flat. The hall beyond was deserted and quiet; only the buzzing of a flickering hall light could be heard in the otherwise silent building. A good reason to live near older people he thought, they were all bound to be in bed, tucked up sleeping like little babies.

He stood in the hallway and removed the surgical gloves from his hands. He removed a handkerchief from the inside pocket of his jacket where his scalpel resided. Holding his handkerchief over his left hand, he leant forward and closed the door, giving the hand a quick wipe so as to not leave any fingerprints. Standing still once more in order to ascertain that the silence remained and satisfied that he was alone, he started making his way to the stairwell. He felt so light and happy he could have skipped gleefully down like a newborn colt, but it wouldn't do to draw attention to oneself. He took his time. Patience was one of his virtues and he had an abundance of that.

Frances Capaldi returned home from her three-week cruise on the ninth of September. She had lived at The Mews for ten years ever since her husband had passed away. They had owned a fair-sized semi-detached town house together, which in truth had been too big for the two of them once the children moved away, but it had proven to be a lucrative investment on selling, and Frances had made a considerable profit, allowing her to purchase the small ground floor flat she now resided in and have enough left over to live in a style she had quickly become accustomed to.

Her favourite thing was a cruise. She had been on several and spent at least three weeks away. This time her holiday had consisted of a glorious summer float around the Mediterranean islands. She was rested and tanned and ready to take up a bridge tournament organised by the local over-sixties' club.

The cab driver driving Frances home had reluctantly carried her suitcase to her flat. He refused to take it any further than her front door, and consequently she had refused to tip him. Quid pro quo as far she was concerned. He had gone off with a disgruntled mumble. Frances could not have cared less. No sooner was she through her front door, the cab driver was forgotten.

The suitcase was on wheels and the only real challenge was lifting it over the threshold. She had taken too much abroad as per usual, and she couldn't resist a knick-knack or memento. She struggled with her case into the flat by herself, promptly leaving it in the hallway. It was so nice to be home. Frances loved to travel and enjoyed her many trips away, but she always loved to come to her little flat. She walked through the hall into her living room which led through to the small kitchenette. There she was gratified to find a bottle of milk, thankfully provided by her neighbour Gladys. At least she could have a decent cup of tea. Going abroad was all very well, but she was yet to find anyone who could make a decent cup of tea.

She disrobed from her holiday clothes and put on her dressing gown while the kettle was boiling. She could do with a good catch up of her soap programmes that she had set up on record while she away, and was looking forward to a good old binge watch so that she could discuss what was happening with her friends when they met for bridge the next day.

Settling herself into her favourite chair, remote control in one hand, feet on her pouffe, she took a sip of her tea. Something caught the corner of her eye and she looked up. Then she frowned. There on the ceiling was a dark red stain that resembled red wine. It was clearly coming through from the flat upstairs and completely ruined her ceiling décor.

Frances Capaldi was not a happy woman. Clearly that young woman upstairs had had some sort of party while she away. It just wasn't on. The flats here in The Mews were designed to accommodate the elderly and retired, not young people about town who wanted to throw wild parties.

She immediately reached for her phone book and cordless phone. She was going to give that landlord a piece of her mind. She was fed up with the comings and goings of the young people he consistently rented his flat to. There had been loud music, constant noises and bangs, comings and goings at all times of the day and night and quite frankly she had had enough.

She looked up at the stain once more, consternation in her mind as she dialled the number. She would refuse to be fobbed off this time and this time he would be responsible for her decorating costs. It would take a considerable amount of money to cover that stain and she had no intention of footing the bill.

CHAPTER SEVEN

Marcus Nicholls returned home on the eighth of September in blaze of front-page publicity and pious indignation.

The headlines splashed about the previous week had proclaimed 'Where is Marcus?', practically accusing him of killing his wife. By sheer coincidence he had been spotted in the South of France and the authorities were alerted. He had then spent a very uncomfortable six hours with the French police before being bundled back to the UK for further interrogation.

Marcus Nicholls was not a happy man. This was all very inconvenient for him. Not that he wasn't devastated by Mary's untimely death, but Marcus found it incredibly difficult to live in the past, and now Mary was definitely his past. He wanted to move on with his life. He was sure the house, the cars and the money would undoubtedly be his. There was bound to be some sort of payout in life insurance and of course there must be a death-in-service benefit. He was already counting the pennies. He might even be able to take retirement. It would be marvellous to live the life he had always wanted.

Deep down, Marcus Nicholls was a cold, calculating, callous bastard. He knew it himself, and Mary had known it too. Unfortunately, in the case of the bastard, there was always a woman who loved them unconditionally and that had been Mary's misfortune. She had been a fool who was head over heels.

Marcus had truly loved Mary at one time but that love had settled into something more platonic. He loved her, but he wasn't in love with her. It was a sad fact that had presented itself to him very early in their marriage.

Mary had come from terrible beginnings. Her mother was a lush and a prostitute and had been a complete waste of space as a parent. The only time Vera ever contacted Mary was when she needed money and much to Marcus's disgust, Mary always gave in and let her have what she wanted, despite Marcus urging Mary to cut all ties and let Vera rot in her own filth.

Mary had wanted to have a child about a year into their marriage. Marcus could understand that need in Mary because she had come from such awful beginnings and he had dutifully allowed her to pursue her dream. The unfortunate thing was that Marcus had bought and paid for a private vasectomy six months after they were married, so procreation was out of the question. Every month, Mary would remain hopeful that she would find herself with child and every month her period had come with the ultimate disappointment. Marcus encouraged her to visit doctors and even said that he had visited himself. "It's not me I'm afraid, darling," he had told her one day. She had been crestfallen, her face crumbling before his eyes in floods of tears. He wanted to feel for her, he truly did, but the fact of the matter was that he didn't want children – never had. The thought of doing such a thing was totally abhorrent to him. He simply wasn't the type of person to have offspring; he loved his life far too much.

He was gratified when Mary eventually gave up on the dream and he didn't have to keep pretending any longer. She threw herself into her career, something which he encouraged. It allowed him the freedom to do his thing, which unfortunately Mary was not up for at all. It was another nail in the coffin of their marriage as far as he was concerned. Mary had liked vanilla sex, no frills – a wham, bam, thank you ma'am. Marcus's tastes tended to something a little more exotic. He was into the 'S&M' scene. Not the real hardcore stuff, but he liked a bit of tying up and spanking.

Marcus now sat in an interview room at the police station, accompanied by one police officer. Truthfully, he knew he hadn't done it and knew it was only a matter of time before he would be released. He would have the press clamouring at his door for the story and no doubt could negotiate a top dollar deal with maybe even a book deal. Inwardly he was clapping his hands together; this could be the best thing that had happened to him for a long time. It was all about acting the part from now on.

On arrival at the police station, he had blustered on, demanding all sorts of action be taken, that the police find out who did this. The blustering had quietened considerably now that he had been sitting in the interview room for almost an hour, with the dowdy little specimen in uniform keeping him company.

It was very irritating that he had been kept waiting. The murder of his dear departed wife was gradually taking a further and further back seat as he contemplated his own fate and the fact that he desperately wanted a shower.

Ginny really wanted to handle this one herself. The high-profile arrival of Marcus Nicholls had the press camped outside the Main Road police station. It was supposed to be a secret that they had negotiated his transport from France and yet the moment he landed at the airport, the newspapers and TV were aware of it. Fortunately, Marcus had been wise enough not to speak to anyone before he had been delivered to their station.

Now he had been kept waiting an hour in the interview room and Ginny felt sure he would be sufficiently pissed off. Pissed off people, in her experience, had a nasty habit of slipping up with their testimonies.

Ginny and Pat made their way to the interview room. Ginny was still sure that she had her number one prime suspect and he was now in her custody.

Marcus Nicholls was nothing like Ginny had imagined. He was older than Mary Nicholls by nearly ten years, but you wouldn't have guessed, as he looked nothing like a typical almost fifty-year-old man.

He was fit and well built, clearly worked out at the gym – not an ounce of fat was visible anywhere. Large muscular biceps were visible from beneath the polo shirt he wore; clearly, he liked weights. A large expensive-looking gold watch sat on his left wrist and a gold wedding ring on his left third finger. A large gold signet ring sat on the little finger of his right hand. He was extremely good looking, almost movie star handsome, with bright blue eyes and blonde hair which showed no signs of grey and was swept back in a modern style. He was very tanned. He carried himself with an air of somebody extremely confident and he would definitely turn heads walking down the street. He could perhaps be considered a blonde George Clooney and every inch of seem to exude an air of charm and self-assurance.

He stood up as Ginny and Pat entered the interview room. He even smelt nice, Ginny noticed, but she wasn't about to be fooled by schmooze.

"Marcus Nicholls." He oozed charm as he held out his hand for Ginny and Pat to shake. Ginny shook his hand and then gestured to the chair he had vacated.

"We know who you are, Mr Nicholls," Ginny stated. "Please sit down." She was business-like, determined not to react in the way he wanted her to. He was clearly aware of his presence and the effect he had on the opposite sex. Ginny had no intention of allowing him to see that she found him extremely attractive. She had to view this matter in a completely clinical way. He was, after all at the moment, her prime suspect.

Marcus Nicholls was used to getting his own way, particularly with the ladies. He turned on his charm and sophistication and usually had them melting in the palm of his hand within seconds. He was reputed to have a woman panting for him in a record-breaking amount of time and had no trouble talking them in to other things. He had no doubt that he could charm his own way with DCI Virginia Percy, so much so that she would be begging for his release. He smiled winningly, displaying super-white teeth, the corners of his blue eyes crinkling at the sides, making him appear boyish and innocent.

Ginny's mouth popped open for a second. He decided that she was totally star struck and in awe of him, as he did with most women. Ginny on the other hand could only think, does he honestly think that is going to work?

"I understand you waived the right to a lawyer at the moment, Mr Nicholls?" Ginny enquired politely now that the introductory pleasantries were out of the way.

"I see no reason to have one at the moment. I'm completely innocent." He drawled the word innocent in a seductive way and leant back in his chair, turning slightly so that his right elbow rested on the back of it. He crossed his left leg over his right in what he must have considered a seductive pose. Ginny almost laughed out loud. Was he serious? She coughed pointedly.

"Could you please sit properly in your chair, Mr Nicholls?" His blue eyes blinked once, then twice. The smirk playing around his lips disappeared and he turned back around on his chair to face her. "Have you not grasped the seriousness of this situation, Mr Nicholls?" She asked him. He was definitely becoming less and less attractive by the second. This man was a cardboard cut-out. She doubted if he had ever loved anything more than himself throughout his entire life. She would have liked to consider him the male equivalent of a bimbo, but unfortunately, she knew he was an extremely clever man. It was the main reason she needed to watch her step here. She could see through the pretence of him using his looks and charm to crawl under her skin, and she refused to let that happen.

"Of course. I completely understand the seriousness of this situation, Detective. And please, call me Marcus." He smiled again. She wasn't an expert in body language but that smile had not reached his eyes and was not sincere. His credibility was dwindling faster than sand through an hourglass right now. Marcus Nicholls was a façade. Ginny was beginning to think they were dealing with a cold fish, someone who had a calculating mind, who knew exactly what he was doing. Was he her killer, as she suspected?

The interview proved inconclusive, much to Ginny's frustration. The questions were fired at Marcus Nicholls and he had answers to them all. If he was at all flustered by the arrest or her questions, he didn't show it. He was arrogant, never once requesting the presence of his brief to accompany him. He presented them with an alibi for the time of the murder and they were yet to find out if he had indeed travelled back to the UK from the South of France at any time during the course of the past few days. At the moment everything needed to be investigated thoroughly.

Ginny felt sure that if Marcus Nicholls had murdered his wife, he had taken great steps to ensure that he wouldn't be caught. She intended to turn over every bit of his life and if he had done it, she was going to take him down.

Ginny had asked for him to be taken to one of the cells. The clock was now ticking. She had just under thirty-six hours to find some concrete evidence that Marcus Nicholls had killed his wife before she could charge him, otherwise he was free to go.

Back up in the incident room, she marched back and forth. She snapped at anyone who spoke to her. There was nothing she could do. There were no leads and no suggestion that Marcus Nicholls had even been in the UK when the murder took place.

The forensics had found very little DNA, which suggested that their killer had been clever enough to cover his or her tracks well. The fibres and hair that they discovered had been tested, but nothing had been found on the database. Whoever their killer was, he or she was not known to them. Currently Marcus Nicholls' DNA was being tested, but he was so uber-confident in his innocence that Ginny knew nothing would be found. Her best hope at the moment was that he had paid someone to kill his wife. But even that seemed far-fetched. Professional hits tended to be quick and virtually untraceable. Whoever had killed Mary Nicholls had clearly enjoyed themselves and taken their time.

Ginny sighed and came to rest before the whiteboard presenting their investigation so far. The top brass was already breathing down her neck, wanting results. The newspapers had reported all the grisly and gory details and as usual that had the left the police looking like a bunch of amateurs, something those above did not take kindly to. They wanted a face in the frame, and they wanted it yesterday.

All her training and preparation had led to working on something as big as this, and she just couldn't seem to make it work. She needed a strong lead, something to go for... to focus on. She hoped that some kind of clue would turn up. The killer had to have made a mistake somewhere along the line. There was no such thing as the perfect murder. She just had to find out what that was. She also knew that she was very much on probation with this case. If she failed, she would be out on her ear, without a doubt. The old boy's network did not appreciate those who failed and if you were a woman, they half expected you to fail before you started. She was determined to get a result on this even if it took everything she had.

"Ma'am?" She turned to see WPC Charlene Wilkinson approaching her. "The Super sent me to find you. There's been another murder." Ginny had a sinking feeling as Charlene provided her with the details of the address.

"I'll drive," Pat volunteered, her ever present best friend and colleague in the right place at the right time

The address Charlene had provided wasn't too far. Pat pulled up outside the building ten minutes later, although in reality, she couldn't have missed the whole shebang. With police, paramedics and blue lights flashing, the whole area was lit up. People were outside their homes or just loitering in the street, watching the comings and goings with obvious interest and Ginny was sure, a great deal of speculation. Much to her dismay, the local press were also on scene. How they had managed to get there before her was a mystery.

Pat double-parked the car in the first spot he could and the two of them made their way to The Mews, a senior citizen retirement village of small self-contained flats. Badges were in hand, ready to flash at the first policeman who accosted them. She didn't have to do anything so drastic however, as Steve King was ready and waiting for her, looking bleary- eyed and very much as if someone had punched him in the gut.

"What have we got?" she asked in low tones when he didn't immediately speak. It was then that she noticed how green around the gills he looked. Ginny swallowed.

They moved away from the cordon towards the flats, coming to a stop at the bottom of a flight of stairs. "It's bad." Steve whispered, his voice cracking with emotion. "She's been torn apart. The bastard's butchered her." Ginny glanced up into his face and saw something she never had before. Steve was beyond shocked. She looked around him towards the top of the stairs, then out to the front of the building, her mind taking in what she saw, calculating.

There was an intercom device that allowed people entrance through a security door. There was CCTV, although at the moment somebody had thoughtfully propped the door open with a large fire extinguisher to allow people entrance to the building without hindrance.

"What the hell happened?" Ginny asked, turning back to Steve, her feet moving automatically to mount the stairs. Steve grabbed her arm and pulled firmly so that she swung to face him.

"I'm trying to tell you." He almost growled at her. She looked at him surprised and stunned into automatic silence. She was never manhandled, let alone by a colleague. She looked pointedly down at her arm where Steve's meaty hand still rested. There was no pressure and it didn't hurt. He let go of her immediately and his arm dropped limply at his side.

"Steve… ?" she was concerned now; she had never seen him like this. Her hand reached out to touch his arm, this time to comfort.

"You need to be prepared, Ginny." His voice was quiet, so quiet she was almost straining to hear it. His eyes were averted towards the floor. He hadn't even bothered to call her Ma'am.

"What on earth is wrong with you? I've never seen you act like this."

"I've never seen anything like this." He shrugged almost helplessly, looking up towards the direction Ginny assumed the victim's flat was before turning his eyes back to her again.

"You have never seen anything like this," he stated flatly. "This girl has been mutilated beyond anything I've ever seen. I've seen death Ginny, I've seen murder, but this… " he looked up towards the flats again. "This is just sick." His words seemed to fail him and his shoulders appeared to hunch inwards.

Ginny swallowed and took a deep breath. If a man like Steve was so affected, then it must be bad. But she had to see. She stepped around Steve and continued up the stairs. He made no move to stop her this time.

As she reached the top, she noticed a young officer sitting on the stairs that went up to the next level. He had his head in his hands. Ginny was sure he was crying, his shoulders shuddered gently, but there was no sound.

Ginny was aware of Pat as she stood at the entrance to Anna Chapman's flat. The door to the flat was immediately opposite the top of the stairs. It gaped open at her like an astonished mouth. Movement could be seen inside, but there was a peculiar kind of hush like everyone was afraid to speak. Steve came up behind them. He had not yet shared what had happened. Whether subconsciously she wanted to delay the inevitable of what lay ahead she didn't know, but her feet refused to move. She knew what she was going to see was bad, but she needed the details.

"Give me the story, Steve."

"Frances Capaldi lives in the flat below. She returned from a three-week cruise earlier today. She spotted a stain she thought was red wine. Apparently, the landlord is always letting the flat to young people and she called him in. He was the one who found the body. The flat belongs to George Allen, a local businessman who owns several properties in the area. He rents this particular property to

Anna Chapman, twenty-five year old and who has lived here for the last eighteen months or so. He believed her to be attending the university. George Allen stated that he has had little dealings with the woman; she paid her rent on time and caused him very little grief. Sounds like she was just a normal student, played her music too loud on occasion and had a few comings and goings with friends and boyfriends. Apparently, Mrs Capaldi was constantly complaining about our victim and other students prior to her."

"What do we think, initial findings. Is it the same killer as Mary Nicholls?"

"Hard to say right now, but I would say yes. Looks like our boy is getting more adventurous, if you could call it that." The emotion in Steve's voice was evident and he too sounded on the verge of tears.

Ginny turned him. "Are you sure you're okay to continue, Steve?"

"Yes Ma'am. Its just that I have a daughter close to her age. You can't imagine… I mean her parents." He looked down at his feet. "I might just stay out here if that's okay Ma'am, I don't think I can go back in if I'm honest." She nodded understandingly and patted his arm, a gesture of comfort

As with any crime scene, there were always more people around than entirely necessary and with the uniforms and forensics milling around the scene, Ginny was galvanised into automatic action.

"I don't want any more people tramping through here destroying any evidence. Get those uniforms downstairs to stop any entrance by anyone and I mean anyone. The gawkers out the front can go on home. I want the neighbours questioned, the other residents here in the flats. Find out who she associated with, any shred of information related to this woman." Steve nodded, already turning to go back down the stairs, relieved to have a task that didn't involve seeing the body of Anna Chapman again.

"And check any known association with Mary Nicholls, they may have known each other." Ginny threw over her shoulder.

Ginny turned to look back towards the open maw of doorway housing yet another murdered woman. That made two murders in the space of a week and she had no idea what or who they were looking for. However, if any link, no matter how remote, turned up that linked Marcus Nicholls to both murders, she just hoped they could find it.

Ginny couldn't procrastinate any longer; she swallowed, removed her forensic booties from her pocket and placed them over her shoes before making her way into Anna Chapman's flat.

The flat reeked of death and blood. There was an overpowering stench in the air that made Ginny want to gag. It was like being in an abattoir.

Lying in a pool of her own blood, surrounded by her own intestines with her belly ripped open was the pale naked body of Anna Chapman. Her mouth was open and slack as if in a silent scream and her eyes were closed. Her left arm was across the left breast. Her legs were bent, her knees flopped outwards. Her face was badly bruised and swollen in places. Her throat had been sliced open. Her intestines had been arranged neatly by her right shoulder, having been removed from her stomach, which gaped open like a massive bloody yawn. There was some kind of cloth around her neck, which was red and soaked with her blood. The scene was macabre and horrifying. Ginny had never seen anything like it. Her gag reflex was in full flow as she turned abruptly from the grisly scene, found the kitchen and threw up unceremoniously in the sink. Now she understood completely what Steve King had meant.

The body had been removed and the forensic team were combing the flat for any clues left behind by the killer or killers. The uniforms were on twenty-four-hour guard to protect the scene. The first two officers on the scene had confirmed that nothing was touched, and that seeing what had been done, they knew the girl was dead and had informed the powers that be straight away. Ginny hoped that was the case.

"I need to speak to George Allen, the owner of the property. What else do we have?" she asked Pat.

"I spoke to one of the neighbours, a lady called Gladys Smith, who lives opposite Frances Capaldi. She said she used to chat with Anna sometimes. She believes that she works in an Italian restaurant in town, called… Castellani's. She said that Anna has had a few visitors, she wasn't sure if they were friends or something more. There was one lad she said came over quite a lot recently, but she didn't know his name. She said Anna kept herself pretty quiet, was no trouble."

"What about the lady who lives in the flat below?"

"Frances Capaldi." Pat offered.

"Yes, what about her. Did she have anything to add?"

"Not really, she didn't really speak to Anna that much and she's been away for the last three weeks on a cruise, returning earlier today."

"It's alright for some. What about family?"

"George Allen was able to provide next of kin details. Mother's name is Mrs Phillipa Snelgrove. We have a uniform from that constabulary going over to break the news as we speak."

"Okay, let's go and speak to her boss, if he can shed any light on her life."

Castellani's restaurant was busy, the early evening business in full swing. Pat and Ginny stepped in the restaurant and were greeted by an older lady with a friendly face.

"Table for two?" she asked, helpfully.

Ginny showed her badge and her face fell immediately. "I'm DCI Virginia Percy, This DS Patrick Paterson, I wonder if we might speak to Mr Castellani please?"

"He's not in any trouble is he? I'm Mrs Castellani." The woman hopped down from the stool she had been sitting on and

Ginny was surprised that the woman was tiny, possibly no more than about four feet, eight inches.

"He's not in any trouble, Mrs Castellani, but we do need to speak to him, and you if possible; perhaps we could go somewhere a bit quieter."

"Of course, there's an office in the back, I'll take you through there. Nico works the bar, he's just over there. I'll take you through and then grab him." She pointed to the bar where an older man was watching, a frown on his face.

Pat and Ginny followed Mrs Castellani through the restaurant, exiting through a door that said 'staff only'. The kitchen to the right was emanating delicious smells as they passed and entered through a door to the left. The office was tiny, with a small desk housing a computer, a filing cabinet and room for two chairs. Mrs Castellani left them there, promising to be back with her husband. Obviously worried that something was amiss, Mr Castellani had intercepted her at the staff only door, and the two of them returned in seconds.

Mr Castellani was an imposing man who stood at least two feet taller than his wife. He offered his hand to the two detectives on arrival in the room. "What can we do for you?" he asked pleasantly.

This was the part of the job that Ginny hated the most, breaking bad news. "Erm… Mr and Mrs Castellani, perhaps you would like to sit down." Ginny gestured to the chairs in the room. Mrs Castellani cast a worried glance in her husband's direction. "Take a seat, Beth," he told her softly. She turned and sat in the office chair.

"There's no easy way to say this, but we are here to ask you some questions regarding Anna Chapman. I'm afraid she was found dead earlier today."

Mrs Castellani took a sharp intake of breath as her husband whispered the echoed world 'dead', Mr Castellani made the sign of the cross. "How did she die?" he asked softly.

"We believe she was murdered." Ginny confirmed. Mrs Castellani burst into tears immediately and Mr Castellani cast her a worried glance.

"She was a good girl," he murmured, turning back to face the detectives but moving to comfort his wife by putting his arm around her shoulders.

"I realise this has come as a shock, but I'm hoping you might be able to give us some details about Anna, any boyfriends or friends she associated with."

Mr Castellani seemed to consider this for a moment. "I only ever saw her with two men who were boyfriends, the first one I'm sorry I don't remember his name. Kelly might. She's one of the other waitresses, she was good friends with Anna. Her boyfriend right now is somebody called Greg."

"Do you know his surname?"

"I'm afraid not. I know he picked her up a few times from work, but if you ask me, he didn't look like a nice boy."

"In what way?"

"It was nothing I could put my finger on, he just looked wrong. He was wrong for Anna." Ginny had the impression that Mr Castellani had looked upon Anna as a daughter.

"How long had Anna worked for you?"

"She's been working here about year and half or so since she first moved here. At first, she only did a couple of shifts with us, but now is practically full-time. She's going to be missed very much." Mr Castellani added sadly. "Do you know who did this terrible thing?"

"We can't release any information at the moment Mr Castellani, but rest assured we will catch and apprehend the person who did." Ginny confirmed.

Ginny and Pat left the Castellanis in the little office, with Mrs Castellani still crying softly. It saddened Ginny that they had obviously cared for Anna Chapman very much.

Their next visit was back to Melanie Watson. Ginny had received a text while with the Castellanis to say that she had completed her preliminary post-mortem report and was ready to share it. Pat drove Ginny to the coroner's office.

Nothing much had changed since they were with Melanie a week ago. Apart from her clothing being different on this occasion, everything else remained the same. She had an open file before her on the desk and once the detectives were seated before her, she began to give the extent of Anna Chapman's injuries.

"Since you asked me to put a rush on this, I have been working straight through. Forgive my hurriedness, but I am rather tired," she began; her austere persona was back.

"No problem, Melanie."

Melanie Watson nodded and turned to her notes. "The cause of death was likely to be a slash to the throat, although this was mutilated further post-mortem. She had been hit around the head at least twice due to the bruising and swelling on her face. I would say that happened prior to her death, possibly to knock her unconscious perhaps. Like I suggest, the cause of death was most likely the cut to her neck; the killer went back to that area and sliced all around her neck as if he was trying to remove her head with a knife. She had a scarf tied around her neck, presumably used as some king of gag. It was tied at the back of her head and had been pulled out of her mouth probably after she died. Her abdomen was cut entirely open, her intestines severed and removed from the body; as you know, these were found by her right shoulder. Her uterus, part of her vagina and part of her bladder had been removed. They were not on the scene. They appear to have been removed neatly and I would say a surgical instrument such as a scalpel had been used. She doesn't appear to have put up any fight, there was no evidence of bruising consistent with attempting to defend herself. I would say that the punches to her face were entirely unnecessary if the intention was to render her unconscious. She had been sexually assaulted, quite violently – what was left of the interior of the vagina was bruised – there was no trace of semen and I believe a condom had been used. Once more, there were no fingerprints, which suggests the use of gloves. There was evidence of bloody footprints that went from the living area to Anna's bedroom. There were no traceable footprints as I believe the attacker was wearing booties similar to those worn by us, but we do have fibres. However, I doubt those will be discovered to be more than run-of-the-mill. Again, the wounds are typical of a left-handed assailant which would indicate that you are looking for the same killer who murdered Mary Nicholls. "

Pat looked quickly at Ginny before turning back to Melanie. "What time do you suppose her death took place?"

"I would say she was killed anywhere between eleven p.m. and three a.m."

"Shit," Ginny muttered. Melanie Watson quirked her eyebrow in question at the detective's expletive, but said nothing. Pat knew exactly what Ginny was thinking. If Marcus Nicholls was the killer of Mary, he couldn't possibly be the killer of Anna, since he had been in police custody the whole time. This meant only one thing; they had just lost their prime suspect and would be forced to let Marcus Nicholls go.

Back in the incident room, Ginny sat at one of the desks, her hands around a hot cup of coffee. Pat, Mark and Steve had joined her.

"What have we got?" Ginny's voice was weary.

"Twenty-five-year-old female, Anna Chapman," Steve King began, perching himself on the edge of one of the desks. His large frame threatened to obscure everything else in sight. Steve was not a small man in any shape or form. His shirt was half tucked in, half out and his tie was skewed somewhere around the side of his neck as usual. Ginny wondered why he even bothered to wear one at all. He had sharp eyes that watched carefully. Rarely did anything get past him. He was a good officer.

Steve continued his report, "She has lived in the flat for about a year and a half, neighbours report a quiet sort of girl, had a few visitors, friends they believe, but no family as far as they know. They thought she worked, but didn't know where. Not reported to be very noisy or very chatty, but pleasant if she did."

"Isn't that unusual for a university student?" Ginny queried frowning Steve nodded and then shrugged before continuing. "They can't all be ragers" he confirmed before continuing.

"Her nearest neighbour, across the hall, is Mrs Gladys Smith. She thinks that Anna attended the university but wasn't sure if she still does. Nobody seemed to know very much about her at all, seemed to keep herself pretty much to herself."

"What about boyfriends, girlfriends?" Ginny questioned.

"Like I say, neighbours report seeing some comings and goings but didn't know who they were."

"That pretty much corroborates what her boss said, although he didn't mention her attending university and said she worked at the restaurant full time. He did mention a current boyfriend, some loser called Greg," Ginny filled in.

"That would be Greg Myers," Mark chipped in. "Known drug user, has been arrested several times for possession of class A substances, with a possible intent to supply, but no tangible proof. He has claimed every time that it was for personal use only, so nothing has stuck."

"Has he done time?" Ginny asked.

"Not as yet, slippery as a bar of soap and has managed to evade going to prison so far."

"Right, let's bring him in for questioning," Ginny instructed. "Do we have any link between Greg Myers and Mary Nicholls?"

"Nothing so far Ma'am." The deliberate use of the title she hated so much gained Mark a look that said as much and he grinned back at her unrepentantly. She studiously ignored him, carrying on with her instructions.

"Let's get on to the university first thing and find out if she was definitely still attending. Find out who her friends were, see if we can find a link between Anna and Mary Nicholls. Good work so far, team." Ginny rubbed a hand down her face.

Charlene entered the office and approached Ginny. "Mrs Snelgrove is here to see you, Ma'am."

"Who's that?" Ginny was at a complete loss.

"Anna Chapman's mum," Charlene informed her apologetically. Ginny sighed theatrically. This was all she needed right now.

The imposing form of Phillipa Snelgrove gave rise to a far grander person than she actually was. Phillipa Snelgrove came from working class beginnings, but believed herself to be elevated to the position of middle class and therefore felt she deserved to be treated as such.

She had had many aspirations as a young woman and had intended to ensure that she married well. She had no intention of being a downtrodden housewife like her mother. Unfortunately for Phillipa Snelgrove, she had got herself pregnant by the then love of her life, Jacob Chapman.

Phillipa had pursued him relentlessly as had most of her peers at the time. Jacob came from a good family with money behind them and therefore he was doubly attractive. Phillipa would broker no opposition and eventually won out against the other girls chasing him. Jacob took Phillipa's virginity. She found the whole experience to be sweaty, wet, uncomfortable and so deeply unsatisfying she had no idea what everyone was raving about. The end result was that Phillipa's rose-coloured glasses were off completely and she no longer had any interest in Jacob Chapman. Unfortunately, nature had other ideas and since no precautions had been taken, Phillipa found herself in the predicament of being pregnant.

Both sets of parents had met, discussed their children and decided the only option was that Phillipa and Jacob marry and raise the child in a settled environment with both parents. Unfortunately, neither Jacob nor Phillipa felt anything for each other and the whole thing was doomed to failure before it started.

They managed eighteen months of marriage before both deciding enough was enough. They wanted to live their respective lives and that did not include being partnered to each other. They separated and soon after divorced. Initially Jacob had shown a lot of interest in his daughter, visiting her often, but even that particular honeymoon period soon wore off, and his visits became less and less.

Despite several suitors, Phillipa's Mr Right remained elusive until she finally met Richard Snelgrove. A confirmed bachelor, having not met *Mrs Right* himself was quite simply blown over by the hurricane force that was Phillipa. She set her sights on the meek, agreeable, but extremely rich man and she won out. For Phillipa, her dreams had come true particularly on the money part, for the rest, she had invested in a vibrator.

Having settled her own life as happily as she could expect, Phillipa had turned her attention and high hopes on her daughter. She had wanted Anna to become a lawyer or a doctor, but when that particular dream came to nothing, she was happy to allow Anna the freedom of attending university to become a teacher. It gave her pleasure to regale the ladies at her club about how well her daughter was doing.

When the police had arrived at her home the night before last, informing her that her daughter had been murdered, Phillipa's world had instantly fallen apart. She could scarcely believe that her beautiful daughter had been murdered.

Ginny entered the interview room and shook hands with Phillipa and Richard Snelgrove, introducing herself.

Phillipa Snelgrove gave Ginny an appraising look, taking in everything from her feet to her hair, before glancing towards the door and then subsequently back to Ginny.

"I'm sorry, officer, we were given to believe that we would be speaking to the detective in charge, not their junior." Her elocution was practised and somewhat forced when she spoke; her unhappiness was evident.

"Yes Mrs Snelgrove, I am the DCI in charge of the investigation of the murder of your daughter," Ginny confirmed.

Phillipa Snelgrove's mouth formed a perfect 'o' as she absorbed that piece of information.

"I see," she snapped, still clearly not happy. "May I ask what your qualifications are?"

Ginny inwardly groaned. She knew she looked young, but being questioned on her qualifications really rubbed her up the wrong way. Sometimes civilians had no idea what the police rank system meant and clearly Phillipa was one of them. Fortunately, Ginny had a knight in shining armour in the form of Richard Snelgrove on this occasion.

"My dear," he touched her arm gently, bringing her focus to him for the moment. "I believe this young woman is the officer in charge on Anna's case. She wouldn't say so if that was not the case, you don't need to know her qualifications." His voice was a soothing balm over Phillipa's emotions. Her eyes filled with tears. "I'm sorry, Richard." He patted her hand and squeezed her fingers while she took a handkerchief from her handbag and dabbed at her eyes.

Richard Snelgrove had never been much of an assertive character, in fact it suited him to be located quietly in the background of any situation, yet now, in what he considered to be his wife's hour of need, he was forthright and direct in his dealings with the police on the matter of his step-daughter's murder. In truth, he had found Anna somewhat spoilt and indulged. She had been a sullen, unhappy child from the moment he had known her and despite Phillipa's best attempts to ensure she was well looked after, Anna continuously rebelled against her mother's wishes. It had been a blessing in disguise when Anna had wanted to go away to study at university.

"What can I do for you?" Ginny took a seat across the table from the Snelgroves.

"We came to... " Richard began, "That is, we were hoping to find out a little bit more about Anna's death. Do you know who did it, for instance?"

"Our enquiries are continuing at this time, Mr Snelgrove. I wish I did have something more to tell you."

"I never should have let her leave for that university. She could have studied much closer to home." Phillipa Snelgrove sniffed and sobbed through that comment, finishing with blowing her nose.

Now was not the time to tell the Snelgroves that they believed Anna had stopped attending the university.

"I'm really very sorry for your loss." Ginny commiserated. "We will be in touch once we know more." She stood up, readying herself to leave. There was nothing she could possibly share with the Snelgroves at the moment, nothing they needed to hear to that would make their loss any easier to deal with.

Richard Snelgrove seemed to understand; he nodded. "When might we be able to take Anna's body home?" He requested softly to renewed sobs from his wife's direction, "for a funeral?"

"We'll let you know as soon as possible," Ginny confirmed. She wanted to bolt from the room, anything to avoid the distress she would view in their faces when she told them the truth about what had happened to their daughter. She wished in that moment that somebody else could be in her shoes to inform them of the details of the grisly crime, but she was faced with the colossal task of having that responsibility herself. Forcing herself to fill them in the details of Anna's demise she eventually slipped out of the room, leaving the Snelgroves to a uniformed officer. She couldn't deal with the remorse at the moment. The Snelgroves, although passive in their request, were looking for answers and she couldn't blame them for that. Unfortunately, she couldn't deal with the aftermath of what she had just revealed. She felt like a coward as she paused in the corridor for a moment listening to the racked sobs of Phillipa Snelgrove.

Ginny entered the incident room. She felt like she had been beaten black and blue.

"You okay?" Pat was instantly at her side, hand on her shoulder. She looked up at his concerned face and gave him a weak smile.

"The Snelgroves are understandably upset, looking for answers that I can't give them." She shrugged helplessly. "I suppose Marcus Nicholls has been released?"

"Went out of here like the king of the fucking castle, arrogant bastard."

"I bet he did. Well that's our prime suspect out of the window. He couldn't possibly have killed Anna Chapman, you can't get a better alibi than being in police custody at the time of a murder. What about this Greg Myers?"

"We've got a couple of uniforms out to pick him up now. With any luck they should have him back here within the next half an hour," Mark confirmed.

"Did you find any link between Myers and Mary Nicholls?"

"If there is one, it's not obvious." Mark replied shrugging his shoulders helplessly.

Greg Myers was brought in fifteen minutes later for questioning and once again Ginny was back in an interview room; it was practically her new home these days.

Greg Myers was dishevelled and looked like he needed a good hot bath. His hair was all over the place and the beard he sported looked like it needed a serious trim. His eyes were red rimmed and bloodshot. His hands tremored slightly – a sign of needing a fix or drink, one or the other, or perhaps both. Ginny noticed how dirty his fingernails were as his hands rested on the table and wondered what Anna had seen in this man.

Ginny introduced herself and Pat, and sat down across the table from Greg. He nodded and rubbed a hand down his face in some kind of attempt to wake himself up. "We'd like to ask you some questions about Anna Chapman," Ginny stated and again Greg nodded. "How long had you been seeing Anna?"

Greg seemed to think for a moment before speaking. When he did, his voice had the gravelly sound of somebody who has been smoking excessively or shouting a lot. "We've been seeing each other a couple of weeks."

"Did you get on well, no arguments?" Greg shrugged in response. "What does that mean, Greg?"

"She could be a bit moody sometimes, like the other night."

"The other night when?"

Greg met Ginny's eyes then. "The night she was killed," he admitted.

"What happened?"

"Dunno really, we was all chilling. Then Tom and Tanya went into the next room."

"Who're Tom and Tanya?" Ginny interrupted.

"My mates," Greg offered. He stopped speaking and looked at Ginny for clarification to continue.

"Carry on," she told him.

"Well I don't remember much, but I know Anna had the hump coz she pissed me off."

"Pissed you off why?"

"Coz she was being boring." Greg sounded like a petulant child.

"You mean she wouldn't have sex with you?" Ginny surmised. Greg looked at her in surprise and then he grinned humourlessly.

"Yeah that's right." He shrugged helplessly.

"When you say it pissed you off that she wouldn't have sex with you, did you hit her at all?"

"Fucking hell, no."

"Are you sure about that? You didn't hit her in the face, in the head?"

"I ain't never lifted a finger to a woman in my life." It was the most alert Greg had been the whole time. He fixed Ginny with a stare, but the passion in his statement sounded truthful.

"Okay." Ginny ignored his look. "What happened next?"

"Anna left."

"Did you go after her at all?" Greg now looked sheepish again and wouldn't quite make eye contact. He seemed to be wrestling with himself. "Greg?"

"No, I didn't go after her." He was now fixated on rubbing his grimy fingers on the table.

"So, what did you do?" Ginny knew he wasn't telling her something. Maybe he had seen Anna's attacker. She didn't expect Greg's answer.

"I went to bed with Tom and Tanya." Greg refused to make eye contact with anyone in the room as he stared pointedly as a spot on the table before him.

There was a pause while everyone digested that piece of information. "Did you have any further contact from Anna?"

"Nothing at all." He admitted ruefully, still refusing eye contact.

"Were you with Tom and Tanya all night?" Ginny had to ask but she had the feeling that he was. Still not meeting her eyes, she whispered yes in response.

He seemed to withdraw in on himself, had clearly been thinking about what had happened. "If I had gone after her, she might still be alive now." His statement was not directed at anyone person, but hung in the air the obviousness of what he said lost on nobody in the room.

Yet another dead end, Ginny thought. This was not going well so far. They would have to corroborate Greg Myers' story, but she had the feeling that he was telling the truth. She also knew that it was unlikely that Greg was responsible for two horrific murders, leaving very little evidence. She doubted he would be able to manage much more than rising in the morning.

The incident room was subdued, the team busy looking through CCTV and other information.

Ginny stood looking at their whiteboard which now contained a picture of Anna Chapman alongside the one of Mary Nicholls. In the picture she looked young and carefree, smiling into the camera at whoever was taking the picture. Such a waste of life.

"Ma'am?" Mark's voice came as a distraction from behind. Ginny rolled her eyes as she turned around.

"How many times have I told you not to call me that? Call me Ginny."

"Sorry." He grinned unrepentantly.

"Have you got something?" the hope in her voice could not be missed.

"I don't know if it's something, but here it is. Mary Nicholls and Anna Chapman." He repeated the names of the victims. Ginny stood waiting, her face blank.

"I'm sure you're about to make a point here, but perhaps you could move it along a little," she said sarcastically. This time Mark rolled his eyes.

"It's the names. It sounds a little far-fetched at first, but I did a little digging."

"What are you talking about?" Ginny glared at him with irritated impatience. "Spit it out, I'm not in the mood for playing guessing games."

Mark rolled his eyes a second time and huffed out a breath. "The first official victim of Jack the Ripper was Mary, sometimes known as Polly Nichols, the second was Annie Chapman." He was warming to his subject now. He considered himself something of an aficionado on the subject and it had in fact been one of the reasons he became a police officer in the first place.

Still his colleagues around the incident room were giving him blank looks.

"Look, the names aren't exactly the same, but they're close. You said you've been looking for a link." Mark shrugged and turned his full focus on Ginny. "What if our killer thinks of himself as Jack the Ripper, is acting out some sicko fantasy. Maybe he's read too many stories, maybe he picks his victims because of their names. He can't find exactly what he's looking for because those particular names don't exist or if they do, they're far away, so he goes for the next best thing, the nearest name to those victims he wants to kill." He could see the realisation dawn on the three people in front of him as Pat and Steve had now joined and were listening intently. "I think we have a copycat on our hands." You could have heard a pin drop as Mark finished speaking.

"Fuck!" Ginny, Pat and Steve said simultaneously.

Ginny was suddenly on her feet, alert and wide awake. "Find out exactly how the Ripper killed his victims and see if it matches what we have so far. Also, if we can think of this, so can the press and it will only be a matter of time before they're scaremongering, printing all sorts of information and panicking people. We also need to know who the Ripper's next victims were and see if we can match them to anyone locally. This killer has done his research; he may already be planning the next one." Ginny was pacing the floor now, firing off instructions.

"Mark, what else do you know about Jack the Ripper?"

Mark grinned. "Well, I can tell you the names of his next three victims: Elizabeth Stride, Catherine Eddowes and Mary Kelly."

Ginny could feel the adrenalin pumping around her body. This was the closest thing they had had to a major lead since the first murder and even though it sounded a little far-fetched, she had no doubt that what Mark said was true. It was too perfect, too neat. "Right we need to check those names, see what comes up, any similar variation and we need to contact those women without causing a major panic."

"Are you sure we're not barking up the wrong tree here, just clutching at straws? It all sounds a little out in left field." This from Steve King. He was a realist.

Mark was sitting at his computer, pulling up information on Jack the Ripper.

"This is uncanny," Mark observed, gaining everybody's attention once more. "I think he's even killing them on the same day as the historical Jack the Ripper."

"How can you be so sure?" Pat asked, sceptical again.

"The original Mary Polly Nichols was killed on the thirty-first of August, so was our Mary Nicholls; the original Annie Chapman was killed on the eighth of September... "

"The same date as Anna Chapman," Ginny finished.

"Holy shit!" Pat exclaimed. "You could be on to something here, Mark."

Suddenly Mark was on his feet again. "Shit, shit, shit... Fuck!" he exclaimed wildly.

"What the... " Ginny started.

Mark turned to look at his three colleagues.

"Mark... ?" Ginny started to ask. "What is it?"

"According to history, Jack the Ripper killed his next two victims in one night. The first was Elizabeth Stride, during which if you believe what the story says, he was interrupted and therefore, apparently unsatisfied... " Mark made little speech marks with his fingers as he continued... "so that he continued to move on and kill Catherine Eddowes. He killed her the same night as Elizabeth Stride."

Ginny paled at Mark's words. "What date did that happen?"

"Thirtieth of September," Mark finished.

The silence was like a heavy weight across the incident room.

"That means if your theory is correct, we have a little over three weeks to find out who his next victims are and who actually did this." Ginny stated the obvious.

"Is Marcus Nicholls still in the frame?" Pat queried. Ginny glanced over at him. She had the purposeful look he had seen on many occasions. She was like a dog with a bone, and once she had the bit between her teeth, there was no stopping her.

"We need to carry out a full background check on every aspect of Marcus Nicholls' life, and I mean a full background check. I even want to know what colour underwear is his favourite. If there is the smallest shred of evidence that links him with Anna Chapman or any potential victim, we have to find it."

"It's a pretty big job, we need more man hours." Mark suggested.

"I'll be in the superintendent's office first thing, believe you me. We need to find out who did this like yesterday," she stated.

"Yesterday could already be a day too late," Pat almost whispered.

CHAPTER EIGHT

NOW

The police knew nothing. He knew everything. He had enjoyed watching the scene unfold outside the house of Anna Chapman. They were like headless chickens, all clucking in different directions, none of them knowing what to do, pecking at nothing on the floor.

The young detective leading the investigation had whetted his appetite, however. He had enjoyed watching her. She had an air about her that was worthy of a Ripper victim. He could imagine himself looking into her eyes as he cut her open from neck to groin. That would be something indeed, and something to look forward to yet.

But he had digressed. She was not part of the current plan.

The Ripper had remained elusive for decades; the air of mystery that surrounded him was as much alive today as it ever was. Yet here he was alive and well and living in the twenty-first century. Those fools had no clue that it was *he* who had worked the streets, ridding London of the foul stench of those faceless women who were disgusting specimens of worthless humanity. Even then they had no clue as to who he really was, bandying around their hapless guesses, slapping each other on the back because they deemed themselves right, and all the time it was *he* who deserved the pat on the back. There were those who surmised he had travelled to America, those who surmised he had died or just decided not to kill any more, those who thought he was linked to the Royal Family. They were fools, all of them. Speculation had continued and yet no suspects were ever really known to the police or the authorities. And well, only he knew the real answer to that. Now, here he was again. Now he was reborn and ready to pick up where he had left off. The game of cat and mouse had become very interesting. With an armoury of internet access and electronic gadgets at his disposal, he was free to discover everything about his victims that he needed.

The police could fumble their way through the quagmire of little clues and bits of evidence left behind, but they would never catch him. He had thought through every avenue of detail, had prepared for the slightest eventuality. He was a finally honed killing machine, his art perfected over decades of time.

His time was here and now. He needed to show that he was back before he continued in his work. The scene needed to be set, and yet it seemed that so far, those imbeciles had no clue who they were dealing with. He had been so meticulous with the first two, making them exact replicas of his first events, down to the last detail.

He smiled to himself. They were in for a treat this time. The next victims were already chosen, his plans already made. The police could shamble around to their hearts' content, but they clearly had no clue. He could relive his past and then the real games could begin; if they were floundering in the dark now, what fun it would be in the future.

He stood in the crowd, a nondescript passer-by. At one point, Virginia Percy had come so close to him, he could have reached out and touched her. He had had to fight that urge, to run his fingers through that blonde ponytail. Her eyes had met his for the merest of moments and he had felt that tug he felt with all his victims. She was his.

He liked to say her name, to roll it around on his tongue. V-i-r-g-i-n-i-a.

Today she was dressed in a red jacket and it brought out the red highlights in her blonde hair. It made her look wanton, not like a dowdy police officer at all. He wondered what she would look like stripped naked. He could imagine her body beneath his, smiling at him, urging him on as he sliced through the soft, smooth skin.

She had luscious pink lips; he had focused on her lips as she spoke to her officers, the way her tongue licked them enticingly. He could feel his heart start to beat faster. The anticipation, the excitement. Oh yes, Virginia Percy would be a Ripper victim of the twenty-first century. Even her name was fitting… "virgin". He scoffed at his own choice of words. There was no doubt in his mind at all that she was very far from That! They were all whores, every woman he encountered, some more blatant than others.

She had disappeared into a car with a big bear of a colleague accompanying her. He wouldn't be with her all the time. Virginia's little stint in the limelight was over for the evening. "But only for a short while, my love".

It was time for him to return home. He had research to do. He had the feeling that Virginia Percy's social media pages would prove to be a very interesting read and he couldn't wait to begin. He had infinite patience. He could wait a very long time before he made his move. He could covet her from afar for as long as it took to know every intimate detail of her life.

Besides, there were other ventures afoot. His next three victims were chosen and their time was coming. But before he could contemplate Virginia, there was also someone else he had in mind. This time the world would live in terror at his reign. No-one would know who would be next. The excitement was almost too much for him to bear and he giggled to himself. Soon the world would know the true identity of the Ripper.

CHAPTER NINE

THEN: RANDALL GOFF 1993

Randall Goff was six years old. He sat at the kitchen table, his school socks bunched around his ankles, his school shoes scuffed. Two large fresh red, angry-looking grazes decorated his knees, his painfully skinny, white legs swinging off the floor. His equally skinny, white arms rested on the kitchen table, his tiny hands curled into fists. His knitted grey jumper was torn, a small straggle of wool escaping and unwinding itself from the rest of the neatly knitted rows – knit one, pearl one. One sleeve was rolled up; his white shirt, also torn on one elbow, was decorated with a trickle of blood from a cut there. His mother was patting at a cut just above his eyebrow. He winced painfully but knew he daren't shy away from her.

"I can't believe you've been in another fight, Randall." His mother sighed, her voice soft. Randall knew better than to trust that voice. "What on earth was it about this time?"

"They fink me name is funny." Randall sniffed and wiped at his running nose with the back of his hand, smearing snot across his cheek. His mother watched that little movement with a studied expression on her face. Randall knew he had done wrong immediately. She was disgusted with him. Mother was always disgusted. "Sorry." He whispered, dragging a dirty and well used handkerchief from his pocket. He wiped his hand and his face before placing the offending item back into the confines of his pocket. Randall's mother sighed before turning her first aid administrations to the cut on his elbow.

"It's think, Randall, with a 'TH' and it's my, not me. Must I always remind you to speak properly? Just because we live… here,"

169

Randall's mother gestured around her but meaning a far bigger landscape than the house they lived in, "one must continue to keep one's standards. I have told you many, many times, so much so that I find it tiresome to continue." Randall watched as his mother inspected her perfect fingernails painted the same glossy ruby red as her lips. She sighed dramatically, as if to emphasise the point. Randall remained silent, knowing better than to speak at that moment.

With her nursing attention completed, Randall's mother turned and cleaned the small bowl she had used, and put away the TCP carefully in the cupboard. Everything had a place in Randall Goff's house and everything had to be put in its place… including him.

"I suppose I shall have to try to sew your jumper, although my sewing is not what it used to be and that jumper has seen better days. You look like one of those refugee children all over the news." Randall's mother had her back towards him as she stared out of the kitchen window. He sat as silently and as still as he could and watched his mother, not wanting to attract her attention more than necessary. "You will retire to your bed now, Randall. Your punishment for fighting will be no supper before bedtime." She never even turned her head the slightest bit as she spoke to him, just continued to look out of the window. Randall, like a bird avoiding a cat, kept his eyes fixed on her the whole time as he got himself out of the chair and removed himself from the room with as little fuss and sound as he could manage.

The kitchen led into a narrow, dark hallway with stairs leading upwards. He crept up the stairs slowly, carefully trying to keep his feet as light as possible. His mother did not like him to make a noise. She would sit in the parlour now, a room like her bedroom, where he was not allowed. He was only ever allowed in the kitchen or his own tiny bedroom. Everywhere else in the house belonged to his mother and was for her use and her use only. He was not allowed to make a mess or create a noise. All of those things annoyed his mother. Still, he had few toys to play with anyway. Mother didn't believe in presents. She said that everything given had to be earnt, and that there was no such thing as a free lunch.

Randall didn't quite know what that meant, except that he didn't get any new toys for Christmas and birthdays. Any toys he had, had been recovered from other people's rubbish and carefully hidden in his room. He only took them out when he was absolutely sure mother would not find them. Woe betide him if she should.

At Christmas she would give him something practical like a pair of socks. Birthdays usually entailed a treat of a cake or some other sweet confection. Randall enjoyed his birthdays.

The other children at school would gabble on excitedly after each Christmas holiday, regaling their stories of the gifts they received and the food they had eaten. Randall would listen enviously and if questioned, would lie about what he got, but the other children remained sceptical at his stories. He was never sure if they just didn't believe him full stop or whether he just sounded like he was telling a story, that what he said was too far-fetched to be true. Either way it didn't matter; Randall didn't have any friends at school, or anywhere else for that matter. The other children rarely spoke to him and neither did his teachers, who seemed to view him with contempt. Most of the time he remained sullen and silent.

When Randall was about four years old, he had strayed into his mother's bedroom. It had held a magical symbolic magnetism that he could not resist. He had only managed a few steps in to that room that held the scent of his mother, intoxicating his senses, before she had discovered him. She had used the belt on him that evening. He had not been able to sit down properly for days and had had to bite his lip from crying out. Mother had warned him not to cry or moan; punishment, she had told him, when due, was just and proper and one should never complain about it. Randall had many punishments delivered to him, usually with the belt that his mother informed him had belonged to his father. Sometimes she hit him with other things, whatever happened to be in her hand at the time when he annoyed her, which apparently was often, although he was not always quite sure what he had done wrong. Mostly she sent him to his room, where he was expected to stay until the following morning.

Sometimes his mother was sweet. She would sit him on her lap and cuddle him and shower him with kisses and tell him how special he was. Those were the days when Randall was at his most happy, however, those days were very few and far between.

Randall was a quick study. He learned his hard lessons and could gage his mother's moods. He knew when he should keep quiet and he knew when speaking would get him in more trouble. He was intuitive for a six-year-old and knew far more than he should; in his childlike eyes, self-preservation was already his number one aim. But sometimes he made mistakes, just like he had tonight.

His stomach grumbled loudly now as he sat on his bed. It was the only piece of furniture in the room apart from one old threadbare rug. A tiny, dirty window looked out at other similar houses in the crowded streets. It was a two up, two down in a run-down part of town and he hated living there.

Randall thought about the reasons why the boys had attacked him today. Gary Daniels was the ringleader, nine years old and master of the universe in Randall's world. He paraded the streets with his gang of lads, ages ranging from five to nine. There was a lot of building work going on where the modernists were pulling down the houses that had been built around the end of the second world war, putting up luxury apartments and high-rise offices. Their little town was being rebuilt but it was a slow process. It presented a playground of sorts for the children who lived there. There was simply nowhere else to go and nothing else to do but hang around the streets. Sometimes, somebody would organise a game of football and they would kick it to each other up and down the street. Randall didn't ever join in. He watched from the sidelines, but only when he could escape notice and only when his mother allowed him to go out.

Randall's biggest challenge of the day was to find a new way home, away from the bullies in Gary Daniels' group. No matter how ingenious Randall was in trying to find a way home without encountering the group, he seldom managed it, but he was fast and could usually outrun the motley crew of young thugs. Today however, uncharacteristically, he had ended up in a one-to-one with Gary Daniels.

Gary Daniels was a notorious pack animal, not very often on his own, but even alone he was nonetheless a bully. Usually it was relentless teasing that Randall could ignore for the most part, but the moment they mentioned his mother, he saw red.

Always, as before, it was silly things the boys teased him over. His dad was dead, his clothes came from the charity shop, all sorts of things that could not only have described the boys themselves, but any of the children living in that particular part of town at the time. Most of the comments were water off a duck's back to Randall, but the comments were usually followed by a punch or kick from one of the gang. That in itself didn't usually bother him either. It was the outcome of the scuffles that left him looking even more bedraggled than he had started out that would incur his mother's wrath. That alone was enough to make him run for home.

Today, however, had been different. Gary Daniels had slated his mother. Had called her all sorts of foul names and accused her of having indecent relations with Mr Pratchett, their headmaster of all people! Randall had seen red. How dare he say such things about his precious mother? She was beautiful and angelic and more than that, she was a lady!

Randall couldn't bear to hear it and before he knew what was happening, he had thrown himself at Gary Daniels and punched him in the face. Gary's nose had exploded in a spray of blood, but Randall just kept on throwing punches in his direction. Gary's half-hearted attempts at fighting back had been hampered by his initial injury. His gang, originally nowhere to be seen, had obviously come in search of their leader. However, either shocked by Randall's sudden onslaught or overcome by his burst of violence, they had stood on the sidelines, neither joining in nor catcalling like they usually did when a fight happened. The fight had been broken up by two burly builders on their way home.

Randall ran towards home feeling elated. He had tripped and gone sprawling headlong along the pavement at one point, his knees and elbow coming up with the scrapes his mother had eventually cleaned. The one cut on his eyebrow had been the closest Gary Daniels had come to fighting back and that hardly hurt at all. Randall was proud of himself, even if he couldn't tell his mother the real reason for the fight. He had stood up to the bullies and protected his mother's honour. He was a real man and in that moment and he felt like King of the World.

He hadn't told his mother what the boys had called her or the rumour about her and Mr Pratchett. Randall didn't believe it anyway, it was all lies.

Randall came out of his daydream, dimly aware of a heavy knocking on the front door followed by a loud shrill voice of a woman. "I'm telling you... you keep your animal of a son away from my Gary. I won't be telling you again." Randall immediately recognised the deep, gravelly voice of Mrs Daniels raised and clearly directed at his mother. He climbed from his bed and crept to his bedroom door, opening it a crack before dropping to his knees and crawling to the top of the landing so he could peer through the bannister rails and see the front door. Sure enough there was Mrs Daniels, a large buxom woman with a cigarette permanently decorating her lip, defying all logic by remaining precariously balanced throughout her tirade. Her hands were on her ample hips, her bright pink velour tracksuit accentuating her ample bosom and ample hips. She looked like a huge pink blancmange wobbling all over the place. Her hair, which was dyed an unnatural blonde colour, formed a curly, frizzy halo around her head and looked to Randall like she'd just been electrocuted. She wore too much make-up. Randall's gaze switched to his mother, so perfect in comparison.

She never had a hair out of place. Her beautiful natural blonde hair was styled within an inch of its life, her skin was the colour of milk, as soft as satin, with nothing to mar its perfect softness. Her slim figure was clothed in a white blouse and brown skirt. Even at home she looked immaculate. Randall could not help but make the comparison, even noting his mother's shoes compared to Mrs Daniels' 'seen better days' trainers. His mother would never be caught dead in trainers.

"I'm sure I don't know what you mean." Eugenie Goff's clipped tones filtered up to where Randall hid. His mother never raised her voice; she said it wasn't ladylike.

"Your son beat the living crap out of ma Gary. Broke 'is nose and everyfin like I said. Had to take 'im to the bloody hospital an all, your son deserves to be locked up for what 'e did and if 'e comes wiv in an 'airs breath of me boy again, I'll fetch the old bill." Mrs Daniel's used her fat, stumpy, nail-bitten finger to accentuate her words, pointing in Eugene's direction accusingly.

"Well, thank you for bringing this to my attention, Mrs Daniels," Eugenie replied, her voice never moving rising higher than a conversational tone, but Randall could hear clearly the thread of anger running through it. His mother was absolutely furious.

"You and your airs and graces," Mrs Daniels sneered, "You fink you're somefin special don't ya? Well you ain't Missuuusss Goff." Mrs Daniels dragged out the 'Mrs' carefully in a sarcastic way. "We know all about ya, don't ya worry about that." And with a loud sniff and a flick of her head, Mrs Daniels turned on her heel and marched off in the direction of her own house down the street.

Eugenie Goff closed the front door quietly behind the departing woman before turning to look up the stairs. Her eyes met Randall's. How did she know, he thought as she gestured for him to come down the stairs? He was in for it now. He knew that look as well as he knew his own face. "Come down here, Randall." She beckoned him.

He stood before his mother wearing nothing but his pants and vest. He was still wearing his socks bunched around his ankles and his hair stood in all directions where he had been lying on his bed.

"That was an ugly scene that I hope will not be repeated, Randall." His mother's voice still maintained the soft tone. Even when she was angrier than words could say, she didn't raise her voice.

"I'm sorry, Mother, but the boys were calling you names." He blurted it out and looked down at his feet, waiting for the slap or some kind of other punishment that would surely come. Then his mother did something that took him completely by surprise. He was expecting the slap around the head but instead she cradled his head and pulled him towards her. His head rested lightly against her stomach as she stroked his hair, he put his skinny little arms around her and inhaled her scent, wanting to remember this moment for the rest of his life. He knew he would remember this moment forever.

"You really can be a good boy sometimes, Randall. Run along now." She had released him almost as swiftly as she had cradled him. He felt suddenly bereft without her arms around him and knew that he craved more of her pleasure. He knew in that instant that whatever he did, it would be so that she would treasure him like she had just then. In the warm aftermath of her embrace, he happily went to bed, all thoughts of hunger and chastisement gone from his mind.

The gang never bothered Randall again. His walk to and from school remained uneventful from then on, with only the odd glare offered in his direction from Gary Daniels. Randall was pleased beyond relief. The events of that afternoon had also afforded him some kudos so that none of the other boys at school bothered him either. They didn't want to be his friend but they definitely left him alone now. The teasing was over.

CHAPTER TEN

NOW: LIZZY STROUD 30TH SEPTEMBER

Lizzy Stroud was sixteen years old today.

She was so excited that she had woken up at five a.m., an uncharacteristically early time for her. With her excitement building, she had tried to go back to sleep, but it had been near impossible; her mind was buzzing with the upcoming events of the day. Not only would there be presents, but her party that evening was the pièce de résistance and she could hardly wait.

There were definite advantages to having rich parents and being an only child. Tonight, there would be servants and champagne, not to mention a live band and a disco. Her father had spared no expense; anything Lizzy had asked for, she had got, including a daringly sexy, designer label dress. It was a one of a kind, straight off the catwalk in Milan and had cost a fortune. And really it wouldn't matter if she looked a little tired, the make-up artist would sort that out and make her look like she had just walked off the cover of Vogue.

Lizzy sat up in bed and drew her knees to her chest, hugging them tightly. She felt light as a feather and so excited she could hardly contain herself. There were still the presents to come from her parents, the party just being an added bonus. She had a feeling that they had bought her a car, even though she wasn't quite old enough to drive yet, but that wouldn't matter really.

Lizzy could bear it no longer; she glanced over at the bedside clock. Five forty-five a.m. She knew she would have to get up. It seemed silly to go and jump on her parents' bed, but she was so excited by the prospect of her birthday that she almost did just that.

However, at the last moment, she decided that she would in fact have a swim instead, that at least would give her parents until six o'clock. Lizzy giggled to herself. Yes, she would have a swim and then go and jump on her parent's bed. It felt like Christmas Day already and yet it was only the thirtieth of September.

Lizzy got out of bed and removed her nightshirt, throwing it carelessly on the floor. Padding over to the large chest of drawers, she opened the third drawer down to reveal several swimming costumes and bikinis. She picked out a red costume that had not been worn before and ripped off the tags before wiggling into it. It really was a pretty costume and she couldn't remember why she hadn't worn it before now. She remembered buying it, or rather her mother buying it for her on one of their countless shopping trips a few months ago, but this was the first time she had actually worn the item. She turned this way and that to look at herself in the full-length mirror.

The red of the swimming costume was stark against her pale skin, but the costume touched her curves in all the right places. She was large breasted like her mother, but had a small waist that curved into wider hips. She had a traditional hour glass figure like the movie stars of the '50s. Lizzy hated her figure if truth be told; she wanted to be super skinny like the catwalk models. She had tried dieting and starving herself, but she never seemed to be able to maintain it; she was just so hungry all the time and ended up giving up before the first day was even over.

The swimming costume was cut out on either side of her stomach, just one thin panel of nylon material between the part that covered her breasts and the bikini bottoms. There was nothing across her back apart from one tie strap and the halter part that fitted over her neck. There were tiny frills on the top of the bikini part as well as one layer of frills around the top of the bikini bottoms that adorned her to her hip bones. It was as skimpy as hell and she knew her father would hate it. He liked to think of her as his little girl still, but looking at herself in the mirror now, Lizzy knew she was all woman. She wished she could actually wear this to the party tonight. She would enjoy the boys' eyes popping out on stalks, especially Andre's if he got a load of her wearing this, especially if she was wearing her red platform sandals too.

Lizzy scooped her ebony hair into a bun on top of her head and fixed it with a black scrunchy. Padding softly into her en suite bathroom, she grabbed a towel from the rail and made her way through the silent house towards the pool at the back.

She loved her house. It was beautiful. Her mother had the best taste and when she had her own apartment in Chelsea or something like that, which wouldn't be long she hoped, she would ask her mother to decorate it for her.

The plushly carpeted upper landing led to a veranda that overlooked the marble floored hallway below. The staircase swept grandly to the right, and was wide with a dark wood bannister that curved to the hallway. Lizzy had, on countless occasions, slid down the bannister and was tempted to do the same today. At the last moment she reminded herself that she was wearing a swimming costume and it wouldn't do to have any traction burns on her legs, particularly as her dress was almost embarrassingly short and if she was going to allow Andre the freedom to explore again, he might find it off-putting.

Lizzy's father had flattened the four-bedroom house that had been on the land when he purchased it fourteen years ago and had purpose built the commodious mansion that now stood in its place. Lizzy's mother's favourite film was Gone with the Wind and she had maintained that she had always wanted a house that looked like that.

David Stroud had dotingly obliged his wife and despite the modern opulence that had later followed, with extensions and additions to the main body of the house, the completed article was nothing short of the Tara replica, complete with columns, white paint and wide veranda. It was certainly a sight to behold when following the drive and coming upon the house.

Lizzy descended the stairs royally, left hand trailing along the bannister, her bare feet sinking into the thick, soft carpeting. She always felt so queenly walking down the stairs like this. She had tried out different methods over the years, running down, sliding down the bannisters, but at the moment it was the queenly descent, head high, one foot in front of the other. In her mind's eye she could imagine her royal subjects standing at the bottom of the stairs, awaiting her instructions, staring at her with abject reverence and love. She imitated a regal wave as she stepped down the last few stairs, giggling to herself. Tonight, she would descend the stairs in the same fashion. She would make her grand entrance to her peers who would stand in the hallway and watch her descend. She was determined to have the best sweet sixteen party of the decade and hoped her peers would be envious.

The hallway floor was marble but heated beneath so Lizzy had no qualms about stepping on to it with her bare feet. With only the tiniest pat as her feet touched the tiles, she made her way to the back of the house and the pool room.

The house was so quiet today with her parents still sleeping and the staff not yet beginning their daily work. She could have been the only person at home. Trudy, their housekeeper, came to work at seven to start breakfast and do the things that housekeepers did; Lizzy wasn't exactly sure what that was, but she knew it entailed housework and stuff like that. Trudy was scary. She was like a Rottweiler in the body of a Chihuahua. Daddy said she was all bark and no bite, still Lizzy found her to be quite intimidating. She bossed Lizzy around, much to her annoyance, telling her to pick her things up, look after them, put them away. What was Trudy for if not to pick up after her? That was what being rich was all about wasn't it?

The pool room was silent apart from the faint sound of the pump that worked continuously. The pool was a rectangle, no deeper than four feet twelve all the way round. Bright yellow and white stripy sun loungers decorated the side of the pool and behind them a wall of glass doors that could be opened up in the summer in order to bring the outside in. The pool room caught the sun all day long and was always warm. Today, as it was chilly outside, the windows were slightly condensated, obscuring the view of the sumptuous gardens that were tended, of course, by two gardeners.

Lizzy padded to the sun loungers and threw her towel on to one of them. She walked to the edge of the steps and dipped her foot in to the water. It felt almost as warm as a bath.

A sudden movement caught her eye through the windows to her right. It was a dark shadow. She turned quickly startled. It must have been a bird or something since it was there one moment, gone the next. She moved over to the window anyway to look out, using her hand to try to clear some of the condensation. She peered through the glass wondering what it might have been. There was certainly nothing out of place. The garden looked as it always did, perfect.

Lizzy glanced over at the marquee that was erected yesterday for her party that evening. It stood like giant beached iceberg, a dominating white presence on the immaculate lawn. One of the flaps suddenly blew in the wind. A tiny piece that had somehow freed itself. Lizzy jumped and then laughed at her own stupidity. That must have been what she had seen just now. She huffed out a breath on the window and drew a heart with an L in the middle, her signature tag that she left everywhere from her school books to the ladies' changing room in Harrods one time.

Shrugging, she turned away from the bank of windows. She never saw the man until it was too late. The dark shape had entered silently behind her and was ready for the moment she moved. His gloved hand was across her mouth before she had a chance to scream, as he dragged his knife across her neck. The gurgling body of Lizzy Stroud fell at his feet.

Sarah Stroud was awake but groggy, thanks to the two sleeping tablets she had taken last evening. She had had trouble sleeping lately and Dr Ahmed had kindly given her a prescription. It was supposed to be one a night, but she was currently self-medicating with two. It knocked her out that was for sure, but she felt like she'd been run over by a bus for at least an hour after waking. She lay back on the pillows, enjoying the warmth of the bed. Her husband was snoring softly, his back towards her. He never had any trouble sleeping. Sometimes that was enough just to annoy the hell out of her. Being married for twenty-five years had its comforts, especially when one had more money than even she could spend in a lifetime, but it also had its disadvantages.

For instance, she was well aware that David had affairs. It had bothered her at first, but she acknowledged, despite the drawbacks of his little entertainments, as she liked to call them, that he always came back to her. He was a successful businessman who travelled abroad on business probably on more occasions than was entirely necessary, but he allowed her the indulgence of living an opulent lifestyle with no worries, and as a result she deemed that she could forgive his little indiscretions for that reason, but on occasion it depressed her.

David had always treated her well and took care of her. Still her depression on occasion could be an enlarging, festering black spot in the pit of her stomach. She was tearful at times, and had put on weight because she couldn't seem to stop eating when she went through the times when she was very low and unhappy. Countless nights she had lain awake, while her husband snored the night away like a baby beside her.

The one thing they were unanimous on however, was their daughter. She was their blessed child and unfortunately the only one they could ever have. After a traumatic birth, Sarah had undergone a total abdominal hysterectomy following complications. It had been a bitter pill to swallow at first as she had wanted more children, but she had come to terms with her situation and was thankful for the one child she did have.

As a consequence of being the only child they would ever have together, both parents doted on Lizzy. She was a mediocre child academically and would never become a lawyer or doctor, but somehow that had never bothered either parent. David adored his 'little girl' as she had always been, even though she was almost a fully-grown woman with all the attributes that entailed.

Today she was sixteen and to Sarah it seemed like no time at all had passed since her first birthday. She could remember with perfect clarity her first steps, her first word, every milestone as it was reached through her child's life and it was all documented by photograph or video as the perfect catalogue of her daughter's upbringing.

The party that had been planned for her daughter's birthday was the highlight of the year's social calendar. The guest list was immense, with stars of screen and TV in attendance as well as certain dignitaries who were due to attend which included a member of the royal family and a couple of well-known politicians. It was set to be the most talked about event of the season. Even OK! magazine had snagged the sole rights to the photography for the evening.

A small photo shoot would be taken at home this morning as well. Several outfits had been planned and purchased, designer of course. Sarah felt better than she had for weeks. She had even managed to lose a few pounds. Being busy seemed to agree with her and she would have to talk to David about the possibility of going back to work.

Maybe she needed to fill the void that had apparently opened in her life. It was a theory that had been bandied around by her therapist for the last few weeks and at first she had not agreed with him. Now with the preparations for the party keeping her focused and feeling useful for the first time in a long time, she was beginning to think he had been right. Maybe that was what was missing from her life and why she had felt so depressed lately. She needed a purpose and being an interior designer had given her a purpose. She was planning to speak to David about setting herself up in business.

Sarah sighed and looked over at the clock beside the bed. She was surprised to see it read eight forty-five a.m. My, she really had slept longer than she intended.

Trudy would have breakfast ready and waiting and no doubt there would be plenty of muttering under her breath because her day's schedule would be all out of sync now. Trudy ran the house with an iron fist and for the most part, Sarah had no problem with it. However, sometimes it was rather like staying in a grand hotel. Breakfast was served at seven thirty a.m. sharp with a light luncheon at one p.m., followed by a wholesome, nutritious evening meal at six p.m. The order of the day was set by mealtimes, with all the chores being carried out in-between. Sarah had nothing to do except plan the meals with Trudy, watch daytime TV or shop. For the most part Trudy was a good employee, but one thing Trudy hated was to have her schedule upset. Appearing for breakfast at nine a.m. rather than the allotted seven thirty a.m. would absolutely set the cat among the pigeons and therefore piss Trudy off royally. Still Sarah shrugged as she got out of bed, at the end of the day, Trudy worked for them and would do as she was told; if she didn't like it, she could leave.

Sarah wished she had the courage to tell Trudy just that to her face, although she knew she never would.

Pulling on her silk peignoir and slipping into her heeled mules, she sat at her dressing table, pulling a comb through her ebony curls that were now from a bottle rather than nature and feeling annoyed at the slight puffiness around her eyes. Damn the sleeping pills. She doubted the three glasses of Chablis she had consumed last night had helped either.

Sarah was surprised that Lizzy had not been in yet either. It was unusual for the child not to come bounding in a like playful puppy. It had been the same every year for birthdays and Christmas since the time she had been able to walk. Perhaps she was still asleep too, although Sarah knew her child to be an early riser, and in particular on Christmas and birthdays.

Lizzy had been in an uncontained bubble of excitement all day yesterday, chattering from the moment she got up and went to school to the moment she had returned home. It had been an incessant babble that Sarah had found quite comforting. Her daughter was a constant comfort to her and she loved her more than anything. She may not have been top of the class or the brightest academically, but what Lizzy fell short of in the brains department, she more than made up for everywhere else. She was certainly a popular child with her peers and that was definitely something for Sarah to be proud of.

She had packed Lizzy off to bed at about ten o'clock, as she had eventually found the constant stream of chat quite exhausting and that was even with a break while Lizzy indulged her favourite pastimes of Twitter, Facebook, Instagram, Snapchat and whatever else was the latest craze with the young these days.

Eventually she had persuaded Lizzy to retire, stating that "The sooner you go to bed, the sooner tomorrow will come." It had been something Lizzy had heard all her life the evening before birthdays and of course Christmas. In fact, Sarah was fond of saying it prior to any exciting event. Lizzy, like she had always done, skipped dutifully to bed, kissing her mother and father goodnight. Her father, for once home before midnight, too seemed swept up in the excitement of his daughter's sixteenth birthday. It was her first grown up milestone after all.

Sarah took a final glance at herself in the mirror. She was suddenly startled to think that she could see her own mother staring back at her. Her mother was seventy-five, so not a good look when one was only forty-one. Thank God the make-up artists and hairstylists would be around today. Sarah wondered what kind of magic tricks they would have up their sleeves. She needed to look the part, and since David was going to be around all evening, he might even want to spend the evening in her company once the festivities were over. She hoped so. Despite everything, she still loved David and found him an extremely attractive man.

Ignoring the reflection in the mirror, she turned and flip-flapped her way to the en suite in her heeled mules to brush her teeth. She gave David a gentle tap on his shoulder as she passed in order to rouse him.

He opened his blue eyes slowly and looked up at her. "Morning." His voice was deep and gravelly from sleep.

"No sign of our daughter, I'm going to go in search of her. I'll meet you downstairs; it's nine o'clock so I'm sure Trudy is cursing the ground we walk on for ruining her schedule this morning." Sarah turned at the sound of her husband's grunt in response.

The faintest noises could be heard from downstairs as the day came to life in the house. Sarah made her way to her daughter's bedroom and tapped lightly on the door. The room was empty, the bed a rumpled mass of duvet, her daughter's nightshirt flung into a heap in the middle of the floor. Ah, her daughter was swimming, as she so often did first thing in the morning. Clearly, she had been a late riser too. Trudy would be dreadfully angry. Sarah almost laughed at that. Sometimes she forgot that it was actually she who was in charge and that Trudy worked for her.

Sarah made her way down the grand staircase to the lower floor. The round Chippendale table in the centre of the hall had already been adorned with a huge bouquet arrangement that included lilies, carnations and freesias. The scent was overwhelming and pungent. Sarah fingered the delicate petals, inspecting the arrangement and nodding when she found it to her satisfaction.

Instead of immediately going through to the kitchen, Sarah turned and walked toward in the direction of the pool room. She had no doubt that if Lizzy had been in the kitchen with Trudy, her excited high-pitched voice would be heard throughout the house.

Sarah opened the door to the pool room. It was eerily quiet. She had never really given much thought into that saying before, but as she stepped into the pool room, the silence was overwhelming. She couldn't place what was missing at first, then she realised what it was – the sound of splashing water, the sound of her daughter swimming. In those few precious seconds which it took for her to open the door and walk in to the pool room, Sarah Stroud had felt pleasure in the fact that it was her daughter's sixteenth birthday; the rest of her subconscious thought was forgotten in the next breath, as the scene opened itself before her.

The pool water, usually blue, was now pink. Her mind was telling her that couldn't be right. As shock tore into her, the brand new red swimming costume she had purchased for her daughter less than one month ago bobbed into view on the water. At first it seemed as though the dye from the swimming costume had stained the water, but as her head turned to the right, she noticed the tiny folded up naked figure of her daughter. She was the reason the pool water was pink. Thoughts flashed through her brain; had she fallen? She took a step towards the pale figure, willing her to make some kind of movement so that she would know that she was alright. Another step and another – her brain was failing to comprehend what she saw. This was no accident, her daughter hadn't slipped and fallen. There was too much blood, way too much blood.

It was in that moment that Sarah Stroud started to wail. It was a high-pitched keening that went on and on. It got louder and louder, "No, no, no, no, no… " until with one final scream she was falling to her knees beside her daughter. She was aware of nothing as her hands went to her daughter's lifeless body. She was still warm, the blood still pumping from her neck in a slow trickle. Was she in time? The sightless eyes of her daughter stared straight ahead. Was that right? Was her daughter still alive?

She barely noticed the footsteps behind her, barely heard the words "Oh my God," uttered by somebody, she had no idea who. She was even less aware when what felt like a just a few seconds later, she was being helped to her feet, a blanket was being put around her shoulders and she was being led away from her daughter's body.

Ginny stood in the luxuriant pool room, looking down at the body of Lizzy Stroud. The body had been found by her mother, who was currently upstairs under heavy sedation. Any report from her would be a long time coming yet. Her husband was with her.

Ginny glanced down at the body again. The crime scene photographer was currently snapping his pictures; each flash of the camera made Ginny flinch as if she was slapped each time. Murders were bad enough when they happened, but those of a child, no matter how old, you just never got over it.

Lizzy Stroud's body was lying on its side, facing the wall. Her left arm was extended, the palm open as if it should have been cupped around something. The right arm lay across her stomach, the back of the hand and wrist covered in blood. Her legs were drawn up so she appeared in the foetal position, her feet close to the wall of the pool room. Her throat had been cut and even without moving the body, Ginny could see it was a deep gash and from the amount of blood the carotid artery had most likely been severed. There was no doubt the cut was deep and immediately Ginny thought of Mary Nicholls and the similarity between the two mutilations. She knew it was their killer once again. Ginny closed her eyes for a moment. What if the killer had sexually assaulted this young girl as he had with the last two victims? She swallowed hard. It didn't bear thinking about.

The cause of death was no doubt the cut to her throat and by all accounts Sarah Stroud had been stating over and over that her daughter's body was still warm, that she was still alive. Ginny doubted that was the case but was firmly of the opinion that the killer had probably been interrupted, perhaps by the arrival of Sarah Stroud in the pool room, which would have meant he could have been nearby, possibly leaving the scene as the police arrived. The grounds, although vast, needed to be searched thoroughly.

Ginny looked out of the pool room windows into the opulent garden. A large marquee stood central to the immaculate lawn, and tables and chairs had begun to arrive, the day's festivities continuing. The police had now managed to intercept any advancing workmen or deliveries, turning them away. It wouldn't be good to have any clues or evidence compromised at this stage by the trampling feet of people to-ing and fro-ing.

Ginny still felt they were chasing down shadows with no fixed leads. With Mary Nicholls and Anna Chapman's death less than a month ago, and still no suspects, the pressure was mounting from above to obtain a result. Now that another body had been found with a similar MO, it could only mean that the gravity of the situation would intensify and Ginny could very well be hung out to dry on this one; something she had no intention of allowing to happen.

Of course, it didn't help that this particular victim was the daughter of a very prominent and powerful businessman, David Stroud. He had connections at Whitehall and Scotland Yard, not to mention rumours that he was friendly with the odd royal or two. That could only spell disaster for Ginny should he decide to pile on the pressure, which she had no doubt he probably would.

The only significant and salient point at the moment was that they appeared to have a serial killer on their hands, and a copycat to boot.

It had become apparent early on that Marcus Nicholls, their prime suspect, had never met Anna Chapman. They had exhausted each and every lead they could and if there was ever such a link between them, it was unfindable. They had been forced to release him after questioning, after the murder of Anna Chapman since there was no evidence linking him to that murder at the time and the fact that he had been incarcerated in the police station at the time of the murder. As alibis went, that was cast iron. It meant they were faced with the massive challenge of 'Who did it?'.

So far, each lead they had had proved to be a dead end. There was no significant CCTV, no significant DNA. They had no links, no clues and no suspect. The only pertinent fact was the Jack the Ripper link Mark had picked up on a couple of weeks ago. They had exhausted every resource they had trawling the internet for similarities or exact copycat names of the Ripper's next victims. The vast spectrum of opportunity had left them not knowing where to start at first. There were so many versions of the name Elizabeth Stride. The mind-blowing connotations of looking for the proverbial needle in a haystack weighed heavily on Ginny. Even with the enlistment of forces across the country, checking on the similarities and watching their homes, she still had the feeling they were somehow falling short. She had the distinct feeling that their killer was one step ahead all the time, probably laughing somewhere about how clever he or she was compared to the police. She had known deep down that it couldn't really have been that simple to crack his code and get to his next victim before he did. The checks on Elizabeth Stride with so many variations had limited their resources. It had been impossible to protect every single person with a variation of that name. Had Lizzy been considered as a variation? Why had they not thought of that? Even with the checks on the actual Ripper's reported fourth victim, Catherine Eddows, they were falling short. That name in itself was practically non-existent and the again the variations were endless. They could spend a lifetime trying to second guess how he was picking his victims. Was there something within their make-up that she or the team were missing? They were researching similarities as they had done with Elizabeth Stride but it was difficult to predict where or when he might strike.

Now that he had struck on the day it was expected, Ginny knew there would be another body. She just didn't know who it would be or where to start looking. She could feel her new job slipping through her fingers at an alarming rate, it was like trying to hold on to water. They were bound to bring in a more seasoned, experienced officer after this. She already felt defeated.

Ginny hoped that maybe with CCTV this time and asking questions they might be able to find something significant that would allow them to start putting a picture together.

Ginny ran her hand over her face and through her hair. She had forgotten her scrunchy today and it hung loose around her shoulders. It was already getting on her nerves. Her mind was working overtime, just looking for something that could be a clue to who committed the murders.

Ginny looked up to see Pat walking towards her, his face grim, eyes studiously not looking at the naked body of Lizzy Stroud lying on the pool floor.

"You okay?" he asked softly as he reached her. She looked up into his unshaven face and smiled weakly.

"Kids are always the worst." Pat nodded in agreement, and continued

"Steve's talking to David Stroud at the moment, but it doesn't look hopeful. Mrs Stroud is upstairs under heavy sedation so I'll doubt we'll get much out of her today or even tomorrow. She was hysterical."

Ginny looked towards the body of Lizzy Stroud. In death she looked even younger than her sixteen years and Ginny hoped to God for the second time that morning that she hadn't been seriously sexually assaulted, as had the other two victims.

"This is the same guy who killed Mary Nicholls and Anna Chapman," Ginny stated flatly. Pat said nothing, but nodded his head in agreement. "The same MO with the cut throat. Hard to tell from this angle, but it looks deep, probably down to the bone, same as before with the others. I need all the CCTV checked again. We need to check for anybody appearing on camera here or there. Anything at all. I need to know who's been here, anyone the family doesn't know." Ginny smiled without humour as she looked outside and gestured towards the marquee.

"Although, my guess would probably be there have been a lot of strangers in and out over the last few weeks. This party was to be the social event of the year by all accounts." Ginny ran a tired hand through her hair again, dishevelling it. "We need to get a result on this, Pat. I'm running out of ideas, I don't mind saying."

Pat felt for her. He too was aware of the pressure that would soon start to implode on the team. It was not unheard of for one team to be replaced by another if no results were forthcoming and so far, they had zilch to go on – just a couple of dodgy statements that would most likely pan out to nothing.

Ginny looked up at Pat again. "Pepe Vasquez said that Mary Nicholls felt like she was being followed, that she was uneasy in her own house. We need to find out from the parents or friends, anyone who Lizzy may have spoken to, see if she had the same impression. I want her movements clocked for the last two months. Who she spoke to, who she met. We need to check out everything on her social media, if she was speaking to anyone. There is a link here, Pat, we just need to find it and if we have to work around the clock to get it done, that's what we all do."

"That's if we're looking for the same killer," Pat added.

"I'm almost sure of that fact if nothing else," Ginny replied, biting her lip. "Let's get back to the station, see what we missed. We need to go back over every detail with a fine-tooth comb. It's there, it just has to be. No murder is ever perfect."

The body of Lizzy Stroud was being removed so that the forensics could continue their work. A baby this time. What kind of sick fuck killed a child?

"Mark said there would be two today," Pat stated the obvious, breaking into her reverie.

She nodded. "Yes, he did." What else was there to say?

They left the pool room together and encountered Steve King coming down the staircase with David Stroud. He was distraught, but managing to keep it together. "This is DCI Virginia Percy, our lead detective for the case." Steve introduced Ginny as they reached the bottom of the stairs.

"David Stroud." He held out his hand for Ginny to shake.

"I'm really very sorry, Mr Stroud." Ginny had no idea what to say. The man was clearly distraught and broken. He ran a shaking hand through his hair.

"Why would he target a sixteen-year-old girl? What possible motive could he have, unless this is some attack against me?"

"Is there some reason an attack would be against you, Mr Stroud?"

He shook his head. "I just don't know, Detective. All I know is that my beautiful baby has been taken from me." He let out a sob and instantly put his fist in his mount as if to stem the flow of emotion. Ginny stepped forward and put her hand on his arm, looking directly into his eyes.

"I promise you we will do everything we can to find out who did this and bring them to justice, on that you have my word." Ginny meant what she said with every fibre of her body. Their killer had risen to the heights of official serial killer now that he had murdered three victims, and for the heinous crimes he had committed, Ginny wanted nothing more than to see him brought to justice.

The incident room was in a loud disarray as Ginny and Pat pushed through the double doors. Voices over voices but no discernible words could be heard.

There were now three pictures on the whiteboards at the back of the room, one of the team having helpfully placed a school photo of Lizzy Stroud next to the ones of Anna Chapman and Mary Nicholls. Ginny found it difficult to look at the image of the young girl who could have been no more than fourteen in the picture. Her face looked so young and innocent, it was heartbreaking.

"Okay listen up," Ginny called loudly over the din, which ceased almost immediately. She perched herself on an empty desk and looked out at the faces staring expectantly back at her. The team was bigger now that extra staff had been enlisted. Some of the faces she recognised, some were brand new.

"I'm sure I don't need to reiterate the fact that we have another murder and this time it's of a young girl aged sixteen today. So far it looks like it might be the same killer who murdered Mary Nicholls and Anna Chapman, but until I have the coroner's report, I can't confirm it. The girl had her throat slashed deeply enough to cause her death, but as you may have heard, mum is claiming that the body was still warm when she found her, and she was convinced her daughter was still alive. I don't think she was alive, but I do think our man was interrupted and had to make a quick getaway, or that it was staged that way, if Mark's Jack the Ripper theory is to be believed. There was no mutilation to the body as in the other cases." Ginny looked around the room at the faces of the men and women she now worked with. A couple of them had children the same age as Lizzy Stroud and she had no doubt that they were feeling it at the moment.

"Obviously, if this is the same killer, what we have is three very different women, from very different backgrounds, their only common interest at the moment was the person who murdered them. I doubt very much that a twenty-five-year-old and a thirty-nine-year-old had any dealings with a sixteen-year-old girl, but if there is link, we need to find it. As far as we know they did not know each other, did not move in the same circles, nor did they live in the same areas. We need to ascertain whether this is actually the case or whether they had met at any time. We need to find out how he chooses his victims. These are not random acts of violence. They are planned and meticulous. In the cases of Anna and Mary he took his time, meaning that he knew nobody was going to be at home or come home. We need to know how he's doing it."

After giving further instructions to the team, Ginny ordered them to get on with it.

She walked to the whiteboard and took her time to look at each picture, imprinting their image into her mind, although she was sure she would never forget as long as she lived. They were missing something, she was sure of it. There had to be more in common than the fact that he was just picking random women off the street. The murders were too perfect, too staged, well planned and thought through. He had obviously meticulously planned each one somehow, but how had he committed the murders in such a short space of time?

Mary Nicholls had been murdered on the thirty-first of August, while Anna Chapman on the eighth of September. Less than a month later, they now had Lizzy Stroud who was murdered today – thirtieth of September. She bit her lip in consternation. She was missing something so obvious, she knew it, but her brain was actually starting to hurt trying to figure it out.

Ginny turned to Pat. The din in the incident room had quietened down to a low rumble now, with everyone busily working on their tasks, and lines of enquiry were being thoroughly investigated

So far, their lines of enquiry had involved questioning nearly every member of staff at Hart, Smith & Dawson. There had been no definite leads from that. It seemed that those colleagues who knew Mary Nicholls liked and respected her and the rest of the staff barely knew who she was, except that she was somebody in charge. A great eulogy if ever there was one.

Phoebe Dalton had been unable to provide any further information than she already had and her statement was completed. She had been unaware that her employer was having an affair, so the likelihood that she knew about any suspicious people following Mrs Nicholls around was slim to none.

Nothing had shown in the toxicology reports for both Mary and Anna. If they were drugged it was something that didn't remain within the body. Melanie had confirmed the date rape drug, Rohypnol was known to leave very little or no trace in the body. Anna had consumed alcohol and evidence of cannabis was in her system. Mary, a known security freak had allowed somebody into her house. Had she known her killer? Had Anna?

"Pat?" Ginny called, turning from the whiteboard.

"Boss?" He was working on a computer but stopped and looked up when she called.

"Let's see if Marcus Nicholls knew Lizzy Stroud or if there is any link between them. Couldn't hurt to check it out."

"You got it." he returned his attention to the computer screen in front of him.

Ginny looked at Pepe Vasquez's statement on her desk. The housekeeper who had worked for the Nicholls family for the last five years had eventually been lucid enough to be questioned and had in fact provided them with their strongest lead so far which was that Mary Nicholls had felt uneasy and that she was being watched.

According to Mrs Vasquez, Mary Nicholls had always been of a fairly nervous disposition and disliked being at home alone. This was an enigma in itself since it seemed that Marcus had clearly worked away from home for a good chunk of their marriage, meaning that she invariably spent many evenings alone. However, on further questioning, although this was something Mary Nicholls complained about fairly frequently, her complaints had been stepped up of late. She even went as far as mentioning to Pepe Vasquez that she thought somebody had been in her house. This was an intriguing thought. What if the murderer had been in the house prior to the night he killed Mary Nicholls? Pepe and Marcus had confirmed that Mary Nicholls was almost anally security conscious. She never failed to lock her car, or lock her house. She was notably afraid of the dark and kept her lights on when at home. She had a security system installed and yet despite all that, she felt as if someone had been in her house.

It wasn't clear from the statement whether she felt the intruder had been in the house while she was out, or whether she had been home. Surely if it was the latter, Mary Nicholls would most likely have called the police?

According to the statement, Mary Nicholls had claimed that her underwear drawer was dishevelled and had accused Pepe of going through it. When Pepe denied the charge, Mary had suggested that someone had been the house, for she had noticed that other things had been moved around her bedroom.

Ginny wondered why, in view of the circumstances, that Mary Nicholls did not contact the police at that stage and why this was never mentioned to her husband.

The team so far had trawled through hours of CCTV footage checking the comings and goings of her street. Unfortunately, the footage could only be collected from adjoining roads, as Mary Nicholls' street itself did not have any cameras. So far, they had matched footage with many of the residents as well as delivery people, the milkman, postman and visitors in general. It was a time-consuming, seemingly never-ending task which so far had not led to anything concrete.

There had been no fingerprints, hardly any fibres or hairs and no bodily fluids to provide a single clue about the killer. He had used a condom and surgical gloves, of that they could be sure. They had found alien fibres on the sofa and around the body of Mary Nicholls, but these were all generic and could have been there before the murder. So far that hadn't turned up anything, although they still needed to speak to plenty of people listed.

The situation with Anna Chapman had again presented no clues at the crime scene, however her social media was a minefield. They had ascertained early on that she no longer attended the university. Testimonies from other students she attended with had turned up very little; nobody had kept in touch other than a couple of friends. Those people had been interviewed and released, with no further leads.

It seemed that Anna was very much living a double life, which her mother was unaware of. Until today with the murder of Lizzy Stroud, the trail was rapidly growing cold. In fact, a guest spot on Crimewatch had been arranged in order to present a reconstruction on Mary Nicholls and Anna Chapman's last known movements. Ginny was becoming increasingly despondent by the concept however, as currently they had no key witnesses, nothing even presentable as a photofit and certainly no poignant clues with which to tempt the general public on who, why or what.

Ginny had arranged to visit Melanie Watson again this afternoon. The austere coroner had agreed to carry out the third autopsy on the body of Lizzy Stroud urgently to confirm if in fact they were looking at the same murderer to both women or now investigating two separate cases. As certain elements of the case had been closely guarded secrets so far including the fact that the killer was left-handed, Ginny was hoping that further light could be shed to provide a suspect. She was also anticipating that if the killer had been interrupted as she had guessed since the body had not been quite so mutilated, that he might well have made some glaring mistakes which would lead to his capture.

"Ma'am." Ginny looked up from her reverie at the face of Mark. She scowled at the interruption. "Sorry, Boss." He grinned repentantly, always the cheeky chappy.

"What is it, Mark?" even the team's clown couldn't snap her out of her mood today.

He waved a CD in front of her face. "Footage from the Stroud house for the last forty-eight hours. They have cameras on the house and in the grounds as part of their security system." He smiled triumphantly at her and she felt herself smiling back.

"Get on it, Mark." He nodded emphatically and moved to a spare desk.

Yes! Ginny thought. This could actually provide them with at least an image of their man. After all, how aware could he have been about every camera and the angle at which they were set?

Mark had the CCTV from Anna Chapman's and Lizzy Stroud's last known movements. He had already pored over hours of footage which had given them nothing. Now he had the high street CCTV, which showed Anna Chapman. The imaging wasn't the best, but they had managed to identify her by her clothing and short hair style.

They had tracked Anna Chapman from the alleged time she left her boyfriend's house. It tallied with his story of the approximate time she left his squat. She was seen walking down the street before waiting at the bus shelter. At that time, she was alone. The grainy image showed a man dressed in black with blonde hair approach the bus stop. They seemed to have some kind of verbal exchange, and then Anna left with him. She was later seen staggering from the pub while the man held her up. He helped her into an old-style Volkswagen Beetle before driving off. They had been unable to trace the car on further CCTV footage so far. They had tried to enhance the image of the number; unfortunately the registration had in fact matched an Audi TT belonging to a Michael Rogers from Mid Lothian who had a cast iron alibi for the murders in general since he was currently in hospital having suffered a massive stroke. The barman in the pub had also been questioned. He vaguely remembered the young woman and the man who came into the bar because she was, as he put it, "off her face" when they left. He was unable to provide anything other than a generic description … tall, blonde. There seemed to be no discernible features, nothing descriptive about the man. Ginny had viewed the CCTV image trying to adopt the grainy image as possibly being Marcus Nicholls. Despite his alibi for Anna's murder, there was still something about him that made her think he was guilty. Unfortunately, there was no plausible proof to back up that concept. She didn't even have a reason to bring him in again. Again, they had reached yet another dead end.

The CCTV footage from Lizzy Stroud's home wasn't much better. Somehow the killer must have been aware of where the cameras were situated and unfortunately the pool room wasn't one of them. Despite having several strategically placed cameras on site, it appeared that several of these had been tampered with a few days before and therefore no valid CCTV footage was available. It meant only one thing… that their killer was extremely prepared. He had clearly visited the property on previous occasions and knew the location of the cameras. He had managed to take out the ones that would assist in their tracking of him by spraying them with black paint. It was impossible to check back as the CCTV reset itself after a week. Any visits their killer may have made to the property in the last few weeks were unfortunately recorded over. David Stroud did not have a security crew to check his CCTV footage on a regular basis; it was more a deterrent in case they were burgled. Again, they were left with very little to go on.

CHAPTER ELEVEN

NOW: MELANIE WATSON 1st OCTOBER

Melanie Watson sat reading through her final versions of the autopsy report of Lizzy Stroud.

She had to admit, never had she encountered anything so gruesome in her life. She was used to dealing with the occasional unexpected death, but now all of a sudden had dealt with three murders in quick succession. She didn't know whether to be completely disgusted or elated by the prospect of her job suddenly becoming a hundred percent more interesting. This was everything a coroner dreamed of when they entered the profession, being involved in a high-profile murder case. Melanie Watson felt more than privileged that she was involved.

As soon as Lizzy Stroud's body had been brought in, she had recognised the name, not just because the body belonged to a sixteen-year-old socialite, but because it had reminded her of something deep in the recesses of her memory.

Something about this case had caught her imagination; she had recognised the name Mary Nicholls from the first, but believing it to be a common name, had no further thought other than her clinical purpose.

Then the body of Anna Chapman had been brought in. She had been mutilated far worse than Mary Nicholls before her and on reading the police reports from the scene, she had no doubt whatsoever that what the police were looking at was a copycat killer.

She had not been sure at first but had downloaded the autopsy reports of the Ripper's original victims, since the information was available online. What she had read so far matched exactly the current victims and therefore she had concluded that the killer definitely fancied himself as some sort of modern day 'Jack'.

It was now the first of October and if the killer had performed exactly as the history books had written, the modern-day Catherine Eddowes was awaiting discovery. Melanie had no doubt that she would very soon have a further body on her table.

She turned to her computer and tapped in the name Mary Kelly. Hundreds of pages returned in the search engine and she grimaced at her computer, exasperated.

She tried a different tack and logged on to her social media account. She entered the name Mary Kelly once more and was shocked to see how many names appeared in the list. She grew despondent immediately. She didn't really know what she was hoping to achieve – maybe inbox a couple of people, tell them to be extra vigilant. She could inbox all the people named Mary Kelly in the UK but that would clearly create some kind of panic, something she was sure the police were hoping to avoid.

Melanie was expecting Detective Chief Inspector Virginia Percy and a colleague this morning for her report on the latest murder victims. She wondered if the boys in blue had cottoned on to the Jack the Ripper theory yet.

Melanie scrolled through the photographs on her computer, hoping for some kind of divine inspiration on how the killer might have picked his next victim. Who among these women would he be likely to choose, or had he chosen already? Was there a similarity in looks? She decided to do some more research on Mary Kelly, the original Ripper victim, to see what she could find out. If the killer was something of an expert on the Ripper murders, then perhaps what was needed was for somebody to follow in his footsteps.

Melanie felt a cold hand of fear shimmer down her spine. This person had so far managed to avoid detection by the police. He executed his victims and he did it precisely. That took time and planning.

Melanie tapped the name Mary Nicholls in to her social media page and waited for the results. Many faces stared back at her, but not the victim's. Clearly that particular account had been shut down. She googled Mary Nicholls and again was confronted with many women of the same name. There must be some way of narrowing this down. She carried out a few more clicks, turning up nothing. She needed to think like the killer. To catch a killer, one needed to think like a killer.

Melanie Watson had no ambition to become a hero in the case of the modern-day Jack the Ripper, but she certainly wanted to know more. The case was intriguing and had caught her imagination. She smiled to herself. It was almost as intriguing as the original Ripper crimes. Nobody knew then who had committed the murders. It was a delicious mystery that had already sucked her in and she was fascinated to investigate further.

If Melanie Watson had known that she was being watched, she may have left well alone, but like all the victims so far, none of them ever had a clue. Until it was too late, that is.

CHAPTER TWELVE

THEN: KATHERINE EDDOWIN
29TH SEPTEMBER

Katherine Eddowin sat the back of the church, whispering conspiratorially with her friend Martha Davies. They had met at school and despite having an immediate dislike of each other, had gone on to become best friends, a friendship that had continued through their adult years and into their thirties. They had survived each other's boyfriends and marriages and had even managed to get pregnant at around the same time. They each had two boys apiece who they hoped would become best friends in the future.

They considered themselves pillars of the community and attended the same church each and every Sunday, but for the most part spent it camped somewhere near the rear, gossiping about the other wives and mothers in the congregation.

They told each other everything, commiserated their worst moments, bitched, laughed and enjoyed each other's company more than anybody else's. They were as inseparable now as they had ever been and even though each of their husbands tolerated the friendship, they could not understand it, nor could they tolerate each other's spouses. It was a matter of consternation that both women successfully ignored.

They had volunteered their services for the church bazaar and were now among the other volunteers, although slightly sat apart. The turnout was good today and both women were of the opinion that they could put in little effort, allowing others to do the lion's share of the work while basking in the glory of the success themselves.

"Did you see her shoes?" Martha asked incredulously, her eyes flicking quickly to the target of her disapproval five rows ahead. The woman so chosen on this occasion was Felicity Rowbothom, a lawyer apparently, Martha had informed her friend disdainfully, with a passion for the latest Jimmy Choos. Today she had appeared at the church wearing glaringly red stilettos, much to Martha's and Katherine's disgust and more deeply, envy.

"So inappropriate to wear in church, even if God is looking the other way, not being Sunday and all," Katherine whispered conspiratorially. "More suited to Sunset Strip than Sunnyside Drive." Martha giggled at her friend's turn of phrase.

"Well maybe she is a high-class hooker asking for the Lord's forgiveness," Martha added, her eyes moving slyly towards the object of their sniping remarks.

Katherine caught a glance from Sally Worthington, sitting in the pew on the opposite aisle, in reprimand as she realised that perhaps their gossip had become a little loud. She lowered her eyes sheepishly.

It was the same every time they got together, whether it was to attend church or the local shops. The two women sat next to each other so that they could gossip freely and make their derogatory comments. It was tolerated to a point but had caused a great deal of contention in the past. Somehow however, they continued to carry on with their backbiting, as if beyond reproach.

Reverend Gordon approached them now, their hushed gossiping meaning that they had failed to hear the last of the planning for the bazaar to take place next weekend.

"Good morning, ladies," Reverend Gordon boomed jovially. He was a large man who wore ill-fitting clothes that incensed Katherine and Martha's derogatory opinions. He had been the butt of their snide comments on many an occasion and while he knew what people said about him, Reverend Gordon was fortunately one of those people who had a very thick skin. He was aware of his size and knew he should do something about it, however he also liked his wife's cooking very much and was loath to give it up.

He had wondered often about the two women sitting before him now. They regularly attended church with their families and volunteered to help out in all occasions including the upcoming bazaar. However, for the life of him, he could not understand their purpose in being so helpful one moment, but so nasty about people the next. It was a most perplexing situation.

Katherine looked up, a frown of annoyance crossing her face at the unwelcome interruption. Martha simpered up to the vicar, telling him exactly what he wanted to hear. Pleased as ever with the wanton praise and servitude afforded him by one of his parishioners, the vicar smiled, his small piggy eyes disappearing into his overblown face, the reason for his interrupting the women in the first place quite forgotten.

Katherine was fed up. She was bored with the gossip and the pretending now. While Martha simpered and flirted with the vicar, her mind wandered in the direction of Henry Davies, her best friend's husband.

Katherine sighed inwardly. She was hot and heavy for Henry at the moment. Their stolen rendezvous were what she lived for presently, not like her wet blanket of a husband who didn't know where to put it, or how to use it, nor what to do with it once it was there. She was truly sick of the misfortune God had bestowed on her. She hated her husband. Charles Eddowin had been the biggest disappointment of her life. She could not for the life of her imagine why she had married him in the first place. He had a pole stuck up his arse the size of a ship's mast and he never failed to make her feel like a piece of crap. Even her sons had failed to gain any favour with him and he had continued to ignore her existence as he always had. She could remember loving him once and wasn't entirely certain when they had stopped. He was pleasant enough and he was extremely wealthy, two of the finer points of remaining married to him. She knew when she married him she would have a certain way of life to look forward to and at first that had been enough. Now she felt miserable and unsatisfied most of the time.

It was fine for her to be paraded on show for dinner parties and the procession of countless council dinners that she had been forced to attend, hanging on his arm like a trophy, while he coldly and studiously ignored her until it was time for the perfunctionary lovemaking, if it could be called that at all. If not for her vibrator and latterly, Henry Davies, she might not know what an orgasm was at all.

Katherine was not a happy woman with Charles. She knew she was falling for Henry in a big way. For the first time in her life she felt like she was beginning to understand what love was. The only fly in the ointment was the fact that the man she so desperately wanted, was in fact her best friend's husband, a fact that would not go down at all well and would no doubt end with Martha being utterly devastated by her betrayal and in the process the loss of their friendship. But she just couldn't help herself. The daytime meetings between her and Henry had become more intense. They couldn't seem to get enough of each other and although the 'L' word had not been mentioned, Katherine was sure it was only a matter of time.

"Kattthhhhyyyyy," fingers snapped in front of her face and brought her back to the room. Martha was smiling at her like a cat who was licking cream.

"Sorry, I was miles away," she responded to her friend, politely.

"Well, yes I could see that, but you missed what Reverend Gordon said." Katherine's face turned quizzically to the vicar.

"I was rather hoping you and Martha would help organise this year's flower festival," the vicar stated clearly for the benefit of Katherine, who had not heard him the first time.

Caught off guard and in no way interested in helping organise the flower festival, Katherine found herself agreeing with an enthusiasm she did not feel.

"Excellent stuff," the vicar responded, lifting his enormous bottom from the pew and waddled over to speak with somebody else.

Lest he get pressure sores, Katherine thought unkindly, while smiling buoyantly in the vicar's direction.

"Oh my God, I am soooo excited." Martha's voice, Katherine found, was getting on her nerves. "This is a real kick in the pants for that smug Rita Martin." Looking up at the object of her condescension, she waggled her fingers in a wave and smiled benevolently while nudging Katherine in the ribs. "What a hoot!" she exclaimed. "Aren't you excited?"

"Very." Katherine agreed, although it was hard to raise interest for the task ahead and she hardly felt much in the way of happiness at the prospect. This was sure to take up much of her free time. Free time she was hoping to spend in the arms of Henry. Katherine Eddowin was a disappointed, bitter shrew of a woman who was also desperately unhappy.

Later that day, Katherine Eddowin drove her children to meet the coach that would take them to camp for four days. She loved her sons but under their father's influence, they were bound to end up being pompous arses just like him. Not only would it do them good to be away for a short holiday, but it would give her the opportunity to spend more time alone with Henry, and his hot and heavy lovemaking. She felt a warmth spread across her nether regions in anticipation. She could hardly wait.

Katherine waved the boys off, climbed into her sensible Volvo and started the engine. Checking the rear-view mirror for oncoming traffic, she pulled into the main road and started her drive into town. She never saw the beat-up old Volkswagen Beetle pull out behind her and follow her route.

Katherine stopped at Martha's house three hours later. She had dutifully retrieved her dry cleaning, dropped off Charles's suits and shirts, had completed her shopping and taken it all home and was now ready for her afternoon with Martha.

She had to admit Martha knew how to arrange a tete-a-tete. It wasn't just her that was invited today; Martha had extended her invitation to Philippa Kitchen and Winona Churchill. Both women attended their church and both were married to successful men, not unlike themselves. It was par for the course as far as Martha was concerned and she was always keen to gather new items of gossip to be picked apart later when it was just the two of them together.

However, Katherine felt a completely different vibe today. Something was not sitting right. She could not recall ever feeling it before, or perhaps she had never noticed it, but there was something definitely not quite right about Martha. She seemed a little too bright, as if she was almost flirting.

Usually there was an abundance of hors d'oeuvre and an even larger abundance of good wine. If nothing else, Martha certainly knew her cuisine and alcohol. Katherine always left her best friend's house with a warm fuzzy glow surrounding her which continued into the early evening, but today she had refused the alcohol, instead opting for fruit juice because she was taking antibiotics.

It had become apparent to her at some point during the lunch that Martha and Philippa were flirting riotously with each other. As the sober one of the quartet, it was becoming more and more obvious. It was an even bigger consternation when Winona, seemingly oblivious to what was unfolding before her, and already very drunk, called time and left particularly early.

Katherine was left with Philippa and Martha who were touching rather a lot and giggling like a couple of silly teenagers.

"Kattthhhyyyy... " Martha's voice grated on her like a knife edge and she inwardly winced while smiling at her friend innocently.

"What is it, Martha, darling?" she questioned politely.

"I think one needs to tinkle." Martha dissolved into a fit of giggles while Philippa joined in at her side.

"My dear, I think you've had one too many." Katherine rolled her eyes.

"Daytime drinking is wonnnderrrrfull, especially when one's children are away from home" Martha trilled, falling against Philippa and giggling like a school girl. It irritated Katherine that Martha felt the need to stretch out her words, particularly her name.

"Help her to the loo, I'll just clear up a bit here." Katherine told Philippa while she stood and began to collect cups and plates from the table.

"Tallyho, old girl." Philippa helped a still giggling Martha to her feet and the two of them disappeared from the kitchen up the stairs.

Fifteen minutes later the table was cleared, everything nestled safely in the dishwasher. Katherine looked at the clock; it was already four thirty p.m. and she needed to get home. If Martha was otherwise indisposed this evening, it might mean she would have a rendezvous with Henry.

She wandered into the hallway wondering what had happened to Philippa and Martha and if they were okay. She wondered if the two of them had passed out in the loo together; they had been gone an awfully long time.

At the bottom of the stairs, Katherine looked up, listening for any giggling or sounds from the two other women. When she could hear nothing, she called gently up the stairs. Still there was no response.

The family bathroom was deserted when she checked it. She wondered if perhaps the women had ventured into Martha's plush en suite and moved in the direction of her friend's bedroom. Nothing could have prepared her for the sight which confronted her as she opened the door. Both women were completely naked except that Martha was still wearing her shoes. Her knees were spread and drawn up with Philippa on her knees, her head between Martha's legs. The moans emanating from Martha were undeniably sounds of pleasure as Philippa performed oral sex on her best friend.

Whether she gasped or spoke, Katherine was unsure but Philippa's head lifted for a moment to turn in Katherine's direction. She smiled and crooked her finger, her lips glistening from her ministrations. "Join us," she called softly.

Katherine's shocked face went from Philippa to her friend lying on the bed, writhing in ecstasy as she whimpered, "Don't stop." When Katherine didn't move, Philippa shrugged and returned to her task in hand. Katherine only had time to hear the elicit murmur of "Oh yes," before she closed the door on the scene before her. She stood on the other side of the door for a moment. The shock that initially engulfed her body made way to two questions entering Katherine's mind. First was how, in all these years had she never known that Martha swung both ways? And two, why had she never made a move against her? What was wrong with her? She left Martha's house feeling let down, confused and if she was truly honest a little bit hurt.

Katherine sat at home in her own kitchen, replaying the events of the afternoon. How could she never have known about Martha? Was this the first time? Had Martha been that drunk? Somehow the resounding no that kept ringing in her head meant that she perhaps did not know her best friend as well as she thought she did.

Katherine put a perfectly manicured nail in her mouth. She had always been one to bite her nails in situations of stress, which was why she spent the money every two weeks getting her nails done with a false acrylic set. She was tempted to bite each and every nail off now.

It didn't occur to her that she had been betraying her best friend with her husband; that piece of relevant information went ignored as she thought about the betrayal that her best friend was in fact a lesbian and had failed to share that vital information with her.

The shrill ringing of the phone interrupted her reverie and made her jump. She turned to answer it. "Hello?"

"Kattthhhyyy, darling." Martha's girlish tones filtered down the phone and Katherine winced. She hated being called Kathy and Martha was the only person who called her that.

"I didn't know you were a lesbian," Katherine blurted out suddenly. Martha laughed heartily at her friend.

"Darling, I have been telling you for weeks that Henry is no longer interested in me sexually. Philippa and I are just good friends with benefits. I am not a lesbian per se, but I do enjoy sex, darling, as well you know." Katherine couldn't fail to miss the insinuation by Martha. It was widely acknowledged between the two friends that Katherine did not enjoy sex, while Martha was the flirty, experimental one. They had not been friends since school without knowing a thing or two about one another.

"Oh come on, you're not going to get all pious on me, are you?" Martha complained at her friend's silence.

Katherine could tell that Martha was getting annoyed and she sighed theatrically down the phone. "It was just a shock seeing you like that, I never knew," Katherine replied sullenly, although it was a blatant lie. Nothing about Martha was ever "a shock".

"Well now you do, so get over it," Martha retorted, her patience sapped. "Anyway, the reason I'm ringing is the flower show." Martha changed tack immediately and was all sweetness and light again, the conversation not two seconds before, completely forgotten. "I think we should get together and discuss how we're going to arrange it. Shall we regroup at the end of the week? Philippa would love to help out too."

Katherine rolled her eyes dramatically. "Of course, Martha, no problem." Even as she agreed, she knew she would have to find some excuse to not go. Perhaps one of the boys would be 'ill' that day. She had no intention of playing third wheel to those two once again.

"Thank you, darling. I should say we will outdo that old hagbag Rita Martin and put her previous efforts to shame."

"Without a doubt." Katherine tried and failed to put some enthusiasm into her voice. Martha continued as if she didn't even notice, which in truth she probably didn't.

"Darling, you are such a treasure. Love you," Martha simpered down the phone. "Ciao for now." The conversation was completed and Katherine was left with the dial tone in her ear.

Charles was not at home and Katherine sat at her breakfast bar in the kitchen, sipping Merlot. The bottle was on the worktop beside her. All thoughts of being on antibiotics were forgotten. She was depressed and needed to drown her sorrows.

She was still in shock from her discovery earlier that day and kept reliving the scene in her mind. It wasn't the fact that Martha was having a lesbian affair that bothered her at all, it was the fact that she hadn't known, and the fact that Martha hadn't bothered to tell her. They were best friends after all and told each other everything, at least that was Katherine's impression of their relationship. Still the fact that Katherine was in fact having a wild affair with Martha's husband failed to register on her radar.

Katherine was starting to feel mellow; the wine was doing its job. Topping up her glass, she wandered through to the living room. She didn't bother to turn on the lights, preferring the comfort of darkness as she settled herself into the sofa. Knocking back the entire glass of Merlot, she placed her glass on the coffee table and stretched out languidly. In a short time, she was sound asleep and that was how her husband Charles found her.

Charles was not a happily married man. He spent a good chunk of his time away from the family home these days, only really pleased to see the boys when he was there. He knew he no longer loved Katherine, but wasn't quite sure how to tell her. He wanted the chance to start a new life, to begin again before he was too old and perhaps find somebody else whom he could love. He had been trying to find the right time to tell Katherine and had been in the pub finding his 'Dutch courage', hoping that tonight he would be able to tell her. It was a perfect opportunity with the boys away for a few days and he was hoping that he could resolve the situation amicably.

He knew Katherine no longer felt the same about him either. It was obvious in the way they both skirted around each other. They never really spoke these days unless it was regarding a decision about the boys.

He stood now, watching his wife sleeping on the sofa, one arm thrown above her head, the other across her stomach, snoring softly. She had been drinking again if the empty glass beside her on the coffee table was any indication. He wondered how many glasses there had been tonight and he hoped she was not drinking in front of the boys. His own mother had been an alcoholic and it had left a devastating impression on him. He did not want his own sons influenced by a similar situation.

Sighing, he turned and made his way upstairs, leaving Katherine on the sofa. There was no point trying to wake her up. She would be aggressive and unbearable. The best way to deal with the situation was to leave her where she was until she automatically woke up herself and staggered up to bed at some point during the night.

THEN: 30TH SEPTEMBER

It was Saturday and Katherine was wiping down the kitchen sink, having completed her morning chores. Her head was pounding thanks to the hefty amount of red wine she had put away last night. She had woken up on the sofa and staggered to bed, only to find Charles already there and sound asleep. It had annoyed her so much she had been tempted to wake him up, but in the end could not be bothered with a fight. She had simply pulled off her clothes and climbed naked into bed. Maybe Charles would be tempted to rekindle sex with her.

No such luck of course, he had awoken early and mumbled something about going to the gym. He had now been missing for three hours.

She had tried ringing Henry, but had got his voicemail, so she sent him a text to which he still had not responded. What was it with men and their inability to commit? She was steadily becoming more and more irate as the time went on and wondered whether in fact Charles had discovered her affair with Henry. Maybe he had? And maybe Henry was currently in hospital after being wounded. The finger was back in her mouth, the temptation to nibble her perfectly manicured nails almost too much to resist.

The doorbell ringing broke into her reverie.

Martha stood contritely on the doorstep holding a bouquet of Tesco Finest flowers.

"For you, sweetness." She thrust the flowers into Katherine's arms as she walked through the front door into the hallway and immediately began removing her jacket. "A little something to apologise for yesterday. I realised in the dead of night that perhaps I should have told you about me and Philippa. It was terribly rude of me. Do you forgive me, darling?" Martha was staring at her reflection in the hallway mirror, fluffing her hair and checking her make-up.

Katherine sighed inwardly. Much as she loved Martha, she was not in the mood for her today. However, she hid her real feelings well and smiled beautifully at her friend. "Nothing to forgive, silly." She moved past Martha and made her way to the kitchen, putting on the kettle then pulling a vase out of one of the cupboards. Martha meanwhile had followed her into the kitchen and sat herself at the kitchen table.

"Do you remember our little lesbian romance, darling?" Martha laughed heartily at her memory of the two young girls' drunken fumble.

"I think that was more you show me yours and I'll show you mine," Katherine chided.

Martha laughed raucously. "It was, rather." A sudden silence descended. "You missing the boys yet?" Martha asked. There was definitely an awkwardness between them.

"The house is very quiet without them," Katherine confirmed, arranging the flowers in the vase and transferring it to the kitchen table. "They're beautiful Martha, thank you."

Martha stared at her friend for a moment before her eyes became slits, a sure sign that Martha was on a bloodhound trail. "What gives?" she queried. Katherine shrugged her shoulders, her eyes inexplicably filling with unshed tears. Martha was on her feet in an instant, pushing Katherine onto a chair. "Whatever is the matter? I thought you were out of sorts yesterday, but this is not like you at all."

Again, Katherine shrugged. She was on the verge of telling Martha everything. A sudden need to come clean and tell her friend about her and Henry was overwhelmingly oppressive. However, she stopped herself just in time. "It's Charles and I, things are not going well." She changed tack at the last second. This was in fact something that was bothering her, and it was as good a subject as any to discuss with her best friend.

"Where is he at the moment?" Martha re-took her seat, holding her friend's hand.

"At the gym he said, although he's been gone an awfully long time." Katherine glanced up at the clock as if to confirm this point.

"You think he's playing around?" Martha made it sound like a statement more than question. Katherine shrugged.

"I think that Charles and I are over. If it wasn't for the boys, I think I would tell him that." Martha patted her friend's arm sympathetically, but as ever in a heart to heart with Martha, the conversation quickly turned to her.

"Darling I know what you mean, Henry and I just don't seem to click any longer as a couple, but the sex is still marvellous." Katherine's ears suddenly perked up at this comment. What did she mean the sex was still marvellous? Henry had, in no uncertain terms, said that he and Martha no longer had sex, that their marriage was an empty shell.

"But if you're marriage is not working why do you still have sex?" Katherine knew she had to be careful, it wouldn't do if Martha thought her friend was jealous, but she needn't have worried as Martha laughed.

"Darling, we both have needs. If nothing else, Henry and I have both have vigorous sexual appetites in common. We both need to have sex on a regular basis. Don't you remember how we fucked like rabbits when we first got together? Nothing much has changed there, we just don't talk as much. More a perfunctionary wham, bam, thank you darling." Martha chuckled again at her own humour and Katherine tried to look like she thought it was equally funny. Inside she was seething. Henry had lied to her! *To her*! He had told her that he and Martha barely spoke, let alone touched. They were living separate lives but together he had told her. She was furious that she had been so easily duped. It was so cliché it *was* almost funny.

Her first affair since being married and she had fallen for Henry in a big way. Whether it was the excitement of sneaking around or whether it was that someone was finally paying attention to her and found her attractive, she didn't know, but she had thought that she was falling in love with Henry.

"Of course, Henry is embarking on a new little affair at the moment." Katherine was immediately back on alert. "You think he's having an affair?"

"Darling, when is Henry not having an affair?" Although she kept her voice light, Katherine could not help but notice the underlying sadness in her friend. They had not been best friends for years without knowing a thing or two about each other. Immediately, she felt so guilty, she almost blurted out to Martha for the second time that day, that it was her who was having an affair with Henry. She was caught between wanting to tell all and admit the truth and wanting to hit Henry over the head for lying to her for all these weeks.

"Why don't we go out for lunch, cheer ourselves up?" Martha asked suddenly.

Suddenly the front door banged open, startling both women. Martha looked up at her best friend's husband as he entered the kitchen, freshly showered, his hair still slightly damp. Martha had always had a bit of a soft spot for Charles and although they had never 'got it on', Martha was never one to rule anything out completely.

"Looking good, Charlie," Martha teased, practically fluttering her eyelashes at him, a fact that did not go unnoticed by Charles, although Katherine, already rising from her chair, missed it.

"Martha, you know I hate it when you call me that." He opened the fridge and took out the bottle of orange juice, opened the top and swigged it out of the bottle. Katherine looked up at him. He knew damn well she hated it when he drank straight from the bottle. His eyes met hers in defiance. "Have I interrupted something?" he queried, glancing from his wife to her friend and knowing full well that he had.

"Not at all, darling, I was just going to invite Kathy here out for lunch when you arrived in the nick of time. Can I interest you both in a spot of luncheon?" Martha, gay as ever, recovered herself quicker than anyone Katherine knew.

"I'm quite alright thank you, Martha, however I do have something rather important to speak to Katherine about, so perhaps we could both take a rain check?"

Katherine felt her heart flipflop with anxiety. What on earth could Charles have to speak with her about?

"Of course, not a problem, some other time." Martha was already leaving the kitchen and putting her jacket back on. Katherine followed her friend to the door.

"Call me later." Martha mouthed and then air kissed each cheek. She waltzed out the door in a cloud of Chanel perfume.

Katherine closed the front door firmly behind her friend and turned back towards the kitchen, each footstep slower than the last.

Charles looked serious. Did he know about her and Henry? She hoped not, that would lead to all sorts of problems including ruining her friendship with Martha. Nothing killed a friendship stone dead than one's best friend having a rampant affair with the other's husband.

Katherine walked back into the kitchen, wringing her hands nervously. She moved to the counter and switched on the kettle, glad for something to do, however mundane. Charles sat at the kitchen table and waited patiently for her to make the tea and finally take her seat.

"There's no easy way to approach this." Charles said softly.

Katherine took a sip of her tea, feeling the trepidation mounting. What was wrong? Had Charles lost his job, had he met someone else? She placed her hand on his forearm. "You can tell me anything, Charles," She informed him carefully. He sighed dramatically before looking her directly in the face.

"I'm leaving you, Katherine." There, it was said, it was out there like a glaringly bright neon pink sign.

Katherine took a moment to process what her husband had just informed her. "Is there someone else?" Her voice almost choked for a moment and she took another sip of her tea.

"No, it's nothing like that. I've felt for some time and I'm sure you have too, that something is no longer working between us. We have nothing in common except the boys and I think we are making each other miserable. I wish I could say that there was someone else, to make it a clean-cut reason, but the truth is, Katherine, I simply don't love you any more."

Katherine was dumbstruck by his little speech. He was leaving *her*. He did not love *her*. It was how she felt herself, it was true, but it should have been her telling him that, not the other way around. She immediately felt betrayed and indignant. He could see the emotions playing across her face, knew that she was on the verge of hysteria.

"I was hoping for a calm discussion." The sound of his voice was beginning to grate on her nerves. How dare he?

"A calm discussion?" Katherine repeated. "A calm discussion." She repeated it again only louder this time, her voice becoming shrill. She stood up, facing him with her hands placed on her hips. A righteous indignation she had no right to suddenly overwhelmed her. "I have done everything for you. You wouldn't be the man you are today without me by your side. We have two children for God's sake and you have the audacity to sit there and calmly say to me that you don't love me, that you're leaving me. HOW ... DARE... YOU?" Her voice had reached a high-pitched crescendo.

Charles had turned to face her. He was still seated seemingly unmoved by her reaction. Her mind was in turmoil. This was the last thing she expected. "I realise that this has come as somewhat of a shock to you, but you must have felt that our marriage was going wrong?" He sounded so damn plausible and correct. She *had* felt it, it was absolutely true, however she had no intention of admitting that fact. There had been a gradual decline for months, probably years if truth be told. It was why she drank and it was why she had embarked on an affair with Henry. She needed to feel wanted, to feel loved and Henry had provided that for her. But, if she looked in the depths of her soul, she knew that what Charles said was true. However, that still didn't make it any easier to hear or accept.

"I have arranged to rent an apartment and I'm moving in tonight. My bags are already packed. I won't contest any demands you put on me for yourself or the boys, I feel I owe you that much, but I think you and I will be happier apart. I will of course make arrangements to visit the boys and I would like to be here so we can tell them together. I wanted to wait until they were on holiday before I told you. I think it only fair that they have the opportunity to enjoy themselves before the bad news."

Katherine heard what he said. She listened to his reasonable voice, stating his reasonable case and in that moment, she hated Charles with such a passion that she could have cheerfully stabbed him. This was her worst nightmare come true. A separation, a divorce, either way it would have a detrimental effect on her standing in the community. What would they think at church? What would the other mums at the school think? She was middle fucking class and the middle classes carried on despite everything. Didn't they? The old English stiff upper lip and all that? "Is there someone else? Really, Charles, I would prefer you to tell me if that's the case." Her voice did not betray the emotions she truly felt in that moment.

Charles sighed dramatically. "No, there is definitely nobody else. I have no reason to lie to you, Katherine. This is simply a matter of falling out of love. It happens, but that doesn't mean that at some point in the future we can't be friends." Katherine could scarcely believe he had just said that very thing.

"Friends?" she spat in disgust. "You're going to take eight years of marriage and throw it down the toilet so we can be friends?" Katherine grabbed the empty tea cups and took them to the kitchen sink. Charles had also stood up. He looked uncomfortable and she knew it had taken a considerable amount of effort to speak to her today. The fact that he had waited until the boys were away at camp also showed a certain amount of premeditation. She was beside herself with anger but still outwardly the majority of those feelings were hidden. She needed to salvage what she could. Any parting would be done on her terms. She had instantly forgotten about any plans she may have had regarding her and Henry.

"Look, Katherine, I'm going to make a move, leave you to think about things. I know there's plenty we need to discuss, but I think it might be better if we have some time to digest this initial split." Charles was already making his way to the hallway. He sounded tired.

Katherine had no thoughts in her head; she certainly wasn't thinking clearly when she realised she was holding the large vase of flowers Martha had so thoughtfully given her earlier. With a strength she did not know she had, she threw the entire contents including the vase at Charles. The vase banged his arm, the contents of flowers and water splashing over him and the kitchen. He staggered to one side, immediately taken by surprise.

"Jesus Christ!" he exclaimed loudly, his hand involuntarily cradling his arm where the vase had performed a direct hit. It was now in pieces on the kitchen floor. Charles was soaked. The sight in other circumstances might have been comical, but neither Katherine nor Charles was laughing. "You crazy bitch," he muttered, leaving the kitchen. She heard his footfalls on the stairs.

"I suggest you get out before something worse happens to you!" Katherine shouted after him, the warning evident in her voice. Her emotions were see-sawing out of control. She was feeling disgusted with herself for her own behaviour on the one hand. She had never resorted to violence in her life, but on the other hand, she also felt a little bit pleased with herself. She had enjoyed hurting Charles and was surprised to find herself wanting to hurt him again.

Charles did not need telling twice. In a matter of moments, he had changed his shirt and had returned to the hall, carrying two large suitcases. He pulled on his jacket and opened the front door. Katherine was shocked to discover that he was so well prepared and it hit her then that it was indeed Charles's intention to leave her. That from tonight she would be alone. For some reason she felt panicked. She couldn't be alone. She didn't know how to be alone.

"Charles, can't we talk about this some more. There must be more to say." He found that her wheedling disgusted him. She was moving towards him with her arms outstretched, a pleading look on her face. His hand came up in a gesture to stop which she did automatically.

"There is nothing further to discuss, Katherine. I've had enough. I can't keep up this charade any longer, the pressure of it is too draining. I dread coming home every night to find you passed out on the sofa from too much wine, I dread spending time in your company because we have nothing to talk about apart from the boys and that conversation lasts mere minutes before we are thrown into silence. I hate your friends. I can't live like this any longer and I refuse to. Oh and I know about your little affair with Henry Davies. I've known for some time and this is how little you mean to me now. I simply don't care about it."

Katherine stood rooted to the spot, her face a mask of incredulity, her mouth open in a small 'o'. The things Charles were spouting were nothing she had not considered herself, but again the fact that it was him saying it to her rather than the other way around was as bad as him stabbing her in the chest. And to top it off even more, Charles knew about her affair. He had known all along and yet he had never said anything. The hurt and indignation that washed over her in those few seconds spurred her on. She wanted to hurt him because she was hurting.

"Well then you'll know that he is more of a lover than you'll ever be. You're a pathetic, weak excuse for lovemaking left me cold all these years, Charles. I needed a real man, someone who could teach me what real lovemaking was all about," she spat nastily.

Charles grinned at her, a nasty grimace that held no humour. "Henry Davies is a dog. He fucks anything that moves and he enjoys the challenge of the chase. You are just one more assignation under his belt that will soon be over and done with. You're a fool, Katherine, a stupid, dense little fool and I don't have the time or the inclination to babysit you any longer." Charles turned and opened the front door, and picked up his cases. As he stood in the doorway, he turned to look at her.

"A colleague of mine will be coming to collect the rest of my things for me tomorrow morning. I have packed what I want to take and the boxes are in the spare room. The house is yours and like I said, I will provide for you and the boys. My lawyers will be in touch, but I think it's safer and easier for both of us if we don't see each other for a while." Charles put down his cases and closed the front door quietly. Katherine was still rooted to the spot in the hall when she heard his car drive away.

Katherine's vision blurred and she swayed slightly as she poured her fourth glass of wine. She glared as the contents only filled her glass halfway. She had finished the entire bottle but still did not feel numb enough to erase the day's events.

Nothing had gone according to plan. The unpleasant scene with Charles had replayed itself in her mind's eye all day. Some parts were replayed more than others. The fact that Charles knew about her affair, the fact that Henry was just using her. Deep down that hurt more than anything. She had fallen for Henry in a big way. She had been taken in by his sweet words, his hard kisses and his voracious lovemaking. For the first time in such a long while her body had come to life, had felt tingly and alive with every nerve ending on fire for him. When she analysed their relationship, she thought that it was possibly the idea of great sex that she had actually fallen in love with or the fact that for the first time in many years she had felt like an attractive woman again. Did she really love Henry? Would she have considered leaving Charles for him? Deep down she knew the answer was no. She would never have hurt her husband or her best friend in that way. She had selfishly toyed with the romantic notion that it could or would happen, but if reality had bitten her firmly on the behind, she would have shunned it with every fibre in her body. The thing that rankled too was the fact that Charles knew her so well. He had known about the affair, but he had known she would never have left him. He also knew Henry well enough to know that she was just one fish in a rather large pond and sooner or later he would have moved on.

It had given her a measure of satisfaction in ringing Henry earlier and telling him that the whole thing was off. His initial response had been surprised but he had not appeared upset in any way. That in itself had made her angry all over again. She wanted him to feel something, to be as devastated as she felt.

She confronted him over what Martha had said and was surprised when he had denied emphatically what his wife had said, brushing it off as complete and utter lies. It seemed that Martha and Henry truly no longer slept together, but as Henry pointed out to Katherine, although they were best friends, it was unlikely that Martha would admit such a thing to anyone.

Martha did not handle disappointment well and not even in front of her best friend would she admit that any trace of her life was a failure. Katherine certainly knew this fact to be true of her best friend and although a small part of her deep down knew what Henry said to be the stereotypical bullshit spouted by men, she accepted what he told her and firmly relegated it to the archive in her mind. She would no doubt take it out and re-examine it at some point in the future, but for now it was forgotten.

In the aftermath of their discussion, Henry was in complete agreement with their affair being over. Rather than feel vindicated in retaining some of her dignity, Katherine now felt dirty and sleazy and had for the first time since it began, a large measure of regret and guilt over going behind her best friend's back.

Katherine hit the bottle with a flourish. There were two bottles of red wine left in the house and she intended to drink both bottles dry before starting on the spirits left over from Christmas.

After cleaning up the kitchen of broken glass, water and ruined flowers, she had retreated upstairs, removed all her clothes and put on her dressing gown. She had piled all the pillows into the middle of the bed and rested herself against them, turning the television on to some nonsense rubbish just for background noise as she drank herself into a stupor. She had toyed with the idea of calling Martha, but just couldn't face the commiserations and questions at the moment. Instead she had polished off half the second bottle of wine and fallen into a drunken sleep at some point.

She awoke now, her dressing gown askew but still belted, her naked body beneath it barely covered. She had slid off the pillows at some point and was lying in a sprawled position across the bed.

Her eyes felt gritty and her mouth felt like the bottom of a budgie cage. She glanced at the clock by the bed and was annoyed to note it was only nine p.m.

Pulling herself into a seated position, she attempted to rearrange her dressing gown demurely. God, she felt awful. She needed to find the Alka-Seltzer quickly before her hangover deepened into something infinitely worse. Pulling herself off the bed, she put her bare feet on the floor, feeling the softness of the carpet beneath her toes. She hoped her legs would hold her up. She glanced towards the mirror on the dressing table, catching sight of her hair and face. The sight did nothing to make her feel any better. Her hair was in complete disarray, as if someone had carefully back-combed it into any given direction. Her mascara had run although she couldn't remember actually crying. She assumed she probably had at some point since she now resembled a caricature of Alice Cooper. Ignoring her reflection, Katherine stood up slowly, waiting for the sudden bout of nausea that rolled through her stomach to pass. She undid the tie of her dressing gown, straightened it and redid it up again before leaving the bedroom and making her way slowly downstairs, using the wall and the bannister rail for balance.

The house had that middle-of-the-night hush, although it was still early on. It had been daylight when she ventured upstairs and now the downstairs of the house was impossibly dark. Switching on the light in the bright white of the kitchen made her flinch and wince. She grabbed a glass and filled it with water, drinking it quickly. Refilling her glass, she went in search of the Alka Seltzer she kept in her medicine chest in the utility room.

Triumphantly she pulled out the pack of tablets and dropped them into her water with the satisfying plink, plink, fizz. She swallowed the concoction quickly. Having the feeling she might need more at some point, she put the box in the pocket of her dressing gown.

Realising that she had not locked up the house earlier, she checked the utility room door that led to the back garden and was gratified to find it locked. She needed to make sure everything was locked now since she was on her own without a man around. She swallowed back the tears that threatened to come upon her at that thought. She stopped herself just in time. She was not going to be one of those women that fell apart just because a man had walked out of her life.

Flicking off the utility room light, she walked back into the kitchen. A tall figure stood in the doorway between her kitchen and the hall. Confusion filled her befuddled brain at that moment. Had Charles returned after all?

"Mrs Eddowin?" the man was soft spoken and tall. He was dressed in dark clothing and his face appeared to be in shadow but this was largely due to the fact that he wore a black beanie covering his head. He was carrying a black bag which resembled an old-fashioned doctor's bag.

His features were indistinguishable and he might have been considered an attractive man in a nondescript kind of way, should one have taken the time to really consider the fact. However, he was the kind of person you simply did not notice, through no fault of his own. He had the kind of face you saw but failed to remember completely once he was out of sight.

The one disarming feature was his eyes, which appeared so dark they could have been black. They were as soulless as those of a reptile.

Katherine could not fathom the reason why this man was in her house at first. Her senses, dulled by the amount of alcohol she had consumed, suddenly sprang to life as she realised that this man was in her house in the middle of the night.

"Are you a burglar?" Katherine enquired wondering what her chances of making it to a phone actually were.

"No, Mrs Eddowin, I'm not a burglar." She realised then that he had already said her name once. That for some inexplicable reason he knew her name. She could not fathom the reasoning behind that, nor could she find the will to remove her feet from the spot at which she stood. Still he did not move either.

He suddenly smiled at the woman before him. The smile never reached his eyes. The smile was a pretence, covering the cold-blooded killer that lived behind it.

Katherine felt the cold hand of fear envelop her spine as the man before her smiled. Suddenly she knew beyond a shadow of a doubt that this man was not a burglar that she had unwittingly interrupted. An inner sixth sense told her that he was here to harm her.

As he stepped into the pristine white kitchen towards Katherine Eddowin, she realised that something awful was about to happen. As slow as her brain was at assimilating the information before, still she did not move. She watched him slowly walk towards her like a cat stalking a bird. His eyes did not leave hers and she felt trapped by his stare.

Too late, he was before her and in a lightning flash he struck, his left arm striking from right to left as he sliced through the soft skin of her exposed throat. The cut was deep enough to severe her carotid artery and an arc of warm red blood cascaded through the air, marring the perfectly clean kitchen and spattering him. Katherine's hands dropped the glass she had been holding and it shattered at her feet as her hands moved towards her throat as if she intended to stop the flow of blood, a look of abject disbelief on her face. She had not seen the knife, she had not known what he wanted, but as she collapsed to the ground and the life began to ebb out of Katherine Eddowin's body, her last thought was that thank God her boys were at camp.

Randall didn't care that he was covered in her blood and he certainly didn't care that the pristine white kitchen was spattered with her blood either. The display was been magnificent. None of the others had bled as Katherine had. Even the spoilt little bitch he had sliced up this morning had not bled like that. She had bled though. He grinned at the memory. He felt himself grow hard at the thought of what had transpired this morning.

Every plan he had executed had been meticulously thought out and carried out without a hitch so far. He had easily entered the premises that promised guard dogs, these being nothing but a fallacy made up by the pompous prick who was her father. Whatever money they had, as much materialistic crap as they had, nothing could stop him from carrying out his plans.

But there was no time to procrastinate just yet. He could repent at his leisure soon enough and recount all the events that had taken place so far. First and foremost, he had to finish his work for today. Two murders in one day took a lot of planning and executing. He laughed out loud at his own pun.

His heart was pounding with excitement as he watched the life force seep out of Katherine Eddowin. Within mere seconds, the kitchen floor and cabinets were covered in her life's blood as it seeped from the deep wound in her neck. She wasn't dead yet, however. Her eyes looked at him pleadingly, a pleasing death rattle emanating from her, the only sound in the quiet house.

"What's that?" he said, leaning forward and holding a hand cupped to his ear. "Why yes, my darling, that's just what I was thinking." He began removing his clothing, his blood spattered top and trousers. He was hard and already wearing a condom. This time he had come prepared. Wearing his beanie, his booties, a pair of surgical gloves and his condom, he knelt down and pushed apart her dressing gown which had already come loose as she fell.

"Well look at that, you're all ready for me," he said and smiled beatifically at her.

As Katherine Eddowin's last breath left her body, he ejaculated his sperm into the condom he wore. His body felt alive while hers expired.

He stared down at the woman at his feet. Her eyes were open and staring, unseeing into nothing. She was dead and his work could continue. It was ten thirty p.m. and he had already accomplished much this morning. He was nearing fruition of the first phase of his work and he was beyond excited by the concept. Today they would know who they were dealing with. Who it was, who was carrying out his work so diligently. He hadn't planned to give the police any kind of helping hand. He had thought to remove that part of original history and let them continue to flounder in the dark. However, he could see the sense of it. He felt glorious and powerful. He wanted to share that with somebody, and who better than Detective Inspector Virginia Percy. He wanted to give her a taste of what was to come, allow her to share in his passion, just this once. He could almost feel himself growing hard again at the thought, but he couldn't allow that just yet. He had important work to be done.

He looked down at the woman before him. She was quite attractive he supposed, but disloyal and a whore just like the rest of them. He had no sympathy for what he was about to do. She deserved it. They all deserved it.

CHAPTER THIRTEEN

THEN: RANDALL GOFF JULY 1998

Eugenie Goff sat at her kitchen table across from Ian Pratchett, headmaster of the local primary school and lover of almost four years. He had cut an imposing figure once upon a time, tall at six foot two inches, with a muscular physique. He had had jet black wavy hair, a large Roman nose, full lips and a dimple in his chin which had reminded Eugenie of the movie star Kirk Douglas.

She had been taken in immediately by Ian's good looks and charm but as she came to know him, it was his quick mind, wit and interesting, well-educated conversation that had captured her heart. He reminded her of her beginnings, a far-flung memory to her past to which she could never return and he was a far cry from the dirty, cheap squalor she was faced with every day.

They had commenced their affair during a far more decorous period when even the slightest whiff of scandal could be the cause for illicit gossiping. The sensational story of the headmaster having an affair with a married woman had circulated again and again. She was blamed and shunned and looked down upon, being seen as a fallen woman in the eyes of those who considered her indecent in every common sense. The stories had circulated the neighbourhood for years and even though what was said was mainly hearsay, Eugenie Goff never escaped the reputation that proceeded her for years, even though she had never in fact been married. However, the taint of an unmarried woman having a baby out of wedlock would have punished her twice as severely, despite the so-called modern times.

Eugenie considered herself a cut above her neighbours, that her present circumstances were the result of a situation she could not have avoided, and it was important to her that she continue to preserve the semblance of the life she left behind, if not for her own sanity.

She spoke well and was well educated, something that belied her current circumstances and implied that she came from an entirely different background. She carried herself with an air of refinement and grace. But in the end, she lived no better than the rest of them, survived the daily struggle for food and to provide for her son as a single parent. In the end, it didn't matter where she came from.

Her high opinion of herself created jealousy. She was always perfectly turned out, from her hair to her feet, and her house was always spotless. People resented the fact that no matter what carried on behind closed doors, she continued to think herself better than the rest of them. She had no friends and no acquaintances to speak of. Ian Pratchett had been the first person who had truly taken an interest in her since she had lived in the area. There were parts of themselves that had formed a kindred bond and recognised that each resided in their own form of purgatory by living where they did. They had unwittingly and unconsciously rescued each other.

The only fly in the ointment was Randall, her son. She had loved that child when he was a tiny baby – had wanted to give him a life he could be proud of. Or had she? Sometimes she wondered if she looked upon that period with rose tinted glasses.

At sixteen, Eugenie had been full of aspirations and dreaming of fairy tale endings, which she had bitterly come to realise did not exist. That bitterness had eaten into her, taken the purity that had once existed and extinguished it along with any hopes and dreams she had. As much as she believed that she loved that tiny baby, the circumstances that prevailed upon her in the aftermath of his birth led her to resent his existence, and the projection of hate she had against his father was transferred to an innocent little boy.

However, Randall had been a strange, woeful little boy, with his dirty blonde hair and huge brown eyes that were so dark, one could be forgiven for imagining they were black. He had been a tiny, skinny little thing, almost appearing scared of his own shadow. Yet he had watched her. His large dark eyes bored their way into her soul, watching her every move unrelentingly. He made her feel uneasy although she could never quite put her finger on why. From the moment he could talk and walk, she had felt Randall with her like an ever-present shadow, watching her, measuring her, like he was waiting for something. It was a feeling of unease that dogged their relationship.

Amidst the unease, Eugenie had felt it necessary to enforce her will on Randall, to give herself the upper hand and ensure that he was unaware she was afraid of her own son. She bullied him and treated him badly. It became as acceptable as breathing to punish him for any minor indiscretion and each time he would look at her with those huge dark eyes, at first as if he was imploring her to love him, then in hate and contempt. He was about four years old when she realised that she had no love for her only son, nor did she think she ever would. There was nothing endearing about the four-year-old boy whom she had given birth to. In every sense he resembled his father, whom she now hated with a passion, but there was also that uneasiness that she felt whenever she was in his presence. She could feel his eyes on her, watching her, and to that end Eugenie never felt completely settled around her son.

As the years passed, Eugenie learned to cope with the concept that she disliked her own child so much. There was nothing specific she could put her finger on as to why she felt the way she did. He was reserved and silent much of the time, absorbing himself in the books he obtained from the library. She had happened upon him reading one day and was alarmed by the macabre theme the books portrayed. They were full of death and murder, and each one he obtained was more sinister and viler than the last. In some dark recess of her mind she knew she should be worried that her son was reading such material and yet she just couldn't bring herself to delve too deeply into that aspect of his psyche, nor did she care enough.

Even the other children that attended school with Randall seemed to offer him a wide berth. He had no friends that she was aware of and seemed to associate with nobody at all.

Still she could not dwell on the subject of Randall for long. It insulted her wellbeing to do such a thing.

Eugenie sat at the small kitchen table opposite the man who had become her life, whom she had fallen in love with and wanted to be with for the rest of her life. She had not thought it could happen again. She had believed that she had loved Randall's father with a romantic passion that could withstand the wrath of her father and that he would be as happy as she was regarding her pregnancy, however the case was not true in either circumstance. By becoming pregnant then, she had ruined her life. The man responsible had little interest in becoming a father and her own father had ostracised her from the family.

"I'm pregnant, Ian." Eugenie spoke quietly. In her head she had envisaged a more serene and beautiful way to tell the man she loved he was about to become a father, but in the end, there was nothing to do but blurt it out.

She had wanted to tell Ian alone. She didn't want Randall to know or for him to overhear what she said. For some reason she had the sense that Randall eavesdropped on everything that went on inside that house, another strike against him that made her wary and uneasy.

"Ah." Ian looked down at his hands, carefully folded on the kitchen table. "I thought it might be something like that when you said you had news." He wasn't smiling like he should be, she thought. In fact, he looked downright miserable.

"Is that all you have to say to me?" she asked, confusion clouding her face. This was not what she expected at all and as if that wasn't enough, the sudden banging of the front door heralding her son's return to the house was too much to bear. "Say something." She hissed across the table at Ian quickly, angry now at his reaction. She couldn't understand it at all. She thought Ian loved her, had been sure of that fact. She thought he would marry her, make her respectable. She would finally be a married lady and not have to suffer the pretence of a dead husband any longer.

Randall sat at the top of the stairs, listening. It would make no difference whether he sat in his room or in the kitchen with them, he would hear either way since the whole house seemed to be made of tissue paper.

"I think we should go out for a walk, take in the night air." Eugenie sounded a little breathy and was trying very hard to keep herself under control. All through her life she had exercised a certain control, did not raise her voice or betray many of the emotions she was truly feeling. Everything was always clamped down tight, never allowing others to see beyond the perfect façade she created.

Now it was difficult to keep those feelings bottled and under control. She felt that poise she worked so hard to maintain slipping, barely hanging by a thread, unravelling at the speed of light due to the Ian's lack of response to her news. She suddenly had a feeling of déjà vu. Reminiscences of a place and time when this situation had arisen before. She refused to let it happen again. Perhaps it was just the shock.

She had an immediate feeling that her conversation with Ian was about to get ugly. For some inexplicable reason, she had no wish for Randall to overhear any of it. The only course of action apparent to her was to take the conversation outside. She didn't want Randall knowing anything about her conversation with Ian. In fact, she didn't want Randall to know anything, full stop. The boy was positively poison these days and she had no idea how to handle him. The dealings of a sullen ten-year-old boy were far beyond her capabilities.

From the skinny little boy whom she could rule with an iron fist, he now stood almost as tall as her. He should not have been able to, but he intimidated her and frightened her. He was strange and guarded, wrapped up in his books that he seemed to pore over for hours, always the same macabre stories of killers, murders and torture. Some of the pictures were so graphic, it had made Eugenie feel quite sick. It was all he seemed to be interested in. As soon as he went to school, Eugenie always breathed a sigh of relief, knowing it was safe to leave the confines of her own bedroom. It was the hours when he was away from the house that she felt completely at peace.

Ian agreed to walk with her. If truth be told, he disliked being in the house when young Randall was around. His presence unnerved him but if somebody should ask him why, he could not have explained it. There was just something odd about the lad, the way he seemed to stand in the shadows, just watching, barely saying a word. Those dark eyes held some kind of malevolence.

Ian stood and helped Eugenie on with her jacket, before pulling on his own. They left the house together, walking side by side in silence towards the end of the road. It was dusk and the sunshine of the day was disappearing behind the houses, creating a streak of pink in the darkening sky.

Without much to be said, they walked together towards the park, an unconscious effort on both their parts to appear normal, like a couple out for a stroll.

They had only followed the path a short way when Ian stopped walking and turned to Eugenie. "Look, Eugenie," he began and instantly she knew he was going to be the bearer of bad news.

"Just say it." Eugenie looked miserably at her feet, not really wanting to hear what he had to say, but willing him on to get it over and done with just the same. The feeling of déjà vu was back. She had been here once before, although the circumstances had been different. This time the man before her was not married, although she had the feeling what he was about to say was very similar in the telling.

"I've been offered a job in Scotland. It's to be headteacher of a prestigious boys' boarding school. It's a fine opportunity and I would be a fool to turn it down. I'm not getting any younger and I'm fed up of trying to teach the children here something that they neither want, nor need to learn."

Eugenie knew that Ian was dissatisfied with his job as headmaster of the local school. It had been his bugbear for several years. He had come to the job an idealist, believing he could make a difference and educate the poor working class, change the status quo. However, he had grown despondent and felt that he had nothing more to give. Eugenie had thought that if he did decide to move on, she would be going with him. Now here he was telling about a new opportunity, but somehow she didn't think it included her.

"So why can I not come with you?" Eugenie asked hopefully, staring up into the lover's face she knew so well.

"The position stipulated a single man only. There is no room for a family." Ian looked apologetic. He hated confrontation, she knew.

"But that's absurd." She spluttered, her dignity and poise rapidly evaporating with the setting sun.

"Be that as it may, the opportunity is too good to pass up, Eugenie." He was trying to placate her. "Look, if it works out as expected, perhaps I can send for you. Once I get the lay of the land and all that."

"Send for me?" she echoed. Eugenie took a step back, her hand fluttering at the beaded necklace she always wore at her throat. She felt like she was drowning, like she was somehow losing her breath. As she exhaled, she noted that her breath trembled. She would not cry. She most definitely would not cry. She had promised herself this all day.

"And what about the baby, *our baby*?" Eugenie queried when she had composed herself enough to speak again.

"In some respects, I feel that our relationship has run its course." Ian's tone sounded wheedling now and it irritated her. "I feel like I'm trapped, like we're married already. That was not my intention, I never wanted to get married. I made no secret of that fact."

"So, you applied for a job as far away from me as you could possibly get, a little extreme don't you think? How long has this been planned, Ian?" Even to herself Eugenie sounded shrew-like. Her control had visibly slipped and she was in no mood to protect that carefully cultivated façade that she worked so hard to preserve.

Ian pushed a hand through his hair, not really knowing where this conversation was going. In his mind it had all been very serene and dignified. He had planned to tell her he was leaving, that he would send for her as soon as he possibly could. She would never have known that he had no intention of doing that. He could have disappeared and moved on with his life. Lord knew he had been wanting to do it for months, but was just waiting for the perfect opportunity to come along. The job in Scotland was perfect but, in all fairness, he would have taken a job anywhere so long as he could move on and make a fresh start. Now there was an added complication. In all the years of them being so careful, Eugenie was now pregnant.

"Look, if it's about the baby, I will give you the money to have an abortion. Nobody need ever know." He realised his mistake as soon as the words left his mouth. The look on Eugenie's face was one of abject horror.

"You want me to have an abortion? To get rid of this baby, *our baby*?" The tears that had been threatening now filled her eyes.

"It's an added complication." He admitted his thoughts out loud. "I can't possibly stay here and take care of you and a baby. I have my career to think about." If holes could be dug any deeper, Ian Pratchett was doing a sterling job of ensuring his was the deepest.

"An added complication?" Eugenie repeated his words, her voice barely a whisper. She had turned her face from his to stare into the darkness of the park. Even in profile in the dimming light, he could appreciate that she was still a good-looking woman. At twenty-six her figure was still firm, her legs strong. She was passionate and strong, a combination of fire and ice in the bedroom that had at one time left him thinking about nothing else. Yet those days were gone now. He had long since lost his blind admiration for her and had settled into a pleasant companionship. He had never inspected their relationship beyond what it was. He had never expected it to evolve beyond anything more and he had thought Eugenie had felt the same way.

"How can you do this to me? What am I supposed to do?" Eugenie appeared genuinely devastated. Ian was exasperated; he had no idea how to handle this. Eugenie was one of the most refined people he had ever met. This blatant display of emotion was a revelation in its newness and it was far from pleasant. Besides, he had just offered up a plan of what he thought she could do.

"I told you I would give you the money to get rid of it," he snapped spitefully, his patience wearing a little thin now. He wanted the subject to be over so he could be on his way home. He had a lot to do still before he moved to Scotland.

"And what if I don't want to get to rid of it?" Eugenie cried indignantly, her voice rising slightly, her head whipping back round so she looked him in the eye.

"Well that would be your choice, my dear. You've done it before, I'm sure you can cope again." He informed her flatly and coldly. Eugenie reached out and slapped his face as hard she possibly could. Her hand stung from the contact and she closed her fist in an attempt to ignore the pain.

Ian let it go, despite the fact that his cheek was now on fire. He supposed he deserved it really.

"You would expect me to go through the pregnancy, suffering the humiliation of another illegitimate child. It's bad enough that

I've had to spend my days exiled in this godforsaken part of the world as it is, living off the odd handout from my mother, but for God's sake Ian, I never thought you would do this to me too."

Ian hung his head in shame. He knew she was right. He was the only person she had ever told the complete truth to, about Randall and the circumstances that had prevailed upon her to end up as she had.

Randall's father had claimed to be in love with Eugenie. In truth he had been so besotted with the sixteen-year-old virginal, nubile young woman, that he had made it his absolute goal to woo her and lure her into his bed. He was successful only because she was an innocent, a naïve child who was flattered by the attentions of an older man, and who had not until that point received much love in her life. She couldn't see that their relationship was doomed from the first and had nowhere to go, that the fact he was married marred any prospect of a union between the two of them.

She had been innocent and romantic enough to believe that he truly loved her, that he would leave his wife and that they would live happily ever after. The sad epilogue to that dream ended in a stark reality. Once he had achieved his goal and the chase was over, he had moved on to his next conquest. Eugenie was left high and dry, finding herself pregnant shortly after.

In a time when it was considered more acceptable to be an unmarried mother, her parents, particularly her father, were old school. As a distant relation to the royal family, her father abhorred the fact that his only daughter would be unable to marry well. His hope had been that she may in fact be introduced and marry into the royal family itself. All her father could talk about was the scandal and the press finding out. His plan had been to send her away, telling friends and family that she was travelling abroad to widen her horizons. She would then return to the family home, less the baby she had given birth to who would be offered up for adoption. It was an old-fashioned notion that might have been more acceptable in Victorian times, but this was the eighties. Some sensibilities might have been offended, but in general it was a wider accepted notion that an unmarried mother in society was the norm.

Eugenie had been fine with being sent away, it was the loss of her child that she objected to. Despite what he did and how he treated her, Eugenie was in love, or thought she was, with Randall's father and as far as she was concerned, if she couldn't have the real thing, the next best thing would suffice.

That next best thing was his child and she was determined to keep that baby no matter what. She had thought many a time about how different her life would have turned out if she had followed her father's instructions, given the baby up for adoption, or as she had thought many times, got rid of him while he still resided in her womb.

Despite her own and her mother's weak protestations, the matter had eventually earned her an unceremonious eviction from the family home, with her father claiming that she was a disgrace and a disappointment. He said that he never wanted to set eyes on his only daughter again and he had stuck to his word. Only a weak contact with her mother had provided her with some of the help she so desperately needed, but other than that that she was alone and foisted into the world with her bastard child.

When she had moved to the house in which she now lived, she had made attempts to befriend some of her neighbours. They were distrustful of the soft spoken, young woman who did not speak like them. She wore a wedding ring, but there was no husband and the rumour-mongers went into overdrive trying to guess what her story was. She claimed herself to be a widow although the circumstances were never fully shared.

Now, it was as if history was repeating itself all over again. She didn't have the life or the energy left in her to go through it all again to bring up a child all alone. Goodness only knew that Randall had turned out a very strange boy indeed. And what would Randall make of it all? Would he shun her as her family had done before?

Would she once more be an outcast in her own home? Could she subject a new born baby to Randall and his strangeness?

Eugenie was not prepared to take the chance. She had no doubt that Randall was a product of an unhappy pregnancy, that the merciless way in which his father had used and abused her had scarred her unborn child irrevocably and created the monster that now resided under her roof. She would not take that chance again. Eugenie refused to see that Randall was the product of her years of emotional and physical abuse. That it was *she* who had created the monster that was her son, by pushing him away and not showing him any love.

Her hand fluttered unwittingly to her stomach; she felt something cold and merciless clamp down on her feelings. The tears stopped and it was as if a switch had been turned off inside her. She regarded Ian coldly as if she was seeing him for the very first time. She saw him as Randall's father had been, a selfish, mercenary libertine who used her and trashed her reputation. She could only imagine what her life would have been like, how it would have turned out if not for the three men in her life.

"If you want me to get rid of it, I will, but I need the money as soon as possible," Eugenie said coldly. How quickly her feelings of love had dissolved in that moment when she discovered she loathed Ian so much. He was unsure at first. Her coldness and flat affect unnerved him slightly and he could see a glimpse of where Randall might have got his personality. However, he brushed it aside quickly, knowing that he had won, smelling his victory in her defeat.

"Of course, my dear, whatever you need." The relief in his voice was enough to make Eugenie want to scream to the rooftops. She looked up into his face, cast in shadow, the only light from the street lamp giving him a sickly yellow look.

"I expect you to have the money for me tomorrow. I will arrange an appointment for the day after. I will come to your house tomorrow night and then I never want to lay eyes on you again."

Ian had to admit that since the beginning of their conversation he had not expected Eugenie to relent quite so easily. He had envisioned tears and pleading across the following days before he might have been able to either persuade her to do as he suggested or slip away quietly, leaving her to it. As he watched Eugenie turn and walk away from him towards her home, he allowed himself a smile. Things were going his way for a change and for that he was immensely pleased.

With every step towards her house Eugenie felt a little piece of her harden until she felt a great tightness in her chest like a freezing cold vice. That last little piece of the child she had once been disappeared forever with the hopes and dreams she had once had.

The polished letter box and door knocker gleamed even in the darkness as she reached her house; they represented glowing beacons that signified her entry to purgatory. She felt trepidation on entering. She had no inclination to see Randall and she felt despair over her situation. Despite her hard exterior she had shown to Ian, there was a part of her that felt apprehensive about her circumstances. How could Ian do this to her? This morning she had been full of hope for the future. She had thought that Ian would be as happy as she was; how could she have been so blind?

Placing her key in the lock, she opened the front door and stepped in to the dark, pokey hallway. She didn't even bother switching on the light, just made her way up the stairs to her bedroom, where she climbed onto her bed fully clothed. She did not have the energy to perform her nightly tasks, nor did she care for once. She lay back staring at the darkened ceiling, her hands unwittingly covering her stomach where her unborn baby lay sleeping.

Randall lay on his bed listening. He saw and heard a lot more than his mother gave him credit for. She really could be so dense at times. Of course he knew she was pregnant. She had been sick over the course of several mornings and had not had her monthly bleed. See, he was much more vigilant than she knew. It didn't surprise him to find out that his mother was a whore, just like the rest of them, just like the women in those filthy magazines. She had probably stripped off and opened herself up like them to Mr Pratchett and now she was paying the ultimate price, she'd got herself pregnant. Well to coin a phrase, she'd made her bed, now she could lie in it.

He listened intently to the sounds of the house as he lay on his bed, smiling to himself. In his mind he could clearly imagine what he would like to do to Mr Pratchett, what he had wanted to do to him for a very long time. The man was insufferable and Randall did not appreciate the way he looked at him, like he thought Randall was a bug to be squashed.

Randall knew all about squashing bugs. He wondered, not for the first time, what it would feel like to squash Ian Pratchett, to feel the life draining from his body, to watch as his eyes died alongside his beating heart. Randall smiled to himself. All good things come to those who wait, he thought to himself. Randall had a lot of patience and he could wait as long as it took.

Nevertheless, Randall was disappointed with his mother. He could remember a time when she had appeared to him to be like an angel. He could still remember how it felt to adore her, and to know how he had disappointed her time and time again. He had tried, tried so very hard to make her smile, be pleased with him, love him. He had even defended her honour when the bullies had proclaimed her a whore having sex with their school headmaster.

The irony was that it was all true. It hadn't taken him long to discover some truths and then he had gone out of his way to pursue the rest.

On going through her things, he had found letters from his grandmother, a woman he had never met. Those letters had proved very informative and had given Randall some insight into his mother's predicament. Clearly, she had asked time and again if she could come home, only to be told that 'Daddy will not hear of it and will not accept your child'. Was that the reason his mother disliked him so much, because without him she could have returned to the bosom of her family? Then he had come across her diary. It wasn't the kind of diary where entries went day by day, but more a collection of his mother's thoughts. There were certain admissions that jumped out at him: '*Randall is such a strange little boy*', '*why does he watch me like that?*', '*sometimes Randall frightens me*' and '*why do I not love something I carried for nine months?*' The last entry had burned into Randall's brain. His mother did not love him, and she never had. Deep down he knew she never had. She had tolerated the child she had brought into the world, possibly believing that at some point she could return to her home. Now he could see why she had treated him as she had. It had finally made sense. He had been born, that was reason enough for his mother to hate him.

He had started to watch her then, to follow her. She never knew he was there, never expected to see him and therefore he could blend into the background. He would follow her to Mr Pratchett's house. On occasion he could hear what was going on. He wasn't stupid. He had heard the boys talk about things as school; he had seen videos and pictures in books. Everything the bullies had proclaimed was true.

He was only ten years old and yet after the first time he discovered what his mother truly was, he had walked home in cloud of anger. His tiny body had vibrated with a rage that was indescribable. He felt so betrayed and wanted to direct that anger towards something. It was the first time he ever killed anything.

The kitten he encountered on his way home was small but friendly. She came to him quickly when he knelt down and called her over. With very little thought in his mind, he had picked up that cat and carried her all the way home. The satisfaction he got as he drowned that poor cat in the bath was immense. The pent-up anger and frustration he had felt dissipated in the instant he looked down at the cat's lifeless body and staring eyes. More than that, the ten-year-old felt something he had never felt in his young life before. Randall Goff had felt power.

The morning after the meeting with Ian, Eugenie sat at her table, peeling potatoes for the evening meal. Randall had left for school at his usual time. Eugenie had been awake all night, unable to sleep or shake the mental images from her mind. In truth, although she had deliberately hardened her heart to what was about to take place, she couldn't help but feel it was wrong. Was it her place to take a life away, no matter how small and insignificant that life might be at the moment? She wondered, for the umpteenth time whether she should just leave and move to another area completely, starting a new life with her baby. After all, it could be girl. She had always wanted a little girl. She could lie again. Tell people her husband had died. Who would know? Perhaps she could start a new life in some rural village where the way of life would be much more to her personal taste. The idea certainly had a sense of attraction and appeal, much more so than ridding herself of the tiny life that resided inside her.

Eugenie sighed miserably. There was only one thing stopping her and it had nothing to do with the new baby she carried. Randall would undoubtedly oppose any move she wanted to make. She would like nothing better than to leave Randall behind as well, but she had no idea what he would think about that idea. She had no idea what Randall thought about anything at all for that matter.

Placing her potatoes in a saucepan, covering them with water and putting the lid on top, Eugenie left them on the kitchen table for later on. For now, she had more important things to do. First thing at the top of that list was paying a visit to Ian. She had every intention of taking his money, whether to use it for the abortion or to start a new life for herself. Pulling on her jacket, she checked her appearance in the mirror above the mantelpiece. Not a hair out of place. Her skin was pale, yet flawless, her make-up applied carefully and perfectly, her lips painted ruby red to match her nails. Pregnancy certainly agreed with her, even so early on.

It was a fair walk across town to Ian's home. Usually to cross such a distance, she would take a bus, but today she decided to walk there and get a bus home. With one final glance at her reflection and satisfied by what she saw, Eugenie Goff left her house.

Standing outside the school gates, she felt trepidation for what she was about to do engulf her body. She had played out scenario after scenario in her head trying to think of exactly the right thing to say or how to react to what he would say. She knew she was a match for him intellectually but hoped her emotions would not betray her and turn her into a quivering wreck. Taking a deep breath, she pushed through the school gates and walked to the main reception.

The young woman sitting at the reception desk glared at Eugenie as she approached the desk. She reminded Eugenie of a powder puff, lots of backcombed blonde hair, pale white skin and startling glowing red lips. Her mouth was moving in a circular motion as she chewed gum and intermittently glanced at Eugenie before staring at her red talon nails.

"I'm here to see Mr Pratchett" her crisp tones giving an air of haughtiness that immediately rubbed the other woman up the wrong way.

"He ain't here." The young woman snapped back unhelpfully.

"Do you know where I might find him, it's very important." Eugenie tried to be pleasant but it was too late.

The young woman before her shrugged just as Mandy Jones, Deputy Headteacher entered the reception area.

Mandy Jones was somebody Eugenie had encountered previously when Randall had started at the school. She was a genuinely kind person who apparently really liked children. Eugenie could not fathom the notion herself, but was willing to acknowledge this was a vocation for some. She turned away from the unhelpful drudge who sat on reception and smiled at Mandy Jones.

Mandy smiled back, a natural reaction.

"Mrs Goff?" she was one of those people who remembered everybody's name.

"Hello Miss Jones. I was here to see Mr Pratchett." She caught the screwed-up features of powder puff out of the corner of her eye.

"I'm afraid he's taken a leave day today. He's going to leave us you know." Mandy genuinely looked upset at the concept. Eugenie nodded in commiseration.

"Yes, I had heard." She muttered.

"Is there something I can help you with? Is it about Randall?" Mandy Jones enquired. She waited politely as Eugenie smiled. The smile did not touch her eyes.

"It's quite alright." Eugenie was back to her aloof self. "I am sure I will be able to catch up with him at another time." She side stepped to the left of Mandy Jones and made towards the door.

"Well if you're sure?" The reception door had already swished closed on Mandy's words.

"That woman is so cold you could freeze ice on her arse." Powder puff commented to no-one in particular.

Mandy Jones felt a certain sympathy for the woman who had just left. In all her years as a teacher she was yet to encounter a child stranger than Randall Goff, or indeed to meet a parent so entirely emotionally divorced from her own child. Mandy felt that she had come across every scenario involved with the single parents, the challenges that they faced, the struggles their lives threw up, yet there was some element of truth in the statement that you could freeze ice on her "arse". Eugenie Goff clearly had emotional issues which she had projected on to her son with frightening ferocity. The strange little boy within their care created uneasiness with all his peers and yet it was easy to see where his learned behaviour had come from. Mandy Jones however, could only wonder what had happened to Eugenie Goff to make her so emotionally moribund that it had affected her only child so much.

Eugenie made her way to Ian's home. The house that was situated within the grounds of the school was a small dwelling much too large for the headmaster by himself, more intended for a family. A small garden was enclosed with a picket fence. Eugenie made her way through the gate and approached the front door with trepidation. She rang the doorbell twice in quick succession.

Ian opened the door wearing his trousers and a vest underneath his shirt which was unbuttoned. A five o'clock shadow adorned his face and chin, his hair was unstyled and hanging loose. Eugenie realised she had never seen him like this. Although their assignations over the last five years were many, he had never actually stayed the night in her house and therefore she had never seen him the following morning. To say his appearance came as something as a shock to her was an understatement. She was completely thrown into disarray. She must have been standing with her mouth hanging open because Ian immediately started buttoning his shirt and tucking it in, while he stood back to allow her entrance to his home.

Eugenie had enjoyed visiting Ian's home in the past. It was clearly designed with a family in mind – a spacious kitchen, with separate parlour and dining room. There were two bedrooms upstairs and a bathroom. There was neat little garden at the back of the house and a tiny lawned area to the front. Ian was fond of growing his own vegetables in the sunny patch at the back of the house and as Eugenie made her way through to the kitchen, she could see the tendrils of his runner beans weaving their way up the poles Ian had erected.

The house was really was too big for a single man on his own and Eugenie had often thought that Ian might eventually ask her to marry him and that she would live there. Another of her little dreams that had been unceremoniously trampled over, and another nail in Ian's coffin as far as their relationship was concerned.

The little house belonged to the school and was based just outside the school grounds, although adjoining the property. The playground usually echoed with the sounds of children's voices, but was silent at the moment because the children were in lessons.

Ian had to admit, Eugenie was a fine-looking woman. Even despite their argument the previous evening, Ian was not averse to the idea of taking her to bed right at this moment, although he doubted Eugenie would be happy to agree. She had an air of haughtiness that he found extremely attractive. It carried an essence of untouchability that had first attracted him to her. She was a lady of breeding – that had always been clear.

At first the circumstances surrounding her demise to this corner of the world had been unknown to him and he could only surmise that she had married beneath her and then her husband had died. At least that was what the gossip-mongers were spreading. She had a cool, classy exterior that presented itself as a challenge and he tried where others had failed miserably, to get beneath her skin. The challenge had been fun and when finally, she became his, she had been a wildcat who kept him on his toes. He had enjoyed their relationship thus far. Now he could see her becoming a drone and he was too much of a young man about town to be tied down, especially with a wife and baby in tow.

"I haven't had a chance to get to the bank yet, Eugenie." Ian followed her through to the kitchen; he knew what she had come for. "I've been busy packing up the house. The new headmaster is due to move in shortly, you know end of term and all that, he wants to move in and get his family settled."

Eugenie turned to him and gave him a divine smile. She knew then that Ian had been planning this for months. The realisation that Ian had perhaps given his notice the term before was like a punch in the gut. How could she not have realised? For the last couple of months, he had been using her, stringing her along. She knew if she had any sense, she should be demanding far more money than she had already asked for. She also knew how much his reputation meant to him. She could easily disparage that but in doing so would also disparage her own. Eugenie was much too proud to do that. Despite the fact of what people thought about her, there was still a semblance of dignity from her former life that filled her with an air that she was far more important and superior than her peers. To admit that she was an unmarried, single parent was just not done, even though each and every neighbour she had was well aware of that fact.

"Not to worry, we'll go to bank together." She waved her hand regally at him ignoring the farce between them. "If you would pull yourself together and get ready." She continued.

"Er, look, Eugenie... " Ian began, "Today is not a very good day for me, perhaps you could come back tomorrow and we could sort it out then."

"NO." Her voice was pure ice, broking no opposition. Ian stopped short, breaking off anything he was about to say. Eugenie smiled serenely at him at once again and instantly he was reminded of Randall. There were definite resemblances between mother and son. "Perhaps you misunderstood me, Ian. I want this matter dealt with as soon as possible. I am not prepared to wait until tomorrow so that you can skip town without giving me a penny. I realise that I am not destined to mean anything more to you than a plaything you can pick up and put down at your heart's content. Use me and then walk away when you've had enough."

Ian looked warily at her. The mild-mannered Eugenie Goff was hiding somewhere and had been replaced by this formidable woman before him. He swallowed reflexively, knowing that she would not leave until she got what she came for. However, if nothing but resourceful, Ian was willing to try. "But you can see, I'm not fit to go anywhere at the moment."

Eugenie stepped up to the man she had loved for the last four years, feeling nothing but contempt for him now. "Pathetic little worm. You listen to me. You will get ready and go the bank. I will come with you. You will furnish me with two thousand pounds and I will be on my way."

"Two thousand quid? You must be out of your mind." Ian wanted to shove her out of his way.

"A small price to pay to have me out of your life forever," Eugenie stated flatly.

He eyed her warily, wondering what was going on in her pretty head. "And if I don't give it to you?" Only one way to test the waters.

Eugenie laughed in a carefree way as she walked around the kitchen table, trailing her fingers across its surface, before stopping and coming to face Ian on the other side. "My dear Ian, if you don't give me what I want, I can absolutely guarantee that you will never work again, either here or in Scotland, at least not in the profession you have chosen. I will make it my own personal crusade to publicly humiliate you and ensure that everybody knows what kind of predicament you have left me in. I am sure that this new school with so prestigious a reputation will be only too glad to find another gentleman to fill the position and when I say gentleman, I mean it in the loosest terms when referring to you." The smile she gave him was so beatific, it was hard for him to comprehend that he had heard the words she had just uttered.

"You wouldn't dare." He spluttered with righteous indignation. "To disparage my reputation would be to disparage your own." Ian felt trapped. He had thought to put fifty pounds in an envelope and pop it through Eugenie's door on his way to the station. He was planning to leave on Sunday evening, taking his train to Scotland to be ready to start his new job for the start of the Autumn term.

Eugenie simply shrugged. "I have nothing more to lose," she stated simply. He knew she was right. People had gossiped about Eugenie Goff for years and yet nobody had quite worked her out. She never told her story and she let people make up their own minds. If it came out, nobody would be surprised, however it could be seriously detrimental to his plans.

The school at which he was planning to work had a very strict moral code. It was the reason they had requested a single man for the job. In fact, Brightcross had very few female teachers at all. It was a completely male-dominated arena and Ian had no doubt that the principal governors who had selected him for the job would be appalled by the fact that he was leaving behind a woman he had bedded for four years, subsequently had got pregnant and was now her leaving behind, unmarried and a single parent. Not exactly the moral code they would want presented to the future gentleman residing in their establishment. Eugenie had him by the short and curlies, so to speak, and although he had to admire her tenacity, he didn't like it one bit.

"If I agree to give you the money, do I have your word that you will never bother me again, whether you plan to keep this baby or not?"

"Ian, once you give me this money, you are dead to me," Eugenie replied coldly. Ian nodded and swallowed once more.

"Give me five minutes to make myself presentable."

"Take your time."

Eugenie pulled out a chair from under the table, smoothed a hand over her skirt and sat down, crossing her legs before her. Ian watched her perform the little ritual he had seen a hundred times before. He couldn't help feeling a certain amount of admiration for Eugenie, even though he was seething with anger that she had obtained the upper hand. In truth he was arrogant enough to think that he had held all the cards, but now he could see that he had been outwitted on this one and although it killed him to hand any money over to her, he was prepared to do it in order to save his own skin. This job was his new start and at thirty-five, new starts were hard to come by. He turned and made his way upstairs to make himself presentable at the bank.

Two hours later, Eugenie Goff placed her saucepan of potatoes on the stove. She was pleased with herself today. She had managed to extract two thousand pounds from Ian successfully and it now sat rolled up carefully and stashed in one of her shoes where no-one would find it. In all honesty, she had been worried that Ian would never go for the blackmail – that he would call her bluff and she would be forced to give up. Now she was two thousand pounds richer and could begin planning her new life. The more she thought about her options, the more excited she became. There was only one problem on the horizon as far as she could see and that was Randall.

Like clockwork, her son entered the house as if thinking about him conjured him up. He dutifully removed his boots by the front door and sauntered into the kitchen.

"Hello, Randall." His mother paused in her cooking to look up at her son. He stared at her, unsmiling, black eyes watching her intently. The familiar sense of unease filled the base of her stomach.

"Hello, Mother," he responded. There was no affection and barely any intonation in his speech at all.

"Dinner will be ready in about half an hour if you'd like to get yourself washed," she said pleasantly, belying any of the true feelings swimming around her at that moment. Randall grunted and left the kitchen, making his way upstairs. Eugenie's hand fluttered to her heart for a moment. She would be lying if she said she wasn't truly afraid of Randall these days. It was something that had grown over the years. Where most mothers' love increased for their children, Eugenie found instead that she felt more uneasy, more genuinely afraid of her only child. And yet if anyone was to ask her what she was so afraid of, she wouldn't be able to explain it exactly. There were no words to describe her feelings towards Randall. How would one describe an innate sense of foreboding every time he was around, or the fact that the way he looked at her sent chills of trepidation down her spine? Even to rationalise it to herself, it sounded absurd.

They ate their meal in near silence. Eugenie found that despite her earlier triumph during the day, she had no appetite. She pushed the food around her plate despondently.

"What's wrong, Mother?" Randall suddenly spoke, breaking her reverie. She glanced up at him, taken by surprise. Rarely did he say more than a few words on any given day. They did not have the kind of relationship where each of them was interested in the other.

Eugenie felt she had little choice except to share something with Randall. "Mr Pratchett and I are no longer seeing each other," she confirmed in a dignified manner. Randall watched her with his unblinking stare and she felt the hairs prickle on the back of her neck. "Although, really it is probably for the best. He has a new job in Scotland and I don't think you or I would like to move that far away." There had been no need to say more, but anything she could do to disarm that unnerving, unflinching way he had of watching her, made her feel slightly better and braver. Randall continued to look at her for a few more seconds before returning to eat his meal. Eugenie felt her breath release slowly. She hadn't even noticed that she had been holding it. What was it about Randall?

Eugenie set about clearing the table once her son had removed himself from her presence. He was now upstairs out of her way and she could breathe easy once again. She still had no idea how to broach the subject of being pregnant with Randall, nor what she intended to do about it.

CHAPTER FOURTEEN

NOW: 2ND OCTOBER

Ginny stared at the three images on the whiteboard.

So far it was blatantly obvious that the three women's lives lost so far were exact replica copycat killings of the original Ripper in 1888, even so far as the dates they were murdered. The only palpable difference was in relation to the names, ages and professions. The women were not related and had nothing in common, no friends, family or acquaintances. So far, every avenue of enquiry was leading to a dead end and it was becoming increasingly frustrating for those involved.

Since the only lead was in relation to the Ripper's original killings, they were pursuing this line in the investigation, starting with the next two alleged possible victims, namely Catherine Eddows and Mary Kelly. The search results so far had been exhausting since they knew they were looking for possible variations to the names as well as the original. The name Mary Kelly by itself had returned thousands of women, all potential victims. The connotations were so far exceeding their given resources, a fact that the entire team was aware of, however Ginny was of the opinion that given the location of the murders so far, this was a local boy and therefore the net of their search was considerably smaller.

So far, they had victims aged sixteen, twenty-five and thirty-nine. It was a far flung idea that he had chosen each victim by their age, but the ages didn't match anything about the original victims. The only exact replica was the way in which he killed each woman, even down to the way the bodies were displayed. They now knew that nothing about the murder scene was random. And still they had no idea who the perpetrator was. He had left virtually no DNA at the sites. He had been wearing gloves and a condom. He had come into close contact with each of his victims, yet none of the fibres found at any of the scenes had matched anything except generic types of clothing that could be brought anywhere. Any suspicion of other DNA found at the scene matched nothing on the country database suggesting that their perpetrator had not been arrested and was unknown to them. There was no DNA under any of the victims fingernails. There was no evidence that any of them had put up a fight, which meant that he was either known to them, or he simply took them by surprise. They had the option of course of stretching their net wider. Interpol were always happy to provide information, but Ginny had the feeling that their killer was of the homegrown kind. The other option at this stage was requesting people to attend for volunteer DNA testing, but again Ginny had the idea that their man would not be very forthcoming with his sample. That wasn't to mention the cost implication involved which she doubted she would receive an agreement from senior management at this point. However, it was something to consider taking to David Stroud. His influence would undoubtedly prove far more fruitful than her own at the moment.

What was far more vexing however, was that the entire team had been unable to ascertain a lead as to how he was tracking his victims and finding out their movements. It had been suggested that perhaps he was using social media as a point of contact, but each of the women's media pages had been explored with a fine-tooth comb and so far, nothing untoward had been uncovered. They were still exhausting their lines of enquiry in this, trying to locate the friends of each victim, but again there were no similarities. For the most part you had to be a friend to gain access to their pages. If he was 'a friend' he wasn't using the same name. But again, with hundreds of people to go through, they were getting nowhere fast.

Again, there were no links or common friends to suggest that the women somehow were related through a known associate. The IT bods had been unable to uncover any significant leads from the women's emails or social media chats to suggest that they had been contacted by anyone they didn't actually know. Yet again, another dead end.

Ginny took the pen she was chewing pensively out of her mouth and dropped it on the desk she was perched on, a frustrated sigh escaping her lips. She turned to look for Pat who was busy going over information with Steve King and Mark Gregson.

"Got anything?" she enquired hopefully. Three pairs of eyes met her balefully and she knew they were no farther forward in the case. Ginny's heart sailed to her boots. They all needed a result on this and fast. *SHE* needed a result.

Francine Blackman came racing through the double doors at that moment. The constable of the team and the youngest was turning out to be an asset. Similar in stature and looks to Ginny, she portrayed a similar colour blond hair which she kept in a dignified, neat bun at the nape of her neck. "Ma'am." She was out of breath, clearly having run practically the length of the station.

"What is it?" Ginny hoped beyond hope that it was good news for a change.

"You have a package," Francine replied.

"A package… " Ginny had no idea what the girl was going on about.

"It's a kidney," Francine spat, horrified. The entire incident room fell silent, all attention on the breathless young woman.

"A human kidney?" Mark questioned, his face paling considerably.

Ginny looked towards him. "Mark?"

"The original Ripper took a kidney from his fourth victim and sent it to the press, I think with a note."

"We don't have a fourth victim," Ginny almost whispered. Her stomach flip-flopped uncomfortably and she could feel her senses begin to whir. If this gift was of the human kind, they were undoubtedly looking for victim number four, or possibly more. So far Mark's information and knowledge on the Ripper had proved invaluable. He had provided them with details about the murders that were uncanny in their preciseness, so that they knew they were looking for a copycat. "Where is it?" Ginny asked Francine.

"Downstairs. One of the admin girls opened it. They've left it where it is for now and the path lab have been called."

Ginny nodded. "Yes, we need to know if it's human. Our boy could be toying with us, but I doubt it. Lead the way, Fran."

The kidney was nondescript. Looking at it, Ginny could not tell if it was from a human or animal. It was wrapped neatly in a sandwich bag. The note that had been found in with the package had been placed in an evidence bag.

"Did anyone touch this?" Ginny asked, hoping that the perp had been stupid enough to leave a fingerprint.

The young admin woman who had been unlucky enough to open the package lifted her hand reluctantly. "Just on the corner," she squeaked as Ginny glared at her.

"What does it say?" Pat leaned over Ginny's shoulder. "Oh my God, is that blood?"

The letter was written in red, which had the resemblance of blood, however they would need to get that ascertained by the lab as soon as possible.

"It says… **I send you half the kidney I took from one woman and preserved it for you, the other piece I fried and ate, it was very nice. I may send you the bloody knife that took it out if you only wait a while longer**," Ginny read aloud.

"He ate it." Pat had paled visibly. "What kind of sick fucking bastard are we dealing with here?"

CHAPTER FIFTEEN

NOW: 2ND OCTOBER

Charles Eddowin was picking up his boys from their trip away. They clambered off the coach in a bluster of non-stop chatter and excitement, running to their father as soon as they spotted him and throwing their arms around him to a collective, "Where's Mum?"

This was the part he had dreaded since he had left Katherine two nights ago. He was surprised that he hadn't heard from her at all. No texts or calls. It had been total silence all around.

Katherine knew he was picking up the boys today; that had been their arrangement all along. She would drop them off, he would pick them up. The fact that he hadn't even heard from Katherine regarding that had him thinking that she had probably spent every waking moment in a drunken stupor since he left. In all honesty he was worried about taking the boys home straight away. He thought he might take them for a McDonalds first.

One thing he knew about Katherine was that she loved her boys and was extremely protective of them. If he didn't turn up at the appropriate time, she would be undoubtedly be on the phone and at least he could ascertain how she was. If she was drinking and far from sober, he would keep the boys with him for the night. He had the feeling that this would be something that might happen more and more.

The boys were more than happy to go to McDonalds. Mum didn't let them, she said it wasn't proper food and therefore when they did get to go, it was considered a real treat.

While Charles waited for his children to eat their meal, he checked his phone. Still no calls or texts. He decided to ring Martha, to get an indication of how things were. He really didn't feel like taking his boys back to Katherine if she was paralytic and he also didn't feel like having an argument, which would undoubtedly happen if she was drunk and he refused to return the boys to her.

"Hello, Charlie." Martha's bright voice shrilled down the phone, making him visibly wince. He hated to be called Charlie and she knew it.

"Er, hello, Martha. I erm... I was just wondering if you had heard from Katherine at all?" He had stood up and moved away from the table where the boys were sitting eating, so that they wouldn't overhear his conversation. His eyes strayed back to them momentarily, gratified to find they were paying him no attention at all, absorbed in their Happy Meal toys.

"No, darling, I haven't. She's refusing to answer my calls and texts. It's really quite rude and I took her flowers. I thought she had forgiven me."

"Forgiven you?" Charles echoed.

Martha sighed dramatically down the phone. "Well of course you wouldn't know, you walked out of the family home." Martha's sarcasm had Charles biting back the retort that threatened to pop out that it was none of her damn business, but she was already rambling on. "We had a little falling out, it was nothing, you know Kathy and I, we've been friends for so long, we're practically related. But I am rather miffed that she's not answered me at all. We're supposed to be arranging the church flower show, don't you know?"

Charles frowned. Now he was a little worried if he was honest. Katherine might have ignored him, thinking in some warped way it might teach him a lesson, but as Martha truthfully stated, they had been friends for such a long time, nothing came between them. "Er, Martha," he interrupted her constant babbling about some inane matter at the church. "I wonder if I might trouble you for a favour?"

"Of course, darling, what is it?"

"I wonder if I could drop the boys to you for an hour or so, just so I can pop home and check on Katherine." The silence was deafening at the other end.

"What's happened, Charles?" Martha's voice was suddenly serious; her tone held an element of concern.

"Hopefully nothing, but I haven't heard from Katherine for a couple of days and if you haven't, I have to admit I'm a little concerned. I just hope she hasn't done anything silly."

"Silly?" Martha echoed. "You mean… "

Charles interrupted, "She was drunk and upset when I left her. She might have fallen down, hurt herself, anything. I would just like to go and check."

"Do you think she might have hurt herself on purpose?"

"No, no of course not." Charles sounded much more confident than he felt in that moment. "I would rather just make sure she's okay before I take the boys home."

"In that case I'm coming with you. We'll leave the boys with Henry," she instructed. Much as Martha irritated the life out of him, he had to admit he would be quite glad to have the company. Either way, if Katherine was drunk and disorderly at least Martha might be able to get through to her; he would present like the proverbial red rag to a bull.

With the boys left with a chagrined Henry, who already looked frazzled having his own two boys home as well, Martha and Charles drove over to Katherine's house. As they pulled into the drive, Charles noted that the curtains were still closed despite it being the middle of the day. This already did not bode well.

Charles and Martha got out of the car. He walked to the front door, Martha slightly lagging behind.

"The curtains are still closed," Martha commented absently. He didn't bother to acknowledge the comment, having already noted the same thing himself.

Charles used his key to open the lock and pushed open the front door. The hallway was dark, all the blinds and curtains seemed to be closed and there seemed to be an unearthly, deathly silence. There was uncollected post on the doormat.

"Katherine?" Martha called, pushing past Charles to step in front of him. Charles noted that her voice shook slightly. He glanced towards her; she carried a frown and he had an idea that his face displayed a similar look of worry. This was so unlike Katherine. Martha turned to look at Charles. "Do you think she could be upstairs?" she whispered, her eyes moving to look towards the stairs.

"There's no need to whisper, Martha." Charles took a step further into the hallway. "KATHERINE... " he shouted. There was no reply. Just the silence that greeted them.

"It doesn't even seem as if there's anyone home," Martha acknowledged. "It's so quiet."

"I suppose it makes sense to check upstairs first." Charles took a step towards the stairs. When Martha didn't move he turned back to her. "Aren't you coming?" he questioned, placing a foot on the first step. It seemed like neither of them really wanted to go in search of Katherine.

"Maybe I'll just check the living room," Martha replied weakly. She had a very bad feeling about this suddenly. What if Katherine *had* done something silly, had taken an overdose and choked on her own vomit, or was hanging somewhere, nasty stains and excrement running down her legs, her eyeballs and tongue bulging? Martha swallowed hard at the mental picture she conjured up. Not that she had ever seen anyone who had hanged themselves or taken an overdose. She really knew nothing of what to expect on that front except what she had read or seen on TV. She watched Charles disappear up the stairs and then turned once again to the closed doors before her. Her brain was telling her to do something, to open one of the closed doors before her, but she was rooted to the spot. She didn't want to move on account of what she might find.

She could hear doors being opened and closed upstairs as Charles made his way through the bedrooms. He was back down the stairs in a matter of minutes.

"She's not up there," he stated, reaching the bottom of the staircase. As if she wasn't even there, he strode past Martha and opened the living room door. She could see the room was in semi-darkness from the curtains being closed, but she could also see no hanging bodies, no best friend who had choked on her own vomit.

Charles spun away from the living room and moved towards the kitchen. This time Martha trotted behind him, feeling slightly more confident at not finding anything. Perhaps Katherine had gone out or something.

Neither Charles nor Martha were prepared for the scene that confronted them as Charles opened the kitchen door. Before the horror of the grisly scene before them could even register in either of their minds, Martha passed out cold, her body dropping like a stone beside him. At precisely the same time Charles Eddowin jammed his fist into his mouth. If someone had asked him in that moment why he did that, he would have said to stop himself screaming. Unfortunately for Charles Eddowin, that failed miserably.

Ginny stood in the kitchen in the home of Katherine Eddowin, staring down the mutilated corpse of the woman it once was. On her feet she wore forensic booties to cover her shoes so that she could move around freely. It was a difficult job to step between splashes of blood and other markers that the forensic team had left indicating that a source of evidence lay in that spot. The body was currently in the process of being photographed. The forensic team were spread out across the house, although initially, it seemed as though most of the activity had taken place in the kitchen.

Katherine Eddowin's body was by far the worst so far and seemingly the work of the same person who murdered Mary Nicholls, Anna Chapman and Lizzy Stroud.

As predicted by Mark, Ginny had expected a fourth victim, but was hoping that as they had got through the rest of that dreadful day on the thirtieth of September that perhaps they were mistaken and that the killer would not strike again, at least not then. The team had entered a honeymoon period of expecting another body at some point but for the past couple of days the investigation had continued, with Ginny feeling much more at ease as each day passed with no further reports of a murder. The fact that a kidney had been delivered to the station had dashed that hope somewhat and now that the pathology lab had confirmed that it was indeed a human kidney, Ginny's hopes of another body not materialising had been dwindling at an alarming rate.

It has been the who and when that had eluded them so far, but now they were confronted with their worst fear.

Although it had yet to be confirmed by the pathologist that Katherine Eddowin had been dead for two days, the fact that Jack the Ripper had killed two victims on same day and that their killer seemed to be mimicking the murders in an uncanny exactness suggested that Katherine Eddowin had indeed been killed on the same day as Lizzy Stroud. This confirmed in Ginny's mind that the killer they were looking for was a delusional monster who thought he could imitate one of the most notorious killers in history, or that this was just the beginning of a killing spree that would go on and on.

Whenever Katherine had been killed, one thing for certain was that her corpse was no longer fresh. The body, in the warmth of the house, had started to putrefy, the particular stench of the dead starting to fill the air with the sweet, sickly aroma that had you gagging and in truth the smell was already quite overwhelming.

Katherine Eddowin lay flat on her back, her arms down by her side. Her eyes were open, staring sightlessly into nothing.

Her belly had been cut open, her intestines being pulled from her body and stretched out, reaching up to her right shoulder, the same as Anna Chapman's corpse. A piece of her intestine had been cut away and was lying between her body and her left arm. Her face had been mutilated and was a mask of blood, obviously having been cut open in several places across her nose and cheeks. Part of the bone was visible and her nose appeared to be completely missing. Her throat had been cut – again, to the bone. Her abdomen had been ripped open, from which her internal organs were clearly visible. The pathology lab would have to confirm if any of her internal organs were missing. To Ginny it looked like a bloody mess. There were further cuts in her groin and her thighs. The dressing gown that she still wore hung about her body. It had been pulled open but as it was towelling, it had absorbed a considerable amount of blood, turning it from white to a deep darkish black in places while pink in others. The extent of her injuries was vast and it was difficult to tell at this juncture what had been the cause of death. Everywhere you looked was covered in blood. It had been splashed about the kitchen like art and to top it off on the kitchen wall, written in blood was the iconic phrase '*the juwes are the men that will not be blamed for nothing*'.

Ginny made her way out of the kitchen. Quite frankly she had seen enough.

Pat was standing by the staircase where Charles Eddowin sat, his head in his hands. He had been particularly distressed but had managed to call the police. Martha Davies however, had been taken to hospital, beyond all coherent speech once she had been revived from a dead faint and had then become quite hysterical. Fortunately, the forensic doctor on site had administered an injection to calm her down prior to her being moved to hospital.

Ginny approached Pat and Charles Eddowin now. Charles was speaking in barely a whisper.

"I had left her, you see," he was explaining quietly.

"So, she was at home alone? For how long?" Pat asked, his eyes meeting Ginny's above Charles Eddowin's head. All she could think was that he had the same look as she currently felt; they were all exhausted from the relentlessness of the murders and still they had no prime suspect. She already had a meeting with DSI Sparkes this afternoon and in light of the murder of Katherine Eddowin, she had no doubt that she would receive her marching orders by being taken off the case. It wasn't what she wanted. It was like a vendetta now. She wanted, no… she needed to find out who the murderer was so that she could bring the bastard to justice and ensure he was put away for the rest of his natural life.

Charles Eddowin looked up at Ginny. Ginny didn't think she had never seen anyone truly shocked in her life, but as Charles Eddowin looked back at her she was struck at how empty he looked. He was a wrecked shell of a man, his eyes bloodshot from crying, his face beyond a paleness that she had seen on a human being previously. He looked like he was hanging on by a thread.

"Mr Eddowin, I'm Detective Inspector Virginia Percy; I'm the lead investigator in this case." She held out her hand and he shook it weakly, holding just two of her fingers for a moment before letting go. She was surprised he managed that much in view of the circumstances.

"Seems Mr Eddowin left the family home a few days ago," Pat informed her helpfully. "Mrs Eddowin was home alone."

"Mr Eddowin." Ginny turned her attention once more to the devastated husband. "Do you recall Katherine saying that she felt unsafe, like she was being watched at any time?"

He seemed to ponder that thought for a moment, then shook his head. "No nothing like that at all. Katherine was always so busy, either with the boys… " His voice trailed off and his eyes filled with unshed tears again. "Sorry." He apologised quickly, wiping away at his eyes. "I just don't know how I'm going to tell my children or what I'm going to tell them."

"I understand," Ginny said simply. What else could she do? "Where are you going to stay?"

"At my mother's. I've rung her. She's already picked the boys up from Henry." He rattled off the address and Pat wrote it down.

"Henry?" Ginny asked.

Charles tapped his forehead with the palm of his hand. "Sorry, Henry Davies, Martha's husband," he finished.

"Katherine's best friend," Pat offered and Ginny nodded.

"They've been friends since they were at school together. If anyone would know whether Katherine felt like she was being watched at all, it would be Martha. They told each other everything," Charles concluded sadly. Carefully, like he was worried his legs wouldn't hold him up, he stood up from where he was sitting on the stairs. Pat took a step back. "I think I should be with my boys now. You have the address if you need me and my phone number." The defeat in his voice was obvious.

"We'll be in touch, Mr Eddowin, we may need to ask you further questions," Ginny told him softly. Charles Eddowin nodded.

Ginny and Pat watched as he made his way to the front door. He studiously made no attempt to look back towards the kitchen, his head down and Ginny suddenly knew what a 'hangdog' expression meant.

CHAPTER SIXTEEN

NOW

Ginny sat before DSI Sparkes, having filled him in on the 'story' so far. He looked as incredulous as she felt on discovering that they had a fourth body and were no further ahead with arresting anybody for the heinous crimes that had been committed.

"I'm sure I don't need to tell you that your days are numbered, Ginny." The fact that he had used her first name and indeed shortened it like everyone else spoke volumes. "Your replacement is currently being sought as we speak. I would expect that you will be demoted or taken off the case altogether, although what you have found out so far could be invaluable so you might be kept on, depends on the person taking over I suppose."

"Yes, sir." What else could she say?

"What's the story with Marcus Nicholls? You had him in custody."

"Not enough evidence. He had a cast iron alibi from his girlfriend in the South of France, plus we were unable to find any records that he had travelled from there to have been able to come back to the UK and return to France again."

"You don't think he could have hired somebody to do it?"

"It crossed my mind, but the death was too messy. Hits tend to be clean and fatal immediately. This killer likes to mutilate his victims, plus we could find no connection between Marcus Nicholls and the other victims."

DSI Sparkes nodded as though he agreed. "Well you have a couple of days or so I would say. Keep going, see if you can't turn something up in the meantime." She nodded at the dismissal and got up from her chair. "I'm sorry it has come to this," DSI Sparkes said as she reached the door.

She turned back towards him. "Sir?"

"We had high hopes for you," he finished before turning back to whatever paperwork was on his desk. She was dismissed.

High hopes indeed, she thought nastily. That wasn't the impression she had had on previous occasions. The rumour on the street was that she had only got the job because her father was high up and had connections. The old boys in the network were probably clapping their hands together and slapping each other's backs on the fact that they were so clever and had been right about poor Virginia Percy all along.

Ginny went into the incident room where she received commiserating looks from her colleagues. They knew her days were numbered as well as she did.

She made her way over to the whiteboard, where four women's faces now resided alongside written details about the case. If only she could have an epiphany and find some way of cracking the case. She was desperate to find out who did it and she wanted to bring the perpetrator to justice herself, not have someone step in last-minute-dot-com and take the glory. She almost felt like crying, but wouldn't give the rest of the incident room the satisfaction of seeing her fall apart. She had no doubt the Supe had spies in her midst, watching every move she made.

Pat appeared at her side. He always seemed to know when she needed him. "How you doing?" he whispered. She shook her head, unable to speak at that moment, her eyes filling with unshed tears. "You can do this, Gin. We all have faith in you. All we need is one good clue, one piece of evidence and we'll have this bastard." She looked up at him then. He had been her best friend since they were ten years old. Ever since she could remember he had had her back, never failing, never faltering. They had both chosen the same line of work and even then, their friendship had endured, no rivalry or animosity even when Ginny's career had overtaken Pat's. He had chosen to remain by her side, in her shadow despite the fact he was an exceptional police officer in his own right and could have gone on to mirror her own career somewhere else.

"I need to go and see Melanie Watson. I asked for a rush to be put on the autopsy for Katherine Eddowin. Let's go and see if the formidable Ms Watson can provide us with that clue, shall we?"

"And she's back in the room." Pat chuckled flippantly. Ginny punched him in the arm playfully.

Melanie Watson sat reading through her final versions of the autopsy report for Katherine Eddowin. She had to admit, never had she encountered anything so gruesome in her life. She was used to dealing with the occasional unexpected death, the odd murder, usually a spouse that had had enough of their partner. The murdered body of the sixteen-year-old Lizzy Stroud had undoubtedly confirmed her first thoughts of a copycat killer on the lose and one with penchant for Jack the Ripper murders. Whoever the killer was he had clearly researched every detail of the murdered women back in the eighteen hundred's and had done his uppermost to copycat those killings in the finest detail.

And so far he was evading every possible angle the police were covering.

She had read the police reports from the scenes. What the killer had done took time… privacy.

The body had been brought in for Lizzy Stroud, not as mutilated as the first two victims. He had acted like he was interrupted as the original Jack had been. He had not sexually assaulted the victim and Melanie wondered if this was because of her age. Was she picked for this particular purpose, to be killed but not raped? So far he had seriously sexually assaulted both Mary, Anna and Katherine. Did this mean their killer had some kind of conscience? He was clearly a sociopath on every other level. You didn't need to be a psychologist to know that.

In order to check her theories, she had downloaded the autopsy reports of the Ripper's original victims. Not only was the killer murdering his victims in exactly the same way as Jack the Ripper had over a hundred years ago, he was even emulating the way the bodies were positioned when they were found.

She had shared her theory with DCI Percy who hadn't seemed at all surprised and it shouldn't have been a disappointment to her that the police were already aware of the fact that the murders were copycat killings, except it was.

It was now the third of October and although it had originally looked as if the killer had failed to create two bodies in one day, it now was startlingly apparent that he had in fact murdered two victims. The shocking reality of reading the way Catherine Eddowes had been murdered compared to what lay on her lab table had been a rude awakening. Katherine Eddowin had been mutilated almost beyond recognition. Even aside from the brutality of a copycat murder, the killer had gone out of his way to mutilate his victims with a desire of relish that was both frightening and shocking.

The stark reality that hit home even more was the fact that if the killer was enacting the way the history books told it, there was to be another body yet, that of Mary Kelly. Perhaps the most infamous of the Ripper victims, her name synonymous with the unparalleled brutality of the murder that took place in Whitechapel on 9th November 1888.

She had already tapped the name Mary Kelly into her computer and discovered hundreds of pages returned in the search engine that there was no way of knowing where to start.

Even on social media, the story was the same. The phrase "needle in a haystack" came to mind immediately. How were the police to protect or alert anyone of that given name or indeed any variation since the killer seemed to like to keep them on their toes?

She didn't really know what she was hoping to achieve, maybe inbox a couple of people, tell them to be extra vigilant. She could inbox all the people named Mary Kelly in the UK but that would clearly create some kind of panic, Something she was sure the police were hoping to avoid.

Melanie was expecting Detective Inspector Virginia Percy and her colleague at any moment to give her report on the latest murder victim. She had been asked to rush it through and despite having several other cases to work on, Melanie had done as she was asked. She had to admit, this case was intriguing her more than any other had.

Melanie scrolled through the photographs on her computer, hoping for some kind of divine inspiration on how the killer might have picked his next victim. Who among these women would he be likely to choose, or had he chosen already? Was there a similarity in looks? She decided to do some more research on Mary Kelly, the original Ripper victim to see what she could find out. If the killer was something of an expert on the Ripper murders, then perhaps what was needed was for somebody to follow in his footsteps.

Melanie felt a cold hand of fear shimmer down her spine. This person had so far managed to avoid detection by the police. He executed his victims and he did it precisely. That took time and planning. Yet even she was aware that no murder was perfect.

Melanie tapped in the name Mary Nicholls in to her social media page and waited for the results. As she looked at the faces that appeared on her screen, she picked out the killer's first victim with ease. Tapping on to her image, she attempted to move forward on to the woman's profile only to discover it had been blocked. She was losing patience. There was no way to possibly find out any details about Mary Nicholls other than what her name was and what she looked like. She could have gleaned that much off the news.

If Melanie Watson had known that she was being watched, she may have left well alone, but like all the victims so far, none of them had a clue.

Ginny and Pat arrived at the pathologist's office an hour later for the post-mortem report on Katherine Eddowin. It was a visit that had been paid three times previously in the last month. Apart from confirming how the victim died, Ginny thought that there would be little new information to glean. They already knew that it was likely to be the same killer who had committed all the other murders, a fact that was confirmed when they finally sat down in Melanie Watson's office.

Pat was slightly enamoured with Melanie Watson and Ginny picked up on this almost immediately. She had of course teased him mercilessly since their first meeting about a month ago.

Her long legs were encased in skinny blue jeans, slung low on her slim hips together with a white polo shirt. She wore a black suede jacket over the top and black boots to complete the outfit.

Melanie Watson was an enigma to be sure. An intelligent, successful woman housed in a body to die for and a face to envy, yet she carried herself with a surly and brusque demeanour that could almost border on unnecessarily impolite on occasions. There were no preliminaries, no pleasantries – Melanie Watson opened her file and began reading the contents to the two detectives before her.

"I'd say she had been dead for at least two days, although with the putrefaction of the body, it's hard to pinpoint exactly. Since the belief is that we have a copycat killer on our hands, I would deem that she was murdered on the thirtieth of September. Rigor mortis had left the body fortunately.

"The cause of death is almost certainly the large gash to her throat which caused a haemorrhage from the left carotid artery. She died almost immediately and the rest of her injuries were inflicted after death. Her larynx was severed as were her vocal chords. Her abdomen had been opened from her breast bone to the pubic area. The incision was made upwards. Her liver had been stabbed with a further incision vertically. A horizontal cut spanned around the abdomen as if he had tried to remove her belly button which left behind a flap of skin. The incision continued to the right and went down the right side of the vagina and rectum and for half an inch behind the rectum. There is a stab wound of about an inch in the left groin, below which there was a three-inch-long cut that went through all the tissues.

"The cuts and stabs were made after death and by somebody kneeling on the right side of the body. As with the other victims, the perpetrator was left-handed. The left kidney had been surgically removed, the renal artery having been cut through. The womb was cut through horizontally, and some of that too, had been removed. All the wounds were inflicted by more than one sharp instrument. I would say a kitchen knife for the most part although it looks as though a scalpel may have been used for the fine work and the removal of the organs. As I said before, I should say that you are looking for somebody who has some knowledge of the internal workings of the body and is able to identify what was where. I would say that the killer has honed his practice. He may have attended medical school, may have learnt the internal workings of the human body."

"So, alongside the use of the household knives, he carries a scalpel of some sort?" Ginny was frantically making notes although she was aware she would be given a copy of the full report, writing it down helped with her memory. She paused for a moment and looked a Melanie.

Melanie smiled without humour. "Yes, but unfortunately surgical scalpels can be purchased on the internet. That in itself would be like looking for a needle in a haystack."

Melanie was continuing her initial assessment and Ginny was brought back to earth, listening intently and making her notes. "I would say that the person you are looking for carried out this attack with a peculiar type of ferocity. He definitely meant it. Judging by the cuts to the throat and the trajectory of the knife wounds inflicted on the rest of her body, I would say that this person absolutely hated the victim. He wanted to inflict pain, although most of it has occurred post mortem, and she wouldn't have felt a thing.

"And the sexual aspect?"

"Intercourse occurred. There is evidence of penetration and would, in this case, have been after he had slit her throat."

"You mean he had sex with her when she was dead?" Pat balked at that thought.

"I would say she was still alive, but barely. I don't think you have a necrophiliac on your hands, but he certainly likes to interfere sexually with his victims."

"Except for Lizzy Stroud?" Ginny wanted to confirm.

"Yes, Lizzy Stroud was most certainly hymus intactus." Melanie Watson confirmed.

"But we definitely have a woman-hater on our hands?" Ginny asked.

"I've only dabbled in psychology, Detective, but I would say that your killer definitely hates women. The ferocity of the wounds he inflicts on his victims shows a considerable amount of anger. The bruises on Anna Chapman's and Mary Nicholls' bodies suggested that he inflicted those with either kicks or punches. In the case of Anna Chapman, he punched her face so hard that he fractured her cheek bone. That unfortunately was something the original Ripper did not do. I think your boy is severely wrapped up in not only mutilating the bodies of these women, he wants to hurt them rather badly as well and if that happens before or after death, I don't think he's bothered. I should say you are looking for somebody who may have definite 'mummy' issues. He may have been mistreated as a child, perhaps spent time in care, either way he has a considerable amount of rage."

"And what about the angle of him being a doctor? The original Ripper stories proclaim that he might have been one?"

"His administrations on the bodies show that he has researched what he is doing but even with the precision implements he is using; I would say that there is a clumsiness to his work. Unless he is a surgeon that has been injured in some way, which is doubtful, I would suggest that your man has a serious grievance against women in general, I would say that you are looking for somebody who has very little medical knowledge at all?"

"A butcher then?" Ginny queried.

Melanie smiled humourlessly. "Detective, this person is a killer, nothing more. He is clearly insane and probably believes himself to be Jack the Ripper, however, I can find no evidence of the fact that he might have any medical knowledge and yes, while he might butcher the bodies, he does so with a frenzied attack that could not be deemed in any professional way. Your killer is just that, a murderer."

"Thank you, Melanie, that's been most helpful."

Ginny stood up, getting ready to leave.

"Just one last thing, Detective," Melanie offered. Ginny looked the other woman sitting across from her, waiting. "This person is just starting on his adventures, if one can call it that. He is a copycat killer, but I would say he is evolving. As you are probably aware, the so-called Ripper's last victim was Mary Kelly. If he intends to kill a person by this name, you need to find a way to alert women to be vigilant. I do think that he puts a considerable amount of preparation into the planning and execution of the murders and to that end he may have already chosen his next victim. I myself have researched women by the name of Mary Kelly and it returned hundreds of possible women. I even looked on social media and still there were so many possible victims. We, of course do not know how he chooses his victims, but I implore you, Detective, find a way to stop this man in his tracks." The austerity of Melanie Watson had disappeared, in its place the first sense of a compassionate, caring woman. In some respects, Ginny felt she was a kindred spirit. They had a similar goal in that they both wanted the killer stopped and the sooner the better.

Ginny sat hunched over the computer at her desk, scanning page after page of personal profiles. All of the women she was scanning were named Mary Kelly and there were simply hundreds of profiles with a hundred more variations to the name. It would be impossible to tell who could possibly be the killer's next victim, or how he would choose her. Ginny had the feeling that whoever the last 'Ripper' victim was, their killer had already chosen her and had every intention of honing his craft and continuing until he was caught.

The leads so far had proved nothing more than a huge disappointment. Four women dead, four forensic scenes and barely a clue to identify the killer between them. Nobody ever saw anything, nobody ever noticed anything, and the forensic evidence barely gave a clue to who the killer might be.

They had been on Crimewatch. The TV programme, while giving some leads, disappointingly had subsequently also proved fruitless. It was becoming embarrassing.

Ginny sighed and turned away from the computer screen to gaze out of the window. It was raining again. The grey sky matched her mood. She stared broodingly out of the window, trying to piece together the most impossible puzzle she had ever encountered.

At first it had been a means to an end, a way to make a name for herself. A top job that she could sink her teeth into and attempt to follow in the footsteps of her father, to be the "son" that her father so craved, a child to follow in his footsteps and make him proud. She had already failed by being born a girl. She had worked so hard throughout her life, forgoing the usual things expected of her such as marriage and children. It had all been tucked away in a nice little drawer, to be taken out at some future date when she was old and full of regrets. None of it had seemed important; only the job was important – being better than the men that were continually competing with her for those top jobs. She had been one of the lucky ones with perseverance that had not fallen by the wayside. And now, at the first hurdle, she was going to fail. It was almost too much to bear.

Ginny turned her attention back to the four dead women. Nothing to link them, they didn't know each other, they didn't have any friends that linked them and they certainly didn't even live in the same vicinity. It was clear that he was picking his victims at random, but how was he choosing them? There was something that attracted these women to him, something that grabbed his attention. She just had to discover what that was.

One thing was apparent, the victims were well known to the killer. He must have spent months watching these women, tracking their every movement. He must have known their comings and goings better than their closest family member. This meant that he had chosen his victims a significant amount of time before he actually carried out the killings. He must have spent hours watching their movements, learning their schedules.

The only thing linking them so far was that each woman had a profile on social media that was not accessible by any member of the public unless they were added as a friend. Whoever the killer was, he had been able to locate places of work and social events, and pinpoint the exact location of each woman on any given day. Looking at what each woman had posted, it would have been easy for anybody to follow them. It was becoming a real eye opener for Ginny, who had used social media herself for many years. Naïve it might have been, but she was fast becoming educated in just how easy it would be for anybody to pick a potential victim, befriend them and use that information. However, it did mean that perhaps the team would be forced to carry out some good old-fashioned police work.

They had already looked through the list of friends added to see if there was a common denominator. So far nothing had turned up a link but it had given them a list of potential suspects. All they had to do was eliminate the people from each friend list to see if they could find their killer. If there was no common denominator through the names, then perhaps face to face was the answer. However, the fly in the ointment at the moment was the number of friends listed and the locations. So far on the four victims they were looking at close to five hundred people in not only different parts of the country, but out of the country as well. There were at least two in Australia. Could she really afford to discount those people just because they were so far away?

If the killer had spent months researching his victims and watching them, it was clear that he had been planning his crime for months. With a dawning realisation, Ginny realised that trawling through the endless Mary Kelly women on social media was a waste of time. The killer had already chosen his victim and was probably watching her even now. What she needed to do was warn the potential victim.

Ginny picked up the phone on her desk and dialled a number she knew only too well. It was answered on the second ring. "Hi Sharon, I need a favour." Ginny had no time to beat around the bush. Sharon knowing that Ginny would only have rung her had it to with her current case was obliging.

"Whatever you need, Ginny. I will have some requirements of my own, just so you know," Sharon Bywater replied into the receiver, no sign that she was surprised to hear from the detective.

"Name it."

"Full and exclusive story rights once you catch the killer?"

"Done." Ginny sighed in resignation. She might be adding another nail to her coffin, but at this stage in the game, she was willing to try anything.

Ginny sat back in her chair, her fingers steepled beneath her chin. It was too late now. Tomorrow a story would run, alerting any woman named Mary Kelly with any variation of that name that she could be being watched by a copycat killer. Hysteria was bound to follow once the story broke. Corners would no longer hide the killer for any woman named Mary Kelly. However, the story might also uncover that one person who was the actual intended victim, that one lead that would nail their perpetrator, because if he had the chance to carry out that one last act as depicted by the history books, her career was finished. There would be no second chances.

CHAPTER SEVENTEEN

NOW

When Sharon Bywater was handed the assignment of covering the murder of Mary Nicholls, she had no clue she would be stumbling on to something so huge. She had been excited, there was no denying that. So far it had been routine stories that filled her time adequately, but nothing massive ever really happened locally. In the year since Sharon had been working for the paper, the biggest thing had been a spate of burglaries in which the burglars had been rather partial to lawnmowers and other such garden equipment. It had led to a big piece on 'shed safety' that she had covered, but so far, her portfolio was looking dire compared to anything the city papers were covering.

She wanted to enter the big time, to make a name for herself and she was shrewd enough to stop at nothing to get what she wanted.

Something about the Mary Nicholls murder had captured her attention. She was a notorious reader of murder mysteries and had read many books about Jack the Ripper in her time. It was obvious to her the moment she heard the name Mary Nicholls that something about this murder was not 'run of the mill', however she kept all thoughts to herself. It wasn't until the murder of Anna Chapman a few days later that she suddenly realised that there might be a serial killer in their midst. It was just too coincidental to be a fluke. The killer was clearly looking for similarly named women to be his victims and at the moment it looked like the police had no clue.

Sharon was nobody's fool. She had her eye on the main chance and she was planning to crack the case, before the police, before any of the big papers and certainly before the killer had killed Mary Kelly. By her reckoning as it was now September, she had a good two months to track the killer. He was sourcing his victims by name and there was only one way she could see how to do that in this day and age and that was through social media. She guessed it was only a matter of time before the police saw the link and she needed to be one step ahead of the game.

Checking the dates and the details of the Ripper killings was a piece of cake. Sharon set about compiling the evidence she had put together. She located enough information about the Ripper's victims in the 1800s, which was readily available in abundance from the internet. Any idiot could look up exactly how the victims were murdered, down to the smallest detail.

Getting hold of the information on the up-to-date murders had been a lot more difficult and time consuming. Her efforts were being thwarted by the police at every turn; they were keen to keep much of what was going on out of the papers.

However, Sharon believed it was her duty to inform people of the news and this was big news. When this story broke, she was going to be bigger than Rupert Murdoch himself.

Then a friend, Virginia Percy, had called and asked her to print a piece about anyone called Mary Kelly. She had known Virginia Percy a very long time, since school in fact. She also knew Patrick Paterson, who she had heard tell was still following Ginny around like a little puppy.

Sharon had always liked Ginny, in fact had had a huge crush on her at one point. Unfortunately, it seemed that Ginny did not reciprocate those feelings. Still they had remained friends, if only at arm's length.

Sharon wrote up her story for the paper. She had already spoken to her editor, who was more than happy to go for it. He himself was also keen to make a name for himself. The story would run in tomorrow's paper and would alert anyone called Mary Kelly to contact the police if they felt they were being followed, stalked or just felt generally uneasy. Since the story of the Ripper's victims had already intimated that they had a copycat on their hands, it wouldn't be hard for most people to work it out anyway. If she played a significant part in the capture of the killer, she felt sure the larger papers would headhunt her. She could really make a name for herself. It would certainly make a change from 'Bywater's By-lines'.

Satisfied with her article, she sent the email to her boss containing the story before closing down her computer just as her doorbell rang. Perfect timing as always. She smiled to herself and walked through her flat to open the front door.

Selina stood on the threshold, holding two bottles of wine.

"I bring gifts," she proclaimed proudly, holding up the two bottles like trophies. Sharon stood back and regally waved Selina's entrance into the flat.

Sharon was happy. She was finally in a relationship that seemed to have some potential. She had met Selina six weeks ago and they had been seeing a lot of each other ever since. At first Selina had seemed like an ice maiden, almost untouchable and aloof, but she had soon turned out to be a tiger temptress, particularly in the bedroom. Sharon had to admit, even in such a short amount of time, she was falling in a big way for Selina. She hoped that Selina was feeling the same way since there was at least ten years age gap between them. Selina looked older than her twenty years, but maybe that was because she held herself with a certain poise, and was mature for her age.

"I brought red and white. I didn't know what we'd be eating." Selina moved into Sharon's kitchen, placing the white wine in the fridge.

"I thought we could order Chinese. I think a small celebration might be in order," Sharon said proudly.

"A celebration?" Selina had turned away, busying herself with opening the red wine, but there was an edge to her voice. Sharon was completely oblivious, continuing to rattle on about being called by the police and writing her story alerting anybody called Mary Kelly. They were going to catch the killer and she would play a pivotal part.

Selina poured the red wine, composing her face as she turned to Sharon, offering her a glass. "Well I shall say that's cause for a celebration." The edge to her voice had gone, but as Selina Jackson smiled, the smile never reached her eyes. Sharon turned to leave the kitchen, feeling good about herself. She never saw the immediate disappearance of the smile on Selina's face. If she had seen her partner's face in that moment, she would have been shocked to see the abject hatred there.

CHAPTER EIGHTEEN

NOW

Ginny stared at the images on the whiteboard for what seemed like the millionth time. It was as if she was waiting for the women to tell her who their killer was, as if some divine inspiration could be gleaned from their faces, their eyes.

So far it was blatantly obvious that the four women who had so far lost their lives were exact replica copycat killings of the original Ripper in 1888, even so far as the dates the original victims were murdered. The only palpable difference was in relation to the names, ages and professions. The women were not related and had nothing in common, no friends, family or acquaintances. So far, every avenue of enquiry was leading to a dead end and it was becoming increasingly frustrating for those involved.

Since the only lead was in relation to the Ripper's original killings, they were pursuing this line in the investigation, starting with the next alleged possible victim, namely Mary Kelly. The search results so far had been exhausting since they knew they were looking for possible variations to the names as well as the original. The name Mary Kelly by itself had returned thousands of women, all potential victims.

The only option Ginny could see was to use the media to their advantage. To alert any women name Mary Kelly or a variation therein to be more vigilant, to put the onus on the potential victim herself. Ginny could only hope that they could reach her in time. The clock was ticking and time was of the essence.

"The story just broke, ma'am." Francine's cheeks were flushed, her excitement palpable. Ginny was alert suddenly, her full attention on her colleague.

"Some local hack called Sharon Bywater just basically broke the story with the link to Jack the Ripper. She's trying to alert any woman called Mary Kelly in the local vicinity and wider. The national press has jumped all over it straight away."

"Damn, that was fast," Pat proclaimed, walking over to join the two women.

Ginny turned to the nearest computer and put in her password, before bringing up the internet. Linking into the BBC website, she was confronted with the news page and followed to the link to breaking stories. Sure enough the main story was about the four murders and the link to Ripper victims. "It was only going to be a matter of time," Ginny mumbled, not sure if she was speaking to herself or her colleagues. She looked up at Pat. "We better get ready for the fallout. We need to prepare a press conference immediately before this thing descends into a three-ring circus. With the press giving out the names of the next Ripper victim, anybody with a similar name will be contacting us."

"Could prove to be helpful in that respect," Pat commented. The pen was back in Ginny's mouth as she thought it through.

"It would give us an idea of who we need to protect, especially around here. Maybe the public knowing won't be so detrimental to our case. At least it might stop the Ripper in his tracks," Ginny conceded.

That afternoon, Ginny sat facing a room full of reporters. It was hot, stuffy and she felt uncomfortable wearing the stage make-up she had been required to have plastered all over her face for TV purposes.

Pat and Steve King had accompanied her and were flanking either side of her, looking like two great bodyguards.

Ginny got to her feet and the room immediately silenced from the rousing chatter that preceded it. "I have a statement to make."

Ginny spoke into the microphone. "There will be no questions at this time. I am sure that you can appreciate this is an ongoing investigation and there are many details that we cannot divulge due to the nature of that investigation." She allowed her first statement a moment to digest before continuing. "Four women have been murdered in the last eight weeks and we believe that the killer has specifically chosen his victims in accordance based on the name shared with Jack the Ripper's original victims of the last century. That is the only link. There is no similarity between the original victims and the current victims. It is thought that he will attempt to murder again and we would like any women bearing the same or similar names to that of Mary Kelly to contact us should they have any concerns. We would urge members of the public to be extra vigilant and take whatever precautions they need to, to keep safe. If you notice anybody acting suspiciously, please contact us immediately on the designated telephone number." Ginny reeled off a telephone number before taking a big breath. Despite stating that she would not answer questions, a barrage of voices started a deluge upon her. She was ushered out by Pat and Steve, leaving the press to assimilate their own stories as no doubt they would do.

HIM

He was captivated by the scenes playing out on the TV. There was definitely something special about DCI Percy. He stroked her face on the TV screen while she spoke into the camera. Her blue eyes had met his on several occasions through the screen and he had felt she was speaking just to him. What she said made no difference. She made him feel special, the first woman who had accomplished that in a very long time. He wanted to feel the softness of her skin beneath his fingertips. He knew he would have to kill her of course, that was inevitable. However, he knew that when he took her life it would be so much more special than any of the others so far. The current whores were just a means to an end, for him to claim a piece of history, to pick up where he left off so to speak. It was only a matter of time before they realised that the pieces of his puzzle were coming together. However, there were flies in the ointment that needed taking care of. He had watched her as he had the others, screened her social media accounts. She was, by all accounts and enigma to him. She didn't prostitute herself out like many other women, in fact seemed totally embroiled in her job, with very little social life. He found her intriguing and wanted to know more about Virginia Percy. She confounded him and in return his obsession with her grew.

His attention was removed from the television set as he turned to look at the local paper. The young reporter called Sharon Bywater had already exceeded the investigations of the police. In other circumstances he would perhaps view her as a kindred spirit of the occult, but she was just a pest that needed exterminating. She had usurped his beloved one, his Ginny. Ginny was the one to discover his secrets. He was saving the best until last and she was the best. How he would rejoice when he finally felt her blood on his hands.

His face screwed up in annoyance as he looked at the social media page for Sharon Bywater. He scrolled through dozens of pictures of her in various acts of depravity. It disgusted him. Sharon in a bathing suit, leaving little to the imagination, Sharon drunk on a night out with the girls, a short mini skirt barely covering her private areas and then later kicking her legs up showing the world her underwear and beyond. She was disgusting and it made him feel sick that women could degrade themselves in this way with no thoughts of the consequences that might take place.

Ginny's social media page did not show such things. It seemed it was rarely used. In fact, he had been hard pressed to find anything about her via the internet at all except for her recent television appearances. He was gratified to find that his angel was as self-depreciating as he assumed she would be. It gratified him to think that she did not cheapen herself as the whores did.

CHAPTER NINETEEN

THEN

Eugenie had counted her cash four times and four times it had come out at the same amount, one thousand, eight hundred and eighty pounds. Eugenie sighed with exasperation. Clearly Randall had discovered her stash and had been pilfering small amounts, thinking she wouldn't notice. Eugenie *had* noticed. She had noticed one week ago when she had had the sum total of one thousand, nine hundred and fifty, and now she noticed that it was a hundred and twenty pounds short. That was to be their nest egg, money to help them start a new life. She could have put it straight in the bank but she was worried that this would somehow be alerted to the authorities who paid her benefits. She couldn't afford to have them sniffing around asking questions about a large sum of money in her possession. She would have to make a new hiding place.

Eugenie had been making plans secretly behind her son's back for weeks. It had taken some considerable thought and a great deal of secrecy to keep quiet the details of not only her pregnancy, but of her planned move. She had found it very difficult to love Randall. He was such a strange little boy. But the more she thought about it, the more she realised he was likely a child of circumstance. She had been ostracised from her family for carrying him and in consequence she felt she may have taken it out on him in some part. Then she had brought him to this place. She looked around the pokey little house she called home. She had tried so hard not to be a snob about it, but it was incredibly difficult. The area itself was little more than a slum. She felt that Randall had not flourished as he should in those circumstances. She needed to get him to the country. She felt sure that at ten years old she still had time to bring out the little boy she knew must be in there somewhere. And besides, the baby she carried deserved a better start in life than she had been able to give her son thus far. Still she was furious about the missing money. What on earth could a ten-year-old want with so much money and what on earth could he have spent it on?

She had no idea what had happened to Randall. She had tried so hard, against all the odds to raise him to be a proper young man. True, she might have been overly hard on him at times, but she believed that that was in order to give him a backbone, to ensure that he grew up to be decent human being who could go on and make something of his life. Goodness only knew, he had come from poor beginnings.

Eugenie sighed, her hand fluttering to her stomach, where the baby she was going to have barely showed. She would do better with this child, she was sure. There was something terrifying within Randall, something she couldn't fathom. She couldn't understand where it had manifested itself from. At times Randall frightened her. There was a very real tangible feeling that her life was in danger each time she came into contact with her son on some occasions. Even something as simple as eating a meal had become almost unbearable, the fear forcing Eugenie's throat closed so that she could barely eat. And each time Randall would stare at her with those dark eyes, almost unblinkingly, like a snake watching its prey. Eugenie had no doubt that her own son, borne of her flesh, truly despised her and wanted to hurt her in some way. Eugenie knew that if Randall knew about the baby, it would increase the risk not only to herself, but to her unborn child. It had not taken much for her to decide on a plan of action. Once she had acquired the two thousand pounds from Ian, it had only been a matter of time before she was able to raise a further fifty pounds by selling some of her belongings.

Randall, despite hardly being at home, must have somehow got wind of her plans or at least that she had the money, and he was quietly siphoning it off, no doubt hoping that she wouldn't notice. Trouble was, she had a daily habit of checking the sum total and had discovered one week ago that it was dwindling, and quickly too.

Eugenie bit her lip and stared into space. She knew she had to confront him about it, but the thought scared her to death.

The sudden bang of the front door startled her out of her reverie and she quickly shoved the money into the pocket of her apron, idly wondering where her new hiding place should be.

Randall barely glanced in her direction as he sidled past the kitchen to the stairs. He said nothing, did not even smile. Eugenie tried to smile with a fondness she did not feel and she knew that her smile would have looked like a grimace as she glanced at the son she felt very little for.

Eugenie felt that time was running out. If Randall knew she had money, he would know she had plans to use it. He hadn't approached her, or asked her about it, which would indicate that he might have an inkling into her plans. Therefore, Eugenie's only choice was to have it out with him, find out if he still had the money and try and get it back. She would have to tell him they were leaving. However, it was too soon. Things were not ready, but Eugenie knew that time would be of the essence. She couldn't afford for Randall to take any more of the money she had carefully accrued. Already the vast sum he had stolen had made a severe dent in her future plans. With her decision made, Eugenie proceeded to move around the kitchen and prepare the evening meal. She would speak to Randall tonight.

Randall stomped up the stairs, a scowl crossing his face as he unlocked his bedroom door and entered the personal sanctuary of his bedroom. He smiled without humour as he glanced around the room. If his mother caught a glimpse of what lay beyond the door, she would have a coronary or run screaming for the hills. That thought warmed him greatly.

She thought she was so clever, that all her secrets were well hidden. She didn't know that Randall saw and heard everything. He knew she was carrying another baby. She had tried to hide it from him, had never mentioned it, but he knew and he hated it. As much as he hated his mother, he hated that baby more.

Mother liked him to have at least washed and changed for dinner. Still trying after all these years to behave like the heiress, a lady with poise and grace which she so carefully cultivated while they lived in near squalid conditions. It made him sick and yet he complied dutifully with her wishes, all the while wondering what noises she would make while he killed her. His daydreams were the only thing that made a meal with his mother bearable. He could barely remember a time when he did not hate her. His entire childhood had been made up of him trying to please her and failing miserably each time. He had tried to act in such a way that pleased her, that would make her smile and yet whatever he did was never enough. She had continued to treat him no better than any of the kids in the street, as though he didn't really belong to her at all, as though she was just looking after him for somebody else and it was the most inconvenient thing in the world. That summed it up really, exactly how Randall felt; he was a huge inconvenience to his mother. No doubt, from her grand beginnings she was destined to be a lady who married well and lived a life of boring civility and grandeur. Randall had clearly scuppered that plan by being born. Well he hoped his mother had been taught a severe lesson by how miserable her life had turned out. She was no different to any other slut using what God gave her between her legs to live a life of debauchery and decline. And yet she had taken that and turned it around on her son and made him pay for her sins and her unhappiness and *He*, Randall Goff, was expected to be happy about that? Never! Randall could feel his heart beating against his ribs. The dark mist that threatened to engulf his subconscious was descending and he knew he was on the verge of becoming severely enraged. It was a like a dam waiting to burst its banks and he could barely control it to bring himself back to order. However, now was not the right time. His subconscious mind screamed at him, willing him to do what was necessary to satiate his need. It was becoming more of struggle every day to stop himself. His time was getting nearer and despite his few fledgling attempts to assuage his necessity to murder, the obligation he felt in carrying out heinous acts was getting harder to ignore. There would be a time, he knew, when his control would be lost forever and he would have no choice.

Randall slumped into a chair at the kitchen table opposite his mother. His dinner was placed in front of him. Meat and potatoes, meat and potatoes. It was the same every day, every night. He stared at the food on his plate and wished for something different. Perhaps the kidney of a victim, just like Jack. Inside he felt himself smile. Yes, he would like to try a kidney very much. He admired Jack the Ripper enormously. He felt he could have been related and who knew, perhaps he really was.

Collecting his knife and fork from beside his plate, he proceeded to eat. Their meals, every night were taken in silence, uncomfortable such as it was.

"Randall… " Eugenie broached nervously. Randall stopped chewing mid-mouthful, black eyes immediately on his mother's face. She swallowed hard, determined to maintain eye contact for as long as possible even though she felt at that precise moment that Randall could see into the very depths of her soul through those obsidian eyes. He waited. She knew he was waiting but sensed at the same time that he knew exactly what she was going to say, to ask him. "Randall," she broached again, "I've noticed some money missing." She almost choked on thin air, such was her nervousness at that precise moment.

"Money?" Randall secured her with a look that reminded her of a snake eyeing its prey.

"Yes," she claimed quietly. Randall gave his mother a disdainful look. Where was the woman who used to bully him? Where was that attitude she used to have? Randall felt a smug sense of satisfaction to know that his mother was actually afraid of him.

Served her right. It was nothing more than she deserved. If she had shown him a small iota of love in the beginning, things might have been different. The only reason she continued to breathe in his presence now was because she was simply... his mother.

"Yes I took your money." Randall admitted directly, causing Eugenie to start at the immediate admission.

"Well... erm, well." Eugenie found she was suddenly lost for words.

"I'll give it back. I needed a few things." Randall resumed eating, breaking eye contact, his attention once more on his plate.

Eugenie released the breath she hadn't even realised she was holding. "What things did you need, Randall?" She was bent on pursuing this matter. What could a ten-year-old boy possibly need a hundred and twenty pounds for?

Randall sighed and put down his knife and fork. He much preferred it when his mother didn't talk to him. What was he going to say, that he needed to buy things so that he could murder her boyfriend, that he needed to buy a train ticket to Scotland?

"I was going to visit Grandma." He lied skilfully. Eugenie was taken completely by surprise.

"Grandma?" she echoed quietly.

"I was." Randall was becoming very good at lying, he sounded completely plausible. "I bought a ticket and everything, but in the end, I wasn't sure how to get there by myself. They wouldn't give me the money back." Eugenie sat looking at her son trying to identify any signs that he was lying. The little boy she had known could not lie very well at all and she could always sniff it out, then she would punish him for it if he refused to admit it. This time she had no such inkling. Her eyes moved over his face as he stared back at her in innocence. She was trying to find any shred of proof that what he said wasn't true, but honestly what else would a ten-year-old boy need a hundred and twenty pounds for?

"I see," Eugenie eventually said, breaking eye contact. "I wish you had told me instead of just taking the money."

"I'm sorry, Mother." It was the first apology she had heard from Randall for a very long time. Over the last four years, something in her little boy had changed, and not for the better. There was an evil lurking in Randall, something she couldn't quite fathom or understand. It was a feeling, a gut reaction. She avoided confrontation and hated herself for it. How could a ten-year-old be dangerous? She glanced at her son through her eyelashes surreptitiously. That feeling that there was something inside Randall persisted. She couldn't shake the sense, the feeling of unease that resided in the pit of her stomach. Was it tangible or was it just a feeling, like mother's intuition? Would moving away help? At this point Eugenie had no idea, she could only hope for the best.

Randall lay on his bed staring at the ceiling. He had wanted to tell his mother tonight that he knew everything. That he knew she was pregnant, that he knew she was planning on taking them to his grandmother's house. He didn't want to go. He didn't want to be around his mother and he certainly didn't want to see that baby. The otherwise mature side of Randall had been replaced by a petulant little boy consumed with jealousy for an unborn sibling.

His mother knew very little about the real Randall. He could tell she was a little afraid of him, although she tried to cover it up well. If only she knew what he had already done. He thought back to a week before, a smile playing around his lips as he replayed the scenes.

Randall had taken some money from his mother's secret stash. She was a fool to keep money in her shoe; if he could think of it, then any potential burglar could think of it. He had taken a small amount at first. He needed to buy provisions for a trip. Then he had found out how much a return ticket to Scotland would cost. He had then taken what he needed, again from his mother's money. Having contacted the school he had left a message on the absence line, impersonating his mother's clipped tones knowing that the imbecile working in the office had no more brain cells than a frozen fish finger and would not contact his home wondering where he might be on that day.

Randall had never been anywhere in his whole life. His mother had taken him to see his grandmother once but he couldn't remember that, so in effect his train trip to Scotland was his first ever trip and he had to admit he was quite excited at the prospect.

He had successfully managed to change trains and never once had anyone stop him to ask why a child so young was travelling without a parent or companion, although he had received a few odd looks.

His journey, meticulous in the planning had taken him exactly where he wanted to go and eventually, he stood before the school gates of Brightcross, an all-boys school housing residential and non-residential students alike from age five to eighteen years. The grounds and the school itself were vast, having originally been a stately home that had been converted. Buildings had been added over the years and now Brightcross was one of the most prestigious boys' schools in the country.

Randall was in search of Ian Pratchett who was now the headmaster of the whole establishment.

Gaining entry to the school had been fairly easy. A ten-year-old boy did not represent a threat or opposition. Randall quickly found his way to the laundry room and located some items of school uniform that he had put on. He had researched the school on the internet, easy to do and had found out everything he needed to know. Wandering around the school had presented no challenge at all. He was not stopped or questioned by anybody, not even to see why he wasn't in class.

He found his way to the private quarters of the teachers that resided on site. He had assumed he might have had to wait for Ian Pratchett to return to his room to see which one it was, but as luck would have it, the names of the teachers were on the doors. Randall quickly located Ian Pratchett's quarters, situated at the end of the corridor.

Randall tried the door to Ian Pratchett's rooms and was not surprised to find them locked. Going outside, he walked around the building, finding it to be a secluded area where tall trees afforded some privacy for its occupants while also allowing complete freedom to come and go from the school itself.

Unperturbed, he located the windows to Ian Pratchett's rooms from the outside. As he was situated at the end of the corridor, he was on the corner and as such had much larger quarters than any of the other teachers. Randall was gratified to find a small bathroom window open. Clearly, Ian thought it was not big enough for a man to crawl through, but had not given consideration to a small child.

Scouting around the area to ensure he could not be seen from any vantage point, Randall returned to the open bathroom window. Reaching up, he could just about touch the sill of the open window. He removed the backpack he was carrying, reached up and pushed it through the opening. With some considerable effort he managed to reach up and hoist his body onto the ledge of the sill before wiggling his body through the window. He had to go in head first and was pleased to discover not only a large ledge on the other side of the window but a sink area which was housed in a worktop, allowing more space to manoeuvre. He pulled himself through and grabbed the taps, which allowed him the leverage he needed to bring his legs through. He landed half on the ledge, half on the sinked area, sending the contents by the sink spinning in every which way and onto the floor. Fortunately, nothing was glass and everything landed with a dull thud. He attracted a few bumps and scrapes on his legs and stomach, but these did not bother him. He lowered himself to the floor and caught his breath, waiting to see if anyone would come running because of the noise he had created. Satisfied with the ensuing silence, he turned to pick up the fallen bottle of shampoo, shaving foam and shower gel that he had sent spinning on coming through the window and replaced them on the window sill before retrieving his backpack.

He opened the bathroom door a crack and glanced into the bedroom beyond. This room was large, having to accommodate both sleeping and some living quarters. As well as his double bed and side tables, Ian Pratchett also had a couple of easy chairs, a large television, a desk with a computer, bookshelves and small kitchen area. There was nothing out of place even though it had been a matter of weeks since he had moved.

Randall moved around the room, looking through drawers and looking at papers, tracking the life of the wayward headmaster. There was nothing really significant, but he did come across a roll of money which he took and put in his backpack. Who knew when some extra money might come in useful?

Randall had no idea of Ian Pratchett's timetable. He couldn't say when the headmaster might return to his room or whether he would at all. However, Randall had patience and was willing to wait it out. Ian Pratchett was going to pay for his treatment of Eugenie and he was going to pay in the worst way possible.

Randall lay under the bed of Ian Pratchett, waiting for his arrival. He had no idea of the time and must have dozed off. He opened his eyes to the sound of somebody speaking and realised that as he opened his eyes, the room was in darkness. He heard the jangle of keys and suddenly the room was flooded with light. He could hear Ian Pratchett's voice, although it was one sided and Randall realised that he must have been talking on his mobile phone. Randall listened intently to the conversation with a growing anger inside him. It seemed that Ian Pratchett had already moved on and was making plans to go on a date and this very evening as well. So much for his proclamations that he needed to be single man for his position within the school.

Randall's anger was beyond description. His whole body was alive with the sensation of rage. He wanted to make Ian Pratchett pay. He had hated the man from the first moment they had met and he knew that the feeling was mutual. Despite what Randall felt about his mother, she was still his mother and nobody was ever going to treat her the way Ian Pratchett did – to palm her off with a measly two thousand pounds and leave her pregnant and alone. If he hadn't heard his mother crying in the night, he might have been willing to leave the matter, but unfortunately for Ian Pratchett he had. He had seen his mother listlessly moving around the house, hardly bothering with her hair or make-up, even on a couple of occasions not bothering to get dressed at all. This was unacceptable as far as Randall was concerned. He might hate his mother for cheapening herself with this man, but he would not allow this man to live any longer.

When Randall heard the water running in the bathroom shower, he crawled from his hiding place under the bed. Taking a large kitchen knife from his backpack he had stolen from his mother's kitchen, he crouched by the entrance of the bathroom door and waited.

It wasn't long before the shower was switched off. Ian Pratchett came out of the bathroom with only a towel around his waist, whistling. He was oblivious to the danger that waited for him. In order for a ten-year-old to overpower a fully-grown man, the element of surprise was all important. Moving quickly, Randall jumped up and plunged his hunting knife squarely into the middle of Ian Pratchett's back. It took every ounce of force he had in his small body, and equally to pull it out again. Ian Pratchett began to turn. It was as if every movement was playing itself out in slow motion. Ian's arm came up towards his back as the blood began to pour; at the same time he began to turn to see who his assailant was. There was a look of abject horror followed by surprise as at first Ian Pratchett saw Randall standing before him, followed by Randall plunging his knife into Ian Pratchett's chest, directly into his heart.

Ian's legs collapsed beneath him immediately. The confusion in his face was evident as he fell to his knees. His right hand came out as if to grab the child and his mouth opened as if he wanted to say something. He fell forward onto his chest and unfortunately, as Ian Pratchett expired, and the last breath left his body, his mind retained the information that Eugenie Goff's weird little spawn had managed to stab him. It was the last coherent thing he ever knew.

Randall stood above the body of Ian Pratchett. He was smiling. He had felt so powerful. It was like the lifeforce of Ian Pratchett had automatically channelled into his body as he stabbed him. He could scarcely believe his plan had been executed so perfectly. He had expected some resistance from Ian, that maybe he would have been knocked down or hurt in some way. Randall had acted on the premise that the man would have been injured and therefore would have been significantly weakened enough that Randall could have gained the upper hand. Randall giggled uncontrollably. This had been so much better, albeit a bit too quick. He had wanted Ian Pratchett to suffer.

The problem was going to be that Ian Pratchett had fallen forward, irrevocably trapping the knife between his body and the floor. Randall tried and failed to lift the dead weight of the body. Eventually using the momentum of his body, he pushed at Ian's Prachett's shoulder and pushed him backwards. He never knew where he got his strength from, but somehow, he managed to rest Ian's body on his left arm. His body was twisted in a peculiar way, his lower half seeming still facing forwards on the floor. Using his right foot to hold Ian's body in place, he used both hands to remove the knife from Ian's chest. It came out with a satisfying suck, the blood it had held in check suddenly pouring from Ian's body and running down the side of his chest. Randall moved around the body and kicked his shoulder so that once again Ian fell forward and landed face down on the carpet. This was the first dead body Randall had observed other than the animals he had killed. He found it fascinating to stand and stare, enjoying the ambience of the silence. Randall wished he had a camera so he could take a picture, keep it as a memento. He felt that he needed to capture this moment in more than just his mind. He was regretful of that fact, but knew he would do better next time.

He bent down and cleaned his knife on the towel that covered Ian's body before placing it back in his backpack. He removed the school clothing that he currently wore and changed these for his own clothes, black trousers and black jumper, putting the uniform in his backpack for disposal later. He also had a black beanie that he put on his head. Before he left, he went through Ian Pratchett's pockets, removing the man's wallet. He was gratified to find a further fifty pounds in cash, two twenties and a ten, which he removed and put into his backpack. There was a bank card as well but regretfully Randall could not afford the time to look for the PIN now. Reluctantly, he replaced the wallet where he found it. It would have been nice to take all his money as well.

Taking one more glance around the room, he left quickly, exiting by the door that led to the long corridor. It was all clear and he moved along the hallway quickly. On re-entering the grounds, he tried to keep as close as he could to the hedges and fences that surrounded the property. It took longer than he thought until he finally reached the school gates while he kept vigilant, looking about him. He needn't have worried; he was a small insignificant form, noticed by nobody. Here he exited the same way he entered and was finally back on the road. A short while later he entered the train station and was gratified to find his train would arrive in twenty minutes. His return ticket was open ended which meant he could return at any time he wanted. He waited for his train and realised from the station clock that it was half past four. It was already dark as the clocks had not yet gone forward to proclaim British summertime's arrival.

He would mostly likely not arrive home until quite late, which might arouse questions from his mother; still, he shrugged his shoulders to himself, he had plenty of time to come up with a plausible excuse that she would believe.

The brutal murder of a headteacher in Scotland hit the news headlines on Sky News and the BBC. Eugenie Goff didn't watch either of these programmes and therefore missed the story of Ian

Pratchett's body being found, but Randall didn't. He absorbed every piece of information about the killing and as far as he was concerned there were no tangible leads for the police to follow. Why would they suspect a child anyway? It was the perfect murder as far as Randall was concerned.

He had returned to his home that evening to find Eugenie Goff waiting for him in the kitchen. She had been crying. At first, he had been afraid that she had found out what he had done, that the police had already been at the door, having tracked him down. As it turned out, his mother had been worried. She had risen from her seat at the kitchen table and wrapped her arms around him. It was the first gesture of love that Randall could remember receiving from his mother for a very long time. She had never been particularly tactile and was not prone to cuddles and kisses, but for a the merest of moments Randall felt cherished in those few seconds. The removal of her arms left him feeling bereft. She glanced down at his face, neither questioning him about his whereabouts for the day, nor asking him any details about what he had been doing. She simply said goodnight and made her way up to bed.

Randall had stood in the kitchen for a moment, wondering if she knew – if his motives had been that transparent that she had been able to guess exactly where he had been and what he had been doing.

The truth would have been harder to bear. When Randall did not materialise after school, Eugenie had not been worried, assuming that he had gone to the library as he very often did. She had been a little worried when he didn't appear for dinner that evening and that worry had grown. She feared that something had happened to her son, that he may have possibly run away, been run over, or kidnapped or something far more abhorrent. Eugenie Goff wasn't crying because something might have happened to her son, that she would never see him again, that the next knock on the door would be a police officer come to give her terrible news. No, Eugenie Goff was crying because she felt guilty. She was wishing those things had happened to her only son, that she would never have to see him again, that the feeling that she disliked her son and had an intense fear of him would be banished forever. Eugenie Goff was crying with relief. The sudden appearance of her son coming home had shocked her once again. She had been so sure that she would never see him again, she had almost talked herself into believing it wholeheartedly. Then, like magic, there he was. She could do no other than put her arms around him in that moment; the mortifying thoughts she had coveted not that long ago needed to be banished from her mind, lest he know what she was thinking. To her relief, Randall never asked her why she was crying that evening, nor did she venture to ask him for an explanation about where he had been, thinking it was so much better not to know and like an ostrich, Eugenie Goff's head was buried in the sand.

CHAPTER TWENTY

NOW

The world was filled with crackpots. Ginny had known that advertising the fact that they were looking for somebody called Mary Kelly was taking a gamble, that every single nutter within an average fifty-mile radius was bound to come out of the woodwork. It was a given.

However, they were frankly unprepared for the fallout from the newspapers and the press release, which had been intense and insane. It seemed that every single person in the county knew somebody who was called Mary Kelly and then there were those who were called Mary Kelly or some variation. They had even been contacted by a transvestite called Vera Mary Kelly who felt like somebody was following her. Every report had to be taken seriously and every report had to be investigated. It had taken a considerable amount of police resources when they might have been better placed investigating the actual crimes themselves. To that end, not one plausible lead could be established. Each line of enquiry had been exhausted and still they had nothing to show for it.

Ginny scrolled through the many witness reports despondently. Ginny could only hope that the killer might have been put off by the media hype or that the Mary Kelly he had chosen was taking ample precautions, watching her back at every turn, being vigilant. It was hoped that if the call came, they would be able to move quickly enough.

Pat came into the incident room and made his way to Ginny's office at the end where she sat. He had a sad look on his face and Ginny wondered what more bad news she could possibly hear. He stepped into her office and it was then she realised he was holding a folded-up newspaper. "What's up?" she asked.

He waved the newspaper around. "Sharon Bywater committed suicide last night," he replied simply.

"What... ?" She was incredulous. "How come, I mean what happened? I only spoke to her the other day." Ginny gabbled her words, she spoke so quickly. Pat took a seat on the other side of her desk, putting his newspaper on top of the desk. She unfolded it, the picture of Sharon Bywater filling the front page of the local rag.

UPCOMING REPORTER TAKES OWN LIFE screamed the headline.

"I don't believe it," Ginny announced, reading through the article quickly.

"Guess it just goes to show, you never know what's going on behind closed doors," Pat said simply, crossing his legs by placing his left ankle on his right knee.

"Sharon was a barracuda." Ginny refolded the newspaper, having speed-read through the article. She laid it back on her desk. "That woman would have sold her own mother for a top story if she thought it would give her leg up in the right direction."

Pat shrugged, "She slashed her wrists in the bath, bled out. Apparently, they found traces of Warfarin in her body. She didn't need Warfarin, wasn't prescribed it, but her mother was. Clearly, she meant business. People don't do that sort of thing unless they're serious, Gin, she must have planned it all."

This time it was Ginny's turn to shrug. "I just don't see it, that's all. Call me cynical in my old age, but if you were to line up several people and ask me to pinpoint who would be most likely to take their own life, Sharon Bywater would not be in my top ten."

"Any more news on the case?" Pat decided it might be helpful to change the subject. He had to admit the death of someone he'd known since school was saddening. Not that he had ever liked the woman, not even when she was a girl – there was just something that didn't gel with him – but he wouldn't see anyone hurt themselves deliberately. All he could think was that she must have felt so desperate thinking she had nowhere else to turn. The whole thing made him sad.

"Zip, zero, nothing, nada... shall I go on?" Ginny answered despondently.

"Oooh, sarcasm, that's refreshing," Pat joked.

"It's all I have right now, Pat, sorry."

"Anything from upstairs?"

"Nothing yet, but I'm expecting it any day, well any hour really. I just... I don't know, Pat, I really want to get a result on this. It's almost as if the answer's out there, but it's just beyond my reach and I'm not seeing it. No murder is perfect, we had that drilled into us, but I'm damned if I can see where he made his mistakes. He's killed four women and yet we have nothing. How can that be?"

Again, Pat shrugged helplessly. "If you can't find the answers, nobody else is going to. We have been over every piece of evidence and yet its turned up nothing. I defy anyone new coming in at this point to prove otherwise."

"Fresh eyes I guess. Maybe we're all just too close now."

"It's just frustrating. He has been a step ahead of us the whole time. He has probably known who his victims are for months. Finding out who is next is like looking for a needle in a haystack."

"Maybe, but whoever he is, he will slip up sooner or later." Pat stood up and stretched. "We're heading down the pub, you wanna come for beer?"

Ginny shook her head. "You lot go, you deserve to let your hair down, I've got a few things to go through here." She smiled weakly at her best friend.

"Alright then, don't stay too late." He turned and left her office, whoever was left in the incident room following suit. In a matter of moments, there was silence and the quiet hum of computers in the background.

Ginny was struck for a moment that this was the same scenario Mary Nicholls had begun her evening in the night she was killed two months ago. The cleaners who worked at Hart, Smith & Dawson had been spoken to and had reported that Mary had been sitting alone in her office working on her computer. They had been put out because it had delayed their finishing for the evening and as one of the cleaners pointed out, they didn't get paid overtime.

What if Ginny were to put herself into the mind of the victims? She had tried and failed to put herself into the mind of the killer, exhausting herself by trying to work out how he chose his victims, what it was about them that attracted him. What if she were to start at the beginning again, but this time imagine herself in the mind of Mary Nicholls? She pulled out the file and meticulously set out the crime photographs displaying the body, studying each one.

Mary Nicholls, a thirty-nine-year-old successful woman, having an affair with her boss. She discovers she's pregnant, a little-known fact discovered on post-mortem and deliberately kept away from the press. It must have been hard keeping that little secret. She hadn't even told Franklin Hart; he had no clue and from what Marcus Nicholls said, the child would have been unlikely to be his since he virtually openly admitted that he hardly slept with his wife any longer. His tastes seemed to run to the more exotic, and he was heavily into 'S&M'. Mary didn't like playing his little games. Mary mentioned to her housekeeper and it seemed only her housekeeper, that she felt like she was being watched. She complained often of feeling that there was someone following her, that she felt someone had been in her house, going through her things, yet she didn't call the police even to file a report. Did she know the person?

Ginny turned to the list of employees at Hart, Smith & Dawson. Most of the staff didn't have many dealings with Mary; when they were questioned, very few really knew who she was except that she had been murdered. It seemed that the top floor was exclusive to only a handful of staff – Ginny went through the list: Phoebe Dalton, her secretary, Franklin Hart MD, David Crisp, an executive, Selina Jackson, Mr Hart's secretary, Bradley Parker, security guard, Richard Ladden, security guard, Guy Preston, security guard,

Jessica Jones, reception, Barbara Arnold, Troy Weir and Victor Child all directors or partners of the company. It was a fairly short list. Since Mary Nicholls spent most of her days in the company of these people, it might stand to reason that they might have unwittingly seen something, although their witness reports belied that notion. Ginny pulled those up on the computer. The security guard Bradley Parker was the last person to ever see Mary Nicholls alive that day other than the cleaners. He had reported greeting her when she alighted from the lift. He stated that he had been surprised to see her still at the office, thinking that everybody had already gone home. He reported that she seemed nervous and he had offered to walk her to her car, an offer she had declined. He had seen her get into her car and drive away.

Ginny tapped Bradley Parker's name into the police computer. Up popped three arrest records under his name. It seemed Bradley, also known as Brad Parker, had been arrested on three occasions in the past, once for indecent assault, once for flashing and once for carrying an illicit substance with intent to supply. How had they missed this? There was nothing reported in the latest reports at all. Had nobody performed a background check or checked arrest records? And if something as simple as a background check had been missed, what else had also been glossed over? Ginny read through the incident reports regarding the arrests.

It seemed Brad had been caught first at age twenty-two, displaying his private parts to schoolgirls on their way home from school. He had eluded the police for three weeks before getting caught, arrested and charged. His second offence had been much more serious. He had followed a woman home from the pub, and when she challenged him, he had indecently assaulted her by putting his hand against her vagina and one on her breast. He had been arrested the very next day for that. Ginny checked the date. That had happened almost a year ago to the day. What if Brad had moved from touching women's private parts to murder? There was every chance their killer had been sitting pretty all this time, probably laughing his socks off that he was successfully eluding the police. If she could prove that Brad had links to the other women murdered, she had her man.

For the first time in many weeks, Ginny felt that old excitement creep back into her body. She was on to something, she was sure of it. She picked up the phone and ordered the immediate arrest of Bradley Parker. While she waited for him to be brought in for questioning, she knew she would need to go through the other women.

Pulling the files up on Anna Chapman, she began trawling through the people known to her. She immediately settled on Greg Myers, Anna's alleged boyfriend and well-known drug dealer. He was a face she instantly recognised as they had picked him up for questioning shortly after Anna's murder. He was a renowned drug dealer in the area and had been picked up and arrested many times for supplying and using. The address he had given police as his abode had been searched. Drug paraphernalia of all descriptions had been found at the address, along with two of his colleagues only known by the names of Tom and Tanya. Greg had not been helpful with regard to their investigations into Anna's death. He hadn't appeared surprised and even less concerned. Ginny didn't believe that Greg could have possibly committed one murder successfully, let alone two. What interested her at the moment was the fact that Greg was a known drug dealer and well known in the area and the fact that Bradley Parker had been arrested for possession. Could this be the start of the link they had been trying to find?

She picked up her mobile and dialled Pat's number. The noise from the pub was immense and Ginny was reminded that the football was playing tonight; no doubt most of her boys were engrossed in the match. Unfortunately, she was about to spoil their fun. The sound of the bar lessened over the phone as Pat obviously took his call outside.

"Gin, you okay?" he asked in a concerned voice.

"Pat," she replied, "I think I may be on to something… " she quickly rattled off her suspicions while Pat listened quietly at the other end.

"I'll be right with you!" he exclaimed when she'd finished speaking. Her excitement was infectious and he could feel it too.

Bradley Parker sat in the interview room. He looked dishevelled and unshaven. Ginny watched him on the CCTV for a moment. He kept rubbing his palm down his face intermittently, his left elbow resting on the table. He said nothing to the officer who waited with him in the interview room. Ginny thought he looked nervous. She glanced at Pat sitting beside her. "You ready?" she asked him briefly.

"As I'll ever be."

Ginny and Pat entered the interview room, and the uniformed officer left. Bradley Parker watched them carefully; he seemed fidgety and slightly on edge.

"Mr Parker, I'm Detective Chief Inspector Virginia Percy; this is my colleague Detective Sergeant Patrick Paterson." They took their seats at the table opposite. "I'm just going to switch on this machine." Ginny reached over and clicked on the recording device.

"Mr Parker, may I call you Brad?" Ginny began. He shrugged back at her. "If you could answer the question Mr Parker, for the recording." She nodded in the direction of the recording device.

His eyes flickered over to it and back to her again. "Yeah, that's fine." His voice was deep and gravelly like he had been smoking forty cigarettes a day for the last ten years.

"Brad, you have been asked to assist us with our enquiries today regarding the murder of Mary Nicholls and I have a few questions I would like to ask." Again, the baleful, almost unblinking stare in her direction. "How long did you know Mary Nicholls for?"

"About five years or so I guess." His gaze flickered back and forth between Pat and Ginny, resting again back on Ginny.

"Did you get on well with her?" He shrugged in answer to that one. "An answer please, Brad."

"As well as anyone else I s'pose."

"Did you ever see her outside work?"

"No."

"Ever ask her on a date?"

"No."

"Can you tell me what happened the night Mary Nicholls was murdered?"

"I already did to the police."

"We're the police, Brad. Perhaps you could go over your story again. It would be nice to hear it in your own words." Ginny pressed and Brad sighed theatrically tapping his fingers on the table.

"Problem?" Ginny queried. Brad shook his head. "When you're ready then."

"Like I told the police before, she came down in the lift, I thought she'd already left for the evening, I thought everyone had left except for the cleaners. She got in her car, that's the last I saw of her."

"What time do you usually finish work?"

"Around eleven p.m. usually."

"That night?"

"It was about eleven."

"What did you do afterwards?"

"Went home."

"Anyone at home waiting for you, a Mrs Parker perhaps?"

"No."

"Is there anyone to confirm you went home?"

"No."

"Did you know where Mary Nicholls lived?"

This time Brad hesitated. "No."

"Are you sure about that, you didn't know where she lived, even the part of town?"

The first cracks were beginning to tell. "I knew where she lived." He confirmed.

"How did you know?"

"I drove her home once."

"What was the reason for that?"

"Her car broke down, it was ages ago… years."

"So, you knew where she lived?"

"Yes."

"So, you just lied?" Brad shrugged. Ginny let that one go. "Ever go to her house after you took her home, visited at all?"

"Nope."

"Never?"

"No."

"Did you like Mary Nicholls?"

"She was a nice lady."

"Did you *like* her, you know in that way?" Again, that annoyed shrug. "You ever touch her?"

Brad looked at her sharply, "No."

Ginny decided to change tack for the moment. "How do you know Greg Myers?" The question caught Brad off kilter. He hadn't been ready for that. Surprise showed in his face and then it dawned on him that the police most likely knew.

"He used to be my dealer," he admitted truthfully.

"Ever go to his squat?"

"Several times."

"Did you ever meet Anna Chapman there?"

The first semblance of fear crossed Brad's face. This wasn't how it was supposed to happen.

"You have nothing on me," he spat.

"Let us be the judge of that. Bradley Parker, I am arresting you on suspicion of the murders of Mary Nicholls and Anna Chapman. Anything you say may be used in evidence against you… "

Ginny watched Brad Parker being led to the cells. The look he gave her was one of pure hatred and it was then she had the impression that she might indeed be looking at the face of her murderer.

DSI Sparkes congratulated Ginny over the phone. "The dogs are officially called off," he informed her. It was a top result and she needn't be worried about being replaced any longer. Now that they had their prime suspect in custody, the investigation could take as long as it needed to, they would back her one hundred and fifty percent.

"Shame they couldn't do that until now," Pat spat in disgust.

"Yeah well, that's the old boys' network for you," Ginny responded and laughed. Nothing could dampen her spirits today.

He watched the news. There she was giving an interview, confirming that they had arrested somebody on the suspicion of two of the murders so far, but she hoped to have a result very soon. She couldn't divulge too much at the moment as the investigation was ongoing.

He rejoiced. Oh, his poor little Virgin. How she had floundered on this one. Still she would learn soon enough. He was unstoppable. He could not be caught. His name would be recorded in the history books once he had become and then he would take her, his precious little Virgin.

Shame about poor Brad, he might have made a willing disciple one day.

CHAPTER TWENTY-ONE

NOW: MARY-JANE KELLY NOVEMBER

Mary-Jane Kelly had been born in Ireland, in a little village in Tipperary. The youngest of six children, Mary had grown up knowing that she only ever wanted to be a one thing – a nurse.

She could have stayed in Ireland. Her parents wanted her to. She came from a close-knit family where every family event meant that the entire family got together for a good old chat and a drink. Being the baby of the family meant that she was constantly being looked out for; in some ways it felt claustrophobic. If she went to town with her friends, she undoubtedly would run into her sister Bridget or her brother Donal. Half the time she felt like a bug under a microscope. She was always being asked to take care of her small nieces and nephews as well at family gatherings, like it was the youngest child's responsibility to babysit rather than join in with the adults. For a long time, Mary had felt resentful of the fact that her family seemed to smother her, not let her be just herself.

The one thing Mary dreamed about was becoming a nurse. Ever since she was a little girl, she had watched every hospital programme on the television, from real life fly-on-the-wall documentaries to the soap-based programmes. Her favourite programmes were 'Casualty' and 'Holby City' and she had devoured every hour of those programmes, imagining herself having a starring role, having relationships with the characters such as Fletch Fletcher or Dominic Copeland. It had inspired her to pursue her career and her dreams.

Her parents had been devastated when she announced she was moving to London. As she had secured her place at the University

of West London to study nursing, they could hardly broker any argument, although they were sincerely unhappy about her moving so far away from her home, particularly to such a vast city where she could become easily lost. So too, her siblings had presented their cases why she should not go, but in the end, Mary was adamant that it was her vocation, no different to being called into the service of the church. Her mother, a devout Catholic had accepted that and being the matriarch of the entire family, all the other family members had fallen in behind her. And so it was that Mary-Jane Kelly had found herself moving to London to become a nurse.

Her visits home had been as often as she could, but she had never returned permanently to Ireland. She had built her life around her career and although her fairy tale childhood dreaming had never quite come true, Mary-Jane believed she was as happy as most people were. She had her job which she loved, she had her own flat and she had the occasional boyfriend. Mary-Jane was still waiting for that someone special to cross her path, but at the age of twenty-nine, she still had faith that it wouldn't be long.

As one of the single nurses, Mary very often pulled the shifts nobody wanted to do. She didn't mind. She understood how many of her colleagues had children and families to return home to and sometimes the shifts such as those on Christmas Day were the best shifts to do.

Mary worked in the accident and emergency department. It was busy and non-stop pretty much twenty-four hours a day, and although many of her colleagues had transferred to wards as the opportunities had arisen, Mary preferred to stay in the hub of the hospital, where you never knew what to expect and every day was different. It was the one thing that kept her job fresh and interesting.

Today was the fifth of November, Bonfire Night, and Mary's shift had started at six p.m. She had no doubt it would be eventful. Last year they had had about nine hundred patients through the doors requiring treatment for firework and fire related accidents.

Mary had no doubt that this year would be just as eventful. She had been right.

A steady stream of accidents and even two deaths had presided in A&E that evening, as well the usual patients suffering headaches, toothaches or general malaise which really couldn't be considered an emergency. Mary had always failed to understand why people would sit in the department for five hours just to receive two paracetamol and be sent home.

Still the shift had been so busy that she had barely had time to grab a glass of water, let alone anything to eat. Now she was nearing the end of the shift, she couldn't wait to attend handover and go home. She had four off days now and couldn't wait to begin her time off.

After handing over details of the shift and the patients still residing in A&E to her colleagues at nearly seven a.m. the following morning, Mary finally left the hospital. She would not be back on shift now until the tenth of November and then she was on days. Days tended to be a little bit quieter for the most part, unless it was the weekend.

Mary climbed into her car for the short drive back to her flat. Her eyes felt grainy with tiredness and her body felt totally exhausted and worn out. It was at times like this she wanted to be at home with her mother. To lay her head on her Mammy's lap while Mammy stroked her hair and spoke to her with her soft southern Irish lilt and told her a story. Mammy's stories were legendary in the family and Daddy often said she should put them in a book.

Mary switched the blowers on in her car, to allow the windscreen to clear. The weather had turned quite cold all of a sudden, a touch of frost, perhaps even snow in the air. Again, that would not bode well for the team in accident and emergency. She had been called back off leave once before during the winter when many staff had come down with illnesses. She didn't relish that thought.

This Christmas, the first for many years, Mary was returning to her home to spend it with the family. She had to admit she was really looking forward to it – the noise and the hustle and bustle of twenty-one people in the house including her brand-new baby nephew Jack, whom she had not yet seen other than in photographs. She knew they would all in their own way try and persuade her to return to the bosom of her family, particularly Mammy. Mary smiled at that. This must be what mellowing with age meant; there would have been a time when she would have baulked at that, not even given it a moment of her consideration. Now? Who knew?

Her screen was almost clear and the car was becoming warm. She grabbed her mobile phone from her bag, suddenly forgetting that she had not switched it on yet. The iPhone sprung to life, and a Snapchat filtered picture of herself and her best friend Flo filled the screen. It was a selfie that they had taken at Flo's barbeque over August bank holiday which they had used a filter on and Mary had saved it. It was a filter that made them appear softer and younger with bright eyes and white teeth and flowers in their hair. It always made Mary smile.

Flo was also a nurse who now worked in the dementia unit. They had met one day in the hospital canteen. It had been a really busy day in the canteen and there were simply no tables available. Flo had plonked herself down where Mary was sitting alone, enjoying a rare quiet moment of relief when she could grab a break and a coffee. Mary often said it was fate that had brought them together. They had started chatting, Flo being the type of larger-than-life character who would talk to anyone. She had had Mary in stitches, laughing until her stomach hurt. They had continued to meet in the canteen on odd occasions and had sat together on those occasions. Slowly they got to know each other.

Flo, otherwise known as Florence Mercy Brown, was thirty years old. She had been born in London but her family were originally of Jamaican descent. She had beautiful, dark, smooth skin, unmarred and unblemished with large dark brown eyes, framed with long lashes. She preferred to keep her own hair short and wore an array of wigs in different styles, although these tended to be shorter for work. She tended to a larger size, but was perfectly proportioned. She often said it was because she liked her food and would never give it up.

She was in stark contrast to Mary who had long red hair and pale freckled skin with the palest blue eyes. The only similarity was that they were similar in size. Mary thought of herself and her friend as curvaceous, each having an ample bosom, smaller waist and wide hips. They made quite a spectacle when they ventured out together and turned heads wherever they went.

They had met about two years ago and had been best friends ever since.

Flo had finally met a man and Mary couldn't be happier for her despite the fact that it had eaten into their girl time. Perhaps that was why Mary was becoming so nostalgic for home lately; Flo had been a permanent fixture in her life for some time. They had eaten together, shopped together and told each other everything about their past lives and the present. It had been a real friendship, something that Mary had never had before, not even when she was at school. She knew that she and Flo would be friends all their lives and hopefully at some point, so would their children.

Glancing down at the picture on her iPhone she remembered the day it had been taken. It was the last August bank holiday, the Bank Holiday Monday in fact. Both women knew they were not working that weekend and had decided in view of the hot weather to hold a barbeque at Flo's. Flo's family had travelled from London to attend, as had many of their friends who were also not working that weekend. The alcohol had flowed and the food had been good. Flo's brother had brought a friend, a thirty-two-year-old divorcee called Luke who was just coming out the other side of a messy divorce, having found out his wife was having an affair. Luke was attempting to get back in the saddle and had hit it off with Flo immediately. They had been seeing each other ever since. Mary just hoped it wasn't a rebound romance and her friend wouldn't get hurt.

Mary sighed and put her phone back in her bag. She had no messages. Still, it was twenty past seven in the morning. The sky was only just beginning to get light and it was freezing. Most people were just getting up for their day or already heading off to work; she was now heading home.

Pulling out of her parking space, she was oblivious of the man watching her from the dark side of the carpark, standing beneath the trees there. She hadn't seen him on the countless other times either.

When news had hit the headlines that anybody called Mary Kelly should contact the police if they felt unsafe or felt like they were being watched, Mary had been inundated with calls and texts from her friends. She had laughed it off, as she did many things. She had been vigilant for a short while, checking behind her on occasions, making sure that the same car didn't follow her from home to work and vice versa. She had soon become bored and stopped looking. Eventually, the news had changed to the next big thing and all thoughts of Mary Kelly were forgotten.

HIM

It amazed him that people never seemed to notice what was going on in their surroundings. There was a murderer on the loose and yet there was an abundance of women who seemed oblivious to that fact, who carried on with their daily lives. Hadn't the news warned people to be vigilant? Still, he supposed it had been a while since the last murder. He was no longer headline or front-page news at the moment. It had been a little over a month since the body of Katherine Eddowin had been found. The grisly details had not been bandied about and the fact that he had sent Katherine's kidney to the police had not been shared with the media at all, although there was some speculation to that end. Clearly, not everyone at the local police station could keep that little morsel a secret. Still, he had been disappointed though that the exact details of his work had not been shared with world. The headlines that screamed '**JACK IS BACK**' had made him chuckle. If only they knew what they were truly dealing with. Jack had indeed been a master; it was the reason he had emulated his hero, had wanted to follow in his footsteps. But that had been in the beginning. Now he understood his real purpose, that being Jack was only the start of something so much more. The next murder would transport him into the realms of history, but it would be like going through a deep dark tunnel where you came upon a door at the end. The door was enlightenment. He would go on and on. There would be no mystery about where he had gone, that his sacrifices would ever just stop. He was eternal and he would live on forever.

The police had arrested someone now. He was happy to sit back and allow that little event to run its course. They would realise they had the wrong man soon enough, but for now it allowed him a certain freedom. They were not looking for him. Nobody knew what he looked like.

He knew that Mary-Jane Kelly was the perfect sacrifice. The moment he had set eyes on her, he had known and not just because of the fact that her name was Mary Kelly, but for all the women he had killed so far, she had somehow meant something more. He didn't know if it was because she was the one who had the same name as the original victim, or something more gravitational pulling him towards her. One thing he knew, it was almost too perfect.

At the moment she had no idea of the importance of her role in the history he was making, but she would. Oh yes, she definitely would. She was the final link in the chain of his becoming. He was almost there, he was almost ready. Soon he would be feared and revered. He could carry out his work and the authorities would remain clueless as they were now. He was clever, too clever for the police. They couldn't fathom how he picked his victims, they were searching for a link, wondering if they all knew each other somehow. It would be impossible for them to guess.

Each of the women he had carefully selected had had something special to him and him alone. It was as if their beings had called to him, that their particular song had hailed his presence. When he saw them, he just knew; they were the One. They were part of his destiny. But there would be others. He already knew who they were.

MARY

Mary decided to have a pyjama day. They were the best. She had stopped at the shop on the way home and brought herself some provisions. It was mainly junk food: microwave chips, microwave dinners, crisps, biscuits and a tub of decadent ice cream. She was all set.

Once she got home and put her shopping away, she made herself a cup of tea and got ready for bed. Fortunately for her, the flats in which she lived mainly housed quiet, professional people and therefore most of them went to work during the day. It meant that when she did nights, she could sleep a good portion of the day uninterrupted.

Mary woke up at four p.m. that afternoon. It was dark of course and a distinct chill was in the air, meaning that the heating had regulated itself to an ideal temperature. Rising from her bed, she checked the thermostat and turned up the heating, before getting herself in the shower. Once she felt clean and slightly more awake, she put on a fresh pair of pyjamas and settled down to watch her TV programmes on catch up. Flo called and they arranged to meet each other for a coffee and a catch up the next day. Her mother called and she caught up on the family news amidst claims of excitement about the forthcoming Christmas homecoming. It wasn't hard for Mary to catch on to that excitement and she had to admit she was really starting to look forward to going home. Usually Christmas was a pretty uneventful affair for her, at least it had been since she moved away from home. She had been invited to Flo's in the past, but for the most part agreed to cover the shifts so that her colleagues could spend the time with their families. This year she would get to spend the time with *her* family. She could recall the family Christmases in the past when it irritated her to be around so many people, to never have the space, or to have some quiet time. Now she found that she actually missed those occasions, that her life was altogether too quiet.

After the night shifts ended it always took a couple of days to right the equilibrium of her days and nights. She found herself falling asleep at odd times while her body got itself back on an even keel.

She met Flo for coffee in town. There was something positively glowing about her friend. She looked so happy and although Mary had concerns that the relationship was on the rebound, Flo confirmed that she was indeed falling in love with Luke and Mary was happy for her.

"Now all we need to do is find somebody for you," Flo suggested, tucking into a piece of dark chocolate fudge cake she had ordered with her coffee.

Mary scoffed at that remark, nibbling on her own piece of chocolate fudge cake. They were not friends for nothing.

"When are you back on shift?" Flo asked.

"I've got three weeks of days and then a week of nights before I go home. I start back on Thursday."

Flo nodded. "I don't know why you don't apply for one of the wards, it would be so much steadier. You might even get a bit more of a social life." It was a conversation that inevitably came about between them at some stage or another.

"I get time off." Flo gave her the look that said really? And Mary laughed.

"You looking forward to going home, anyway?" Flo changed the subject skilfully. Mary had confided in Flo about how unhappy she had been at home and she knew she had not been home on many occasions since.

"I am as a matter of fact," Mary admitted.

"Don't think your mum will have lined up husband material to keep you firmly in the Emerald Isle?"

Again, Mary laughed, but heartier this time. "It would never surprise me."

After her coffee meeting with Flo and a catch up of all the news, Mary came home and promptly fell asleep while watching television. It was how she found herself sitting up, being wide awake at one a.m. in the morning, Facebook-stalking some of her friends' lives. In truth, Mary was falling out of interest in Facebook. She used to spend each spare minute logging in and checking statuses, who was doing what and when. She had many friends and friends of friends, some of whom she had never met but had formed a virtual acquaintance with online. At one time it had been considered quite a status symbol to have as many friends as you could. Now she found the whole thing quite mundane, the same old, same old pattern of 'look what I had for dinner', YouTube videos of something stupid happening to a cat with the odd occasional 'look where I've been on holiday' thrown in. However, she still felt the need to have a look, to trawl through those holiday photos to catch up with the lives of people she hardly knew.

It was how Mary's existence played out day after day. She was a creature of habit, living her quiet life, sometimes living in the unreal life of the dramas on television to the exclusion of all else going on around her.

By Wednesday, Mary felt she was going a bit stir crazy. She had been cooped up in the flat for two days straight, barely moving from her sofa. She looked out the window on a bright sunny November day and knew she had to get out, even if only to walk around the park. She decided while getting dressed that she would maybe feed the ducks. Once dressed, she bundled herself up in a warm coat, hat, scarf and gloves. Grabbing her bread, broken into small pieces in readiness for the ducks, she walked the ten-minute journey to the park.

HIM

He could not believe his luck. Today was the day and he was beyond excited, so much so that he could hardly wait. His Mary was a creature of habit. She was less slutty than other women he had so far encountered, but nevertheless she could claim that title as much as any other; he had seen the evidence with his own eyes.

How to get her alone in her flat had presented quite a challenge and a lot of thought. Her flats had security entry for which you needed a fob and then there would be the challenge of her opening the door and allowing him entrance. She might have come from some tiny village in Ireland, but he had the feeling she was far from a country bumpkin with all the guile of a turnip. He had the feeling that Mary would prove quite savvy in whom she allowed entrance to her property.

He had watched her for some considerable time now. He knew her movements, knew she spent very little time outside her workplace. She had few friends and no family around to mention. She lived quite an exclusive existence and was more a creature of habit than he had encountered so far. Still, he loved a challenge and had carefully thought through how he would approach her.

Now, even better, here she was coming out of her flat and seemingly doing something out of the norm. He was intrigued and started following her.

He watched her enter the park, and followed her while she made her way to the duck pond. Here only a couple of people could be found due to the coldness of the day, despite the bright sunshine. One woman sat on one of the benches around the pond, clearly arguing with someone loudly on her phone, while another woman had a small child in a pushchair. Both wore warm clothing, the child throwing clumps of bread into or near the pond for the ducks.

Mary sat down on a bench and opened her own bag of bread. He watched as she started to throw some, attracting the attention of the ducks which were soon swarming around near her on the water's edge.

Moving forward, despite there being at least one other empty bench, he came to sit down on the opposite end to Mary. She turned to smile briefly at him and he returned the gesture. "Hungry little devils, aren't they?" he murmured, seemingly amused.

She chuckled. "They certainly are."

His face lit up in pleasure. "You're Irish!" he exclaimed.

A small frown crossed her brow for moment. "For my sins." She replied, vexed at the stranger and whatever he might mean.

"I don't mean any offence, it's just that I absolutely love the Irish accent, I could listen to it for hours," he said quickly.

Mary seemed to relax slightly. "Oh, I see." She allowed a small laugh once more.

"Sorry, didn't mean to sound weird." He tried again, using his body language to turn slightly as if he had truly offended her.

"It's really okay."

He asked her a few other questions, like what part of Ireland she came from. He seemed genuinely interested in her.

"I'm Mary by the way," she offered after they had chatted a bit more.

"Roger." He replied almost instantly, using his previous alias. This was going well so far; the ice was well and truly broken. "This might sound cliched, but do you come here often?" he laughed at his own joke and she again laughed with him, not in the least perturbed. She was used to being around strangers, to having brief conversations out of thin air, it was part of her job. She turned to look properly at the man who sat beside her on the bench. He was quite good looking in a boy-next-door sort of way. Although wearing a thick coat and clothing for the kind of weather, he looked like a large man, muscular like those who worked out regularly. He had blonde hair and while she wasn't usually attracted to blondes, he had an undeniable something. She wondered briefly what he might have been doing in the park in the middle of the day.

"I don't, as a matter of fact," she answered his question. "I came here on a whim today. To be truthful I was going a bit stir crazy indoors on my own and needed the fresh air."

He nodded as though he understood. "Yes, I know that feeling. I was made redundant two weeks ago and I haven't found a new job yet. If I'm honest, I was feeling a little stir crazy myself."

"Oh dear, what did you do?"

"Stock broker," he replied, looking suitably sheepish. He held up two fingers in the sign of the cross in front of him. "Don't hate me," he said and laughed. She laughed along with him. "What do you do?" he asked pleasantly.

"I'm a nurse."

"Impressive and a much more respectable profession than stock broker." Mary found herself laughing again. She had to admit she was quite taken with the handsome stranger.

They chatted a bit more while she fed the rest of her bread to the ducks.

The chill of the day was starting to seep into her bones and she was ready to go home. However, something about this man was quite alluring. She felt comfortable chatting to him and he seemed harmless enough. "Look, I'm feeling a bit cold, I think I'm going to head home now." Mary stood.

"Oh yes, of course," he replied softly. He looked crestfallen and for some inexplicable reason, Mary felt guilty.

"Would you like to come back to mine for a cuppa?" She had no idea where it had come from – an invitation she would never usually offer to a stranger. Very few of the men she had dated had even been invited back to the sanctuary of her home and yet here she was, half an hour into a polite conversation, asking a perfect stranger back to her flat.

She was gratified to receive a beatific smile. "That would be absolutely fantastic!" he exclaimed enthusiastically. "To be honest, I don't get out much. I don't have too many friends these days, especially those who don't work," he admitted ruefully, shrugging his shoulders. Mary felt like he was a kindred spirit. There was something disturbingly familiar about his description of his own life and it suddenly dawned on her what it was. His life mirrored hers almost exactly. It was uncanny really.

She liked the look of him and on first acquaintance he seemed like a nice man. As a stock broker he might have made some money for himself; his clothes certainly looked expensive. He might even have had a good redundancy package which would mean he could wine and dine her. As he fell into step beside her, strolling in the direction of her flat, Mary mentally brought herself up short. She was practically planning her marriage and all they were doing was having a cup of tea together. She wasn't exactly a man magnet. So far, her love life had resulted in a couple of relationships, one of which lasted for six months and the other was just for a few dates, which had left Mary considerably unsatisfied in the bedroom department. That had been only a couple of months back. She had tried and miserably failed to maintain a relationship, and although a very nice man, he just didn't do it for her where sex was concerned.

She turned to look at the profile of the man by her side now. He was quite tall, she noted and had a very self-assured way of walking. Their acquaintance, although brief, had been enjoyable and she was starting to find him more and more attractive. She found herself wondering if she would be his type. He looked like he should have a very sophisticated, beautiful brunette on his arm, wearing the latest designer fashions. She sighed aloud without realising and he stopped and turned to her.

"Is everything okay, Mary? If you've changed your mind, it's okay, I am after all a perfect stranger." He took a step back as if to emphasise his point.

In all of Mary's life she had played it safe, done what everyone else wanted her to do. The one thing she had done on her own, for herself, was travel to London to learn how to be a nurse. But still after gaining her qualifications, she had continued to be a people-pleaser, to do things for other people and ensure their lives were made easier before considering her own.

It was time she started doing things for herself, to try and make her life better. If this turned out to be just a cup of tea and a chat with nothing more, so be it. But sometimes you just had to take a leap of faith, to take a chance to see what would happen next.

"Everything is just great, Roger, this is where I live." She gestured to the entrance of the flats they had come to rest outside. "Come on up, I promised you a cup of tea and a cup of tea you shall have." A thread of determination was apparent in her voice.

"Lead the way." Roger was overjoyed and it showed in his face. He looked as if Christmas had come early and Mary was suddenly struck that maybe, just maybe, there was such a thing as love at first sight and that Roger had fallen head over heels for her. It gave her a warm glow thinking about it.

It was early evening and Roger had spent the best part of two hours sitting in her living room. They had exchanged many details about their respective lives and the more Mary heard, she had to admit the more she liked. To her it felt comfortable with Roger in her living room.

"Would you like another cup of tea?" Mary asked. They had already had two a piece, plus half a packet of biscuits and she wished she had something stronger to offer him. She rarely drank alcohol herself and therefore didn't ever buy it.

"Let me make you one this time, I think I know my way around a kitchen you know." He smiled brightly while picking up their mugs, disappearing from the room to enter the kitchen. A moment later she heard him fill the kettle and snap it on.

Mary smiled to herself. Just what was happening here? She never did things like this.

Overwhelmed by a sudden sense of needing to tell someone, she picked up her mobile phone and sent Flo a text. '*OMG you won't believe it, I'm with a man… in my flat… and he is gorgeous xx*'. An instant response was received. '*You go girl, give me all the gory details later, or tomorrow xx'* The text was followed a thumbs up emoji. Mary smiled to herself, placing her mobile back on the coffee table as Roger returned with two steaming mugs of tea.

He smiled at her as he placed the cups on the coffee table before retaking his seat next to her. Was it her imagination or was he sitting closer?

Mary kept giggling. It was as if she was drunk but so much more. He could not believe his luck. How much better could today have panned out? To be invited into the sanctuary of Mary's home and he barely even had to try. Now she was drugged with the Rohypnol that had been in her tea. The most difficult and challenging part of the day was sitting with her, making small talk. Where he had gathered the information from that he fed her, even surprised him. He should have taking up acting. She was lapping up the tales he told as they chatted.

Once she was suitably drugged, he knew he needed to get her to the bedroom. He had already done a quick reconnaissance on the proviso that he needed the loo since he had not had the opportunity to gain access to her flat previously. It was a nicely decorated, spacious, one bedroomed place. Mary was obviously a neat freak since not a single thing was out of place and there was not a spec of dust to be seen. She had a large double bed in the bedroom under the window. To the right stood a large mirrored double fronted wardrobe. There was a chest of drawers and a small dressing table adorned with a couple of bottles of perfume and a make-up bag. The décor was in shades of blue which were pleasing to the eye. He returned to the living room.

Mary was lying back against the arm of the sofa, her eyes closed. He removed his surgical gloves from the pocket of his coat and put them on. Placing his left knee on the sofa, he leant into her.

"Hello, Mary, darling," he called softly. She opened her eyes blearily and half smiled at him. "I'm going to take you to bed now." She giggled once again. He helped her to her feet and she staggered, almost losing her balance. Allowing her to lean against him, he half walked, half carried her to the bedroom, allowing her to fall onto the bed at the first opportunity. She was by far the heaviest of the women he had killed so far. It took some considerable effort to remove her clothing and position her in the centre of the bed. She was now a dead weight in the stupor she had fallen into and he was sweating profusely by the time he had finally managed to remove every piece of clothing she wore. Although at least a size sixteen, her body was nonetheless firm and pleasing to look at. Her skin was the colour of milk all over as if she had never blemished herself with a suntan. He released her red hair which had been pulled into a pony tail and allowed it to fall around her shoulders in rolling waves. He was pleased to notice that her pubic hair matched, a true redhead.

As this was to be the piece de resistance so far to his work, he wanted things to be absolutely perfect. He had a long night and a lot of work ahead of him, but first he decided to indulge in the pastime of enjoying her body before he took her life. By the time he had removed his own clothes, his cock stood to attention, ready and waiting the ministrations that would be to fuck the woman lying on the bed. He really wished that he could take her without the aid of a condom. He wanted to feel his skin against hers, to know what her insides felt like. He pondered on this thought for a moment. He had never been arrested in his life, the police had no DNA. His DNA was untraceable and besides he was going to mutilate her body beyond all recognition. He stroked the length of his penis slowly and ended by cupping his balls. He caught a glimpse of himself in the full-length mirrored wardrobes and found the whole scene incredibly erotic. He watched himself for a moment in the mirror before turning his gaze back to Mary. Moving to the bed, he pulled her legs apart and looked upon the womanliest part of her body. He wanted to savour this moment, to remember Mary as she was now. She lay invitingly, her legs pulled wide apart. Her large breasts lay flattened, but nonetheless erotic, her pink nipples hard and erect in the chill of the bedroom without clothes. Her left arm lay by her side, while the other was bent at the elbow, her hand curled into a loose fist, which rested upon her right cheek. Her head was turned slightly to the right and although her eyes were closed, a small smile played around her rosebud lips. She looked luscious and for the taking, like she was just waiting for him.

He could wait no longer and climbed onto the bed before her. He pushed into her moist entrance with a certain force. Mary's eyes fluttered and she glanced up at him as if taken by surprise. Her pale blue eyes met his and for the briefest of seconds a look of alarm crossed her face before being replaced with something more erotic. He continued to pound his cock into her, his ministrations on her body causing her to melt and undulate beneath him; her breathing increased as did his. This was the best sex he had ever had and as he thought about what he was about to do to her next he suddenly ejaculated, his hot sperm spilling into her body. His arms and legs felt weak as he collapsed onto her body. The aftershock spasms of his almighty orgasm caused his cock to twitch in the warm, moist confines of Mary's body. He felt comfortable against the softness of her body, her breasts providing a pillow for his head. Her hand came involuntarily to his head and she wrapped her fingers up in his hair, a gesture he had long associated with his mother.

The overwhelming feelings of disgust enveloped him immediately and he pulled away from Mary as if her body had burnt him. He almost leaped off the bed, a look of abject horror on his face. What had she nearly accomplished? He had been bewitched by her; her womanly guile had almost managed to make him forget, to become so consumed in the moment of enjoying her body that he might have forgotten his reason for being there. He was furious with her. She would pay for this, oh yes, she would certainly pay. He wanted to beat her with his fists, to pummel her face until it was a bloody mess, to feel that contact – perhaps her nose would break, he could imagine the splat of blood if he did that. He wanted to kick her between the legs. To mar that perfection he had been so enamoured of a few moments before. She had worked her magic on him and he had succumbed. He was filled with such an intense anger towards her he could barely function; the black rage that had engulfed him so many times before threatened to wipe out his rational existence.

He turned from her body a moment, taking a deep shuddering breath, trying to right his equilibrium. He needed to remain focused. He had been presented with the opportunity of a lifetime here. He had thought to gain entry to her flat on the pretence that he needed a nurse for his sister who lived in the same flats, having pushed all the buttons until somebody allowed him entry. He could scarcely believe his luck at not having to use that tack. It had not been necessary to lie to gain entry because Mary, as guileless as she was, had fallen for him and his charm. The rest had been a piece of cake and he couldn't afford to waste that opportunity.

Taking a further deep breath to calm his anger, he turned and left the bedroom, extracting the largest knife from the knife block. While making tea earlier he had discovered that she had the knife block and he hoped that they would be sharp enough for the task in hand. He picked the largest now, testing its sharpness on his own thumb. He was gratified to find that it was extremely sharp. He strode purposefully back to the bedroom to find Mary where he had left her. Without further thought or premise he knelt on the bed to the right of Mary's sleeping form and pulled the knife across her throat, applying considerable pressure so that it would cause as much damage as possible. The instantaneous arc of blood that shot upwards indicated that he had severed her left carotid artery. Her neck began to pump like a mini geyser was lodged in her body. He relished in the scene as he watched her life's blood pump from her body and soak into the bedding beneath her. Mary's eyes remained closed the whole time. She never regained consciousness and never knew what atrocities would be inflicted upon her body.

Many hours later, he had finished. The work had taken a very long time, longer than he had first envisaged. The bedroom looked and smelled like an abattoir. The bloody mess on the bed was unrecognisable as the person it had once been. She had bled out considerably, it had splashed up the walls, the bed was soaked through and it seemed there was blood on every surface in the room, from the wardrobes to the carpet to the dressing table. Even he was drenched from head to toe. He looked like he had taken a bath in Mary once she had been cut open.

He was proud of his work. This was destined to be the pinnacle of his work so far, and he had to admit it was just that. It was like looking at art and he could do no more in those moments but take a step back and admire what he had created. He felt proud of himself; he wanted to share it, to stand on the rooftops and proclaim his mastery.

Sighing happily, he made his way into Mary's small bathroom and looked at himself in the mirror over the sink. He needed a shower, but couldn't take the risk of leaving any DNA behind. The most he could accomplish at the moment would be to wash off as much of the blood off his face as he could, clothe himself and make his way home. He needed the cover of darkness to move freely. During the daylight hours something amiss would be noted and he couldn't take that chance. Right now, it was about three a.m., the witching hour. Very few people would be around at this time of day and the street lights would be off, which would mean he could move freely, undetected.

Keeping on his gloves so that fingerprints couldn't be taken, he washed his face, removing as much blood as he could. He marvelled that it had even got into his ears. He had grabbed the kitchen paper earlier and now used this to dry himself off. He washed the mug he had used for his tea and wiped over anything he could that he thought he had touched with damp pieces of kitchen paper. Finally, he pulled on his clothes. The blood had mostly dried in places all over his body and he felt incredibly dirty and uncomfortable. He was gratified that his clothing was dark so that when finally, he was fully clothed, none of the blood was visible any longer. He put on his coat and black beanie, ensuring that any trace of his blood-spattered hair was covered under the hat. He would burn and dispose of the clothing later. He then quickly walked around the flat, confirming that he had all his belongings and that any trace that he had been in Mary's flat was eradicated. He went to the front door and opened it slowly, checking the hallway for any movement or people. Feeling secure in the knowledge that there was no-one around to see him, he closed the front door behind him and trotted down the two flights of stairs to the ground floor before leaving through the security door to the street. Carrying out a quick scan of both sides of the street, he turned right and began walking in that direction.

Alison McKenzie was sixty-seven years old and lived alone, as she had done for the last seventeen years since her husband passed away. It was three a.m. and she was up and wide awake, much to her chagrin. It was becoming a ridiculous round of dropping off at a reasonable time, only to wake up at some ludicrous hour of the morning and being unable to get back to sleep. She had tried sleeping tablets, relaxation techniques and mindfulness but nothing had worked. She still woke up in the middle of the night. Sometimes she would read until her eyes felt heavy enough that she could actually grab another hour or so; sometimes she tried to watch television. Tonight however, she had made herself a cup of hot milk and was currently ensconced in the recess of her bay window seat, covered in a blanket and watching the world go by her window. Except that there was no world to go by, as it was three a.m. She had no lights on in her flat, preferring the darkness. She had pulled up her blinds, giving her a full view of the street. The street lights were turned off at two a.m., not to be put back on until five a.m. and only the light of the moon cast an eerie white light. The shadows were long and dark and to Alison, it seemed as though the scene she viewed was that of a negative photograph. Had she been an artistic-minded sort of person, she might have had the urge to snap some pictures or perhaps draw the scene before her. As it was, she sat sipping her milk, her knees pulled up in front of her chest. Despite the fact that she was unable to sleep, she had to admit she enjoyed the serenity of the darkness. It was an hour where virtually nobody was around. One could almost imagine themselves at the end of the world.

A sudden movement across her street caught her immediate attention. She watched a man, at least she thought it was a man due to his size, leave the entrance of the flats. He was dressed like a burglar in her opinion, all in black - black trousers, black coat and black hat. From where she sat, his face was an indistinguishable blur, but it wasn't so much what he looked like that caught her attention. For all she knew he could have been on his way to work, but something about his demeanour made Alison McKenzie think that he was up to no good. She was an avid fan of crime and mystery stories and this person looked shifty as he alighted from the building opposite. He seemed to be far too vigilant, like he was scanning the street, making sure there was nobody around. People going to work didn't do that. The burglar turned to his right and moved off down the street. Alison moved from her position and stood pressed against the window, trying to watch where he went next. She could just see to the end of the street from her angle and she followed his progress to the end of the street, watching as he turned right again, disappearing around the corner where he vanished from view.

She sat back down on her seat for moment, pulling the blanket back around herself again. She was absolutely wide awake now, all thoughts of even trying to sleep gone from her mind and body even despite the warm milk. She decided to sit in the window a while longer to see if the burglar came back. She had nicknamed him the burglar. It didn't hurt to remember little details; who knew when the police might want a witness for a crime that had been committed?

CHAPTER TWENTY-TWO

NOW

Shelley McKiernan was the matron on shift in the accident and emergency department on the tenth of November. It was a Thursday, which was always a bit of an odd day, the calm before the storm of the weekend, when everything from a stubbed toe to a major heart attack would stumble through their doors. Shelley was hoping that today would be quiet. In truth she hated working A&E. She couldn't bear the noise and people who entered through those doors. It was nothing like the fly-on-the-wall documentaries that were seen on TV. In those, the romantic side of life was shown; you didn't see the abuse that was screamed at you when patients were forced to wait in the waiting room for hours on end or the drunk who would throw up everything inside his stomach all the way down from your hair to your shoes and you would spend the next seven hours with the stench of vomit under your nose. It wasn't pretty and certainly not the serene scenes portrayed by the television.

Shelley glanced at the clock by the nurse's station. She was waiting to carry out handover. Nurses who had been on the last shift would update the new team on the patients currently residing in A&E so that the patient care could continue with the minimum of fuss. Shelley was awaiting the arrival of one last member of staff, Mary Kelly.

Shelley admired Mary, and she admired very few of the staff she worked with. Mary had shown dedication and care far above and beyond what was expected of her. She was always willing to cover a shift when required, would stay to complete tasks if asked and was always considerate towards every patient, no matter how young or old plus everything in-between. It was how Shelley saw herself twenty years ago and Shelley hoped that the tarnish of disappointment and disillusionment would never jade Mary's life as it had hers.

Staff were required to contact a senior member of staff to let them know as early as possible that they were unable to attend their shift so that time could be made to find and contact a temporary member of staff to cover the shift. Shelley was concerned that she had not heard from Mary at all. There had been no call as far she was aware, still she covered the shift and hoped Mary would contact her at some point to explain her absence.

Later that day, Florence Mercy Brown sat in the hospital canteen in her lunch break. She had made arrangements to meet with Mary, her best friend. Unfortunately, Mary was a no-show. Thinking Mary was caught up in the hustle and bustle of A&E, she decided to do a detour and pop in there on her way back to the dementia ward.

Shelley McKiernan, the austere matron whom nobody seemed to like very much, had informed her that Mary had not shown up for work today and had not called to say why. Shelley was a formidable woman but also in a more senior position. You didn't want to piss of Shelley McKiernan because she was the sort of woman who would have you on bedpan duty for the rest of your natural life.

Flo tried to text her best friend again, wondering if Mary was ill, too ill to pick up the phone. It was so unlike her. If Mary hadn't shown up for work and was currently AWOL, there was a very good reason. Flo decided to pop round to Mary's on her way home from work to check on her best friend.

She had buzzed the door four times and still there was no answer. Flo didn't have a key to Mary's place. They had often discussed sharing their house keys just in case some fate should befall either one of them. Unfortunately, this had never gone beyond the discussion part. Flo was inordinately worried. She had been unable to gain access to the flats by other means and was intermittently ringing Mary's mobile without success. Flo knew Mary too well for this to be prank. A dim recollection of the news that morning fleeting flew through her brain about a report of Mary Kelly on the news. Unfortunately, Flo did not pay much attention to the news. As far as she was concerned the doom and gloom of the world could be found right on her doorstep without watching it on TV too. She tended to ignore any kind of news on TV, never brought a newspaper and hardly ever followed the social media pages. It was to be to her detriment in that moment.

The only thing Flo could think was that her friend had had some kind of accident and was lying hurt. It was what prompted her to phone the police. She knew Mary would be pissed off at having her door broken down, and should everything be fine and dandy, Flo had it in her head that she would foot the cost of a replacement door; it would be the very least she could do in the circumstances. While she waited for the police to arrive, she called Mary another couple of times, getting the eventual result of her voicemail as she had done on the several other occasions she had called.

No-one could have been prepared for the sight that greeted them when the police finally broke into Mary Kelly's property. Although the protocol would have been for the police to check everything out first, Flo had pushed her way forward, shouting that she was a nurse and she needed to help her friend. It was only when she stood at the entrance to Mary's bedroom that she realised there would have been nothing humanly possible she could have done in that respect.

Ginny was on the scene. She was gutted. The grisly remains of Mary Kelly were all over her bedroom. Two of the officers attending the scene and breaking in had been violently sick. The entire flat smelt of vomit and blood but Ginny, although she felt nauseated enough to throw up herself, and in fact having done so on viewing the murder of Anna Chapman, managed to keep the contents of her stomach in situ on this occasion.

She could scarcely believe it when the call came in. Bradley Parker was currently residing in the cells at the station while they gathered evidence to charge him with two further murders and all that time, the real murderer had been killing his final victim. It was unclear at this stage how their murderer had gained entry to the flat.

Mary's best friend and work colleague had said Mary had texted her last evening stating that she was with a man here in her flat. The text had been light-hearted, no evidence of anything sinister or untoward going on, unless of course the murderer had texted Flo as part of his cover. Ginny doubted it. She had no doubt that somehow the murderer had charmed his way into Mary's flat. Either that or he had been well known to her.

Melanie Watson had been called to give her opinion on the body. Everyone was reluctant to move it at the moment, just in case any fresh evidence was removed, such was the extent of Mary's mutilation.

CHAPTER TWENTY-THREE

NOW

Melanie stood back, surveying the scene before her. She swallowed hard and wished that she had not eaten before she came here today. She should have known. Hadn't she read extensively what injuries to expect? Even to a seasoned professional such as herself, the reality was starkly different.

Wearing her required forensic outfit, complete with booties and double layered surgical gloves, Melanie set forward to examine the remains of Mary Kelly. DCI Ginny Percy had joined her and was ready to take notes.

What was left of Mary was naked, lying in the middle of the bed; her shoulders were flat against the bed, but her body inclined towards the left, her head being turned on her left cheek. Her left arm lay bent by her side, her forearm lying at a right angle across what was left of her abdomen. The right arm was abducted from the body resting on the mattress. Her legs had been spread wide apart. The whole surface of her abdomen and thighs had been removed; her abdominal cavity had been emptied. Her breasts had been removed and her arms had several jagged wounds. Her face was unrecognisable, having been heavily mutilated. Her neck was almost severed to the bone and her fifth and sixth vertebrae were clearly visible.

The killer had placed her uterus, kidneys and one breast beneath her head; her other breast was by her right foot. Her liver had been removed and was between her feet. Her intestines, like in other victims, had been removed and resided on the right side of her body; her spleen lay on her left side. The pieces of skin that had been removed from her abdomen and thighs resided on her dressing table. The bed was saturated in blood, which had seeped through the mattress to the floor below. An arc of blood had splashed against the window under which the bed sat, but had also splashed onto the full-length wardrobe mirrors. The killer had slashed Mary's face, cutting her nose, cheeks and above her eyes, and had removed parts of her ears. Finally, her heart had been removed and was currently missing.

"What was the cause of death?" Ginny asked. Everyone seemed to be speaking in hushed tones at the moment, such was the shock felt by everyone at the crime scene.

"I would say he slashed her throat. You see that arc?" Melanie pointed to the spray of blood that covered the window and part of the wardrobe doors. "It's in line with her throat. I would say it's definitely our left-handed killer again. Same MO as he's used all the other times – similarities in the way he stabs and slashes his victims, despite the murder weapon being different each time. I would say she was unconscious at the time of death, possibly asleep."

Ginny was busy making notes, but stopped and looked up. "Any chance she was sexually assaulted?"

"Won't know that until I get her back to the lab, but I would say there is a good chance of it as it's his MO. I'll need to take further tests of course. I did wonder whether he drugs his victims, but there's been no trace of anything in their bodies." Melanie looked pensive for a moment.

"Date rape drug." Ginny spoke at the same time as Melanie said "Rohypnol."

"But how would he get close enough to give it to them? We have CCTV footage of Anna Chapman going to a bar with a man. She was either drunk or drugged when they came out a short time later," said Ginny.

"There was evidence of alcohol and drugs in her system, but no Rohypnol which is known to evaporate. She had been smoking cannabis which was noted in my toxicology report," Melanie pointed out.

"So he puts the drug in Anna's drink in the bar somehow, while she's not looking. Then how did he do it with the other victims?"

"He would have to have been with them. The effects of Rohypnol can last anything from two to eight hours. He couldn't take the chance of it wearing off before he had the chance to kill the women."

"Then somehow, he managed to either break in, or they let him in," Ginny surmised.

"He couldn't have got in here very easily. Mary would have had to have let him in through the entry system and then open her front door."

"Okay, I'm going to head back to the station, I need to check a few things out. Anything more you have, give me a call on my mobile. I've got a man in the frame sitting in custody at the moment. There's no possible way he could have done this so I think I'm going to have to let him walk." Ginny was gutted.

Melanie gave her commiserating pat on the shoulder. "I have a few things to still do here before they move the body, I'll keep you posted."

It seemed as if an unlikely alliance was forming between Melanie and Ginny. Both women, although doubtful of ever being real friends, had a healthy respect for each other and their work, particularly in relation to this case.

CHAPTER TWENTY-FOUR

THEN: EUGENIE GOFF NOVEMBER 1999

Eugenie knew she was in labour. It had started early that morning about four a.m., just a minor tightening of her lower abdomen, like a mild period pain and the pains were at least half an hour apart. She had seen Randall off to school and by then the pains were coming at least twenty minutes apart and were slightly stronger, although nothing unbearable. Eugenie knew that a second baby was generally much quicker than the first and she was fully expecting, hoping in fact to have given birth by the time Randall came home from school.

Randall had almost withdrawn from her completely. Their meals, which had never been chatty affairs, were now carried out in silence with Randall studiously avoiding even looking at his mother these days. His dark, unblinking stare was no longer the focus of her world. In some respects, it was a pleasant relief, yet Eugenie knew her son watched her when she was not looking. She could feel his icy, threatening stare upon her, but whenever she turned, he appeared to have averted his eyes. She didn't know what was more eerie, the full intense stare of her son's dark eyes upon her, or when he refused to look upon her at all.

Something had changed in Randall a few months before. He had not come home from school one day and had eventually returned to the house at a time far too late for a child of ten years old to even be out. He had point blank refused to answer any of her questions. Still he refused to speak to her about it. Eugenie had no idea where he had gone.

Randall had always been a little boy who could instil fear in her with a single glance. His dark eyes had always held a certain malice and animosity. Evil, she had thought at times. On occasion she had felt like he could see down to the very depths of her soul, and knew what she was thinking. She wondered time and time again if she had been the cause of what had become of her son. She knew she had never shown him enough love, and had reacted to every situation throughout his young life with disdain and disapproval. In truth she hadn't disapproved of her son so much as disapproved of her own life and had taken it out on him. She regretted that now. Children were the product of their parents and were to be guided by them. She had failed miserably where Randall was concerned. The fear she had always felt around him, the uneasiness in his gaze, she realised was probably a coping mechanism. He expected to disappoint her, to not receive any love from her. She hated to admit she had never disappointed on that front.

Now with a new baby on the way, she had so many regrets. Her life had certainly not turned out how she envisaged.

She vowed that she would never make the same mistakes with this baby. She would love and nurture this baby as she should have done with Randall. Randall was still a little boy in many ways and she felt sure she might even have the chance to change things with him, to give him the life he deserved. He needed to know what love was, to know how it felt. That was her job and she had failed him.

A sharp pain through her abdomen brought her back the present. She gasped in surprise at the fierceness of the contraction, and tried to concentrate enough to count how long it lasted. It seemed to pass fairly quickly. She checked her watch: nine fifteen. She tried to relax in the chair. Not less than five minutes later another contraction tore through her abdomen once more; the pain was intense and lasted longer this time, she was sure. She could barely concentrate enough. She just managed to pick up her mobile phone before another contraction attacked her. Just as she dialled 999 to summon an ambulance, her waters broke.

By the time the ambulance arrived, Eugenie was too far gone to be taken to hospital. The paramedics proclaimed that they would have to deliver the baby right there in her house.

Without the aid of the gas and air or pethidine as she had had with Randall, at two forty-five that afternoon, Eugenie Goff gave birth to a baby girl.

CHAPTER TWENTY-FIVE

THEN: RANDALL GOFF NOVEMBER 1999

Randall refused to look upon the body of his mother; the sight was abhorrent to him. Her belly had continued to swell with the growth of the baby that would become his sibling and Randall hated everything about it. He hated his mother for allowing this to happen to herself and he hated the unborn baby.

The hate had festered inside him, creating an insidious black void that seemed to reach the very depths of his soul.

Randall had returned from Scotland in a self-proclaimed cloud of glory, congratulating himself on his prowess for carrying out the seemingly perfect murder. The news reports had given nothing away except to say that there were no leads in the case. Randall could feel his confidence grow with every passing day. No police arrived, nobody came to take him away and as the realisation dawned on him that he had indeed committed the perfect murder, Randall was buoyed up by the self-assurance that he could in fact do it again.

He began to read through articles on the internet at the library. At first it was information about the murder. He absorbed every little detail reported in the press – soaked it up like a sponge.

With his first taste of what it felt like to be a murderer, Randall started to research other unsolved crimes. In a very short space of time this led him to perhaps the most famous unsolved crime of them all – the murders of Jack the Ripper.

The story immediately had him hooked. He pored over article upon article that he could find. He found books at the library and took them home and still his thirst for more knowledge continued.

It fascinated him that this person had eluded the police for over a hundred years. Still to this day they had no clue who had committed the murders. It fascinated him to the point of obsession.

In a lot of ways, he felt like Jack, could imagine himself as Jack with the power at his fingertips to indiscriminately kill. Jack had made whores his preferred choice of victim. Randall had so many others he could think of. Soon he was making plans, building his dossier on how he could commit further murders, how these would be undetectable by the police. He found it exciting to discover new ways of murdering people. He started to read information about other serial killers: the Yorkshire Ripper, Brady and Hindley, Mr Christie. Commendable in their crimes, but all were caught eventually. That was the one thing that set Jack apart from the rest as far as he was concerned; he had never been caught.

Randall wondered time and again what it would have felt like in Jack's shoes, to have that absolute power at his fingertips.

Randall started to observe his peers, people that crossed his path in life, his teachers, people in shops. He wondered what it would feel like to kill them, to get away with it. One thing he found disturbing was the indiscriminate way women would act. The girls in his school would chase the boys, wanting to kiss them or to be kissed. They would flirt, attempt to use their wiles and this, Randall discovered, could happen at any age. He started to notice little things in others, adults mainly. He could sit in town and watch the world go by; every passing woman seemed to preen and flirt, attempting to attract a man.

He realised even his own mother was not exempt from this behaviour. Had he not witnessed such behaviour when she was around Ian Pratchett? Randall became aware of what it was that gave these women power, what had men keeling over, doing whatever was asked of them. It was sex, that secret place a woman kept between her legs.

He had been fascinated when he had discovered his mother's monthly bleed. He had watched and learnt the monthly cycle which plagued her. Where did the blood come from and why? Was she being punished? When Randall researched it, he was not surprised to find out that yes, women were indeed being punished and that that punishment was given by God. If God could punish women, why couldn't he?

Randall and Jack, Jack and Randall. He could barely find a distinction. He could feel Jack within him, guiding him like the father he never had. He opened himself up to that feeling, allowed it to take root.

The plan when it came to him felt like divine intervention, that Jack's hand was guiding him. He knew beyond a shadow of a doubt that the unborn child his mother carried had to be sacrificed. He had to find a way to dispose of the infant once it was delivered into the world. He would have liked to stab it now while it resided in the warmth of his mother's belly, but unfortunately, he still required the presence of his mother. He knew what happened to children without parents, that they were taken into care and sodomised by the people responsible for them. Randall would allow no such thing to happen to him. He was weak at the moment, but that wouldn't last forever. Soon he would grow and he would be strong. That would be when he could rid himself of his mother.

The sight of his mother's swollen belly disgusted him. He found he could not look upon it for fear of the urge to stab the unborn infant inside his mother's stomach. He could barely manage to spend any time in his mother's company. He withdrew himself from her – even in her company, refusing to interact. His mother tried, he had to give her that. He could sense a change in her. She wanted to care for him now. She asked him things, pretended to be interested. Randall could not accept it. She had not wanted him before, preferring to offer herself like a whore to the first man who showed an iota of interest. Randall would not take the crumbs offered on her table. He would never be second choice. Besides, he had Jack and that was all he needed.

Randall made his plans to kill the baby when it arrived in the world. He was still buoyed up by the murder of Ian Pratchett and therefore the thought of killing a tiny baby presented no challenge to him.

His plan was simple; when his mother was not looking, he would simply suffocate the baby with a pillow. As far as Randall was concerned, it was simple and effective. His mother would assume the baby had stopped breathing and that would be that, all back to normal.

On the day his mother went into labour, Randall had suffered at school. The peers he was forced to spend his day with had put him in an absolutely foul mood. He had wanted to kill them all, to find a way to commit a mass murder. He had walked home with a black cloud descending upon him. The ambulance outside his house had brought him up short.

Randall entered the house to find the paramedics bundling up his mother onto a chair. One of them held the baby, but he couldn't see it; there was no sound. Was the baby dead? Shouldn't it be squawking?

"Ah just in time, Randall, this is my son, Randall," Eugenie explained to the paramedic covering her in a blanket.

"Would you be a darling, Randall, and bring my bag?" Eugenie pointed to a bag in the corner. It was the baby bag! Randall grimaced but did as his mother asked. He held out the bag and she placed it on her lap.

"Would you like to see your baby sister?" The paramedic holding the abomination had spoken to him. Did he really want to see that? No, he certainly did not. Instead of answering, he shrugged belligerently.

The paramedic knelt down and pulled back the white blanket surrounding the baby. Randall, as if his feet were controlled by somebody else, took a step forward. He looked into the swaddled bundle and was greeted by a pair of the bluest eyes he had ever seen. Unusually for a newborn baby, she gazed back at him with a seemingly unblinking stare. He was instantly captivated. Without conscious thought, Randall put out his hand and the baby latched onto his finger immediately, her tiny fingers curling around one digit.

Randall felt like his world had imploded. Any thoughts he had had regarding killing this tiny infant were gone, replaced with a feeling so unfamiliar he was unable to name it.

"She likes you," the paramedic murmured, breaking the connection of her blue eyes meeting his dark ones. Randall glanced at the paramedic before turning to look at his mother. His mother was smiling at him... at him.

"She's beautiful, isn't she?" Eugenie asked him. He nodded involuntarily, his gaze turning back to the baby.

"What will you call her?" Randall asked, still in awe.

"Do you like Selina?" she asked.

"S-e-l-i-n-a," Randall repeated. He smiled down at the baby. He could have sworn that she smiled back at him. He turned to his mother. "Selina is just perfect," he confirmed.

Again, his mother gave him a genuine smile, perhaps only the second genuine smile she had offered in his entire ten years of life.

CHAPTER TWENTY-SIX

NOW: 10th NOVEMBER

Ginny sat in an interview room opposite Alison McKenzie.

As soon as Alison had seen the news report on TV about that poor nurse being murdered, she just knew she had to come forward and tell the police what she knew, which wasn't much to be sure, but she felt that her small contribution might make a difference.

"What time did you see this man?" Ginny asked.

"It was three a.m. I knew because I couldn't sleep and had just made myself a glass of warm milk. I sat in my window seat. At first there was nobody about, then I saw the man come out of the flats. I thought it was odd immediately."

"What was odd about it, Mrs McKenzie?"

"The way he looked up and down the street, like he was scanning it for possible witnesses. My Gerald, that was my husband, was in the army don't you know, he was in surveillance. So, I knew straight away you see. He was far too shifty, of course there was the way he was dressed as well."

Ginny had to hide her amusement. Mrs McKenzie's information would be undoubtedly helpful, yet she gave her statement like she was sipping tea at a garden party.

"How was he dressed?"

"Like a burglar!" she exclaimed triumphantly, like she had been waiting to deliver that line all along. "Dressed all in black with some black hat on his head."

"Did you get a look at his face at all?"

"Unfortunately no, dear. It was too far away and my eyesight's not what it was."

"Was he white, black?"

"Definitely white."

"What kind of build would you say?"

Mrs McKenzie thought for a moment. "I would say he was tall. It was difficult to tell how big he might have been, but he was definitely a man, he had the physique."

"Had you seen him before perhaps going into the flats? Do you think he may have lived there?"

"Certainly not. I am an old woman, I don't go out much these days but I do like to sit and watch what's going on outside. Sometimes it can get very entertaining."

"You're sure you haven't seen him before, he couldn't be a relative of any of the residents for example?"

Mrs McKenzie shook her head. "Absolutely not, dear."

"Well thank you for your time, Mrs McKenzie, this has been very helpful."

Alison McKenzie looked absolutely chuffed to bits at the compliment and she gave Ginny a big beaming smile.

"Why don't I get one of our uniformed officers to give you a ride home in style?"

"Why thank you, dear, that's very kind. Saves me getting on the bus."

Ginny smiled and thanked Mrs McKenzie again. She made her way up to the incident room. "Mark?" she called on entering through the doors. "Get me the CCTV footage of Anna Chapman, will you?"

"Right away, Boss." he replied, jumping up immediately. He followed her into the office, showing the location of the file on their shared drive.

Ginny watched the CCTV of Anna Chapman at the bus stop. The assailant was wearing exactly the same outfit as Mrs McKenzie had just described.

"Is there any way of getting this image enhanced?" Ginny asked over her shoulder to Mark, who was still standing in her office.

"I've asked the techy guys and they had a go, but the image is far too poor. The cameras along that stretch of road are old and therefore the image when enlarged has no real definition, certainly not enough for a photofit."

Ginny huffed in frustration. "Oh my God, somebody must have seen this guy."

Alison McKenzie was feeling pretty pleased with herself. She had arrived home in a police car and was even escorted to her flat by the young officer. To her it was star treatment and she would finally have some news for her sister that didn't involve what was going in the latest soap operas.

Alison made herself a cup of tea, took up her favourite seat in the living room and switched on her television to catch up on the daytime TV she had missed that morning.

She was disturbed by a ring on her intercom later that afternoon. Tutting to herself at being disturbed, she answered it in a brusque manner. "Yes," she snapped.

"Mrs McKenzie?" came the disembodied female voice at the other end.

"Correct."

"I work with DCI Percy, we need to clarify a few more questions, I wonder if I may come in a for moment?"

"Oh." Alison McKenzie was surprised; she thought that everything had been covered at the police station that morning. "Yes of course, dear, come on up." She pressed the buzzer, allowing her visitor entrance to her building, and then went down her hall to open her front door, before moving into her kitchen to put the kettle on.

"Mrs McKenzie?" a voice came from the front door a moment later.

"Come on in, dear, I left the door open for you. Would you like a cup of tea?"

There was no reply and as Alison McKenzie turned to see if her visitor had heard her question, she was confronted by a tall blond woman wearing a clear plastic rain coat standing in her kitchen. Alison McKenzie had always been a practical woman. The thought entered her head almost immediately that it was not raining today and as she was about to say as much, the woman stepped forward and plunged the hammer she had been holding directly into the head of Alison McKenzie, immediately crushing her skull and killing her instantaneously. Her body collapsed to the floor of the kitchen and the woman stepped forward, quickly removing the hammer which was lodged particularly deeply into Alison McKenzie's brain. It made a satisfying 'squish' as she removed it. She was wearing a pair of surgical gloves and stepped over the body to turn on the tap at the kitchen sink. She quickly rinsed off the blood and pieces of brain from the hammer, before stepping back. A pool of dark red blood was seeping from the wound in the woman's head, she noticed.

She looked down at her clear rain coat and was gratified to notice that only a couple of spots of blood had reached her. There were many spatters around the kitchen.

Hunkering down, she couldn't resist the urge to look closely at the body. Death fascinated her; the lifeless body of Alison McKenzie with her now sightless eyes and bloody ruined head could have held her captivated for a while, but there was no time on this occasion.

"You should never have gone to the police, old woman." She spoke precisely like she had received elocution lessons, but the intonation of her voice had no emotion. "It was a very silly thing to do." She sighed and stood up.

Walking through to the hall, she removed her rain coat and folded it so that the blood spots would be on the inside. She wrapped the hammer inside the coat. Bending down to her tote bag that she had left in the hall on entering the property, she removed a hat and a pair of dark glasses. She put them on before putting the rain coat and the hammer in her bag. She then left Alison McKenzie's home without so much as a backward glance.

CHAPTER TWENTY-SEVEN

THEN: SUMMER 2006
RANDALL AND SELINA

The summer holidays stretched ahead of them, six weeks of not having to go to school. Of course, for Randall it was something more permanent since he had completed his GCSEs and was now embarking on the adult world. Still he expected to spend a good portion of the holidays with his little sister Selina.

Selina and Randall. Randall and Selina. They were inseparable, spending so much time together. Randall had never had anyone to share his interests with, but little Selina had embraced it with open arms, had shown a keen interest and had very soon become his protégé. Selina had no qualms about killing animals, in fact she relished it. Randall could recall he wasn't much older than her when he had started killing animals and it made him so proud that Selina had taken to it like a duck to water. Each death held a certain fascination for her. She would sit for hours watching the body of a cat that she had killed, as if waiting for something more to happen. When Randall had asked her what she was doing, she had told him that she liked to watch the moment of death happen; she said it gave her power.

Randall had liked that description very much. It was true killing that gave you power.

Randall loved his sister more than anything else in life. It had bothered him for some time that he needed to tell her about the death of her father. Selina had never once asked about whom he was and had never questioned their mother on his whereabouts. Eugenie too, had never volunteered any information.

Randall had qualms about telling Selina the story, but he needn't have worried in the end. Selina absorbed the story in childlike fascination, wanting to know all the gory details, questioning him on how it felt when he put the knife in Ian Pratchett's heart. Randall loved his sister even more after that if it was entirely possible. To her there was no association between her and the man who had biologically spawned her. To her he was just another animal to be killed and dissected.

To Randall, Selina was more than just a seven-year-old child. Since the day she had been born, her eyes had held a certain knowledge as if she could reach down and see what was in the depths of his very soul and she found a certain comfort there. They were two halves of the same whole.

It was the reason he had decided to involve Selina in his plans.

All through the summer term, Kelly Farmer and Andy Mitchell had seemed to make it their personal vendetta to attempt to humiliate him whenever possible. Andy Mitchell thought he was a face, a hard man gangster well known to his peers in their little part of the world, it might have been true since he was probably the most popular boy in school. The object of his affection was Kelly Farmer, quite simply one of the most beautiful girls Randall had ever set eyes on. Unfortunately, she was more than aware of this herself and used it to her advantage. Kelly Farmer had held a certain fascination for Randall for almost a year. At first it could have been viewed a schoolboy crush, but as he came to know her better through hours of watching, he realised that she was nothing more than a shallow, spiteful, empty shell of a person. Most of the children at school were in awe of the golden couple and fawned over them. If you didn't fall into that particular crowd you were ostracised and ridiculed for whatever particular reason – whether it was because you wore glasses so you were called 'four eyes' or the fact that you were a little overweight so you were called 'Fatty'. It was all done in such a derogatory manner as to make others feel uncomfortable, but had everyone laughing either because they were embarrassed or genuinely thought it was funny.

Randall fitted in to the ostracised group. Their favourite derogatory comment to use for him was 'weirdo' and Andy Mitchell muttered it whenever Randall walked by, followed by fits of giggles by the entourage. Randall himself found it amusing that they could neither conjure up anything new and that the lemmings found it funny every time it was said. Did they never grow bored of the same shit?

On one particular day Randall decided to play a little game. They were all quite wary of him, mainly giving him a wide berth. There was always something that they could never quite put their finger on that made them all feel uneasy and although Andy Mitchell thought he was full of bravado, he never seemed to do much more than mutter under his breath.

It was lunchtime and the 'cool kids' liked to hang out by the netball courts, where they continued their sport of bullying others. Randall deliberately made a beeline for their little group and on hearing the usual phrase 'weirdo', stopped short in his tracks. Taking his time, he turned very slowly, a smile adorning his face. Later the other young people in that group would have said that his smile was pure evil. It displayed no humour. The object of his smile was Andy Mitchell, who in turn had had the smile wiped off his face when Randall stopped. Randall stepped in as close as he could in front of Andy Mitchell, refusing to allow their bodies to physically touch. It wasn't hard to see that Andy was a good six inches shorter than Randall when they were standing together like that. The other kids had grown quiet, waiting to see what would ensue. Randall waited a heartbeat before he spoke. His voice remained quiet and controlled, but there was an air of malevolence about him that had Andy Mitchell's heart doing a little flip flop.

"Georgie Porgie, pudding and pie, kissed the girls and made them cry. When Randall Goff came out to play, Andy Mitchell ran away." It was a strange rendition of the old nursery rhyme, but nonetheless menacing in its delivery. Andy Mitchell's eyes looked up and met Randall's dark ones. The seemingly fathomless depths stared back unblinkingly and Andy suddenly knew what prey felt like, held in the captive unblinking eyes of a snake. For the first time in his life he was truly afraid of another person. It wasn't as if what Randall had said was particularly scary, but Andy Mitchell had the sudden impression that he was looking upon evil personified, that at any moment Randall would reach out and break his neck.

Andy Mitchell took a deliberate step back and broke eye contact in an attempt to diffuse the situation. He turned to look at his peers, who seemed to have withdrawn into their own bubble of self-preservation, mainly looking at the floor or their shoes.

To everyone's surprise, Kelly Farmer stepped forward, hands on hips, a grimace altering her lovely face into something much uglier.

"Why don't you just fuck off, Randall, you're nothing but a freak of nature. Why don't you just run home to Mummy and piss your pants?" She used her index and middle fingers to imitate legs running as she spoke. Randall's cold gaze turned to her, again in a deliberately slow movement.

"And you are nothing but a dirty little whore," he responded, slowly looking her up and down for emphasis. Her two sidekicks gasped and Randall laughed. He hadn't meant to react, but couldn't seem to help himself. Every one of those young people felt as if a cold hand had reached into their chests and grabbed their hearts at that sound. It was something that they would never forget. Randall did no more but turn on his heel and walk away.

That was when he started to watch them. He knew there would come a time when he could strike out his revenge. It had been on the cards for a very long time with Kelly Farmer. She was a whore who deserved to die.

Selina wanted to help. She wanted to be part of it. Nobody would thwart her brother and get away with it. She wanted to make them pay, perhaps more so than Randall.

Randall had watched and waited for a very long time, for the rest of the school year in fact. During that time Selina was used to follow the group and see where their hideouts and haunts were. She was inconspicuous and went unnoticed, giving her the ability to blend in and report back what she learned to her brother. It was how he discovered that the group very often met in a shed on the allotments.

It was a large shed, with blacked out windows. It must have belonged to one of the group's relatives but Randall could not care less which. The group would spend hours in there, smoking weed and pawing at each other.

Randall and Selina forged their plan; it was flawless in its planning and they hoped it would be too in its execution.

It was Saturday evening, and on this occasion, Andy Mitchell had somehow managed to procure two three-litre bottles of cider. The group met in the garden shed and the drinking and smoking began. It couldn't have been more perfect.

It was the height of summer, and it had been a very hot day. The gardeners were all gone for the day as the sky turned luscious shades of pink and orange against the setting sun.

The group in the shed were oblivious to the outside world. Randall, having visited the allotment the evening before, had managed to put a metal stake in the ground, which he stolen from a building site. It now resided by the side of the shed. He tied a piece of rope around the stake and now his plan just had to be executed. Walking with great care so as not alert the occupants in the shed, Randall walked around the shed, taking his rope with him. He did three circuits before he was satisfied and tied off one end. If they wanted to escape, they would not be able to since the only exit was now blocked. For good measure he used a garden spade under the handle of the shed door. He could hear music from inside the shed and clearly things had escalated in the sexual department due to the wet smacking sounds also coming from within. Randall was tempted to look in through the window, but couldn't take the chance that he would spotted. No, he had a job to do and was needed to see it through to the end.

Taking one of the two petrol cans he had brought with him, Randall set about pouring the contents around the shed and over it, until he had completely emptied both cans. Stepping back slightly, he struck a match from the box he was carrying and threw it toward the shed. There was a sudden 'whoomph!' and in a matter of seconds the shed was surrounded by bright yellow flames. Terrified screams could immediately be heard from within.

They tried to open the door, the tightness of the rope preventing their exit.

Although he wanted to stay, to watch what would happen, Randall compelled himself to walk away from the scene. He appeared unhurried. Selina waited for him at the gate to the allotment. She grinned up at the brother she adored. He took her hand and they strolled away from the allotments together. Nobody batted an eyelid at the two children walking along the street, an older brother looking after his younger sister. They stopped and watched as a fire engine roared by, its sirens wailing. Still they attracted no attention. On that day nobody would remember seeing the two children at all; it did not register in anyone's memory since it was nothing untoward or unusual.

The following morning, Eugenie told her children of the seven deaths that had occurred at the allotments the previous evening. Seven of the children had been horrifically burned, never to recover from their injuries, five of them dying at the scene. The police suspected foul play but had no motive or suspects. Two further children had died on arrival at hospital, their burns too severe to recover from.

There had been one survivor from the atrocity. Kelly Farmer had been badly burned, never again to be the most beautiful girl at school. She spent many months in hospital receiving treatment for her injuries, some of which she would never recover from. When Kelly Farmer first saw what was left of her face in the mirror, she was inconsolable. Giving no thought to the boyfriend and friends she had lost in the fire, she could not bear what she had become... in her own terms a freak. She eventually killed herself by jumping in front of a train.

It was poetic justice as far as Randall and Selina were concerned and it was also the start of their killing spree.

CHAPTER TWENTY-EIGHT

NOW

The murder of Alison McKenzie had come as shock. Her body had been found in her kitchen, bludgeoned in the head with what Melanie Watson later confirmed was most likely a household hammer, although no such implement could be found at the scene. Alison McKenzie had mercifully died instantly.

DCI Virginia Percy sat looking at the CCTV of their prime suspect. They now knew it was a woman who had killed Alison McKenzie, although she had clearly known the location of the cameras since they couldn't get a clear visual of her face. She also wore a hat and sunglasses.

Ginny watched the footage again for what must have been the nineteenth time. There was something familiar about the woman and the way she walked. Ginny was absolutely convinced she had seen her before. But where? She was wracking her brains trying to work it out. Again, she watched the woman. She was so cool, like she had not come to commit a murder at all. She wasn't dressed for it in her pencil skirt and stiletto heels. She looked like a businesswoman attending a meeting. It was at odds with the world.

"Oh my fucking God," Ginny suddenly screamed. It hit square between the eyes where she had seen that walk before from whom.

"Boss?" Pat was at her office door in a flash.

"I know who the fucking killer is!" she exclaimed excitedly. "Who was that posh tart with the attitude who I had a run in with at Franklin Hart's office, can you remember her name?"

Never one to forget a pretty woman, Pat had the answer immediately. "Selina Jackson."

"Fuck yes, Selina Jackson." Ginny smacked her palm on the side of her head. "It's her." She pointed to her computer, showing a freeze frame of Selina Jackson entering Alison McKenzie's building. Pat looked at her computer dubiously. Mark, Steven and Francine had also approached and were standing in the doorway.

"I dunno, Gin, you can't see her face." Pat just couldn't see it.

Ginny blew out a breath in exasperation. "It's her, I God-damn guarantee it," Ginny confirmed again. She had never been so sure about anything in her life.

"But why would Franklin Hart's secretary kill Alison McKenzie?" Mark interjected.

"Alison McKenzie was a witness," Francine offered. Four pairs of eyes turned to her. She shrugged. "Well she is… I mean was."

Ginny was almost buzzing. "You're right, Francine, Alison McKenzie *was* a witness. She saw the murderer leaving Mary Kelly's property in the middle of night. It was splashed all over the newspapers, they gave her name and where she lived. He knew there was no-one around that night because he was checking the street, Alison made that clear in her statement. He had no clue Alison had seen him until that story hit the papers. He has no idea what she did or didn't see and that's the trouble. As far as he's concerned, she could ID him."

"But why Selina Jackson, it just doesn't make sense." This from Pat.

"Maybe it's her boyfriend?" Ginny offered helplessly.

"You've got to have something more tangible, Boss, if we go out and arrest her, we've got to have concrete evidence that she can be placed at the scene. At the moment you have a body on CCTV, but you can't see her face. It would never stand up in court and you would most likely end up with a false arrest suit on your hands."

"Arrrrrgggghhhh!" Ginny screamed in frustration, slamming her hands down on her desk "If I don't get a result, I'm off this case by the end of the week." Her eyes filled with tears that she refused to allow to fall. She would not fall apart.

"It's her." She pointed to the stilled image on the computer screen. "That person is Selina Jackson and I would bet my life on it."

Pat, Francine, Mark and Steven had left her to it. They were right and she knew it, but it was killing her to admit it. She needed to find something more tangible in order to nail this woman as being at the scene of the crime; she couldn't go around arresting somebody because they favoured the same kind of clothes. It was a question of why at the moment. Clearly, she knew the murderer, was protecting him in some warped way, which meant that they believed that Alison McKenzie had seen him, could identify him.

Ginny just had to figure this out.

Selina Jackson – they had first met at the offices of Hart, Smith & Dawson. She knew Mary Nicholls, the first victim. Had Selina Jackson known any of the other victims? No, they had cross-checked all the names of possible friends and family and every piece of information through the social media pages of each victim.

Ginny pulled up the Facebook page of Mary Nicholls. Sure enough, one of her friends was Selina Jackson. She clicked on the link that led her to Selina's pages. Very little adorned the pages at all. There was no personal information suggesting that she had a partner or family. It wasn't the privacy settings, there was simply nothing completed. It was like Selina Jackson had just created the page, but it didn't look like she ever used it. There were a couple of photos of Selina but none of the usual blurb that accompanied Facebook – no holiday photos or pictures of boyfriends or trips out. It was bizarrely bereft of any life information. It was like the page had just been set up simply as a ghost. An idea was starting to form in Ginny's mind.

She called up Anna Chapman's page. There were many more friends on this account and it took a bit of time for her go through all the pictures of those who had been accepted as friends. About half way through she came across a picture of Selina Jackson; it was exactly the same set up as the page she had viewed linking Mary

Nicholls, except this time her name was Selina Brown. Ginny knew she was on to something. Pulling up the Facebook pages of Lizzy Stroud, Katherine Eddowin and finally Mary Kelly she went through each and every photo. She found the aliases of Selina Jackson, Selina Brown, Selina Johnson, Selina Taylor and finally Selina Goff; it seemed this particular young woman had been a very busy person indeed. The reason the link hadn't been found previously was because they had only checked the names, not the photographs. Five identical Facebook pages, five different names and if the date of birth was to believed, the young woman was only twenty years old. She was undoubtedly the link that would lead them to the killer.

"Pat?" she called out to the office. He appeared at her door. It was late and he was the only one left in the office.

"Gin?" He grinned unrepentantly at using her name so loosely.

"We need to bring in Selina Jackson," she told him simply.

The following day, Selina Jackson sat at her desk outside Franklin Hart's Office. David Crisp was perched on the corner of her desk, his favoured spot of choice when he was waiting to speak to Franklin, despite the fact that two chairs had been placed outside the office for just that purpose.

David Crisp irritated Selina to the point of wanting to murder the smug-faced son of a bitch. It irked her that she was forced to be nice to him. She had treated him with aloof disdain since the day she had met him, yet he continued to think that he was the answer to her womanly prayers.

"What are you doing this weekend?" he asked her, cheerfully swinging one leg and inspecting his manicured nails.

Wishing she could have answered with something more colourful in response, she more ignored the question. "I'm very busy," was her ambiguous reply while she pretended to do things around her desk, hoping that the annoying specimen would take the hint, get bored and move on.

"Ah ha." David Crisp was oblivious. "You want to grab a bite to eat and a drink?" Selina had to stop what she was doing and look directly at him for a moment to see if he was actually pulling her chain. The man was a voracious idiot. He was so self-absorbed that he hadn't even noticed that she had already responded. Removing his attention from his cuticles, he glanced over at her and smiled. She didn't return it, only raised one eyebrow. "I already told you... " she enunciated every word so he might this time take the hint. "I'm busy."

"Oh." Rather than looking crestfallen at being turned down yet again, he said, "Maybe another time then." Before she could bite back with any retort about not bothering because it was never going to happen, Franklin Hart opened his office door.

"Come in, David." he called.

David slipped off her desk and pointed a finger. "Catch you later, gorgeous." And then to add insult to injury, he winked as he sauntered into Franklin Hart's office and closed the door. The man was absolutely insufferable. Either he knew exactly how she was feeling and this was a complete wind up to push her buttons, or he really was that obtuse. She thought of the hammer residing in the bottom of her filing cabinet by her desk and was tempted to take it out for use later, but Randall had forbidden her from doing anything else nefarious. The police had no clue as to her identity and he wanted to keep it that way.

The phone on her desk rang, the difference in tone indicating it was an internal number. She glanced at the extension and knew it was Jess, receptionist from ground floor reception.

"Yes?" she answered the phone brusquely.

"There are some police officers here to see you, Miss Jackson," came the clipped reply.

Selina barely missed a beat. She had done it before; she could do it again. "Send them up please." She put the phone down without saying another word. She needed to compose herself. What could they possibly want now? Her only link in this matter was to Mary

Nicholls. She frowned. Should she alert Randall? No. She would see what they wanted first.

She waited for the lift to arrive on her floor and watched as the tall, good-looking detective who had come before stepped out with two uniformed officers. He approached her desk; the two uniforms flanked him either side.

"Can I… " Selina started.

"Selina Jackson?" She stared balefully at him; he knew exactly who she was. "I am Detective Sergeant Patrick Paterson. I am arresting you for the murder of Alison McKenzie. You do not have to say anything, but it may harm your defence if you do not mention when questioned something which you later rely on in court. Anything you do say may be given in evidence. Can I ask you to come with us please?" Selina stood up slowly. She could see that everyone in the open-plan office had also stood up and was looking in her direction like a frozen tableau, clearly having heard every word.

"May I get my coat?" she asked, her voice betraying no emotion whatsoever. They stepped back to allow her access to her coat from the umbrella stand close by her desk. Pat assumed she wouldn't be running very far in the three-inch stilettoes she was wearing.

Wearing her coat and holding her handbag, she accompanied the officers to the lifts. Turning back briefly, she noted that Franklin Hart and David Crisp had come out of his office and were watching; somebody must have rung through to alert him.

Selina Jackson had been sitting in the interview room for half an hour. She had been given a plastic cup of water, but so far nothing more. She knew this was some kind of delaying tactic by the police to make her sweat for a bit.

Finally, the dynamic duo arrived in the guise of Ginny and Pat. Ginny introduced them once more and took a seat on the opposite side of the table to Selina.

"Miss Jackson," Ginny began. "As you know, you have been arrested for the murder of Alison McKenzie, but first, if I may, can I ask you to confirm your full name?"

Selina blinked slowly. She sat on the chair opposite, straight backed, seemingly unworried about her predicament. There was no emotion on her face.

"Selina Jackson." She enunciated her words slowly.

Ginny frowned. "Is that your real name?" Still no sign of emotion from the ice maiden and no reply either. "It's just that we have discovered several aliases that you use and I just wondered which one might be your real name."

"Isn't it your job to find out, Detective?" Selina said sarcastically, making 'detective' sound like a dirty word.

"We can find out, yes, but it would be so much quicker if you could just confirm to us here and now." Ginny was trying to be reasonable. She had already had a run-in with Selina Jackson at the beginning of their investigation when she had gone to question Franklin Hart. She hadn't liked her then, and did so even less now.

"Look, Selina. We have conclusive CCTV footage that shows you arriving and leaving Alison McKenzie's flat around the time that she was murdered." It was a little lie, but wouldn't hurt if it was a means to an end. "We have also discovered that each of our murder victims had you added as a friend on Facebook. You obviously used different names, which I must admit was clever, because it put us off the scent for a while. But unfortunately, you used the same profile, same pictures, everything. Now all of those women coincidentally have also been murdered. Now we're pretty sure that it wasn't you who actually committed the murders, but I am guessing that you know who did. So perhaps it might be a good idea for you to start cooperating with us because believe you me, though we might not have all the details now, we will find out everything and at the moment you are in a lot of trouble."

Selina stared vacantly at Ginny, still no emotion playing on her face. Not so much as the slightest frown.

369

"So, I ask you again, can you confirm your real name?" Ginny tried again. No response. "Did you know Alison McKenzie?" No response. "Can you tell us what you were doing on the twelfth of November?"

"I can see why he likes you," Selina said suddenly. The response caught Ginny off guard for a moment.

"Why who likes me?" Ginny recovered her composure quickly. Selina gave a small smile that said I know everything, you know nothing, however she refused to offer anything else. In fact, despite Ginny repeatedly asking her questions, frustratingly Selina Jackson said nothing more. She was either very clever or very stupid. Ginny had her returned to her cell.

Entering the incident room, Ginny approached Mark. "Got anything?" She had instructed Mark to work through the aliases used by Selina on the Facebook pages, to see if it turned up any real names or whether there were any links on the Facebook pages to other people she knew. The latter had proved fruitless, although they were going to get the ID technology wizards to double check on that front. The only plausible name so far was Selina Goff, who currently held a valid driving licence and passport. The picture matched Selina's. He reported his findings to Ginny.

"Okay, there's our lead. I want every stone about Selina Goff's life overturned. I want to know where she lives, who she associates with, and any minor detail you might think is relevant, I want to know about it." The incident room was hive of sudden activity.

Pat approached Ginny's office a while later. She waited expectantly.

"Selina Goff, born November 1998, lived here all her life and still lives at home with her mother. Never been in trouble with the police, not even so much as a parking ticket. Went to the local comprehensive and then secretarial college. Started at Hart, Smith and Dawson almost two years ago, was promoted pretty quickly to Franklin Hart's secretary and has been there ever since. She has one brother called Randall Goff, ten years older than her. There's not much more personal information other than that. There are no links on the other Facebook pages she was using, other than the one under her real name. There were other people listed as friends, but Steve's checking them out now," Pat concluded.

Ginny chewed pensively on the end of her pen. "Do we know anything about the brother?"

"Checking him out too as we speak."

Ginny nodded. "Good stuff."

Steve appeared at her office door. "What have you got?" Ginny asked, already knowing by the look on his face that something was amiss.

"That reporter you knew."

"Sharon Bywater?" Ginny felt her stomach drop to her boots.

"Yes." Steve confirmed. "Seems that Selina was also friends with her. There's not much on Selina's pages but if you go into Sharon's pages, there's pictures of two women together. I would say they were having some sort of relationship."

Pat looked quickly at Ginny. "You did say you didn't think she was the type to top herself."

"Too fucking right, she wasn't. She was hard as a bed of nails. You know what this means?" She looked at both men standing before her desk before continuing. "That Selina Goff is very likely responsible for the fake suicide of Sharon Bywater as well as killing Alison McKenzie."

"But the coroner turned a verdict of suicide in the case of Sharon Bywater," Steve offered.

"Yes, he did." Ginny agreed, getting to her feet and grabbing her jacket from the back of her chair. She pulled it on, before continuing "But this is new information. We need to prove that Selina was in the right place at the right time. Sharon's case didn't cross our door because it was a suspected suicide. But I want every bit of information you can gather about Sharon Bywater's death. Any CCTV footage of her apartment building, anyone seeing them together. Also find out any information about the brother, where he lives etcetera and any other information from the Facebook pages. Try and search the Facebook picture of Selina, see if she pops up anywhere else on Facebook with another alias. I want the net to close in on this lady, big time." Ginny was heading out the door. "Come on Pat, let's go and pay a visit to Selina's mum." She passed through the incident room in flurry. "Good work guys, keep it up," she called to her colleagues. She was so proud of all them; they had done a magnificent job so far.

Eugenie Goff was caught off guard with a visit from the two detectives standing at her door. She had never had any dealings with the police and immediately thought something terrible had happened to one or other of her children. Her hand went to her heart, her fingers fluttering there when they showed their badges to her. "What is this about?" she enquired softly.

"May we come in, Mrs Goff?" Ginny asked. Eugenie had a terrible feeling of foreboding as she stepped back and allowed the two officers into her home. She sat them at her kitchen table and put the kettle on.

Ginny observed the slim woman who would have only been around forty-six or forty-seven. She looked amazing with a figure a twenty-year-old would die for and long shapely legs encased in a pair of slim trousers. She wore a blouse tucked into her trousers and her hair was beautifully styled and put up. Her make-up was in place and one could be forgiven for thinking that she was a lot younger than she was. It wasn't hard to see where Selina got her looks and poise.

Having prepared a tray of tea, Eugenie placed it on the table and took her seat with the police officers. There as a timely old-worldliness to Eugenie's demonstration of tea making. She had brewed fresh tea in a pot, placing three bone china mugs on her tray with a sugar bowl and spoon as well as a milk jug. It was very reminiscent of yesteryear and, Ginny felt, unusual for a woman of Eugenie's age.

Eugenie had immediately ascertained that her children were safe before she made the tea and was now calmer in the knowledge that they had just come to ask her some questions.

"Before we start, Mrs Goff, I feel I should tell you that we currently have Selina in custody helping us with our enquiries." The china cup Eugenie was holding was dropped onto the table, fortunately empty, and not having far to fall, it didn't break.

"Selina?" Eugenie could hardly believe it. "What has she done?" Eugenie was clearly concerned, her gaze darting back to first Ginny, then Pat and back to Ginny again.

"I'm afraid I'm not at liberty to say anything about that at the moment, I just need to ask some questions about Selina if you don't mind?"

Eugenie looked suitably distressed. "Well of course I will help you in any way I can," she confirmed. She just couldn't get her head around it. Now if they were here to ask questions about Randall, that would be a different matter, that would not have surprised her at all.

"What does Selina like to do when she's not at work?" Ginny asked, something nice and easy to get started.

"Well she works a lot of hours actually, stays late and goes out early. She's a personal assistant. She hardly ever goes out, stays in much of the time really, up in her bedroom." Eugenie pointed to the ceiling to indicate the whereabouts of Selina's bedroom.

"Does she not socialise with friends, boyfriends etc.?"

"Not really." Eugenie shrugged.

"Don't you find that a little unusual, that a twenty-year-old woman wouldn't go out with her friends?"

Again, Eugenie shrugged. "She never has been one for going out much, even when she was a little girl, she preferred to be at home. She spent most of her time with her brother." Eugenie wondered if it *was* wrong. She didn't think it was that strange not to have friends; Eugenie had never had friends herself.

"Would that be Randall?" Ginny continued with her questions.

"Yes, my son," Eugenie confirmed.

"Does he live here?"

"No, he moved out about ten years ago when Selina turned ten. They used to share a bedroom you see, but he decided that she needed her own space as a growing girl. He's ten years older than her."

"Do you have an address for Randall? We'd like to speak to him as well."

Eugenie smiled sadly. "Unfortunately not, my son doesn't tell me where he lives. Selina probably knows, they still see a lot of each other. My son and I are... " She thought for a moment, seemingly struggling to find the right words, "I supposed you might say estranged," she concluded finally.

"It's a little unusual that you don't know his address. Do you still keep in touch with him?"

"My son and I barely speak to each other, if not for Selina we would probably have parted long ago, never to acknowledge each other even if we were walking on the same side of the street."

Eugenie lifted her hand and smoothed back her hair, although there was nothing out of place. Emotions seems to pass over her face as if trying to find the most suitable one to be displayed. "My son hates me, Detective." The words were spoken quietly as if admitting them too loudly would incur a consequence. Ginny felt for the woman before her. Clearly it was something she had thought about on many occasions and perhaps this was the first time she had ever admitted it out loud to another living person.

However, Eugenie felt she should elaborate further. "I was thrown out of the family home when my father discovered I was pregnant. I was only sixteen and had had an affair with a married man, a friend of the family in fact. The man was twenty years older than me at the time and it would have caused quite the scandal except that my father would broke no such sully on the family. He asked me if I would get rid of the child and when I refused, he asked me to leave. My mother was heartbroken when I accepted. My father vowed that he would never accept my child as a relative. We have connections to the royal family you see." Eugenie glanced through her lashes at the detectives to gage their reactions before lowering her eyes once more to her hands in her lap. Ginny and Pat were suitably impressed. "Anyway, we moved here." Eugenie gestured with her hand to indicate her house and her face again told the story, her emotions visible in that one gesture that they should know that where she lived was beneath her. Who knew, maybe she was right.

"I had Randall because I thought I loved his father. I think in my little girl dreams I imagined that he would come and rescue me from the persecution I had deliberately erected around myself. Obviously, that didn't happen and I believe I must have taken that out on Randall to some extent. I didn't mean to. It's just that looking at him reminded me so much of my past disappointments. And really, he was never a naughty boy, just a bit strange."

The story had been heard before; boy meets girl, boy takes advantage of girl, girl gets lumped with all the flack. It was nothing new but Ginny couldn't help but feel sorry for the woman sitting before her. She clearly had expected to live in a very different world to where she had ended up and she defied anyone not to feel bitterness especially as it seemed she might have come from a very affluent family that had connections to the royals. That said, Ginny was already picking up on the remarks Eugenie made about her son. "When you say Randall was strange, what exactly do you mean?"

"Well he was always so withdrawn and serious, sullen most of the time. That was until Selina came along."

"How so?"

"He adored her, still does. Randall lives for Selina. The two were virtually inseparable when they were children, to the exclusion of everybody else, including myself." Eugenie used her hand to emphasise that point by placing it on her chest. "They were like two halves of the same whole, if I can describe them in that way, like they had always been destined to be together. Sometimes it felt like they would have this secret language and could communicate just by a look alone. I have often wondered if they were telepathic."

Ginny smiled back at Eugenie. She felt a moments chagrin as thoughts unwittingly bounced into her head: 'or both totally psychotic', something she didn't say aloud. Ginny had to admit it was looking like Randall might be who they were looking for in regard to the murders. If Selina and Randall were as inseparable as Eugenie seemed to think, even now, the likelihood was that they had planned and plotted this together.

"Do you have a photograph of Randall at all?"

Eugenie stood up from the table. "I do as a matter of fact, it was taken last Christmas. A photo of Randall is as rare as hen's teeth, but I managed to snap a couple of them together." She left the room, returning a moment later with small wooden frame. The photo wasn't the best, but it clearly showed Selina and Randall standing together before the Christmas tree. Selina Goff was tall, standing around five feet, nine inches and Randall beside her must have been at least six foot, three inches. He, like the rest of the family, was blonde. He wasn't smiling in the picture, but looked relaxed, his arm around Selina's shoulders. He was clean shaven and fairly good looking in a nice boy next door type of way. He looked like the kind of man you would immediately trust. The only thing that really betrayed that look was his eyes. They were dark, appearing black in the photograph, compared to the blue eyes of Selina and Eugenie. Whether it was because she knew that he was looking more and more like their killer all the time or whether it was those eyes she didn't know, but Ginny couldn't help but feel the first trickle of uneasiness down her spine. There was something malevolent in his stare; even from the photograph she felt he was seeing her, watching her. There was something even worse that was bothering her too. Ginny was ninety percent convinced she had seen his face before. She didn't know when or where, but she knew she had seen him.

"Do you have any other photos that we could take with us, or perhaps you would permit us to copy that one?" Ginny asked, handing the frame back to its owner.

"I have a spare of this picture," Eugenie said. I printed three photos, thinking the children might want a copy, but they never did." She looked a little sad and disappointed when she said this, but disappeared again into the other room, returning in a few moments with the photograph in hand.

"Do you mind if I take a look around Selina's room, Mrs Goff?" Ginny asked finally, standing up.

"Not at all, up the stairs, first on the left." Ginny looked at Pat who got the message loud and clear. He was to wait with Eugenie Goff while she scouted around upstairs, just in case Eugenie should suddenly get the urge to ring her son and warn him that the police were there. As nice as people might seem, they always expected the worst.

Randall couldn't believe it. How could they have taken his Selina. How could they have known. It had something to do with the Alison McKenzie murder of that he was sure. But how had they discovered it was Selina. She was so careful, so meticulous. She was a further extension of himself.

Now the police were at his mother's house. His mother would have nothing to tell them. She knew nothing of the lives of her children. Her simpering pathetic existence was to not last for much longer. He and Selina had planned it, neither one needing her in their lives. She had been a means to an end while they grew up but she was no more than superfluous to their requirements now.

Selina would never talk, of that he was a hundred percent certain, but the fact that they had taken her angered him just the same. In fact, he was beyond normal anger, he was enraged. He wanted to kill something, to rip someone apart. On discovering that Selina was taken, he had returned home and thrown everything around in his flat, breaking his things in a fit of temper. Instead of releasing the anger he had inside, it had only served to incense him further. He was breathing hard, his eyes wild and bloodshot, the adrenaline coursing through his body.

He left his home, a purposeful plan in mind. If they could take his sister, he would take Virginia. Simple. He would hold to her ransom and when he got his beloved sister returned to him, he would send Virginia back, they didn't need to know it would be a little piece at a time. Randall smiled to himself. If anybody had witnessed that smile at the time, they would have seen the benevolent evil that resided there and they would have been afraid.

Two streets from where he lived, resided the stolen beat-up Volkswagen Beetle which he proceeded to drive to the police station. He had changed the plates for other stolen ones in his collection. He parked across the street from the police station, staring at the comings and goings as if willing his sister to come out of the building. While waiting he recognised the car Virginia Percy's colleague often used. As it drove past him, he spotted Virginia sitting in the front seat. He did a U-turn and followed them to his mother's house.

He was parked a safe distance away, being able to see them go into Eugenie's property. He had pounded and pounded on the steering wheel in frustration. This wasn't how it was supposed to happen. He had so much more work to do yet. How had they found him before it was time? He had only just become, he couldn't be ripped away from his tasks so soon, it just wasn't fair.

As he gradually calmed down, he tried to assimilate his thoughts and work out how this had happened. What possible lead could the police have found to lead them to his sister? The only thing he could think of was the Facebook pages. It had been Selina's idea to use different names. She had been of the opinion that the police would most likely choose names as the common denominator rather than the photographs themselves. And it appeared that she had been right. But had she been? They had certainly found some reason to arrest her. There was nothing to suggest it could have been the Sharon Bywater murder. That had been investigated and gone to coroner's inquest where the verdict had come back as suicide. That was free and clear. He was sure that there was nothing to suggest any link between Selina and Alison McKenzie. It had to be the Facebook link. He felt sure if Alison McKenzie had provided an ID, he would be viewing pictures of himself everywhere, a full-scale manhunt ensuing. As it was, Selina had insisted on taking out the old woman just in case. Could it have been that? Randall hated not knowing things. He felt out of his comfort zone and he didn't like it one bit. He was used to being the one who held all the cards and as a consequence, the knowledge.

Randall drove back to his flat, dumping the car on the way. He had to create a plan. How long could they keep Selina? He wasn't sure. Could she be let out on bail? Would their mother pay it? These would be things he needed to find out. He also needed to know what the police knew. As far as he was concerned, there was only possible way and that would be to take one of the officers, squeeze all the possible information out of them and then kill them. The trouble was, he would have to move quickly. He had no doubt that his mother would have been very cooperative with the police. He should have killed her years ago when he had the chance. Now it would be too late.

Randall had been experimenting with making his own chloroform. He had been surprised to find out how relatively easy it was to make, using household products and a YouTube video. The prototype for chloroform had been used on small animals and unfortunately he had succeeded in killing of them. At this point he could have cared less if his captive died or not so long as he got his sister back. If his captive turned out to be Virginia Percy, all the more, the better.

Randall returned to the police station, this time in a battered Ford Fiesta he had stolen a few weeks ago. This too had stolen plates and as far as he knew was virtually untraceable. He had no doubt that the police would track him by camera, locating the route he would take in an attempt to find out his whereabouts.

Randall had been visiting the police station often of late as part of his plans to take on the formidable Virginia Percy. There was something about the small blonde woman that he found irresistible. He wanted to taste her, to feel her, to know what she felt like on the inside and eventually he wanted to open her up and see what she looked like on the inside. He wanted to watch the life leave her eyes while she looked at him.

In his pursuit of Ginny, a woman that he had mistaken for her on a couple of occasions from a distance had come to his knowledge. Francine Blackman looked a lot like her boss, particularly with her hair down and out of uniform. They had the same colour hair, same slim build and stature. From behind it would be difficult to decide who you were looking at. That was where the similarity ended however. Where Ginny had small features: small nose, small lips, green eyes and wore very little make-up, Francine had a nose which was a little too large for her face, brown eyes and rose-bud lips. She wore a lot of make-up with base and contours. She had pencilled in thick dark eyebrows that to Randall looked like two huge caterpillars camped out above her eyes; she seemed to favour fake eyelashes and was never seen without her lipstick in situ, a bright red slash across her mouth that made her look like she had a permanent pout. She had intrigued Randall almost immediately just because her overall appearance was like Ginny, then you were confronted by this face. He had thought from the first that Francine was nothing but a painted whore.

Francine had accepted a friend request two months ago from Selina Khan which had enabled Selina to keep tabs on her as a potential victim. Selina had combed every inch of the Facebook page and other social media she gained access to as an honorary friend. It never failed to surprise Randall how trusting these people were and how easy they had made it for themselves to be intruded upon through the element of social media. Most of the women shared every innermost private thing on their social media pages, from their most embarrassing photos to detailed information about where and when they would be at any given time. All Selina had to do was infiltrate their lives by becoming their friend; even if these people had never actually physically met her, they were willing to assume they had. Selina would inbox them and say, 'Oh we met at so and so... ' and that would be it, the friendship would be accepted since most of the locations entailed a lot of drinking or use of drugs and nobody could remember who they had met.

Once the link was achieved, it was easy for Selina and Randall to accumulate all the information they needed and Randall would take up the mantle of following his chosen victim.

From an early age, Randall had inspired Selina with his interest in Jack the Ripper and other such serial killers. When he had pored over countless books and even more internet accounts, she had followed in his footsteps, finding the same things to her taste as he did. There was never a brother and sister so in tune with each other, thinking the same thoughts, knowing the same things. It had been so since Selina had been born. Now they had taken his beloved sister and held her captive, and oh how they would pay dearly for that crime.

The object of his pursuit on this occasion, would have, at some stage, met her untimely end, yet for now it was unfortunate for her that it was having to be brought forward. As though his thoughts had summoned her, she appeared, leaving the police station, having changed from her uniform into her civilian clothes. Her hair had been released from the confines of the tight bun she usually wore and was curled down her back. On any other occasion, she would have roused his appreciation, but this was set to be a purely functional pursuit... at least for now.

He waited, beanie in situ to cover his blonde hair, dark clothing in place. He could see her approach under his lashes but kept his head down. She had put in her headphones, which disappeared into the handbag residing in the crook of her elbow. Even better, he thought. As she passed by his car, oblivious to his presence, he reached into his glove compartment and took out a foil covered bottle. Opening it, he poured the entire contents onto a hand towel and then got out of his car. She was strolling along in a world of her own, unaware of his approach or that she was being followed. She was coming upon a back street that led behind some warehouses and he knew this was his opportunity. Making a sudden run for her he reached out and put the towel across her face, holding it in position. She made an attempt to struggle, he gave her that. Tried stamping on his feet or elbowing him, but the effects of his homemade chloroform had the desired effect in making her sluggish and slow moving. It was only a matter of seconds before she succumbed completely and was out cold in his arms. Checking again that he hadn't been seen, he dragged Francine Blackman's body down the side street, lying her beside some industrial bins. He left he the towel in situ on her face so that she would continue to receive the effects of the chloroform before running back to get his car.

In a matter of moments he had returned and parked beside her body. He opened the boot and took out the roll of duct tape and hand cuffs residing there, ready to be used. Using the duct tape, he taped up her mouth, allowing her the use of oxygen through her nose. The then put her arms behind her back and handcuffed her wrists together. Although she now weighed something quite considerable due to her unconscious state, he managed to lift her body and place her in the boot before using his duct tape to tie her ankles. When she came round, which would likely be very soon, she would be unable to move and would present no challenge to him to overcome. Checking again that there was nobody in the side street watching him, he climbed into the stolen Fiesta and drove away from the scene.

CHAPTER TWENTY-NINE

NOW

Francine Blackman hadn't always wanted to be a police officer. At first, she had wanted to be a princess and marry a handsome prince. It was all she had ever talked about since being a little girl. Her parents used to laugh, thinking that their only daughter would become a secretary or a teacher. Francine's father often said she was his princess and in truth she was daddy's little girl. Eventually, as she grew older, she set her sights on joining the police force and eventually pursued her dream. Just like she knew she would, she loved it.

Her father was the proudest dad alive when she achieved her goal. He would constantly brag about her achievements to everyone. Pictures of their daughter were everywhere around the house, from her baby years to her school photos and eventually pictures of her in police uniform. She still lived at home, being happy to stay where she was well looked after while she saved up the money to afford her own place.

She didn't really have a boyfriend, which suited her dad just fine since nobody was good enough for his Francine anyway, but she had lots of friends whom she socialised with often.

To Derek (Del) Blackman, Francine was the apple of his eye. There was nobody he loved more than his daughter, not even his wife. Equally, Francine loved her dad to bits. He was a bit overbearing sometimes, but she knew deep down that was just because he cared. He had been in the army but was now retired. He had fought in the Falklands war and had been a decorated survivor of that conflict. He rarely talked about his army days and Francine knew he had suffered a great deal, having witnessed many of his friends being killed. On returning from the Falklands Del Blackman had been sent on two tours of Northern Ireland. Fortunately, by the time Francine was born, he had been decommissioned which meant he was able to spend every moment enjoying his daughter. He had doted on her from day one. She could never remember an unhappy day in her childhood. She loved her mum equally, but there was a special relationship between her and her dad.

Francine often thought he was part of the reason she wanted to join the police force. She had looked up to him, admired what he had accomplished and while she knew she wasn't quite cut out for the army life, she believed the police force would suit her much better.

When Francine was eight years old, she had wanted desperately to play football. She had always been a bit of a tomboy and tried and tried to play on the team with boys. The coach, at the time, had a strict rule of no girls. He was old school and as far as he was concerned, girls wouldn't, shouldn't and most definitely couldn't play football. It was one thing that Francine played with the boys during playtime. They accepted her as they would any other and in truth, she had been quite good, even they had to admit (for a girl). Yet when it came to playing in the five-a-side tournament between all the primary schools in the area, the coach had not allowed Francine to play.

Del Blackman was having none of that; if his Francine wanted to play football, then play football she would. Marching down to the school, he had given the headteacher a piece of his mind about equality, diversity and discrimination. The very next match, Francine was on the team, much to her delight. Her father had instantly been risen to the exalted position of hero and it was there he had remained through much of her childhood and into her adult life. The term of playing football was short-lived as had been many of Francine's pursuits over the years since, but her father had always encouraged her to try to something new. Due to Francine's inability to stick to anything for longer than a few weeks, her dream to become a police officer was, at first, thought of as another fad, but surprisingly she had proved everyone wrong. Since graduating she had gone from strength to strength. She loved her job and aspired to a be Detective Chief Inspector like her current boss DCI Virginia Percy.

Del Blackman had never been so proud of his daughter than when he discovered she had been recruited to be on the investigating team for the murder investigation team and subsequently in pursuing the current copycat killer. She had discussed some details of the case with her dad, although she knew it was something she wasn't technically allowed to do. Discussing police investigations with your family was strictly taboo, but with her dad, Francine had wanted to thrash out some of the details, see what his take was on things. They had discussed the details sometimes into the dead of night. Del Blackman had been sworn to secrecy and never even divulged the details his daughter shared with his wife. As far as he was concerned it was a sacred bond between dad and daughter.

Francine Blackman was waking up. Her senses were reeling as regained consciousness. She felt nauseated, probably the effects from whatever she had had put over her face, she deduced. She could feel the momentum of a vehicle and knew she was most likely in a car, probably the boot since it was also pitch black and due to the small confines she found herself in. Her hands were tied behind her back and she couldn't move her legs. She was scrunched up into an uncomfortable position in the small space. Although Francine could work out quite quickly all the elements of her situation and current predicament, she had no idea who had taken her and why.

She had no clue as to how long they had been driving, although she had tried to count in minutes once she was aware of where she was. However, she was also aware that they had most likely been driving for a while when she had been out for the count, and unfortunately, she had no idea how long that had been.

Eventually, the car seemed to slow down and she was aware of the undulation of the car as if it was going slowly through multiple pot holes. Shortly after, it came to a complete stop. She listened as she heard the driver open his door and close it. She waited for what seemed like an interminable amount of time before the door to the boot was flung open. The light flooded into the boot and she squinted her eyes uncomfortably at the sudden onslaught of daylight. Francine blinked rapidly trying to focus on the black shape above her. He said nothing to her, just half lifted, half dragged her out of the boot of the car. She felt like a rag doll being tossed around. She was disorientated and slightly dizzy. Outside of the car, her legs felt jelly-like and he allowed her to slip to the concrete floor where he left her, she using the back of the car for support. She had yet to get a good look at her assailant, but knew it was equally important to gage details about her surroundings should she need to pass the information to her colleagues.

There wasn't much to see. She was clearly in some old disused warehouse. It was a large, commodious building with dirty windows near the roof space, many of them broken and blackened with years of dirt. The whole building seemed to be made of corrugated iron, which was formed in an arc shape as though they were in some kind of tunnel. The corners of the building were black and fathomless, yet the entrance had no doors and formed the same arc shape as the roof.

Francine listened to the sounds around her. Apart from the movement of her assailant, it seemed fairly quiet where they were. The distant sound of traffic could be heard, but there was no way of telling how far away it actually was. Francine assumed he had brought her to some farm and other disused area. She knew there were plenty of them around on the outskirts of the town, large dysfunctional places that had once been the hubbub of industry until the companies decided that industrialisation was the key and moved closer to town.

Francine twisted her body from where she sat, trying to see her abductor. She could hear him rummaging about and presumed he was going through her bag. The sounds stopped a moment later and he materialised before her but walked straight past. He held a hammer and she swallowed visibly for a moment before she realised that his intention was not to plunge it into her skull, but to pulverise something infinitely smaller. She realised with dismay that he had removed her SIM from her mobile phone and subsequently smashed it with his hammer.

She could see him clearly now. He was tall, well over six feet she estimated, wearing black trousers and black jumper. He also wore surgical gloves. He had blonde hair and although she would probably describe him as being fairly nondescript, he could be considered fairly good-looking in a boy next door sort of way, just not her type really.

Having shattered the SIM card to nothing he lay the hammer on the wooden box he had used as his base before turning to look at her. He seemed to pause for a moment as if wondering what to do with her, before strolling towards where she sat. He hunkered by her feet where her outstretched legs were still bound up by the duct tape he had used earlier.

"I will remove the duct tape from your mouth," he told her. He had a soft melodious voice, which in other circumstances might be quite pleasant. "Do not attempt to scream, there is nobody to hear you. We are completely isolated. If you do attempt to scream, I will cut something off you. Do you understand?" Francine nodded. He reached forward and ripped the duct tape from her face savagely. She gave a little yelp of pain, her face smarting with the same sensation as really bad sunburn.

"I'm pleased that you can comply with my instructions. This means that we will get on just fine," he told her. Francine nodded again, not trusting herself to speak at the moment without screaming. The realisation of who her abductor was had suddenly dawned on her. His description matched that of Mary Kelly's killer from Alison

McKenzie and also from the CCTV footage they had on Anna Chapman's last movements. He was the copycat killer they had been seeking for many months. She had no intention of antagonising this man for fear that she would end up like his last victim. She would do exactly what he said and hopefully she would come out the other side alive.

Ginny and Pat returned to the station, having interviewed Eugenie Goff. Ginny had looked around the young woman's bedroom in consternation. There was nothing out of place she could find. Make-up, perfume and other beautifying products adorned a small dressing table in an otherwise neat bedroom with the bed perfectly made. Ginny had gone through each drawer and the woman's wardrobe and had checked for any secret compartments or information to suggest that Selina Goff had squirrelled away any trophies from her and her brother's killing spree. Despite the lack of evidence at the moment, Ginny was ninety-nine point nine percent sure that Randall Goff had committed the atrocities while Selina Goff, killing at least two people was somehow involved with the other murders. They just had to find the proof. Ginny was disappointed to discover that there was nothing to be found at the Goffs' house.

Steve King waited for Ginny and Pat as they came through the door, accosting them almost immediately. "Boss?" Steve King had an urgent look about him that suggested he had found something that couldn't wait.

"You got something?" Ginny responded, giving him her full attention.

"You asked me to check Selina's picture in case there were more Facebook pages."

"Yes?" Ginny was impatient, this bated breath stuff did nothing for her.

"Well I found three more."

"Three?" Ginny was incredulous. How much further were the Goff children willing to go before they got caught?

"Yes, Boss. The problem is one of them is Francine."

"Our Francine?" Steve nodded. "Shit!" Ginny looked at Pat.

"Where is Francine now?" she asked, turning back to Steve.

"She left here an hour and a half ago. We contacted her parents, she hasn't got home yet."

"You didn't alert them to anything, did you?"

"No."

Ginny nodded. "Good. Do we know where Francine is, has she gone out with friends or anything?"

"We're just trying to locate CCTV from outside the station to see if we can track her movements. She's not answering her mobile, its going straight to voicemail." Steve King was worried, he didn't mind admitting. He had looked upon Francine as a daughter and hoped that nothing had happened to her.

"What about the other two Facebook pages, the women?" Ginny asked.

"We've got uniforms attending their addresses as we speak to provide a protection detail." Steve responded immediately anticipating her question.

Ginny started walking up and down the office, her preferred act when she was thinking. "He hasn't got a premises this time, unless he's planning to kill all the Blackmans." Ginny stopped suddenly. "We have no choice, we're going to have to tell them that their daughter's missing, or that we can't locate her. We can't take the chance that he won't take her to her parents' home. Let's get uniforms to them as well, make sure they're protected."

"On it." Steve King moved to pick up a phone immediately.

"Pat, we need that CCTV footage ASAP. We need to follow her route home, with any luck she's met up with some mates and is in a pub somewhere." Ginny sounded more confident than she actually felt. If there was one thing about the killer that she was aware of, it was that he was a careful planner, not leaving anything to chance. If he had taken Francine, it was an act of desperation and therefore all the more dangerous.

The CCTV footage was obtained in double quick time. It showed Francine leaving the station and making her way down the road. They watched as a man dressed in black stepped out of his car as she passed, who then proceeded to follow her. They tracked the CCTV along the main road, seeing the man put something over her mouth and then drag her into a nearby side street that was flanked with warehouses. At that time of day there would have been virtually nobody around by the warehouses. Unfortunately, there was no CCTV available to know what happened next, except that then the footage showed Francine's assailant materialise once more. He returned the way he came and got into his car, doing a three-point turn before driving down the side street between the warehouses.

"Zoom in on that registration," Ginny called to nobody in particular. Her bidding was complied with and in a matter of seconds they had the registration plate of the car.

"Do any of those buildings have CCTV?" Ginny asked. She was seriously worried now. The assailant was clearly the man they had been looking for all these months and it was clearly Randall Goff. There was no doubt about it this time. The CCTV was good coverage and the picture clearly matched the photograph his mother had provided earlier that day. They had their killer; they just had to find out where he had gone. "I want every inch of CCTV combed within a twenty-mile radius. That car has gone somewhere and the bastard has a good two hours head start on us. Distribute his picture to all the local stations and an all police alert that this man is wanted in connection to the copycat murders. But no-one attempts to front him up. Make sure they know he is armed and dangerous."

"Armed?" Pat queried.

"I'm not having some have-a-go hero attempting to take him down and getting hurt in the process. This guy is completely off the chart mentally and will most likely stop at nothing. We can't have anyone putting themselves at risk." The team couldn't help but agree.

Mark Roberts suddenly stood up, his face ashen. "Boss."

"What is it, Mark?" She asked, her attention still on the CCTV.

"It's him." Ginny's head shot up and she closed the gap in two seconds. Mark held his hand over the receiver. "He wants to talk to you," he mouthed. Ginny nodded and took the phone.

"Randall?" She questioned down the receiver.

She heard a pleasurable sigh in reply. "I always wanted to know what it would sound like when you said my name," he purred down the phone. Her skin crawled.

"Where is Francine?" Ginny ignored him, going straight in for what she needed to know.

"Alive at the moment." He had such a reasonable manner and that in itself was positively frightening. He had no fear of the police or the repercussions. She glanced at her team and mouthed 'trace'. At least two thumbs up came in her direction.

"I know you will trace this call so listen and do not interrupt." His voice immediately became forceful and commanding, despite keeping the soft tones. "If you alert the media, I will cut pieces off of Francine and post them to you until there is nothing left. I want my sister and I am happy to exchange her." The phone line went immediately dead. Ginny looked at her team.

"Not long enough. The signal's gone," Mark confirmed, frustration evident in his voice.

Ginny sat down on the nearest chair. She rubbed at her forehead with her left hand. They could only hope that he would call again.

"Have we traced Francine's mobile?" Ginny queried with nobody in particular.

"Already attempted that Boss, nothing." Mark responded regretfully.

"He said he wants to exchange his sister for Francine." Ginny informed the team.

"You can't listen to him, Gin," Pat responded anxiously.

She looked up at him. "We have to find a way to arrange it so that he will think we are going to carry an exchange; they we are going to do what he wants. He's desperate now, desperate to have his sister back. It might mean that he's not thinking clearly, that we can have the upper hand."

"You're surely not going to contemplate releasing Selina Goff. We have her for at least two of the murders." Pat was incredulous.

"We have no evidence. There is no murder weapon for Alison McKenzie and although we might have her on CCTV, the jury could throw it out straight away, we don't have a confirmed ID of her face. A pair of legs is not going to be considered conclusive. The murder of Sharon Bywater is already known as a suicide. We have nothing to go on." Ginny almost screamed at him.

"What about all those Facebook pages? She is the link between all the victims. You can't let her walk out of here, Gin." For the first time in his career, Pat was openly disagreeing with Ginny.

"What do you want me to do, Pat? The most we get her for is being an accessory. We have nothing more concrete to suggest she was directly involved in the murders. Even if we charge her as an accessory, she's gonna walk until her trial." They were face to face now, openly shouting in each other's faces.

"Not if you get the CPS to agree that she goes on remand until trial. YOU CANNOT LET HER WALK."

The incident room was in total silence as the two most senior detectives on their team went at each other. Ginny turned to look at her team as she realised that they were sitting in absolute silence watching the scene play out before their eyes, hard not to with the decibel level. The others refused to meet her eye gaze. Ginny slumped into the nearest chair and held up her hands.

"Fine Pat, you win. We'll try and see if she can stay on remand until her trial." The defeat in her voice was evident.

"This isn't about winning, Gin," he told her.

"No, it is Pat, it most definitely is. Randall Goff is winning at the moment. He holds all the cards and he has a member of our team. He's going to kill her, I just know he is and there's not a damn thing I can do about it." Her eyes filled with unshed tears. Never in her life had she felt so helpless.

FRANCINE

Francine had heard Randall on the phone. Would the police consider a swap? She doubted it. Her kidnapper wasn't very happy, she could tell. He was furiously pacing up and down in an agitated state. He had placed fresh duct tape across her mouth and she was forced to sit and watch his incessant marching up and down while he talked to himself.

Suddenly without warning he stopped. He turned to look at her and she was suddenly filled with a sense of dread. He had a vacant look in his eyes that suggested he was not really there anymore and Francine Blackman was given a small insight into what he must have looked like when he killed his victims. It was a chilling view.

Like a large cat stalking its prey, he walked towards her, taking small controlled movements. He hunkered down beside her and again removed the duct tape from her face in a fierce sudden movement. She screamed this time and squeezed her eyes tight shut, the burn from the last removal still fresh on the sensitive skin on her face, the second creating even more pain. Her eyes filled with tears. She opened her eyes and looked up at him. He held up a large knife, which she instantly recognised as a hunting knife; her father had one which he used when he went fishing.

"When I was ten years old, I used this knife," he told her softly in an almost sing-song way. "I killed my sister's father – stabbed him through the heart." He glanced at the knife before turning back to her and smiling. "Stick out your tongue." He instructed. She shook her head, the tears that had filled her eyes starting to roll down her face. He brought the knife in very close to her face.

"Your tongue or your eyeball. You choose." He said it reasonably, like he was asking her to choose between chocolate or vanilla milkshake. Francine didn't want to lose either. She watched as he lowered the tip of the knife towards her eye. She wriggled frantically, panicking at the thought of what he was about to do. He grabbed her around the throat with his free left hand, pinning her in place against the car. "Your tongue or your eyeball." He said again, this time with more menace.

Very slowly, Francine Blackman poked out her tongue. In a blink of an eye Randall grabbed it and sliced through the appendage, removing a good portion. The pain was immense, her mouth immediately filled with blood and she was sure she would choke as a lot of it went down her throat. With what seemed like deliberate slowness he walked around the other side of the car. She heard him open the door and felt the car move as he rummaged around a bit. He returned to her a moment later and held a white towel against her mouth.

"Let's stem the bleeding, shall we, I don't want you to die on me too soon. Open your mouth." He put the towel into her mouth as soon as she did. He stood up abruptly and opened the car boot above her. "Now I have to leave for a little while so I'm going to put you back in the boot," he told her, helping her to her feet. She moaned softly in protest which he ignored. First hoisting her up by placing his hands into her armpits, he lifted her easily until she was sitting inside the boot, before roughly grabbing her legs and twisting her so that she was once again inside the boot. "Now I wouldn't move around too much, it will make the blood flow quicker and try to stay on your side, just in case you choke." Francine watched in horror as the lid of the boot came down, plunging her into complete darkness. She heard his footsteps as he moved away from the car and a few seconds later heard another car start up. She recognised the distinctive throaty sound immediately as an old Volkswagen Beetle. She heard the car pull away and leave, the sound dimming quickly.

Francine wriggled around on her side so that her feet rested on the back of the rear seats of the car. Using every bit of force, she could she kicked out at the seats which suddenly fell forward with a satisfying thump. The interior of the boot of the car was suddenly filled with light. Her shoulders were crying out with the awkward way her arms were tied behind her back but she ignored it, her determination to escape so great.

Shuffling her body bit by bit she pulled herself onto the back of the rear seat of the car and swung herself into a seated position. She placed her legs through the gap between the two front seats and took a moment to look outside the window to ensure that Randall had definitely left. She half expected to see his grinning face looking at her through the window, but was relieved when the whole warehouse appeared empty.

She wanted to much to spit out the towel from her mouth, but she was in agreement with Randall about the fact of not bleeding to death.

With her arms tied behind her back, she tried to use her hands for balance as she shuffled along on her bottom until her legs were in the front of the car and she was poised on the edge of the back seats.

Using the heels of her feet, she attempted to manoeuvre forward while scooting her bum forward. She knew it was going to hurt when her bum landed on the car's handbrake, but fortunately it didn't hurt as much as her mouth, which was currently throbbing, did.

It was a difficult challenge to squeeze her bum through the gap between the seats. Somewhere through sheer thigh power she managed to wriggle until she was able to pull herself into a sitting position in the front passenger seat. Taking a deep breath through her nose, she turned to her right and felt with her hands until she located the door opener, which she used both hands to pull. The passenger door swung open with a gratifying creak. Wiggling around again so that she could swing her legs round, she placed her feet firmly on the concrete outside the car and stood up. She felt wobbly, no doubt from the blood that was probably pumping out of her tongue at the moment, but after a moment to steady her equilibrium she began a slow shuffle on two feet. It was fortunate she was wearing jeans, since they gave her a bit more leverage with the duct tape. She figured that sooner or later the duct tape would start to get looser. All she had to do now was get to the road and get somebody to stop for her. It was going to be a slow process. The cars had sounded as though they came from quite far away and she had no idea where she was. She just hoped she could do it before Randall returned.

"Boss, the car is an old Ford Fiesta registered to a Molly Perkins who reported it stolen about a week and a half ago," Mark Roberts informed Ginny. "We've tracked some good images of where it went through town, but then it becomes sketchy."

Ginny was exasperated. Was every lead determined to be a dead end? "So, we don't know where it's gone?" she queried her voice exasperated.

He looked a little sheepish as he admitted that they had lost it. "We're still searching the camera footage," Mark confirmed.

"Let's get a map of the area set up. He's got to have taken Francine somewhere pretty secluded. Let's start trying to narrow down where those places might be," Ginny requested.

Steve King put down the phone he had been speaking into. "Derek Blackman's here to see you, Boss." Ginny let out a breath; a small part of her had been expecting this. She nodded without saying a word and stood up.

Del Blackman was a broken man; his only daughter was missing. He was pale with red-rimmed eyes and although a large man by any standards, today he looked kind of smaller as if he was shrinking in on himself.

Ginny took him into one of the side interview rooms. "I'm afraid I don't have anything good to tell you, Mr Blackman." Ginny used her 'I'm at a funeral' voice she reserved for giving bad news to relatives.

"Is she… " He seemed to take a moment as though composing himself. "Is she alive?"

Ginny knew she had to find a way to console this man. He was after all the father of a member of their team and while not directly related to anything to do with the investigation, she couldn't help feeling that she owed him in some way. She reached out and touched his hands with her own. "We believe she is alive and we are doing everything we can to find her." She hoped that she sounded as sincere as she meant to.

Del Blackman nodded. "I know you are, it's just that bastard, what he did to them other women. I can't have him doing that to my Francine, I just can't." Ginny had seen very few men cry, but it always brought a lump to her throat when she did. As Derek Blackman broke down in front of her, she wanted to tell him that everything was going to be alright, that they would find Francine and he would get his daughter back in one piece. Unfortunately, she was unable to make that promise because from her point of view, she didn't know it to be the truth herself.

After her meeting with Del Blackman, Ginny returned to the incident room despondently. She felt like the stuffing had been kicked out of her and she was tired. She went to her office and sat down at her desk, putting her head in her hands. In all honesty she felt like crying herself, especially after seeing Del Blackman's reaction. She knew there was a small part of everybody believing they could find Francine alive. Unfortunately, hopes were failing.

Ginny sat up straight. Her post had been left on the edge of her desk. Without Francine around, nobody else had bothered to open it. "Bastards," she muttered to herself. It made her feel better to use obscenities at the moment. The small brown package on top of the pile had caught her attention. It was recognisable immediately since a few weeks ago she had received something very similar containing the removed kidney of Katherine Eddowin. "Shit!" Ginny exclaimed. "Get forensics!" She more or less screamed from her office alerting the team that something was very wrong. "Pat, bring me gloves," she instructed two seconds later.

"How the hell has this bastard delivered anything else without us knowing about it?" Ginny shouted at nobody in particular.

Ginny put on the surgical gloves and started to open the package before her. Inside was the requisite note, written in red to represent blood and a small blood-ridden thing that Ginny wasn't even sure what it was.

I send you her tongue. Next time an ear.

"Oh my God, he cut out her tongue." Mark Roberts sounded almost hysterical as he looked upon the grisly bloody mess inside a sandwich bag.

"We need to get this to the lab, ensure its Francine's. He could be fucking with us," Pat said, patting Mark's arm in a comforting gesture.

"It's Francine's," Ginny confirmed. She didn't need the lab to confirm it.

"You can't know that," Pat said, turning on her.

"Oh come on, Pat. He hasn't let us down so far. He said it was Katherine Eddowin's kidney, and it was, why shouldn't we believe this tongue is Francine's?"

"It's different this time. This is not a well-thought-out, well-planned murder. This is him acting out because we have his sister and he wants her back. If he kills Francine, he loses his leverage." He was clutching at straws and Ginny couldn't blame him, but the entire team were getting far too emotional about this. They needed to accept that Randall Goff had Francine – he would probably kill her – they had to be working on that proviso. Expect the worst and there would be no disappointments. Ginny stood up slowly.

"Gin?" Pat grabbed her arm as she moved to walk past him.

"I want every bit of CCTV in this station combed within an inch of its life." Her eyes met his and the determination was clearly evident as she spoke again.

"This bastard is fucking with us and I want him caught. He has somehow managed to walk into this station and hand deliver a woman's tongue under our noses. How the fuck does that happen?" the last part was announced as a growl.

Ginny pulled her arm from Pat's grip and strode past him.. "I want to talk to Selina Goff again," she snapped at nobody in particular.

Selina sat in a grey jogging suit. They had taken her clothes and provided her with the grey jogging bottoms and a grey sweat top. Without her expertly applied make-up and her hair pulled back into a loose pony tail, Ginny was struck by how young Selina Goff actually looked.

"I know you don't want to speak to me, Selina," Ginny began. Selina sat in the seat opposite, still seeming to have that aloofness that she entered the police station with. Some things about her appearance hadn't changed. "Prison is not a nice place, Selina," Ginny told her softly. "If you talk to us, tell us what you know, it would look good on you in court, might even get you a lighter sentence. After all it's Randall who did most of it, right?"

Selina fixed them with a sullen stare that seemed to go right through them, her blue eyes barely blinking.

"You do understand what this means, Selina, if you don't speak to us." Ginny was trying everything she could to get through to the girl.

Like a switch had been flicked Selina suddenly gave them a mocking smile. "You have nothing, Detective," she informed them. With deliberate slowness, she looked up at the camera position in the corner of the room. "I'd like to go back to my room now." The smile was still hovering about her lips as she turned her gaze back to Ginny.

Ginny knew at this point she had little to lose. "Randall has one of our officers, Selina. He is asking for us to swap you for her."

Selina stared at Ginny, saying nothing.

"I hope you said your goodbyes." Selina's voice was barely a whisper but none the less menacing.

"Take this piece of shit back to her cell," Ginny instructed in disgust.

They would get nothing from Selina. Randall was right when he said she would never talk. They were so engrained in each other's lives that they were more or less one and the same. Even Eugenie Goff, when she had come to visit her daughter, had failed to get her to engage in a conversation.

Mark snagged Ginny as she re-entered the incident room.

"He walked in off the street bold as brass." For a moment Ginny had no idea what he was referring to, but suddenly the penny dropped.

"You are joking me. I full scale man hunt and our killer walks in off the street?" the incredulousness was evident in her voice. Mark nodded bringing up the offending CCTV.

Beyond any belief there was Randall Goff looking like the boy next door with his blonde hair glinting in the sunshine as he entered the police station. Wearing a generic pair of faded jeans and white t-shirt he strolled purposefully towards the front desk. The words were lost to sound, but as he stopped at the desk he looked up, turning his face directly towards the camera whereupon he smiled before turning back to the desk.

He was seen handing over the small brown package and saying something before nodding and turning back towards the exit door. As he approached, he stopped and turned once more looking back at the camera where he held up one hand as a salute.

"I want whoever was sitting at that desk fucking sacked." Ginny shouted. She turned in a furious circle seemingly not knowing which way to go.

"I can't believe the fucker stepped into this station bold as brass and not one fucking plod knew about it." Her voice cracked and almost disappeared she was so furious with the entire situation.

Pat who was busy circling potential sites on a map that now adorned one of the walls of the incident room had stopped what he was doing and was staring at Ginny as was every other member of the team.

"What?" she snapped realising she was the single point of attention in that moment.

"I think we're on to something here." Pat responded placidly as if the outburst had never taken place.

Ginny strode over to Pat glancing at the circled areas on the map. So far he had identified three places. Ginny looked with interest her anger abating as fast as it had arrived.

"She still not speaking?" Pat threw at her over his shoulder.

"Nope." Ginny replied. She stood behind her best friend for a moment. "I'm sorry, Pat, for the way I acted earlier." He turned to her then and wrapped her up in a bear hug which she reciprocated gratefully. Lifting her off her feet, he placed her back down and released her, grinning unrepentantly. She couldn't help but smile back. "What are these?" she asked, stepping closer to the map and pointing at the areas he'd marked, her attention back on the job.

"These are potentially deserted sites within a ten-mile radius. Mark tracked down some more camera footage and we followed his direction which seems to point him in this general direction." Pat gestured with his hand to a certain area on the map. He could have gone further, and we're checking out possible CCTV images against time trajectories. But we reckon what he does takes time. Melanie said it took hours for him to carve up Mary Kelly, so I figure he's gonna want somewhere he can operate without fear of being found."

"It's Melanie now, is it?" she raised her eyebrows in question.

Pat coloured up immediately at her teasing. "We've had a couple of dates," he confirmed sheepishly.

"And you didn't tell me, Pat, I'm heartbroken. I thought I was your best friend." Ginny was teasing but there was an element of truth in that statement. He was her best friend and he hadn't told her he was seeing someone. That just went to show how much their relationship had deteriorated lately. She changed the subject, turning the attention back to the map. "So where are these locations?" she asked peering closer at it.

"There are three abandoned quarry sites in fairly close proximity to each other." Pat gestured on the map. "If he went towards the other two locations, we would have picked him up on camera around here." He pointed to the map again, "And here." He gestured to another spot. "By our reckoning, he was most likely heading in this direction and this is the best spot."

Ginny turned to Steve and Mark. "Anything further on the cameras, could he have gone further than that quarry?"

"We think we've just picked him up again, Boss," Mark confirmed, looking at his computer screen. Displayed were several boxes, each relating to a particular camera, each with a number in the bottom right hand corner. Mark pointed to the top left box. "This is forty minutes after he took Francine, and then he gets picked up here." Mark pointed to another image. "We seem to lose him, but then we pick him up again here." Yet again Mark pointed to another image. "And then nothing, its like he just disappears."

"That's the general area of the quarry," Steve confirmed. "Either that or he has an address there that he's taking her to."

"But," Pat interjected over by the map, "if he turns in here, this is the entrance to the quarry. No cameras. If he were to carry on where would he have been picked up, Mark?"

"We should have been able to capture him on this camera here." Again, Mark gestured to another box on his computer screen.

"Are you sure you couldn't have missed him?"

"No way." Mark was indignant.

This time it was Ginny's turn to grin. "At this point we have nothing to lose. Let get over to that quarry with everything we have. Full body armour please, this guy is a nutter and who knows what weapons he might have in his arsenal."

FRANCINE

It was hard work shuffling along and it had been a slow process. Baby steps. The duct tape around her ankles had given slightly with her movement, but still her legs were firmly tied. Francine had managed to make it to the entrance of the building and was pausing to gather her strength. Her mouth was throbbing. She had spat out the towel and now a trickle of blood kept escaping and dribbling down her chin. With her hands tied behind her back, she had no choice but to keep wiping her face on her shoulder.

She glanced around at the outside of the outbuilding she had been brought to. It was some kind of disused quarry, although she didn't recognise it. A large stretch of ground was before her in all directions, flanked by trees on each side. To her right were some gates. They were open and large enough for vehicles to pass through. This must be the way to the road, she thought. It must have been the entrance for the lorries once upon a time when it was a working quarry. She knew that once these areas were completely finished with, they tended to be made into some kind of nature reserve.

Francine knew that the direction of the gates and beyond was where she needed to go, but she also knew that Randall Goff could return at any moment.

She started to shuffle towards the gates, taking her time more so now due to the unevenness of the ground. It wouldn't do for her to fall, with her hands tied behind her back, she would have no way of protecting her face against smashing into the ground.

She made it to the gates and took another moment to catch her breath, trying to evaluate the best way to go. If she remained in the open and Randall returned, he would have no trouble spotting her. She needed to get under the cover of the trees. She was hoping that she might come to a house or find some way of finding help away from here.

Once she was through the gates, she realised she was on a bridge of sorts. To her left were a few trees, but even in the gloom of the evening she could see the overhead rails that signified she was near train tracks. To her right was a path that moved upwards into the forest. Straight ahead was a dirt path that looked like it led nowhere, except that it was wide enough for a vehicle and was clearly the way Randall would re-enter.

Francine decided to go towards the right. She felt that the trees would afford her some protection should Randall return before she was safe.

It was a difficult progression. The duct tape was proving to be an enormous hindrance with the uneven ground. It had rained recently and the floor of the forest was quite boggy with slippery mud which slowed Francine's progress even more than before. She hadn't gone very far and was considering maybe using the roadway when she heard the unmistakable sound of a Volkswagen Beetle. Francine's heart pounded in her chest. She was so afraid and wanted to run as fast as she could to get away. Tears started to run down her face as she began to panic, frantically searching for somewhere to hide.

Eventually she moved sideways and stood against a large tree. She shimmied herself down and sat on the floor, hoping that should Randall come looking for her he would run right by. She could only hope at the moment that her colleagues knew she had been taken and were frantically looking for her.

RANDALL

Randall pulled the Volkswagen Beetle into the disused quarry building and switched off the engine. It had been risky, but he had taken the cut off piece of Francine's tongue and boldly delivered it to the police station. He had half expected an ambitious police officer would have stopped him and arrested him on the spot, but as fate would have it, he had managed to walk right up the reception desk and hand over his package, requesting it be delivered to DCI Virginia Percy as soon as possible. The officer behind the glass panel had looked at the package quizzically before taking it. "It's evidence for her investigation." Randall had told him obligingly and the officer had nodded.

"May I take your name, sir?" the officer had asked, pen poised.

Randall gave him a winning smile. "My name is Freddy March, I work with Melanie Watson." He had made it up on the spot.

"Oh." The officer had said and dutifully took the package by opening a side door and removing it from Randall's outstretched hands. Other people were coming into the police station to report their crimes or queries and Randall was able to leave. He deliberately looked up at the camera in the corner and smiled as he left. They had his picture and they had his sister. Now nothing mattered.

Randall started the drive back to the quarry. He knew the police would never trade Selina for Francine, it was a pipe dream to hope otherwise. The net was closing in on him and he had a feeling it was only a matter of time before he came face to face with DCI Virginia Percy and he knew the meeting would not be on his terms as he had wanted it to be.

Randall was almost beyond all sanity. Reason had escaped him as he acknowledged that his dream of surpassing the greatest serial killer who had ever lived was now beyond his reach. He could feel his dream slipping away. In the muddle of his mind, Randall had gone beyond reasonable thought. All he could think about was his baby sister and the fact that she had been taken away from him, that she was beyond his reach. They had been inseparable since the day she was born and he found himself enraged at the thought of never seeing her again. Those who had taken her would pay dearly for what they had done, of that he was sure and he knew just where to start.

He climbed out of the car, having killed the engine. The silence was complete and he took a moment to breathe deeply while he stood with the darkness surrounding him. He turned to the Fiesta and noted immediately that the passenger door stood open. He walked around the car and opened the boot, knowing all the time that Francine was no longer in the car.

His backpack was stashed behind a large stone that resided at the far end of the building and it was there he now went to retrieve it. He removed his hunting knife from its sheath and turned towards the entrance of the building. He had been gone at least an hour. In her condition, how far could she have got?

Purposefully, Randall strode towards the entrance of the building. He needed to look at this logically like Francine would have done. She clearly hadn't taken the path that led to the exit of the quarry, he would have spotted her, so that left two possible ways to leave. Either she stayed in the open and followed the path left, or she went into the trees to his right. Randall walked towards the wooded area. It had been raining and the mud was all boggy. Sure enough, he could clearly make out the shuffling prints that Francine had made. All he had to do was follow them. It was a matter of moments before the shuffling came to an end. Randall looked carefully around him in the gloom and spotted Francine sitting at the base of a large tree. He made no move towards her at first.

"Tut, tut, tut, Francine. Were you trying to play hide and seek with me?"

She didn't answer, just stared at him with abject terror. He took a step towards her and hunkered down before her terrified form.

"Not very fucking good at it, are you?" He said in a reasonable voice.

Her eyes filled with tears and she tried to blink them away. Her tongue had continued to bleed and her chin was covered in blood. In the dimness of the available light, it looked black. Randall lent forward and licked at her chin. She tried to moved away from him, disgust evident on her face. She opened her mouth, allowing more blood to escape its confines.

Randall twisted around and used his knife to cut the duct tape around her ankles. He stood up, holding her by her right arm, hauling her to her feet with him. Francine staggered momentarily, her blood loss and terror causing her to stumble.

Randall began dragging her back towards to the disused quarry building and Francine was shocked to discover what very little ground she had covered. Her legs felt like lead. What was wrong with her? She needed to fight, to kick him right where it hurts and make a run for it now that her legs were freed.

Suddenly he swung her round to face him. The force of the spin caused her to land against his chest and in that instant his right arm came up around her back. In his left hand he held his knife which he now held against her cheek. "You think to run away from me," he whispered. Francine wriggled against him, frantically trying to free herself as she whimpered softly. His face was uncomfortably close to hers. "I would like you to run away from me. What a sport it would be to hunt you down." He moved his head towards her as though he was about to kiss her. She flung her head back in horror, once again trying to release herself from his grip. He placed his knife against her throat and she stilled immediately. "Yes, that's what I thought," he told her before turning once more towards the building. They were almost at the entrance now and he forced her back into the dark confines. This time he walked passed the cars and towards a large concrete slab that sat in one corner of the building. As they reached it, he threw her against it roughly. She lost her footing completely and went down with hard on the concrete face first. She let out a small cry of pain followed by a sob as she turned and lowered herself to the floor. "I could have just killed you." He was pacing up and down before her, not really talking to her, more at her. "But now I've thought of something better." He stopped suddenly and Francine jumped. She was terrified. He bent down towards a mound on the floor which she realised was some kind of bag – a backpack. From the confines he pulled out the roll of duct tape. He held it up triumphantly and smiled before stepping before her. His knife was in his left hand. He put down the duct tape and pulled her legs flat to the floor and sat on them. She was pinned, unable to move any part of her body except her head. Using the edge of the sweatshirt she was wearing, he pulled it up and wiped the blood away from her chin. "Don't open your mouth." He told her and pulled off a large piece of the duct tape. He stuck it across her face, pushing down against her cheeks to make it stick. He then pulled, took the tape and wound it once more around her ankles.

"There you are. What a good girl." He smiled again. Francine could only watch helplessly as her captor did exactly what he wanted with her and all the while she could only think the he was becoming more insane by the minute. She could taste the blood in her mouth. She didn't think her tongue was still bleeding as much but with every throb she was sure more blood came out. She just hoped she could survive this before she choked. Would he let her go?

Without warning, he suddenly hauled her to her feet and spun her round, bending her over the stone slab which in some ways now resembled some kind of altar to her. She turned her face to the side and her cheek rested against the hard concrete while she wondered what he would do next. He placed his body over the top of hers. She could feel his erection digging into the top of her buttocks and she whimpered. He reached up and stroked a hand across her hair. "Do you know, from behind you looked exactly like Virginia Percy," he whispered against her ear. He suggestively rubbed himself against her as he spoke and she whimpered again, involuntary tears falling from her eyes.

She suddenly felt lighter as he removed his body from hers. Francine had no idea if he was going to kill her. She just wanted to go home, to see her mum and dad and feel safe in her bed. Tears were streaming from her eyes as she cried silently willing her colleagues to find her and rescue her before it was too late.

She felt something cold in the waistband of her jeans and tried to turn around. In his hand he was holding scissors and began busying himself cutting through the material of her jeans. She tried to wiggle, tried to tell him to stop, her muffled words lost under the duct tape.

In a matter of moments, Randall had cut her jeans away until they hung in strips around her knees. He had then done the same with the thong that she wore. "Only whores wear this kind of underwear," he had muttered while he did it, although she wasn't sure whether he was speaking to her or himself.

Again, she felt that he had moved away and she attempted to move herself, to stand up. It was difficult with her hands still tied behind her back. Before she had managed to extricate herself from her predicament he was on her again and this time to her dismay, he was naked, or at least he had pulled down his jeans.

He forced his entry into her vagina from his position behind her. The pain was immense, causing her to cry out, her sobs being taken with gasping breaths through her nose. He pushed her face against the rough concrete as he pounded into her, his grunts of sexual gratification becoming louder as his strokes came hard and faster. Eventually, it was over, his hot seed entering her body. She gagged, attempting to breathe through her mouth, but finding only her nose as the source of air. Blood bubbled up from her mouth and found its way through her nose, blocking her airway completely. Her body started to convulse as she began to suffocate and choke to death on her own blood. Randall had pulled out of her and stood just behind as Francine frantically tried to find a way to help herself breathe. She tried to rub her face against the concrete slab in an effort to remove the duct tape. Randall stood back and watched it all in absolute fascination. Finally, Francine's frantic war dance of trying to breathe and remain alive ended when she collapsed to her bottom on the floor. She fell against the concrete slab, her eyes beseeching him to remove the tape so she could breathe. Instead Randall hunkered down beside her once more. He watched with interest as Francine suffocated to death, choking to death on her own blood, a trickle emanating from her nose. Her eyes rolled back in her head as she struggled to extricate the flow but with nowhere to go it only served to block her airways.

When he was sure she had died, he lifted her body and lay her on the concrete slab. Now he would cut her to pieces just because he could.

They were twenty minutes away. Ginny with Pat, Mark with Steve, in their unmarked cars, the armed response officers in their vehicle and at least twenty uniformed officers in several police cars, sirens blazing, were heading towards the quarry at a frightening speed. Eventually they reached the turn-off towards the quarry. They had already ascertained from Google and the overhead maps that there were two possible ways in. One was the old road that led directly to the quarry and one was a more rural approach. Ginny and her team cover the first option, while the second team took the other way. The road, if one could call it that, was filled with large potholes that prompted them to take caution as they drove. In convoy they followed the length of the road until they came to a gate. Ginny and Pat, in the front car, stopped and Ginny jumped out. She ran to the gate and was surprised when it opened against her push.

Beyond that gate was a wide stony area. Trees and forestry flanked the whole way around providing shelter and muffling any sounds that came from the nearby road. To the left of the gate stood an old abandoned corrugated iron building, in the shape of an arc. The opening of the building looked like a large screaming mouth, anything beyond in total darkness. No sound could be heard coming from within. It looked exactly what it was, a deserted area.

Ginny walked through the gate, joined by Pat, Steve and Mark and flanked by several armed officers, their torches cutting through the dark with lines of white light.

They approached the building with caution, reaching the edge and stopping before going any further. Ginny looked into the building. Two cars could be seen in the gloom, the missing Ford Fiesta and a beat-up Volkswagen Beetle. Ginny couldn't see anything else at the moment. The officers walked into the building, torches shining. At the far side of the building, which couldn't be seen from the entrance as it was behind one of the cars, was what looked like a large stone slab. Lying on the slab was clearly what remained of Francine Blackman. Sitting on the floor, with his back leaning against the slab, was Randall Goff. He put his hand up to shield his eyes from the bright light of their torch. When he realised who stood before him, he started to laugh. It wasn't a little chuckle. Randall Goff laughed like he found the whole thing hysterically funny. Ginny looked at her colleagues, who looked as confused as she felt.

She took a step towards Randall, an armed response officer by her side, his rifle trained on Randall's chest. "Can you put the knife down please, Randall?" Ginny asked. Still he continued to laugh; there were actual tears rolling down his face in his mirth.

Louder this time. "Randall, please release the knife." He carried on chuckling.

"PUT DOWN YOUR WEAPON NOW." The booming voice of the armed officer at Ginny's side made everyone but Randall jump, however he looked down at the bloody knife still in his left hand before throwing it to his left. "Randall Goff, I am arresting you for the murders of … " Ginny reeled off the names of the victims and completed his rights while Pat and Steve moved in. They each took one of Randall's arms and hauled him to his feet. He was still chuckling as he was handcuffed and led to one of the waiting police cars. Even when he was placed in the back of a police car, he continued to smile, his gaze trained on Ginny the whole time.

The remains of Francine Blackman were still on the slab; awaiting removal to the morgue. Melanie Watson had arrived and was currently examining the body, although it was pretty clear what had occurred.

Francine had been ripped apart. Her arms were still tied behind her back; Randall had cut off her clothes and they hung in strips in places, her arms still encased in the sleeves. He clearly hadn't taken any care when cutting things away; several small cuts adorned her legs. The duct tape still resided across her mouth, but he had cut off part of her nose and her ears which he had placed beside her head. He had cut off and removed her breasts; these were also found beside her body. Her abdomen had been ripped open and Randall had been in the process of removing her intestines when he had been disturbed. He had not cut her throat and it was deduced by Melanie Watson that she had suffered a cruel demise of choking to death on her own blood. On completion of Melanie's investigations later that day, it was clear that Francine had been severely sexually assaulted; Randall hadn't even bothered to use a condom and his semen was still inside Francine's body. It was unclear whether he had raped her post mortem or not.

Ginny and Pat sat opposite Randall in the interview room. Like his sister before him, he was seemingly unmoved by the fact that he had been caught and arrested and now potentially would stand trial for the murder of six women. He grinned unrepentantly at Ginny.

"I'm going to ask you some questions, Randall," Ginny started.

"There's no need. I will tell you everything you need to know. Would you like me to start the beginning…?" His candidness took both Pat and Ginny by surprise.

"Well, if you feel you would like to confess, then by all means," Ginny confirmed.

"Well then." Randall Goff smiled across the table at Ginny. It was a smile that never reached his eyes, which appeared like fathomless pools of obsidian. Ginny knew she was looking into the face of pure evil.

Randall told all, from the time he was ten years old and had travelled to Scotland to kill Ian Pratchett, to the arson of an allotment shed that had killed five young people. There were others along the way – an unexplained death here, a murder there. He had been consistently killing since he was ten years old and although every death would need to be looked into, Ginny had no doubt that what Randall told them was the truth. He went on to explain that

412

when Selina told him she worked with a woman called Mary Nicholls, he immediately knew what he had been put on this earth for. It was fate that had literally brought them together. He had followed Mary for a year and the others for many months. Their deaths were part of his becoming, he told the police. He told them that everything was building up to what he would become. When Ginny asked what that was, he confirmed that he was the greatest serial killer who had ever lived. To some extent, Ginny could agree; his notoriety when his story came out would surpass any other killer who had lived in their time.

"My mistake was taking Francine, I see that now," Randall said finally. "I was angry that you had taken my sister. She is an innocent in this."

Hardly that, thought Ginny. Selina Goff was residing in a woman's prison on remand awaiting the trial. She had continued to refuse to speak about her crimes, but it wasn't necessary now since Randall had filled them in. She was to be prosecuted for being an accessory to the murders.

They had not had any evidence of her involvement in the murder of Alison McKenzie until, luck would have it, Franklin Hart had contacted them to say that when they cleaned out Selina's desk, they had discovered a hammer in the bottom of her drawer. Forensic tests confirmed that it was the hammer that had been used to murder Alison McKenzie and it was covered in Selina's fingerprints. The only thing they were unable to pin on her was the alleged murder of Sharon Bywater.

A psychiatrist had been called into assess Randall's mental state. Randall never professed to being insane, but he didn't really have to, his crimes spoke for themselves. The psychiatrist was shocked to come across such a complete sociopath as Randall Goff. Never in his experience had he come across such a controlled, cold mind who had no empathy for the feelings of others or the enormity of what he had done. It was clear that he had enjoyed what he had done. As far as Randall was concerned, he had become what he had always wanted to be – Jack the Ripper, and yet in Randall's mind he was far more than that; he had surpassed his hero.

CHAPTER THIRTY

1st MARCH

Randall Goff was brought to the Crown Court in the prison transport. He was the only occupant. He alighted from the bus dressed in a smart, grey suit, pristine white shirt and blue tie. His blonde hair was styled and he was clean shaven. He looked like a handsome boy next door and you would never believe that he had committed such atrocities. His prison escort held one arm, helping him from the transport, his hands handcuffed before him.

He smiled at the crowd before him, basking in the glory of being the centre of attention. The camera's lapped it up, snapping in uncontrollable flashes that made onlookers blink at the onslaught of bright light.

Del Blackman had been distraught. There was no consoling him over the mutilation of his beautiful daughter and he wanted revenge. When it came down to it, his old contacts in the army had made it exceeding easy for him to locate a gun. The nine millimetre semi-automatic pistol had resided in the pocket of his coat. He had waited patiently for the arrival of the prison transport and when it finally arrived, he had no other thought in his head but getting revenge on the scum that had murdered his daughter.

The press were clamouring around the transport, trying to get the best pictures of the suspect. The police had a makeshift cordon and they were refusing anybody access. This was quite possibly the biggest case the country had seen. None of that bothered Del Blackman. Before anybody knew what he was doing he had pushed through the press and retrieved his gun from his pocket.

As Randall Goff was brought down from the prison transport, Del pointed and fired his weapon at Randall's head. Del was oblivious to the screams that suddenly erupted at the sight of a gun before them, but nobody could react in time.

The prison guard handcuffed to Randall was sprayed with his blood across his face as the bullet landed squarely in the middle of Randall's forehead and exited the back of Randall's head, spraying the prison transport with blood and parts of his brain. The screaming was intense as people were panicking wondering if they were next to be shot.

The police, ever present and alert for any conflict could be heard to shout: "ARMED POLICE, PUT DOWN YOUR WEAPON"

Before the armed response unit could respond any further, Del scored another shot, this time squarely in Randall's chest. His army training had come in useful. The shot to Randall's head had killed him instantly; the shot to his chest just finished the job as far as Del Blackman was concerned. The armed response police were shouting at him to drop his weapon again and as those voices finally filtered into his mind, he dropped his gun on the floor. As Del Blackman was taken into custody, he felt a sense of calm come over him. Never again would that bastard hurt another woman.

Selina Goff heard about the death of her brother from a prison officer escorting her to the trial. They were in a taxi and she was sitting in the back of the car, handcuffed to the officer. Selina said nothing on hearing the news; she didn't seem to react at all. The trial had to be postponed and Selina was returned to the prison. Nobody could understand her reaction or lack of one.

Selina was returned to her cell. On the outside she preserved the cool exterior she had always presented so well. On the inside she was falling to pieces. Randall, her Randall was dead and gone. She had never had the chance to see him again. She wanted to rage at the world, to kill someone for taking the one person who she loved.

All her life, Selina had only known one person who represented everything to her, father, mother, brother. They had been everything to each since the day she had been born, a protégé child who could learn from the master when he worked.

Selina felt bereft, there was nothing in her life left to live for, nothing that meant anything. Her mother was just a cheap imitation, a cardboard cut out who essentially had meant nothing to either of the Goff children.

Where had it all gone wrong?

Selina Goff was found later that day, having hanged herself in her cell. Somehow, she had managed to twist up one of her sheets to make a noose and had tied the other end to the top of the bunkbed she shared with another inmate.

EPILOGUE

Eugenie sat in the pew of the church, having just had the funerals of both her children. It was an occasion that had been attended by nobody except Eugenie Goff and the reverend who presided over the service. It had been a nice service and now her children's bodies were going to be cremated. She had requested not to be given the ashes.

Eugenie Goff couldn't help but feel responsible for how her children had turned out. Had she not known that Randall was strange from the first? She recalled him being about four years old, his sweetness then. But in truth Eugenie had never really loved her son. She knew that deep down, and it took sitting in church, before God, to admit that. From the day he was born she knew she had made a terrible mistake and should have rid herself of the child while he still resided in her womb. She had placed herself into purgatory and had blamed Randall every day for it ever since. The mother's love she should have bestowed on him was always absent and what he had become was her doing.

When Selina had been born, it had been easy to rely on the then eleven-year-old Randall to take charge and take care of the baby. She had felt some love for her daughter, she couldn't deny, but even that wasn't enough.

It was a bitter pill to swallow, but Eugenie Goff realised that she was indeed the most selfish of all people. She hadn't really cared about her children and in a lot of respects she was glad they were dead.

She had known that something was amiss when they stayed out together for hours. The night of that terrible fire, when five of Randall's school friends had been horribly burned alive, hadn't it crossed her mind, even fleetingly, that her children were in some way responsible? Selina's clothing had smelt of petrol that night and still, Eugenie refused to acknowledge anything about it. Even when she heard the news the following day, part of her knew that it was something to do with her children, but she blocked it from her mind, refused its existence and therefore it wasn't true. Then to discover that Randall had murdered Ian Pratchett when he was still such a young child. Ten years old and committing a murder of such ferocity. She should have been surprised, but even when the shocking news that her son had committed such a crime at ten years old reached her, it had not affected Eugenie as much as it should. She could recall that night when Randall had returned so late. She had been convinced that something terrible had happened to him, and in truth was hoping that something terrible had happened and then, there he was. It all made perfect sense now.

Eugenie realised that she was no less a monster than her children had been. They were after all a product of her.

Sighing, Eugenie stood up from the pew. She had made her peace with God now and with any luck he would forgive her. She was returning to her family. Her mother was frail and needed care, her father had long since passed away. It was a good excuse for Eugenie to return now and given that her father had died many years ago, there was nothing to stop her.

Eugenie stood on the steps of the church, pulling on her black gloves. A movement caught her eye and she saw a little boy, perhaps no more than five years old, peering through the railings that surrounded the churchyard, at her. For moment she was struck at how much he looked like Randall, the same blonde hair, the same physique. It was like looking at Randall so many years ago, when he had adored her beyond anything else, just before he lost his sweetness. It was uncanny. She held up a gloved hand in a wave to the child. His pale little hands gripped the railings and he continued to watch her a moment longer through the bars, not waving back, his dark eyes trained on her as if accusing of her something. Eugenie took a step forward, intrigued at how much this child looked like Randall. Her movement must have frightened him because he took off down the street before she could do anything more. She watched him disappear from view before getting into her car. She had a long drive ahead of her.

THE END